Praise for *Living Magic*

"For anyone wanting to explore magic but not sure where to begin, this book is a gold mine. At least one of the authors has worked as a counsellor, and that might explain how these interviews, as well as the chapters that address basic questions about magic—the mistakes, the politics, the different schools, the relationship with science, the fetish of legitimacy, etc.—manage to be simultaneously profound, sensitive, and really down to earth."

—Ramsey Dukes, author of *SSOTBME Revised:
An Essay on Magic* and *Uncle Ramsey's Little Book of Demons*

"In the too often stuffy environment of contemporary occultism, *Living Magic* is not merely a breath of fresh air but a cleansing wind. No matter what kind of magic you practice, no matter what tradition (or lack of tradition) guides you, you will find plenty in this book to challenge you, irritate you, and make you think more deeply about what magic is and what it can be."

—John Michael Greer, author of *The New Encyclopedia
of the Occult* and *The Mysteries of Merlin*

"The pathways described in this book by Frater U∴D∴ and his distinguished colleagues show the individual magical practitioner, regardless of tradition, how to succeed on a higher level. The contents of this book, honestly read, practiced, and understood, will open new doors of power and invite you to enter."

—Edred Thorsson, author of *Futhark: A Handbook of Rune Magic*

"Now, after decades of practice and reflection, Frater U∴D∴ and three other original members of the Workshop provide us with a collection of writings that brings lessons, anecdotes, and insights (gleaned from actual practice) together with theory, history, and discussion. In regard to history, the book gives the reader a welcome overview of the modern magical tradition, from the Hermetic Order of the Golden Dawn, the Societas Rosicruciana in Anglia, Aleister Crowley, the Ordo Templi Orientis, the Fraternitas Saturni, Austin Spare and the 'Zos Kia Cultus,' the Illuminates of Thanateros, Chaos Magic, and Ice Magic to such practices as sex magic and sigil magic."

—Angel Millar, author of *The Three Stages of
Initiatic Spirituality: Craftsman, Warrior, Magician*

"*Living Magic* is a unique book, written by members of an informal group who met regularly for three years in the early 1980s in Bonn, Germany, to experiment with practical magic. ... Its real value lies in the insights it offers into highly diverse mentalities of modern magicians."

—Rafał T. Prinke, author of *The Deceptive Garden of Errors:*
Alchemical Writings Until the End of the 18th Century

"Reading the first few pages of *Living Magic* was enough to convince me that here was a truly authentic text. ... Authenticity and authenticism will become keynotes in describing magical texts in the months and years to come, drawing a clear line between books such as *Living Magic* and the coming plethora of books that will pretend, quite preposterously, as some already have, to have been written by magi. Occultists diverse of cloak and creed will want *Living Magic* on their shelves for inspiration and for frequent reference."

—Ray Sherwin, author of *The Theatre of Magick* and *The Book of Results*

LIVING MAGIC

About the Authors

Frater U∴D∴ is a writer, poet, and magician. A German diplomat's child, he grew up in Africa and Asia. He holds a master's degree in comparative literature, English literature, and Portuguese studies from the University of Bonn, and is co-founder of the Bonn Workshop for Experimental Magic. Founder of pragmatic magic, ice magic and co-founder of the Magical Pact of the Illuminati of Thanateros (IOT), he is one of Europe's most renowned practical magicians and contemporary occult authors. He studied with yoga and tantra masters and has been involved with the practical aspects of occultism in general and magic in particular for more than half a century. He has many years of experience as a translator and interpreter and is the author of more than forty books, many of which have become modern-day classics, including *High Magic* and *Practical Sigil Magic*. His works have been translated into many languages, including English, French, Spanish, Italian, Russian, Czech, Estonian, and Japanese. He is known for his undogmatic approach to the black arts and has translated works by Peter Carroll and Ramsey Dukes, as well as Aleister Crowley's *Book of Lies*, among others.

Axel Büdenbender was born the son of two teachers. He attended a convent boarding school and has been a devoted fan of Pan since very early on. He worked for several years as a street theater actor. Trained as a nurse, Axel has worked in the fields of neurology and psychiatry, in homes for seniors, and in a hospital for those with lung cancer and tuberculosis. While living in an apartment-sharing community, he immediately furnished his entire room as a magical temple. For several years he lived in seclusion in a remote forest house, pursuing his magical studies. He is a founding member of the Bonn Workshop for Experimental Magic and was a temporary member of the O.T.O. He lives in Bonn, Germany.

Harry Eilenstein is a highly prolific writer, life coach, and magician. He was trained by Catholic nuns as an embroiderer, studied Egyptology, astronomy, and ballet dancing, and is a gifted amateur goldsmith. He has also penned a veritable library—over 130 books—on a wide variety of subjects. His series on Germanic and Norse gods alone comprises some 88 volumes. He is regarded by his colleagues as one of the most productive thinkers of contemporary magic. Whether Kabbalah, ancient Egyptian magic, Tantrism, Eastern and Dakota traditions, or the mythologies, religions, and mystery schools of the entire world, there is hardly a subject he has not explored in depth, always paying attention to its practical applications. He is a founding member of the Bonn Workshop for Experimental Magic.

Josef Knecht studied humanities and ancient languages at the University of Bonn, Germany, in the 1980s, where he was a founding member of the Bonn Workshop for Experimental Magic. In addition to research work and publications in the humanities, he has long been involved in investigating methods of alternative medicine. Today, Knecht lives as an author and blogger in a small town in southern Germany.

LIVING MAGIC

MAGIC

CONTEMPORARY INSIGHTS and EXPERIENCES
from PRACTICING MAGICIANS

FRATER U∴D∴
·AXEL BÜDENBENDER·
·HARRY EILENSTEIN·
·JOSEF KNECHT·

Llewellyn Publications
Woodbury, Minnesota

FIRST EDITION
First Printing, 2021

Cover design by Kevin R. Brown
Interior chakra figure by Mary Ann Zapalac
Interior hand gestures and grips by Eugene Smith

Llewellyn Publications is a registered trademark of Llewellyn Worldwide Ltd.

Library of Congress Cataloging-in-Publication Data (Pending)
ISBN: 9780738766799

Llewellyn Worldwide Ltd. does not participate in, endorse, or have any authority or responsibility concerning private business transactions between our authors and the public.

All mail addressed to the author is forwarded but the publisher cannot, unless specifically instructed by the author, give out an address or phone number.

Any internet references contained in this work are current at publication time, but the publisher cannot guarantee that a specific location will continue to be maintained. Please refer to the publisher's website for links to authors' websites and other sources.

Llewellyn Publications
A Division of Llewellyn Worldwide Ltd.
2143 Wooddale Drive
Woodbury, MN 55125-2989
www.llewellyn.com

Printed in the United States of America

Other Books by Frater U∴D∴

High Magic: Theory & Practice
(Llewellyn, 2005)

High Magic II: Expanded Theory and Practice
(Llewellyn, 2008)

Money Magic:
Mastering Prosperity in Its True Element
(Llewellyn, 2011)

Practical Sigil Magic:
Creating Personal Symbols for Success
(Llewellyn, 2012)

The Magical Shield:
Protection Magic to Ward Off Negative Forces
(Llewellyn, 2016)

Sex Magic:
Release & Control the Power of Your Erotic Potential
(Llewellyn, 2018)

There are only two things that need be done:
the necessary and the impossible.
Ibn 'Arabi

Contents

Foreword
"Not That Book!"

Decades ago, there were four occult bookstores in Austin, Texas. In those steamy days, before the internet, a young would-be magician walked into one of them and asked for a certain tome, but the owner said he would never carry that book.

"Why?"

"Because it works."

As a practitioner and teacher of esoteric arts for three decades, I can say there are less than thirty books in the world that fit that description. You're holding one of them.

Humans claim to want freedom, until it sticks its big, green, ugly head in their door and snorts. Then they've got a large, farting dragon to remind them every night who oversees their happiness. And it's hard to banish It.

So be forewarned that this book is about attracting that dragon through the sane and rational acquisition of magical powers, techniques, and bliss without giving up the benefits of rationality.

Let's look at the three ways to avoid magic and freedom, and then at the Bonn way to obtain Magic and Freedom.

1. Be an entertained consumer. Buy those books, buy those tapes, buy that new Tarot deck based on the macrobiotic diet/Enochian sex magick. It feels a little like freedom when you read.

2. Be the leader of your group. If you (for whatever reason) have more magical power than other folks, you can dominate your peers. That feels a little like freedom, until you try to get everyone to come to the meetings. Your power is gone when you say, "What about next Tuesday at 8?"

3. Join a group with a great reputation. Then, if it's legit (like my group the Oversexed Space Anteater Group), you can feel freedom after being in rigorous training for a long time. Or if it's not legit (like the Sex Obsessed Secret Decoder Ring Group), it may feel like freedom when you're breaking taboos for your superior—like buying him grass, having sex with him, or helping with his decoder ring.

Or you can dare the Bonn Way. You see, a British occultist named Aleister Crowley said exactly what to do.

Exactly.

And was ignored by thousands of his followers. In the subtitle of his magazine *Equinox*, Crowley put the Way to Freedom: *The Method of Science—The Aim of Religion*.

The scientific method has six steps.

1. Ask a question—so work outside your dogma.
2. Do background research—other people have investigated this—don't search the internet for a minute.
3. Make a hypothesis: "I think letter magick will do…"
4. Experiment: 99% of all magicians think everything they do is perfect—and thus avoid the burden of freedom.
5. Analyze and record your data—precisely, honestly, dispassionately.
6. Honestly share your results—with people who can replicate your experiments.

(Wow, that sounds hard!)

Of course, for the method of science, you smart, dedicated individuals are willing to put personal prejudices aside. The Bonn Group had that.

The aim of religion:

1. It must fulfill physical needs.
2. It must be repeatable.
3. It must fulfill emotional needs.
4. It must reflect the changing nature of the seeker, encouraging them toward growth, ethics, bliss.

(Wow, that sounds nice. I didn't know what religion was for.)

Most groups can't put their tiny earthbound egos aside for #4. Modern humans forget that #1 starts and ends quests. Most magicians lack the self-honesty to talk about #3. And #2 is true gold.

So, in Bonn, a stable and employed group of sane people with unbending intent followed Uncle Al's words. They chose the scientific method over dogma; they recognized their personal emotional needs. They did this democratically. They shared successes and failures and some of the truly Wyrd things that only magic will bring. They were gentle on themselves; they were hard on themselves.

Some of them became successful magicians or noted sorcerers, some so successful that we even hear of them in the insular world of English language occultism.

All of them lured the freedom dragon into their homes.

But none of that is important. I mean good for them. But what about me? I just got this book, and I'm reading this intro. What about me?

They left breadcrumbs.

They are completely transparent about method, struggle, and results.

You could do it. You can do it.

Read this book. Reread it. Then get that ad out there on Craigslist. Look for honest, sane, hardworking men and women from different backgrounds. Look above all for honesty, desire, and vulnerability.

Do your experiments. Keep notes. Know your failures, your successes, your moments of wonder.

The dragon will show up. I've done my due diligence in warning you. THIS is the most powerful book on magic. Best to throw it away now. I know some places that wouldn't sell it.

Don Webb
Ipsissimus Temple of Set

Introduction
Magic in a Vanguard Group:
The Bonn Workshop
for Experimental Magic

We wanted to be magicians, to become sorcerers. And some of us even seem to have succeeded—perhaps all? We cannot know for sure, as we are only partially in contact with each other these days. Four of us who still are in contact have designed this book.

At the end of 1979, a good dozen people came together at the Horus esoteric bookshop in Bonn, which had just been opened. Despite their lack of resemblance in terms of personal origin and biography, life experience and world view, they agreed on one common point: all of them were keenly interested in experimental magic and wanted to attempt to pursue it together, practically as well as theoretically.

Their ages ranged from the mid-twenties to the early thirties, and the ratio of men to women was almost balanced. At the time, the majority of them were university students, albeit spread across a wide variety of subjects: astronomy, Egyptology, English studies, ballet, biology, German studies, Indology, comparative literature, medicine, physics, sociology and comparative religious studies. There were also three participants from the nursing professions, including a Korean national and her German husband. One participant was currently working on his master's thesis, while also acting as managing director of the bookstore mentioned above, which means that he could be reckoned as a bookseller, too, as could his two business partners who also co-founded the workshop discussed here.

The group consisted of two married couples (another couple married shortly after the group's inception); of members who had been long-term friends already; of common-law partners; and of unattached singles. They all met for the first time as a group in this specific combination.

What's more, the magical background of the participants could not have been more varied. From the total greenhorn to the experienced Bardonian, from the expert in magical herbal knowledge and mythology to the academic researcher of tantrism, from the Wicca scholar to the sigil magician, from the rune vitki to the kundalini yoga adept, the group's accumulated wealth of experience and knowledge, each related to one or more of its members, was spread over such diverse areas as rune magic; the neo-hermetic Golden Dawn tradition; astrology; radiesthesia; natural magic; ancient Egyptian Heka; talismantics; Kabbalistic magic; Freemasonic symbolism; telepathy and parascience; medieval alchemy; Sufism; Afro-Caribbean cults of obsession; Eastern wisdom teachings from the Vedas or the religion commonly described as Hinduism; Buddhism; yoga philosophy; mantra techniques; Western magical fraternities and orders; sex magic; the tradition of German interwar period occultism; and numerous other subjects.

Undoubtedly, much of this was at first little more than reading-based half-knowledge, but that was exactly the point of the venture: to take up these manifold impulses and translate them into practical experience. All in all, the degree of magical erudition was significantly above average. Furthermore, there was a treasure trove of practical, diverse experiences of individual members, which should not be underestimated and from which everyone was to benefit together. In addition, the upcoming magical work and practical training of most participants would not be limited to the group meetings alone. At home, for example, many participants would often continue to work on their own initiative, either alone or with select partners, sharing during pursuant group meetings their personal experiences, the insights they had gained, and the questions that had cropped up.

But to return to the founding phase, after a lengthy discussion on how to define magic in general and experimental magic in particular, the group agreed to hold regular meetings and to develop a basic framework for further action. In doing so, we primarily took our cue from Anglo-Saxon, predominantly British, magic authors such as Crowley, Spare, Regardie, Dion Fortune, Butler, Conway, King, Grant, and others. This was mainly due to the fact that these writers differed dramatically from the predominantly authoritarian, dogmatic, and prescriptive style of German, French, and other Romance occultists by their rather relaxed pragmatism and their eminently practical didactics.

There was no elitist hierarchy implemented, no leadership, no high priestess, no chief ideologues of the group. All decisions were arrived at in an egalitarian democratic consensus. We refrained from establishing a formal association, did not impose membership fees and neither did we keep any membership lists. Thus the Bonn Workshop for Experimental Magic was created.

The Seven Mountains area (Siebengebirge), situated on the right bank of the Rhine river south of Bonn, then the capital of West Germany, is often referred to as a magical region. Myths and legends have penetrated and surrounded the·region since time immemorial. The best known is probably the Dragon's Rock (Drachenfels), where Siegfried is said to have slain the lindworm. Further, there are remains of Celtic castles of refuge, natural and artificial caves, and—ever since early nineteenth-century Rhine Romanticism at the very latest—the wooded region has generally been regarded as enchanted. From the top of the Dragon's Rock you can look down on the mighty river that winds through the Rhine Valley and flows around the two islands of Grafenwerth and Nonnenwerth. When the weather is clear, the outlines of the distant Cologne Cathedral can be discerned, as you can behold the Eifel region, a vast hilly forest area extending just behind the western riverbank, and the Godesburg castle, itself situated on an ancient Odin sanctuary, well into eastern Belgium.

Only a few years later, the Magical Pact of the Illuminates of Thanateros (IOT) was founded in an extinct volcanic crater not far from here. It was an organizational derivative of the previous, largely virtual, British order Illuminates of Thanateros (IOT), and it was from here that chaos magic finally set off on its triumphal procession across the magical world.

But it was primarily practical considerations that made this area our main operational base. We had access to an artificial cave, part of an underground system that served as an ammunition factory in wartime. After a short hike through a kind of vestibule, we climbed onto a spacious platform where we could work undisturbed, unnoticed from the outside. A large part of our ritual activities took place here. However, this was not exclusive: occasionally we would work in the Kottenforst forest to the left side of the Rhine river, and we also met now and then in the privacy of our homes.

We organized Pan invocations and planetary rituals; we consecrated amulets and talismans; we worked under the guidance of an African fetish priest whom we had invited specifically for this occasion; we explored elemental magic and techniques of Wicca; and we tried our hand at past life regression and oracle divination. We researched the mechanics of astromagic, analyzed horoscopes, practiced extensive trance work, experimented with pendulums and dowsing rods, and generally devoted significant scope of attention to success magic. On a weekend retreat in the Westerwald region, we concentrated solely on rune magic.

Not all members would partake at every meeting; frequently and additionally we would work in smaller subgroups at home. For example, two of our authors regularly conducted extensive hypnosis experiments with each other apart from the larger circle. Three of them met one Christmas Eve for an evocation based on the *Necronomicon*, well aware of the completely fictitious nature of this work once invented by H. P. Lovecraft, of which three entirely different versions circulated on the market at that time.

In fact, for a few of us it was these workings, independent from the group proper but always involving at least some of its participants, that constituted the actual impulse-giving part of the general project.

Everyone contributed what they were familiar with from their own praxis, what they were particularly interested in, or what they had only recently discovered. Our lowest common denominator was the Golden Dawn tradition. For example, the rituals usually began and ended with the Lesser Banishing Ritual of the Pentagram and a final release formula. Usually, after the magical operations, an extensive evaluation was called for, though sometimes we would follow through with it only at the subsequent meeting. In any case, the perpetual critical examination of our own workings played an eminently important role in our approach.

This applied equally to the theoretical treatment of magic. We discussed the most diverse magical authors, schools, and doctrines; dealt with Eastern and Western secret lore of all kinds; put the most common explanatory models to the test and, in doing so, brought our own observations and mishaps into dispute; discussed experiences of success and possible hazards of magical praxis; combined literary and personal anecdotes with philosophical ideas; considered, pondered, doubted, and confirmed; occasionally asked for help, offered advice, and gave active support; and often we simply ranted and speculated to our hearts' content.

Thus we gradually created our own experiential ecotope of magic without necessarily downright pursuing it. The result was not so much some canon of earth-shattering, unique insights, but rather the perception that the paths of magic are characterized by an almost inexhaustible diversity, which is why every fatuitous dogma that inadmissibly simplifies everything far removed from actual practice is bound to fail miserably.

Another essential aspect of the whole undertaking that cannot be overstated was the fact that each participant was always able to verify—simply by taking a single glance about—that there were indeed other magicians around, that you were not alone in the world in your struggle for the High Art. And finally, the sheer delight in experiencing the adventure of magic played a prominent role for everyone as well.

And at some point, after about three years, things had run their course: without any controversy or strife, the group finally disbanded in all composure and the members separated again. A few of them retained contact with each other, and continued to work together, some of them even to the present day; the rest simply lost sight of one another.

Human paths in life and processes of spiritual history are often very convoluted, difficult to grasp in detail and to determine precisely. What may seem to the observer and chronicler initially to be the cause often turns out to actually be an effect when looked at more closely in hindsight, and vice versa, so that we continue to be confronted with the well-known chicken and egg problem.

Thus also, the broader impact of this regional working group, originally limited to comparatively few members, cannot always be clearly determined. And yet there are some lines of connection and events that do permit us to draw some reliable conclusions.

For example, pragmatic magic was developed within this framework, and later the magazine *Unicorn* was created, in which numerous participants presented their magical experiences, insights, and reflections on a quarterly basis, thereby contributing decisively to the large-scale development of a magical scene in the German-speaking world. At the same time, the publishing house Edition Magus began its activities, itself headed by a workshop member, where several works written by participants were to see the light of day.

After *Unicorn* had stopped publication a good three years and thirteen issues later, Edition Magus subsequently launched the magazine *Anubis*, which owed decisive impulses to the workshop group even years later, and which itself contributed to the further evolution of German-language magic. The familiar image of the stone creating ripples when thrown into water could not be more appropriate when describing the Experimental Magic Workshop's repercussion.

With the renunciation of the traditionalist dogmatism that had shaped Western magic, partially excluding the Anglo-Saxon realm, well into the 1980s; with the systematic questioning of organization-centered hierarchies of mediation and authoritarian, almost exclusively patriarchal, structures of dominance; and finally with the evolution of pragmatic, rational, hence fundamentally discerning and, at their core, postmodern approaches, contemporary magic thoroughly changed its appearance in the course of the past forty years. It would certainly be presumptuous and misguided to attribute this solely to the Bonn Workshop for Experimental Magic. However, it is quite indisputable that, within this overall historical context, the workshop can certainly claim vanguard status.

The authors of the present work were all founding members of the workshop group and belonged to it up until its casual dissolution. Their aim is not only to draw a merely episodic conclusion from their collaboration at the time, but moreover to convey their current insights and knowledge in the field of magic. If they can offer some useful, constructive hints to any reader who also wishes to be a magician, become a sorcerer, and perhaps even contribute some inspiration to the continued pursuance of the Great Work of Magic, this book will have fulfilled its purpose.

The Authors

Chapter 1
Folk Magic vs. Library Magic:
Genetics or Enlightenment?
Of Low, High, Black, and White Magic

Frater U∴D∴

In classical magical literature, much ink has been spilled to highlight the difference between "low" and "high" magic. This ongoing tendency reached a climax in the works of Franz Bardon, who disparagingly described the representatives of the former as "deficient wizards" while the "true" magic belonged solely to the cosmically initiated adept.

By "low" magic, we are given to understand, since Theosophy at the latest, any magical action that is carried out from "selfish" motives or pursues purely material goals. Even a maverick like Aleister Crowley, who was demonstrably anything but unfamiliar with this kind of magical operation, rose to the statement that any activity not directly aimed at bringing about "union with the divine" was an act of black magic. We can see from this that the dividing line between "low" and so-called "black" magic, otherwise generally defined as malevolent spells, is often very blurred even when addressed by acclaimed authorities of the magical world. Nowadays people will generally refrain from the moralistic derogatory term "lower magic" and will instead refer to the neutral term "success magic."

In classical magic literature, "high" magic is generally regarded as a discipline that is based on a moral ethic that is only very diffusely defined in Christian-pietistic terms, and that is partly borrowed from Mahāyāna Buddhism, committed—at least in principle—to mysticism, adopting its aims as its own: be it Crowley's *unio mystica*, the labor on the "great edifice" of creation, a concept borrowed from Freemasonry, or any kind of "higher development" either of one's own individual or, preferably, the collective soul.

Before returning to this, let us take a look at another discipline of knowledge that in its own way comes to a very similar distinction important to our scrutiny: religious anthropology.

Magic and Religion: Chicken or Egg?

Until well into the 1950s anthropological religious studies were dominated by the view that magic was a form of high religion that fell victim to decadence and was broken down to the simplest conceivable level—superstition in pure culture. Still, in the late '60s, Theodor W. Adorno called spiritism, standing in for occultism in general, the "metaphysics of the dimwits." This academic narrative was itself characterized by the most harrowing simplism and utter ignorance of the actual cultural anthropological significance of magical ways of thinking and practices. It was only by way of the systematic shamanism research, starting with Mircea Eliade, and the incumbent field research results of anthropological structuralism, that it finally lost its sweeping dominance.

Until then, there was general agreement that the high religions (which themselves represented an overcoming and, finally, an elevation of preceding "primitive" cults by means of the "spirituality" developed by them) prescribed the basic matrix of what would later "degenerate" into mere magical superstitions.

Superstition—this very elastic term, known since the twelfth century, which etymologically connotes a "subordinated, false faith"—is a fief translation of the Latin *superstitio* (literally "super-faith"), which in Old Latin originally insinuated being out of oneself, i.e., ecstasy for magical-mystical purposes. At other times, *superstitiones* simply referred to fortune tellers.

It was the Stoics who early on branded *superstitio* as excessive fear of the gods, while Augustine of Hippo later converted it into a fighting word for the blanket designation of all non-Christian religions. Under Nero the Christians were in turn defamed in this manner. In the eighteenth and nineteenth centuries, following the Enlightenment and the Counter Enlightenment, it finally served as a propaganda term in the polemic against irrational-religious, dubious, or unorthodox worldviews, including Mesmerism and hypnosis as well as occultism in general.

The fact that the high religions themselves engage in magical practices on a large scale (think, for example, of the transubstantiation of the Christian Lord's Supper or Holy Communion—itself an act of theophagy, i.e., the physical ingestion of a deity; of the sacramental doctrine of both Catholicism and Orthodoxy; of the blessing of churches and secular buildings; of the striking of the sign of the cross; of holy water; of the cult of saints with its miraculous phenomena, etc.) was intentionally ignored. In brief, then, the formula was: "First came religion, then magic." The fact that this was merely a continuation of the ancient church doctrine remained largely unreflected, namely that miracles, i.e., supernatural phenomena came solely from God whereas magic was pure imitative devil's work—a controversy that goes back to the New Testament Epistles of Paul and the Acts of the Apostles (keyword: Simon Magus).

Superstition, Shamanism Research, and Folk Magic

If, for example, the formula *hoc est corpus meus* ("this is my body") from the Latin Mass is pinched and corrupted to the popular "hocus-pocus," we seem to find the mechanism described above confirmed: a liturgical declaration is misunderstood, taken out of its context, and transformed into a folk magic formula. An intrinsic magical power is ascribed to Latin in its role as the dominant sacred language. The grandfather of an Alsatian naturopath and magnetizer whom I knew in my early days used to express this in allusion to ecclesiastical exorcism: "The devil comes in German, but he only goes in Latin." It's certainly hard to deny that the already very eclectic folk magic which feeds itself from many heterogeneous sources often makes use of such borrowings from the prevailing religious context.

The same phenomenon can be observed in other religions and cultures. In the Nordic region, for example, there have been numerous discoveries of memorial stones and amulets that were decorated with pseudo-runes: rudimentarily rune-like but meaningless signs that apparently only imitated the actual runes of the Old Norse religion, and which were used by ignorant people who cheated their paying clientele with pretended magical knowledge. Today we would term them charlatans. In West African Islam, the widespread *marabous*, often referred to as "holy men," perform the function of pre-Islamic animistic tribal magicians and fetish priests, hiding their pagan magical activities only scantily behind an Islamic facade. For example, they will craft amulets and talismans from Koranic surahs (so-called *gris-gris*), which are in ubiquitous demand among the populace and are worn, for example, in small leather caskets on the arm. These *marabous* are also responsible for other magical commissioned works that are generally based on animistic practices, and that will often require animal sacrifices. Although this form of magic is strongly rejected by Islamic orthodoxy because it views it as polytheistic idolatry, it is indispensable in the West African world, as are the countless shrines regularly visited by nominally Muslim pilgrims to invoke miracles.

We also find similar practices in Central and Latin America, where a multitude of pre-Columbian cult sites, at best superficially Christianized, have been frequented by the populace since time immemorial, as they were long before the advent of the Spanish conquerors, often even at the same ancient seasonal festivals to this very day.

The still-young science of anthropology finally cleared up the misconception that magic was only a kind of waste product of conventional high religion. In fact, the exact opposite is true. For it is entirely legitimate to define religion as a form of organization whose main concern is to monopolize magic in order to be able to perform its actual function: namely to establish, consolidate, and perpetuate the dominant social order and its hierarchical power structures. To accomplish this, the magical will and actions of the community members must be channeled in a controlled manner. Thus a full-time priesthood emerges, which takes the place of the former tribal magicians and medicine women. At the same time, this process reflects the transition from nomadic to settled societies.

From now on, it is religion, functioning as a social lubricant, which regulates all existential aspects of life: from nutrition to reproduction to the rules of interpersonal relations, child rearing, jurisdiction, and, not to forget, land tenure and ownership conditions. There is no place within such a framework for the remnants of socially difficult to control, fundamentally anarchic folk magic, which is usually only passed on within individual families among blood relatives, and which is committed neither to society as a whole nor to its rulers and the moral ethics and legal codes imposed by them. Consequently, all folk-magic action is perceived as competition by the rulers and the caste of priests working for them, and is accordingly ostracized: an uncontrolled ulceration that should be stopped and exterminated at all costs.

It would, however, be ahistorical to accuse these ruling elites and their priesthoods of exclusively power-obsessed cynicism and pure bigotry. For there is every reason to believe that they were just as convinced of the fundamental effectiveness of magic as were their congregations and subjects. For this very reason, it was developed into a technology of domination in the first place: magic was regarded as a highly effective weapon of world design, the deployment of which by dissatisfied, hostile, or even rebellious groups of the population could certainly endanger the status quo.

For a similar reason, astrologers were persecuted in Rome during the imperial era; setting up the imperial horoscope was punishable by death. And indeed, the political propaganda of various conspiracy groups was already working with falsified horoscopes of the rulers at that very time, as it was to happen again centuries later in Martin Luther's time, and even as late as World War II.

Such prohibitions were issued because the rulers were thoroughly convinced of the validity of astrological insights. Certainly, in the Roman Empire of this epoch, there were among the intellectual elite already large numbers of skeptics who deemed such doings to be outright nonsense. But the long-established Roman custom of always erecting an altar and offering sacrifices to the "unknown god" so as not to inadvertently enrage some overlooked divine entity proves that, in general, a pragmatic "one can never know" attitude prevailed.

The worldwide cross-cultural field research of anthropology and ethnology also made it abundantly clear that common superstition must by no means be sweepingly lumped together with folk religion and magic. Folk magic, as we understand it here, is not a codified or uniform system of magical practices. What's more, only in the rarest of cases is it theoretically reflected upon by its practitioners, and it's not even considered to be learnable as a general matter of principle. As a rule, it manifests itself by some people, regardless of gender, at some point coming out with skills that are generally regarded as magical or supernatural. These magical powers are usually considered innate, but often they also constitute specific, proprietary magical knowledge that can or may only be imparted within the bloodline:

in short, a family craft. The transmission is frequently organized by strict regulations regarding gender or generational affiliation. For example, in one case the talent is only passed from grandmother to granddaughter, in the other from father to son, and so on.

In the course of imparting this knowledge, a form of initiation often takes place, or an awakening of the previously latent paranormal or magical aptitude is brought about. Ethics and morals of society as a whole, if at all called up, play only a marginal role at best: clan ethics goes beyond social ethics.

Basically, the spectrum of inherited or imparted magical skills is very broad: it ranges from clairvoyance ("second sight") and oracle art, to healing powers and weather spells, to protective magic. It includes love and damage magic, the "selling" of warts and shingles, as well as obstetrics and promoting the fertility of humans, livestock, or arable land.

However, only a very small selection at most comes to the fore with the individuals in question. While for example in a given family clan clairvoyance alone prevails, another is perhaps limited to making rain or practicing hail magic, whereas a third family is primarily focused on selling warts, healing animals, or cursing disagreeable rivals in love. Thus, magical universal talents are rather rare in this context. In addition, these talents almost never affect the entire family, but will always be limited to only a few of its members: a sort of folk magic specialization.

Even in the twenty-first century, almost every village still knows its "wise woman," its "cunning folk," its female or male "witch." However, this is usually kept secret from strangers. Even though these magically active people may often seem eerie or even threatening to their neighbors, as they have done for millennia, people like to make use of their skills to cope with their own life crises, to catch a glimpse of the future, or to help their wishes come true.

Often, those affected will complain in personal conversation that they had no other choice: whether it be that the skills in question "erupted" unintentionally, or that their family tradition required them to assume the role intended for them. The manifestation of one's own otherness and the frequently associated social exclusion are often perceived as a great personal burden. If one assumes, for example, that a person can provide for a rich harvest or extensive rainfall, the suspicion quickly germinates that the same person could also be responsible in the event of poor harvests or periods of drought.

In fairy tales, myths, and legends, the witch or warlock often lives either on the outer edge of the settlement, isolated in the woods, or in impassable terrain, if not right at the end of the world. We can see in this a symbolic hint that they were usually only granted a role as social outsiders. They used their magic skills all right, but at the same time they were surrounded by a nimbus of danger: ofttimes respected, always feared, but never loved.

Let's not forget that the time of witch hunts is by no means over. In some parts of Africa and Papua New Guinea it is still the order of the day, as it is in many parts of Asia and Latin America. And perhaps it is only a matter of time before it breaks out again in one way or another, even in our supposedly enlightened latitudes. Today's civilized funeral pyres may no longer consist of stakes of torture on shimmering stacks of wood, but they are of a media and digital nature, or may take the form of administrative harassment measures such as unfounded investigations into alleged ritual murders, judicially mandated admissions to psychiatry wards, or the withdrawal of parental custody on suspicion of belonging to a cult. Those who follow the international Western media of the past hundred years will repeatedly come across corresponding, hair-raising examples.

Literate Culture and Western Magic

Only with the culture of writing did the concept of "high" magic develop in the West. It is the product of theologically influenced—and accordingly biased—scholars. The oldest written documents known to us today, Babylonian cuneiform tablets, are indeed tools of trade and industry: delivery and stock lists, orders for merchandise, and complaints. But it was not long before administrations and religions also discovered the cultural technology of writing for themselves and developed it into an instrument of societal organization and power. For thousands of years it was to remain the monopoly of a few system-supporting specialists in most cultures.

The acquisition of the skills of reading and writing required expert instruction; it demanded study, effort, and time, generally securing no immediate return, and thus it was completely unaffordable to the overwhelming majority of society, plus being irrelevant to the management of average everyday life.

Even in the early Middle Ages, the lower clergy consisted almost exclusively of illiterates.

The higher ranks of the ecclesiastical hierarchy were different: not only did they cultivate their religious literature since the turn of time, but after the decline of the Roman Empire, they were also responsible for the operation of libraries, schools, and the later universities, and so for centuries they produced the majority of scholars, even if over a long period of time they required the translation work and the commentary efforts of their initially culturally far more advanced (and accordingly intellectually and epistemologically more sophisticated) Arab Islamic colleagues in order to at least partially restore the lost pagan writings of antiquity.

It was out of this impulse that medieval scholasticism developed, one of the focal points of which was not least the so-called philosophy of nature. According to the understanding at that time, magic was an organic part of this, but until the Enlightenment all this had to be conceived of within the Christian-biblical, i.e., theological paradigm prescribed by the Church. Any deviation from this was quickly sanctioned as a mortal heresy.

It is noteworthy in this context that the late medieval persecution of witches, which to a large extent took place on supposed as well as actual representatives of folk magic, only began to gain traction on a significant scale that touched the entire Occident after scholars had begun to legally equate witchcraft (which is generally synonymized with folk magic) with heresy. This development may have contributed decisively to the mania of later authors of grimoires to present their own works as prime examples of pious, godly, and thus "high" natural magic, even if their content often proved these assertions a blatant lie.

Since scholasticism, scholars were concerned with understanding magic as a real, tangible force of nature, and sought to master it. This took place in intensive discourse with other natural philosophers, based on an extensive study of classical sources. So it was inevitable that the scholarly dialogue would eventually develop into what we here—not without a modicum of irony—want to call "library magic."(In today's academic religious studies the term "learned magic" is more commonly used.) It was often considered abstractly, subjected to a priori basic assumptions and dogmas of a theological-cosmological nature, and theoretically justified. In the end, it mutated into a pure reading product whose representatives themselves had no discernible magic-practical experience to draw upon. The question of a magical talent that might conceivably be necessary for the exercise of magic receded completely into the background; instead, it was solely a question of their intellectual grasp and the myriad of theoretical rules they allegedly constituted.

Only Theophrastus Bombast von Hohenheim (ca. 1493–1541), better known as Paracelsus, as a trained and front-experienced field surgeon who had always been a proven man of practice, was to vehemently break away from academic medicine and magic, which were exhausting themselves in theoretical considerations. Although he was himself temporarily employed in university service, he enthusiastically plunged into the lowlands of folk magic, constantly seeking dialogue with the "common people" (still predominantly illiterate), in order to learn from them everything that concerned his art of healing and his mystical ambitions: herbalism and folk medicine as well as the magical practices that were then—and in many respects still are today—inseparable from them.

The Ever-Vexing Talent Question

The question as to whether the exercise of magic necessarily requires a given talent, or whether it can also be mastered without such a talent by study alone, does not normally arise for the folk magician. In any case, such abstract considerations do not play a significant role in folk magic, as we have already demonstrated.

On the other hand, it now moves many contemporary representatives of library magic, even though it has unmistakably not yet been clearly illuminated. There are good arguments for both positions, but both of them also have to live with numerous counter-examples being led into battle by the opposing side. For some, magic has become, to put it in contemporary terminology, first and foremost a question of genetics, while for others it is a matter of enlightenment and education.

Unfortunately, the fact remains that magicians, whether natural talents or "semi-skilled," in Western society—and by no means in the West alone—usually do not enjoy an easy life and are largely ridiculed, shunned, and marginalized by the mainstream.

Magic Special Forces: Beyond the Goats

At least the military world seems to be significantly less selective in this respect. The first time I came across this fact was when the magical student of a long-time English friend and colleague told me explicitly about it. He hailed from a very remote northern English village—the kind of closely knit community where a family, even after fifteen generations, is still considered to have "just moved in." This pupil, let's call him P., came from a family in which an above-average number of members had clairvoyant abilities, some more pronounced, some less so. This was apparently typical for the entire area. In the English folk tradition such people are usually called "cunning folk." We find an analogy to this in the German-speaking Alpine region of central Europe, where they are referred to as "wise men/women," a term that also aptly mirrors the English term.

P. reported that the British military regularly employ demographic maps showing the increased manifestation of paranormal abilities among the population of the British Isles. In these areas, the special armed forces are increasingly carrying out recruitment measures. They are particularly interested in young people with skills in telepathy, remote perception, and precognition. These subjects are preferentially recruited and then subjected to appropriate tests. After their general military training, they are finally combined into platoons and drilled for their actual purpose. As is customary with special forces, they are deployed primarily behind enemy lines in conflict situations, where they are usually entrusted with reconnaissance and sabotage tasks. Thus P. himself was recruited and was finally assigned to special missions in both Gulf Wars.

The Russian special armed forces (Speznas), which are subordinated to the GRU military foreign intelligence service, also proceed in a similar way. Within these circles the Russian martial art *Systema* was developed early on in the Stalin era. To this end, the most diverse indigenous and, above all, East Asian martial arts styles were analyzed and separated from their metaphysical and speculative attributes, after which their most efficient elements suitable for military use were combined. The result was—and still is today—a martial art, which does without any theoretical superstructure, but whose experienced representatives can reliably demonstrate physical effects which for thousands of years were generally ascribed only to magicians or sorcerers. The spectrum ranges from the contactless defense against several opponents via remote paralysis to pain control and physical resistance, as well as a degree of agility normally only ascribed to Eastern fakirs, to name just a few select examples. I have been able to convince myself of this personally at numerous seminars and meetings with Russian and German Systema trainers.

Vladimir Vasiliev, the director of *Systema* responsible for the North American region and a former Speznas member himself, describes in his book *The Russian System Guidebook: Inside Secrets of Soviet Special Forces Training* how the recruits in his Speznas basic training were systematically trained to develop their paranormal abilities as resiliently as possible.[1] This included, for example, holding colored surfaces apart with their eyes blindfolded, the contactless determination of displaced and stolen objects in a completely darkened room, and the like.

It is also remarkable that this takes place on a purely materialistic, empirical basis, i.e., without any metaphysical or esoteric-magical explanatory concepts. The military is known for its pragmatism. Whatever works and is considered to be useful is adopted as far as possible, whether academic science accepts its existence or not. Among experts, it is also agreed that most probably just about all special armed forces in the world are likely to be operating on similar lines. However, though this assumption seems extremely plausible, it cannot unfortunately be verified independently beyond a doubt, as such matters are generally classified with a vengeance.

Finally, the well-known feature film *Men Who Stare at Goats* (2009) by Grant Heslov (starring Ewan McGregor, George Clooney, Kevin Spacey, and Jeff Bridges) merits mentioning. This movie features a secret US Army special unit in the 1960s. In addition to the use of hallucinogens and meditation techniques, they also carried out exercises to kill experimental animals (primarily goats—hence the title of the film) by means of willpower through merely staring at them.

It doesn't take too much imagination to envisage the benefits the military might expect from such an ability, which can reasonably be called magical. But even though the film comes across as an amusing comedy, it is essentially

---

1. *The Russian System Guidebook: Inside Secrets of Soviet Special Forces Training* (Visalia, CA: Optimum Training Systems, 1997).

based on verifiable facts: the unit in question did indeed exist, although it was later dissolved as an experiment largely considered to have failed.

Magical Synergies to Be Wished For

Folk and library magic, innate talent, and magical abilities acquired only through intensive study, persistent practice, and practical experience do not necessarily have to be antagonistic to one another, even though this was usually considered to be the case in the past. While military special forces recruit people's magic talents, they continue to train them in accordance with parapsychology, as the example of the Russian Speznas and the above-mentioned unit of the US Army go to show.

Our Bonn Workshop for Experimental Magic, which united both magical natural talents and largely talentless aspirants (like myself; but see also Josef Knecht's self-description in this book[2]), has again proved that a collaboration between the two can be extremely fruitful if the resulting synergies are made use of. So it does not have to remain an either/or scenario; the as-well-as can readily take its place. In any case, it is worth noting that the last word on this subject is still far from being spoken.

---

2. See Josef's views in chapter 9, "Some Questions on Magic."

Chapter 2
My Path from
Wish Magic to Da'ath Magic

Harry Eilenstein

When I was 21, I was sitting one day under my favorite tree in the city park of Bad Godesberg (Bonn, Germany), recently hit by a major life crisis and wondering what would happen next. All of a sudden someone immediately behind me responded to my inner question: "Learn magic!" When I turned around, however, there was nobody to be seen. Thus, another question mark popped up for me.

Nevertheless, I did actually follow the suggestion by going to the library and my local bookshop to have a look at all the books about magic I could get hold of. But I realized right away that conjuring up white rabbits from black top hats couldn't really be what the voice had meant by "magic." So I eventually returned to the park and sat under my tree again.

Then, a school colleague of a friend of mine came by and invited me to a party. Since I had grown up very much like a forest goblin of sorts and had never been to a party before, I decided to go along, thinking to myself: "This is a really strange day..."

At the party I met a lady who told me about her holiday in France. Suddenly I saw the landscape and the lady's surroundings before my inner eye and was able to expand on individual scenes of her narrative on my own without any further cues from her. This day was indeed becoming ever more strange—but in fact it wasn't over yet.

In the shared apartment where the lady in question was living, among her housemates was an herbalist, a drummer who frequently traveled to India to meditate, an astrologer, a lady interested in tantra, plus Axel, a self-proclaimed black magician—however, as it turned out, a totally good-hearted fellow.[3]

When I came into Axel's bedroom and saw all the symbols hanging on the wall, the crystal ball on the table, and the huge mirror, I immediately realized that I had finally arrived at the place where I could learn "real" magic. I told Axel about the voice and my wish, whereupon he prompted me to close my eyes and tell him what I sensed. A bit confused, I did so and reported that I felt like I was swaying, being pulled back and forth. Apparently he was satisfied, responding: "Open your eyes again. You are now my sorcerer's apprentice."

Since Axel was inclined to live by the maxim "the more it sizzles and makes you dizzy, the merrier," I quickly experienced all kinds of things with him, from telepathy and mirror magic to remote hypnosis, and from the citation of spirits to astral travel and the summoning of demons.

Apparently there was something in me that felt that these things were all part of my life and that I should learn them now. This would radically expand the view of the world I subscribed to at the time.

Before my encounter with Axel, I had been utterly shaken in my originally naive, romantic, and nature-based worldview by my first girlfriend, who was in her way fundamentally a diehard pessimist. This led me to reappraise my entire weltanschauung and, above all, my own way of thinking. As a result, I began to not believe in anything anymore, and to question everything.

To me, cerebration and reasoning seemed to consist, at least as far as I myself was concerned, of compiling observations, which I would subsequently examine for regularities in order to be able to apply these rules in everyday life. This attitude actually facilitated my access to magic tremendously because I simply accumulated lots of new experiences via Axel and scrutinized them for regularities accordingly.

First off, I became acquainted with telepathy (remote hypnosis, etc.) and telekinesis (e.g. when a candle suddenly veered through the room during an evocation) as basic elements. The explanation model applied was the life force, which could also be deployed for astral projection and many other things. In this model, the astral body was viewed as a framework of vital force whose organs are the chakras and whose bloodstream is the flow of the

---

3 This was Axel Büdenbender: see his contributions in this book.

kundalini. I became more acquainted with the chakras and the kundalini in greater depth by working with rune magic.

Essentially, for me, the life force was an invisible substance that you can sometimes see like a milky-white glow with a slight blue shimmer and feel as tingling warmth. Moreover, with its help you can achieve effects in the outer world just like you can with the physical body. Apparently there were rules governing this life force as well, as demonstrated by astrology, which I studied auto-didactically at the time. These rules were, to all appearances, parallels, parables, and analogies.

One day I found a diagram of the kabbalistic Tree of Life in one of Axel's many voluminous tomes. I immediately thought: "That's it! That's it! That's exactly what I was looking for!" But to be honest I really didn't have the slightest clue what that could actually be.

Over the next few years I discovered that the Tree of Life diagram is a structure that is contained in everything—from your vacuum cleaner and the structure of the German constitution to a biological cell and a colony of bees, the history of mankind, and the innate formation of a star.

So now I had two distinct systems at my disposal that described the world as a system of analogies: astrology and the kabbalistic Tree of Life (see illustration). Tarot, telepathy, telekinesis, and most forms of magic could also be described as "applied analogies." The world was obviously ordered both by causality and by analogies. Combining the two revealed the image of a perfect symmetrical mandala unfolding like a kaleidoscope in which each and every part was related to all the others.

However, I found it a bit odd that magic sometimes worked and sometimes didn't. Telepathy was quite reliable, astrology always seemed to do the job for me, but calling for desired objects, encounters, and events was a bumpy affair—sometimes it was successful and sometimes it wasn't. What was the reason for this?

Were my analogies inaccurate? Hardly, no. Did I concentrate too little on the consecration of the talismans with which I wanted to summon something? Not really, either.

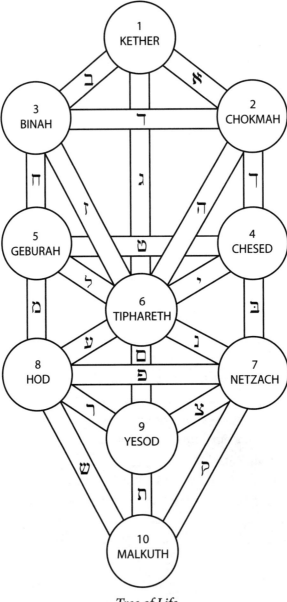

Tree of Life

When I took a closer look at my magical desires and their effects and at Axel's as well, I got the impression that my magically projected desires were actually being answered quite precisely—but the analogy world seemed to "think" more holistically: whenever I wished for something, the result did not merely match my desired image as such, but rather my desired image *including all associations tied to it.*

In practical terms, this obviously meant that if I had wished for a relationship, but at the same time was actually scared of relationships in general, what I got eventually was a relationship with a woman whom I was terrified of.

This allowed only one possible conclusion: if magic is to lead to agreeable results, you must heal the images in your own psyche. In magic, inner contradictions will lead to conflicting results.

At that time I was reading *Techniques of High Magic* by Francis King and Stephen Skinner. One evening, after some further "magic adventures" with Axel, I read him a chapter of the English book, translating it into German from time to time because Axel doesn't enjoy reading English very much. This book describes a "dream travel" meditation with the help of which you can find your own "Higher Self." I knew immediately that I would practice this meditation daily until I had found my "Higher Self" (whatever that might turn out to be).

After two years' meditation, first my power animal and then my soul appeared to me. I had never heard of spirit animals before but the encounter felt like a reunion with an old friend.

Between the ages of eighteen to twenty-two I often wondered what the meaning of life might be. Everything I checked out to see whether it could constitute the meaning of life—from truth to God to beauty—had only ever led to plenty of contradictions or circular reasoning. Finally, I came up with the idea of asking myself how I would actually recognize my purpose in life if I ever did come across it.

I determined several different criteria: it had to make sense immediately; it couldn't be anything that felt strange in any way; and it had to be there already, even though I had obviously overlooked it so far. With a little further musing I decided that the only thing that fulfilled these three criteria was I myself. So my purpose in life is to express what I am.

When I met my Higher Self in the course of my meditation, all questions ceased at that very moment—I saw what I am at the core and what I want to express in my life. This Higher Self is obviously the soul, i.e., what has incarnated in me. It is the meaning of life.

As long as one has not yet identified oneself with one's own soul, i.e., as long as you haven't yet recognized it as your own core and center, it will appear from the outside as a "guardian angel."

I assume that it was my soul that originally said to me in the park: "Learn magic!" She finally made me recognize her with merely two words—a rather effective approach.

Obviously it is most useful to connect any magic to your own soul, i.e., to practice "soul magic." However, the question arose whether the soul is not already radiating, i.e., expressing itself—did I really have to wish for anything in a magical manner? Actually, it was quite enough to heal one's own psyche for the light of the soul to radiate into the world, unhindered by fears, addictions, misguided ideas, etc. According to the principle of analogy, what happens in the world around me should thus correspond to the essence of my soul—a spontaneous fulfillment of the meaning of life, as it were, since the self-expression of my soul is my meaning of life.

So the goal in magic (at least in terms of my own art) is to heal yourself so that your own experiences, magically induced and otherwise, are in accordance with what the soul wishes to express.

With this approach there was still the issue that magically projected "yes, but..." wishes led to results with a snag to them, but at least the path to pursue was now perfectly clear: self-healing.

During my community service in a nursing home for the elderly, I used to ride my bicycle for a good hour in the morning and again back home in the evening. As I was freezing in winter, I told myself at some point that as a sorcerer's apprentice I should really try to solve the problem in a magical way.

So I came up with the idea that I could alternately inhale and exhale with every stepping into the pedals, inwardly saying "fire" and imagining that I could draw fire from the earth's interior or from the engines of the passing cars while inhaling and that I could then channel this fire into my body and, above all, into my ice-cold hands while exhaling.

As this proved quite successful right from the outset, my motivation and, consequently, my concentration was very high. At the time I was not aware that I was unwittingly applying the essential elements of the Tibetan *tummo* meditation, which lamas in Tibet practice to keep themselves warm out in the freezing cold.

This meditation had an unexpected side effect: I woke up. Until then I had only known deep sleep, dream, and waking consciousness, but with the fire meditation on the bike I woke up beyond the normal waking state itself. This experience was simply awesome: I was literally radiating, there was a deep peace inside of me, an all-fulfilling warmth, and I could suddenly fathom the smile of the Buddha statues and the ancient Egyptian statuettes—apparently they knew this state, too.

After about half a year of "cycling in ecstasy," suddenly something happened that I had never heard of before: I was heading toward a crossroads near the flood plain of the river Rhine when I abruptly perceived myself standing at the edge of a bottomless abyss and sensed the mute invitation to take the jump. I panicked, pedaled wildly, and sped away, cursing God and the world just to get away from that abyss.

After I had calmed down again, I began to suspect that I had accosted an important inner place—albeit rather unsuspectingly and totally unprepared for the encounter.

After some further deliberation I noticed that on the kabbalistic Tree of Life there is a place called "The Abyss." You get to it when you've gotten to know your own soul and pushed on with your search.

That was my first encounter with the boundlessness of Da'ath: the call to jump into the bottomless abyss. For this confrontation you actually require total confidence, trusting in this leap into formlessness, surrendering in free fall.

Following this experience, I was still able to keep warm with my fire meditation, but the fulfilled state of awakening did not manifest anymore and neither did the encounter with the abyss.

Around that time, about a dozen people met in the newly founded esoteric Horus bookstore in Bonn; we all hailed from different backgrounds and we were all interested in magic. These monthly meetings, which Axel and I both attended regularly, lasted for about three years. It was refreshing to meet other people who were also aware of and actually practiced magic. Our mutual approach was to explore magic in its totality: how did it work? What could you do with it? What were the decisive experiences in magic?

Apart from the fact that I met Josef[4] and Frater U∴D∴ there, an encounter with a fellow member named Peter was especially significant to me. Initiated by the anthropologist Johanna Wagner, he had learned of an African tradition focused on activating the "clan animal" or "clan being." To effect this, he would simply sit down drumming and thus called up the "clan being." When I finally became aware of it, I realized that this "clan being" was identical with my soul.

In the writings of the Sufi philosopher Ibn 'Arabī I found an image that spoke directly from my soul, if I may put it that way: he describes the world as a perfect sphere—and the innermost being of this sphere is Allah. Every human being is a part of this world and thus also a part of Allah's self-expression. If one imagines a human being as a part of this sphere, one can also imagine extracting him out of this world. The surface of this world fragment (i.e., the person in question) corresponds exactly to the surface of that place in the world from which this particular fragment was excised. This in turn means that what a human being expresses is in harmony with the events of the world. All events in the world will thus fit the person who experiences them: this is Allah's care for all people.

Obviously, this is only an image and you may choose to interpret it differently. But when reading the Ibn 'Arabī text describing it, I suspected for the first time that there could be a more comprehensive worldview in which the effect of causality and the analogies that structure the world are thought through to the very end—and that an entirely different attitude to life will result from this worldview: the outside is a mirror image of the inside—and vice versa.

Several years later I dropped by on Josef and told him about a feeling of mine: I had the distinct impression that it was time to get to know Da'ath. Da'ath is an area on the kabbalistic Tree of Life that describes a continuum, an area without boundaries. For various reasons I had the impression that this area was where my path would lead me next.

When I told Josef about it, he replied that this was exactly what he himself felt when scrutinizing his own path. From then on we met fortnightly for several years and conducted dream journeys to the eleven areas and twenty-two

---

4. This was Josef Knecht: see his contributions in this book.

paths on the Tree of Life. By doing this, we got to understand many things a whole lot better than before. Above all, we also experienced things whose existence we had only suspected until then: the "archive of incarnation" in Chesed, the boundlessness in Da'ath, the security in the community of Binah, the light storm of the creative impulse in Chokmah, the fulfilling unity in Kether.

Some years later again, I asked myself how I might get back to the abyss and into Da'ath—I vied for a more constant "awakened state" again. To this effect, I interviewed Christian healers, Japanese Zen roshis, Tibetan lamas etc. and told them about my experiences, but they invariably harbored the suspicion that I was overdoing it on drugs—though I had never done drugs before in my entire life! Thus, I had to pursue my search all by myself again.

Which meditation or ritual might help me in my quest? If nobody could tell me, I would have to design something on my own. For this to happen, I had to better understand the essence of Da'ath: ideally as a mathematical formula, a physical graph, or something similar.

Since the best-explored field of knowledge is cosmology, i.e., the combination of astronomy with nuclear physics, I worked my way into this subject for half a year and searched for a suitable formula or structure describing Da'ath. Physics' equivalent to Da'ath is the transition from matter (delimited forms) to energy (boundless energy fields): Einstein's famous equation "$E=mc^2$."

Finally, I found what I was looking for: the so-called "SO3"-symmetry. This is a matrix, a table describing how protons, neutrons, electrons, neutrinos, photons, etc. can be transformed into any other of these particles. This was a kind of "transformation mandala."

In any mandala meditation, the meditator must be familiar with the elements of the mandala and describe the entire world and their own experience as part of that mandala. The four elements, which appear all over in magic and which are also arranged as a mandala in the four cardinal points in the Lesser Pentagram Ritual, are obviously best suited for this particular mandala.

First of all, I meditated on the four elements as components of the world, i.e., I imagined all things as consisting of these four elements. Next, I transferred the four elements into the psyche and imagined myself as being made up of them: fire is power, water is love, air is truth, and earth is prosperity.

Then I started to transform each element into the other in meditation—both internally (psychic phenomena) and externally (material things). In the psyche, for example, fire transforms into water when power gives you the courage to love. Truth (air) leads to prosperity (earth); love (water) leads to strength (fire) etc. On the outside, water can become a part of the earth when plants grow; fire becomes a part of (hot) water when cooking etc.

Through this meditation, I got used to the fact that there is no demarcation and I could subsequently let go of more and more forms until I finally felt comfortable in the demarcationless Da'ath behind the leap into the abyss.

This eventually led to a new form of individuality that was no longer based on the demarcation from the "non-I" but on the certainty of one's own innate quality.

After I had conducted this meditation for a while, I also understood what the Buddha meant by the four boundless qualities of an enlightened being: boundless serenity (equanimity), boundless mercy (compassion), boundless love, and boundless joy. This is quite simply the state of Da'ath.

- In Da'ath one does not try to draw borders anymore but rather experiences everything that is as best can be—boundless equanimity.
- In Da'ath one experiences oneself as part of the whole and therefore loves the world as oneself—boundless love.
- In Da'ath one no longer experiences a separation between inside and outside and therefore develops an enlightened (and accordingly wise and effective) egotism that encompasses the welfare of the entire world—boundless mercy.
- In Da'ath one experiences the resonance of oneself with the entire world—boundless joy.

While there was no actual need for it, it was nevertheless a pleasant and welcome confirmation that Buddha apparently knew the state of consciousness of Da'ath. I was obviously on a good path.

We can also represent the phases of this path with the help of the Middle Pillar of the kabbalistic Tree of Life:

My path commenced in Malkuth, in the physical world.

Then my soul interfered and sent me to Axel to become a sorcerer's apprentice and study magic. There, I got to know the vital force with which one can accomplish "ordinary magic"—this is the sphere Yesod on the Tree of Life.

Next, I came to Tiphareth and got to know my own soul. Thereupon I connected my antecedent "Yesod magic" to Tiphareth, i.e., I strove simply to let the essence of my soul in my heart chakra radiate outward through my psyche unhindered.

The next step is the arrival in the demarcationless area of Da'ath, where the "extraordinary magic" becomes possible, which I will describe later in this book.

Finally, there is another step on the Middle Pillar that leads to Kether. The Kether state can be described as achieving unity, resting in God, or similar, depending on one's own view of the world. We can assume that one will then connect the magic of Da'ath to God in Kether—just as Yesod magic is connected to Tiphareth after getting to know one's own soul.

Chapter 3

Bending the Arm of Chance:
When Does Magic
Really Become Magic?

Frater U∴D∴

It's not every day you get to meet the man who killed Aleister Crowley. This was exactly what happened to me in the early summer of 1979 when I traveled through Great Britain to establish contacts with suppliers of esoteric accessories for our Horus bookshop in Bonn, Germany, which was to open in fall. One of the most important wholesalers in the United Kingdom at that time was the Metaphysical Research Group in Hastings in the south of England, the very place where Aleister Crowley had spent the last years of his life, and where he died in 1947.

The Metaphysical Research Group was the business arm of the Society of Metaphysicians, established in 1944 and headquartered in Hastings since 1947. Both were founded and headed by John Jacob Williamson, an elderly, very sociable gentleman at the time of our meeting. Williamson enjoyed being addressed as a "doctor," was extremely eloquent, drove a green Jaguar (which he was wont to do like a veritable devil, as I was sorry to learn when he kindly delivered me to the train station after our next meeting), and knew the contemporary esoteric scene in Great Britain like the back of his hand. He was also the author of various esoteric works in which he dealt, for example, with astral projection and what he termed "New Metaphysics" (tagged "Neometaphysics"). Some of his books are still available today (he died in 2012). Essentially a kind, mild mannered, and somewhat woolly spiritualist, he did not give you the impression that he could so much as hurt a fly.

Hastings, 1947, Crowley: it was only natural that I asked him about all that soon after we shook hands. And he proved perfectly amenable to respond. Yes, Aleister Crowley lived only a little stretch down the road from them, almost if not quite an immediate neighbor. No, they had never met each personally, though he had glimpsed him once very briefly on the other side of the street. So far, everything came over as harmless as one could hope for. But that should change quite unexpectedly.

Shortly after opening his company offices, he continued, they received a visit from two young men, obviously Crowley's followers, who appeared to be the Master Therion's guests for a few days. One talked shop about occult affairs in an amiable atmosphere during afternoon tea.

However, soon after this encounter utter chaos set in without any warning: business partners and associates suddenly became entangled in disagreements, merchandise orders that they had been confident of were canceled entirely out of the blue for no discernible reason, financial irregularities popped up, their entire material existence began to waver.

Becoming suspicious, Williamson finally inspected his premises—and promptly found what he was looking for. Hidden in a corner, he discovered a magic chalk mark on the wall of the room: quite obviously a souvenir left behind by his recent visitors.

"So I picked up a piece of cloth," he reported, "and wiped the sign off." Then, after a brief dramatic pause, with sparkling eyes and a grimly ironic mien, came the real punchline: "And in the same night Aleister Crowley died. Coincidence, of course." There was no denying that the affable Dr. Williamson, like any good esotericist, did not believe in happenstance of whatever ilk at all, most certainly not inasmuch as this grisly anecdote was concerned.

I visited him again later, as mentioned before, and we actually maintained a very good and reliable business relationship for several years. However, he never came back on the episode described above.

I later recounted this anecdote in a somewhat abridged form without naming the then still living J.J. Williamson for reasons of discretion in my (German) article "Coincidence, of course! The Problem of Magic Success Control."[5] Nothing has changed regarding the basic problem discussed therein to this day.

---

5. "Zufall, natürlich!' Das Problem der magischen Erfolgskontrolle," in: *Unicorn. Spirituelle Wege und Erfahrungen* (No. 7, Winter 1983), pp. 225–229.

It was also in 1979, quite at the beginning of my first courageous steps on the deceptive ground of practical magic, when one evening I stood with my then-girlfriend on the right bank of the river Rhine and we spontaneously decided to perform an improvised ritual right on the spot. Cheerfully tuned, very much in love, a bit exuberant, and foolishly ready for just about any mischief, we immediately put this project into practice. We didn't have any tools such as magical weapons with us and so we had to imagine the magic circle as well as the other paraphernalia we knew rudimentarily from the Golden Dawn tradition. So we started off with the Lesser Banishing Ritual of the Pentagram, the Kabbalistic Cross, etc. The invocation followed. At the climax of the Venus ritual thus performed, my girlfriend suddenly embraced me and whispered in my ear: "Conjure me a flying elephant!" It was a request we both thought quite funny but nevertheless a jokingly absurd idea.

We finished the ritual good and proper with a parting thank you, the obligatory release formula and the concluding Lesser Banishing Ritual of the Pentagram. When we finally made our way back, we suddenly spotted a giant pink elephant hovering high above the opposing bank of the Rhine: obviously a captive balloon which a regional brewery had launched for advertising purposes. I still have no words today to describe our utter bewilderment.

And I still cannot say with certainty what unsettled us more about this event: the entirely unexpected all-too-real apparition itself or the sudden, breathtaking realization that it must have something to do with our newly completed ritual, that it was in all likelihood its immediate consequence.

Coincidence, of course—really?

In view of the emotional intensity of such experiences, the usual vulgar-rationalist explanations ("relational delusion," "cognitive dissonance," "hallucinatory linking of disparate events," "irrational projection of meaning" etc.) will invariably prove to be lame and sorely inadequate. The experience of what Carlos Castaneda—admittedly not an unproblematic character himself—once called the "gap between the worlds" cannot even remotely be grasped precisely and it certainly cannot simply be explained away in this fatuous manner.

Nobody understood this better than C.G. Jung, who ennobled such phenomena academically by assigning them the technical term "synchronicity." But while this child may since have adopted a scientific name, it doesn't really explain anything, and the fundamental break with the materialistic rationality of causal thinking remains unresolved.

In all likelihood, this issue won't be settled within any conceivable time frame, and the sooner the magician realizes this fact, the better for everyone involved. Not that in the history of magic there has been a lack of effort to try it anyway. In my comments on the models of magic, we find an overview of such magic explanatory models[6] which aim not only to plausibilize magic per se but also to bring it into harmony with the material, mundane, everyday world as we generally know it.

Probabilistic Sorcery

The English idiom "to bend the arm of chance" (its German equivalent being "to help chance along" [*dem Zufall nachhelfen*]), is taken quite literally in chaos magic. Its understanding of magic is based on chaos mathematics, quantum physics, and information theory. At its core, it is about probabilism: chaos magic wants to be the art, so to speak, of helping chance to take a leap. If, for example, the probability that a certain event will occur, or by inversion won't occur, is the same, the magical act as a pointer on the scales should prove to be the decisive factor one way or the other.

This way of thinking is due, among other things, to the statement frequently found in magical literature: namely, that the results of magical actions often look like pure coincidences, albeit sometimes quite strange ones.

For example, you have conducted a sigil magic operation to support your application for a job. Suddenly the other competitors drop out for some reason—be it that they have changed their minds at the last moment, missed the train and don't show up for the interview, simply sweating the appointment, or whatever other "coincidences" may be at work. Consequence: you get the coveted position. And at the bottom line remains the pragmatic conclusion: goal achieved, success chalked up.

Probably everyone who devotes themselves intensively to practical magic over a longer period of time will be familiar with such "coincidences."

However, this doesn't always have to go off lightly. In my early days as a freelance translator, for example, I went through a period of great financial hardship. So I decided to perform a magical operation to improve my

---

6. See chapter 20, "Models of Magic in Practice."

material situation. In the following two weeks I suddenly received out of the blue more translation commissions than I had previously managed to get hold of in an entire year. And of course every one of them was more time critical than the other: an unprecedented deadline pressure. But since I was in no position to refuse even one of them because I needed the money so badly, and because it would have been extremely problematic from a magico-psychological point of view to pull the hand brake right in the midst of the magical manifestation, I had to suffer from months of massive overwork, which also drove my health to the very limits of my resilience.

In an old edition of the Larousse dictionary we find the beautiful, very French definition of the term "chance": "*chance*—assumed cause of events whose real cause we do not know." The absurdity of the entire undertaking cannot be better expressed: the inexplicable is positively not explained by the inexplicable; it just isn't, period.

People—the esoteric scene is abundantly populated with them—who are constantly on the move with a meaningful "there are no coincidences" on their lips, may perhaps refuse to accept this realization: namely, that even natural science knows no real Why but only a How or two. In fact, on closer inspection, the blithely evoked concept of causality isn't really that much to write home about.

It is in the nature of chance that there is something arbitrary about it and that it eludes precise interpretation. Accordingly, it is difficult and doubtful for the magician to use chance as a testimony to the effectiveness of his magic. Ultimately, it remains a matter of interpretation or, put more constructively, intuition. Certainly it may not always work flawlessly. Error is never excluded—it is our all-too-frequent bedmate, in fact—and all too often desire (or fear) proves to be the real mother of thought. What's more, this approach also has its indisputable downsides.

One conjures, for example, in order to alleviate financial hardship and shortly afterwards one's beloved grandmother dies and leaves an inheritance behind. How to deal with it now? An aggravating burden of guilt or a flippant "coincidence, of course"? Such events, and they are anything but rare, have convinced quite a few practitioners that the real problem with magic is not *whether* it works, but that it actually does.[7] In this fashion you may achieve your desired goal, but not always in the way you had hoped for. Once the "law of undesirable consequences" shows its ugly face, i.e., when dramatically confronted with magical collateral damage, the moral or ethical dilemma of the magician can sometimes be monstrous. More than one promising magician's career has been shattered by this in the end.

The fundamental problem in determining whether seemingly magical phenomena are actually "real" magic is ultimately of a philosophical nature. Anyone who equates magic with an exact science or linear technology, or simply confuses the two, be it consciously or unconsciously, will come across it time and again. This hardly fails to happen because all of us, whether we like it or not, have been molded this way socio-culturally since the Enlightenment at the very latest, at least as far as Western culture is concerned. In fact, ever since that time we have been living within the confines of a largely scientistic worldview, one in which the well-nigh blind belief in science overshadows everything else.

Such a view of the world is not particularly suitable for dealing with coincidences, be they controlled or not, for it focuses solely on predictable control and absolute foreseeability. Neither the subjective experience nor the no-less-subjective intuition really have their place in this realm. Neither does chance or contingency itself. Rather, they are all regarded as disruptive factors that must be eliminated as utterly as possible. For this reason, abstract, universally-valid laws, measurability, and reproducibility are made the all-dominant fetish. As long as the magicians insist on seeing magic primarily as a control of coincidences, they must not expect any help from the prevailing rationalistic-scientistic world view and its agents.

No ingratiation will help: the countless attempts of magical authors to bridge the gap between magic and science have failed without exception. Neither have they managed to bring about a meaningful dialogue between the two worlds, nor did the disciplines in any way advance each other.

In astrological practice we often encounter a very similar problem. Traditionally, astrology builds on a very comprehensive set of rules, though these may vary considerably from one school to the next. Ultimately, however, it

---

7. See chapter 16, "The Problem with Magic Is Not *Whether* It Works, but That It *Does*."

only serves to release our intuition. Here are just two examples from my personal experience.

When I once interpreted the natal chart of a friend who was very skeptical about astrology, merely undertaking the task for the fun of it, I suddenly had the idea, while investigating the position of the lunar nodes, to ask him about a certain month's date. Did the time around this day have any special significance to him? Completely amazed, he told me that the day following was his wife's date of birth.

About a year later I discussed another friend's natal chart with him. And again I noticed (or remembered?) a certain date when I studied the lunar nodes and asked him about it. This time I even landed a hundred percent hit: it was the birthday of his deceased brother (of whose existence I had known nothing until then) with whom he had been very close and whom he had accompanied for months while on his deathbed.

I never succeeded in deriving a halfway reliable astrological rule from these events at the time, and I was never able to reproduce the same effect in other natal charts later.

Coincidence, of course—well, maybe.

In the 1980s I was hired as an interpreter to translate at seminars of the Peruvian shaman Don Eduardo Calderón Palómino and his student, the acclaimed American ethnologist Alberto Villoldo. Since Don Eduardo was not allowed to carry out "real" healing rituals in Germany for legal reasons, he decided to simulate a demonstration of such a ritual. This took place on a windless summer afternoon in the front garden of the conference hotel near the Externsteine, arguably one of Germany's best known ancient holy sites.

Sitting on a wooden bench, Don Eduardo spread out his shamanic mesa on the lawn before him and deposited various magical objects. Immediately in front of it, he inserted a row of rods with different headpieces into the ground. I myself was sitting about three-and-a-half feet away in the grass. The seminar participants, on the other hand, stood about thirty feet away in a semicircle on the edge of the lawn, with a full view of the action.

"When I perform such a healing ceremony at home in Peru," Don Eduardo explained next, "I have the patient step in front of the mesa. And then, when one of these rods starts vibrating, it tells me I have to use it for the healing operation."

Now he had a volunteer step forward to perform the demonstration. The latter stood about two feet away from the rods and the mesa without touching them.

It didn't take a minute until one of the rods sticking in the ground actually began to wiggle violently—without any gust of wind or other discernible external influences. Not unfamiliar with stage tricks, I looked very closely to rule out that there wasn't an invisible nylon thread in the game: a complete failure! My eyes almost fell out of my head and I had to pull myself together rigorously to continue my interpreting without interruption.

Don Eduardo, on the other hand, pulled the rod in question out of the ground as a matter of course and proceeded with his demonstration unmoved.

A leap in time: a few years later I held a seminar in Hamburg, Germany, where I introduced various magical techniques. In the afternoon it was all about a demonstration of a shamanic healing ritual.

On a blanket on the floor this time a volunteer participant lay on her side with her back to me so that she was unable to see me or follow my actions. I was sitting behind her on the floor about three feet away. The other participants sat in a semicircle on chairs a little to the side of us, also behind the volunteer person's back.

After starting the demonstration with incense and a rattle without speaking or explaining anything, I spontaneously put the rattle aside, clenching my right hand to a fist and making a movement as if vigorously pulling an invisible thread attached directly to the back of her head. (Of course, there was no such thread in play: it was all imaginative.) As soon as I pulled a little to the left, her head suddenly jerked in my direction. When I gave in to my movement, her head returned to its original position. When I pulled on another imaginary "thread" at shoulder height, her upper body buckled up to form a hump in my direction and immediately receded as soon as I yielded the movement. The same thing happened about half a dozen times on different parts of her body.

As I said: she was lying on the blanket with her back to me, she could not perceive my movements, and there was no verbal or gestural suggestion put to her. (And no, there were no mirrors hanging on the wall either!) The participant couldn't possibly know what I would do; in fact, I didn't know it myself before acting it out by sheer spontaneous intuition.

Frankly, I was at least as dumfounded by the effect demonstrated as were my seminar participants.

Coincidence, of course? Don't think so, dude.

Perhaps the natural magical talent differs from the not innately "talented" magician primarily by the feeling of undramatic self-evidence with which it encounters magical phenomena—or even their absence. For a folk magician like Don Eduardo, the vibration of his magical rod, as "physically impossible" as it might be, was merely part and parcel of his everyday experience about which it wasn't worth wasting many words. For me, on the other hand, the Western-socialized magical autodidact who grew up in a culture of fundamental skepticism toward anything magical and "irrational," it still had something monstrous about it, hence it also seemed worth reporting on and reflecting about.

Certainly, with growing magical practice the "extraordinariness" of its effects is increasingly receding into the background, meaning that we will start approaching magic as a fundamental experience of human life, just as it has been witnessed for millennia. Perhaps this is indeed the key to a truly continuative handling of the magical art.

Chapter 4

Different Perspectives in Magical Thinking and Experiencing Magic

Josef Knecht

The experimental magic workshop group in Bonn in the early 1980s was very influential for my understanding of the human condition and of world views in various respects; it extended my ideas, which up to then had mainly been influenced by the relevant literature.

Very different characters and interests came together, from ritual-magic-oriented people who tended toward magical orders to people influenced by nature magic and who were more interested in neo-paganism and the modern witchcraft scene.

In any case, the common denominator was our willingness to immediately try out any and all ideas, ideological hypotheses, and experiences that we had only read about before. The group therefore called itself the "Workshop for Experimental Magic." We used the term "magic" in our circle as a common cipher for all sorts of spiritual activities that in other circles today are more commonly called "shamanic," or could also very broadly be defined as "spiritual."

For me, one of the essential lessons of working in a group lies in the realization that for all concepts, the understanding of which one takes for granted, there are quite a number of entirely different interpretations and possibilities of comprehension. Even if you choose to stay with your own view, you will nevertheless have to confront the fact that it isn't the only one.

This is particularly the case with a dazzling concept such as magic. Everything and nothing can be projected onto "magic," from pure naive wishful thinking to highly complex ideological constructs.

To understand modern experience-oriented magic and spirituality, it is necessary to let these different ways of seeing and experiencing stand side by side without having to judge them as either right or wrong—at least if they are based on real experience.

In this chapter, I would like to describe some of the many possible views and practical orientations of modern magic, to distinguish them, to share my experiences with them, and to reflect upon them further.

Basically, we can distinguish between a more inwardly directed magic—which is about the maturation of the "soul," the unfolding of the spiritual potential—and a more outwardly directed magic, for which the influence on the prevailing environment, on the circumstances of life, or on certain events is more important. A similar distinction is made for alchemy, which is either about the "Great Work", i.e., the enlightenment of the alchemist, or the manufacturing of gold from base metals to make a prince or—even better—the alchemist himself rich. Certainly, the ability to create effects in the outside world can be used as a token that certain stages of development have been successfully completed. But my point here is the basic intention in spiritual work.

These two orientations are often referred to as "high" and "low" magic, a distinction and designation that we authors of this book also use in different ways. Like many clichés, the distinction has the advantage of being simple and understandable, and the disadvantage of transporting unnecessary value judgments and never quite getting it right. With this reservation, however, we will occasionally use the cliché to illustrate certain ideas.

In a social discourse shaped by Harry Potter and other fantasy books and films, "magic" is first associated with the outwardly turned form where the aim is to achieve obvious effects and manipulate the material or personal environment, whereby there is an overlap with paranormal effects; usually it also presupposes a corresponding talent for such things.

So-called "high magic," on the other hand, largely corresponds in its aims and often also its methods with the spiritual efforts of other traditions, and in many respects strongly resembles Tibetan Buddhism, for example, which also knows and uses a wealth of structured rituals. In its framework, the inner development is driven by a series of journeys through mandalas, and one has to deal with a comprehensive hierarchy of non-embodied beings, which in the Western tradition we would name demons, spirits, angels, and deities, and which in the Tibetan language expectably bear other names. All spiritual traditions in their "high" form share the common goal of allowing the soul of the practitioner to unfold its full potential through a series of defined stages of development, and finally freeing it completely from the web of conditionality—called *samsara*, *maja*, wheel of fortune, or cosmos, as the case may be—and connecting it with its spiritual origin. The attainment of abilities or skills that are commonly perceived as magical or, scientifically, as paranormal can be accepted or even demanded in some traditions as proof of certain stages of development, but in the end they play only a subordinate role and are not aimed at for their own sake. They are even classified by some as obstructive and distracting (in Zen Buddhism, for example, in contrast to the Tibetan Buddhist approach).

This universal path of development has been thoroughly described by Carl G. Jung for a modern understanding based on the psychological model. Where the older traditions have met gods, spirits, and demons, Jung speaks of archetypes of the collective unconscious, which he interprets in an inner-psychic fashion but nevertheless correlates with, and assigns to, the traditional images. In addition, Jung knew from his own experience and that of his patients that such images of the unconscious can manifest themselves through external effects.

The inner logic of Jung's theory of archetypes and the imagery assigned to it are so plausible and saturated with experience that they are repeatedly used as patterns of interpretation within modern magical schools, and have proven themselves there. Concepts such as that of the shadow, the anima, the great mother or the mandala originate from this depth psychological approach and are now commonly accepted.

Another fundamental distinction that is helpful in understanding the many varieties of magic and other forms of spirituality refers to the attitude toward nature: is the spiritual world of symbols and the context explored for the inner work actually found in "nature"—here meant in the plain straightforward sense of the word—or rather in abstractions?

A typical example of an abstract form of magic would be the Kabbalah and the rituals and journeys to the Sephiroth and the paths connecting them. Exemplary for a form of magic focused on nature would be shamanism in most of its forms, whose power animals, nature spirits, symbolic cardinal points, and elements are based directly on the experience of "nature out there."

The fact that I understand "nature" here in the very straightforward sense of the word is an essential remark, because a kabbalistic magician can certainly object that the spirits of nature are only symbols and that the Sephiroth of the kabbalistic Tree of Life also refer to living experiences with human nature. Sure. Nevertheless, the perceived difference in the world of images remains, as well as the simple fact that the metaphors of nature magic can immediately be understood by every child, while most abstract concepts can only be worked with if one has studied them in reasonable depth.

But this distinction is not only about different forms of metaphor and the world of images, which would ultimately be interchangeable. Behind it all there is a different emotional cast and mindset. In my personal experience, romanticism plays a very important role, especially for beginners of magic. And these romantic ideas and longings strongly determine which style of magic one is attracted to and where one intuitively feels at home and at ease.

In my experience, people who tend toward nature magic also have ecological interests, are often politically engaged, have a positive attitude toward gender justice, and like to combine spiritual exercises with direct experience of nature. In this direction belong the numerous shamanic and witchcraft groups that have formed since the socially and ecologically very turbulent '70s and '80s, and which still play an essential role in the esoteric scene today—the shamanic groups inspired by Native American spirituality arguably more so than the "witches" around whom it has become rather quiet again after a boom in the '80s.

In the latter groups, an attitude of inner connectedness prevails, as does the mystical search for union with the whole of nature. Again, in my experience, individualistic fantasies of power are more likely to be found among those who practice symbol-oriented ritual magic.

A special kind of magic is to be mentioned here in passing, which was only developed by Frater U∴D∴ long after the end of our workshop group, and with which I hence have no experience myself: the concept of "Ice Magic." In purposeful contrast to all other approaches, this one is not about changing the circumstances of life, fulfilling wishes, or maturing of the soul, but about fundamentally breaking through our constructions of reality, breaking up causality as such, and thus ultimately overcoming the kind of world that is the only one we know. In this respect, we can speak here of a Gnostic form of magic that is neither about this world nor the hereafter, but about "tricking the demiurge," as it says in a modern Gnostic text. It is against this background that the initially strange term "Ice Magic" is to be understood. The "ice" is used as a metaphor of the Unworldly, which contrasts with the "world conflagration" or ekpyrosis of entropy as the permanent self-exhaustion of material energy.

As in all Gnostic forms of spirituality, we find here a turning away from the world as such, not in the sense of an attempt to improve the grievances of the existing world, but as a much more fundamental rebellion against being in the world, against being subjected to the laws of an existing reality that we cannot chose or determine. The world as such is always an experience of powerlessness, as Frater U∴D∴ points out again and again in his book.

Some magicians apparently succeed in breaking through the tight web of collective reality here and there. How one may experience this in concrete terms is beyond my knowledge and my own experience. But I have not yet encountered a consistent and stable mastery of causal references, which of course only makes this a statement about me myself and not about the matter as such.

In any case, Ice Magic in its radicalism and fundamentality forms a unique and erratic block in the modern Western magic tradition that deliberately eludes any classification and explication. In this respect, even in the only work available ("Eismagie"/"Ice Magic" by Frater U∴D∴), exercises and practical implementations are only hinted at because breaking out of the web of reality cannot be practiced or taught, but can only be carried out as a unique act, to paraphrase the words of its founder.

I see another interesting polarity in the inner attitude of "seekers" and practitioners in the fact that some tend to strive for a fixed ideological orientation and like to commit themselves to a system that is finally recognized as truth, while others are more concerned with the inquisitive exploration of ever new inner spaces.

Differences like this—and probably all others—are essentially a question of character and fundamental attitudes toward the world, which will be reflected not only here but likewise in other realms of life of the practitioner. Whoever seeks a guru and a firm structure for their spiritual development will also generally have a higher need for security in life than people whose access to life is marked by curiosity and the urge to make independent decisions.

A fixed system of interpretation for both the outside and the inside world, preferably with clear instructions for further development, provides a point of reference for life and makes it easier to bear with the existential exposure in this world that is difficult to understand and even more difficult to manage. Curiosity means the readiness to expose oneself to this ever and again, to risk one's own perspective of life, and to accept possible changes with each new experience if it goes deep.

Part of the distinctions made here are of course those ones made by Frater U∴D∴ in his chapter "Models of Magic in Practice," which I will therefore not line up here again, encouraging you to read them there.[8]

Among these, the psychological model seems to me to be the most widespread in modern times, although it has the disadvantage of not being able to explain many concrete experiences conclusively. It was C.G. Jung, with his expanded model of the collective unconscious and the archetypes, who first created the possibility of being able to classify profound psychic experiences in a psychological model. In the latter, all gods and demons could be incorporated to find a psychologically acceptable place.

In this context rituals will be understood as the way we communicate with our unconscious, just as dreams and visions are the way the subconscious tries to communicate with our everyday self.

While I am in the process of considering the psychological interpretation of magical activity, a comment on the psychological motives and side effects may be interwoven here as well. Depending on the structure of their individual character, some practitioners carry "magic" or witchcraft like a blazon in front of them and thus provoke their environment purposefully and often quite effectively. Even today, magic is still considered a taboo in many circles—not because it is un-Christian or evil, but because it is the peak of irrational superstition and a nuisance in the modern materialistic world.

---

8. See chapter 20, "Models of Magic in Practice."

For people with an extraverted urge for self-recognition, this is an excellent opportunity to grant their urge free play, which can also be served quite well by the typical accessories worn in the Goth scene.

And vice versa: we see others whose mentality is structured rather anxiously and who therefore keep their hobby secret at all costs, appearing in public only under pseudonyms, and for whom secret brotherhoods and hidden cult meetings are an integral part of the fundamental fascination within their slightly paranoid imagination.

When such different modes of emotional cast and of perceiving the world collide, sometimes comic to bizarre scenes can emerge. I remember a customer who, after a while of hanging around in an occult bookstore, steps up to the bar and whispers the question with his eyes shut tightly: "Do you sell grimoires here, too?" The expectation that the bookseller would reach into a hidden drawer with a conspiratorial look and present him with a worn-out old copy with a gloomy cover is literally imprinted on his face whose features promptly slip away as the bookseller stands up, walks to a shelf, and says broadly into the room at normal volume: "Black magic can be found here in these three shelves!" On the one hand, the good man found more grimoires immediately available than he had ever dreamed of; on the other hand, they lacked the nimbus that his dark romanticism was all about, freshly printed and easily restocked as they stood there.

In the same context of psychological needs and effects, we can also see whether someone uses magical-spiritual work as a tool to engage more intensively in the world and gain strength and orientation for that engagement (more on this in my chapter on the political aspects of magic[9]), or whether magic becomes a tool of escapist desires and serves to withdraw into an inner world experienced as better and greater. It is important to point out that the latter variant is not specific to magical or spiritual interests but can occur in many areas of activity. Especially today, the internet, social media, and computer games or sports broadcasts certainly play a far greater role with regard to escapism and the flight from the world, and can fulfil this function with a much lower threshold and with greater social acceptance than esotericism, magic, or spirituality.

---

9. See chapter 21, "Political Dimensions of Magic."

In practical implementation, many of these distinctions only play a role if one commits oneself to a certain cult or a fixed ritual group such as an order or coven (i.e., a fixed group within the witchcraft tradition), and spiritual practice is determined solely by it. In an experimentally oriented circle you can, of course, work with any imagery and try everything out, work on any need.

This brings me to another important and final distinction that played a role in our work, and which is most likely to be placed on the scale between serious and playful—meant without any judgmental connotation here. A more playful approach allows trying out different approaches with a high degree of inner freedom, while a more serious approach usually carries with it the advantage of greater discipline and consistency. Both can, of course, also be experienced in discrete phases.

At the serious end of the spectrum, magical practice will at some point become life-determining and the practitioner will commit themself to an order or a set group. As you can easily see from the different chapters in this book, our group was at first located rather at the playful end of the scale and quite open to any and all experiments. When some members, after about three years, decided to follow more firmly structured paths and to commit themselves to magical orders or order-like systems, our paths separated, because this cannot be reconciled well with the loose and non-binding attitude with which we had set off originally.

At some point it became apparent that the various preferred styles were pushing us in different directions and that the time of unselfconscious joint experimentation was over.

Chapter 5
A Contemporary Magician's Biography

Axel Büdenbender

(Interviewer: Harry Eilenstein)

Harry: How did you originally come to magic?

Axel: Well, it kind of fell into my lap, really. I saw a movie in 1965 or 1966 with Christopher Lee ...

This was *Dr. Terror's House of Horrors* and it featured tarot cards. A stranger read the cards for another stranger in the train. Then the story was built on it. That's when I saw tarot cards for the first time—the cards "The Devil" and "Death." It fascinated me so much ... And in '73 I saw the tarot cards again in a James Bond movie, the first one with Roger Moore (*Live and Let Die*)—once again "The Devil" and "Death" ... and following that, I tried to get hold of tarot cards myself.

What I got was the *Witches Tarot*, which was also called the *James Bond Tarot*—that was terrible ... I found it in a toy store in Bonn.

Next, I bought myself a book that I think was by a certain Werner Keller—that was ... I don't remember the title anymore ... And on the same shelf in the bookshop in Bonn there was another book, *Morning of the Magicians* by Pauwels and Bergier. There are truths, half-truths and total fiction in it—but that's where I first heard about Aleister Crowley, about the novella *The Great God Pan* by Arthur Machen—it fascinated me so much, it was so insane! Then some stuff about Helena Blavatsky. I came across the names—and then I started looking for literature.

But you just try going to the city library back in the seventies, asking: "Do you have any books by Aleister Crowley?" They hadn't the foggiest what I was going on about, they'd never heard the name before.

So then I ordered the German monthly *Esotera* in a somewhat round-about way. It was all about esotericism, which I didn't really care for one bit. But there were classified ads in the back and that actually made it exciting. Amongst other stuff there were people who offered sex magic, and instructional letters of the Fraternitas Saturni were being advertised, too. And there were crystal balls on offer! I got myself one for forty or sixty deutsche marks.

Harry: Yes, I remember that crystal ball well.

Axel: Right, and that was a resounding success, that was my—how can I put this—inauguration. I used to come home in the evening from my late shift and would unpack it. I was a total pragmatist at that time. I'd simply place it in front of my bed, but I didn't light any incense sticks or candles, no fancy stuff. All I had was a lamp with a shade that was pretty dim. There I lay down in front of it, with a white background—reflection was perfect—and concentrated on the ticking of my alarm clock. Somehow I intuited that—only on the ticking, not on the alarm clock itself.

After five minutes my eyelids became heavy. An inner voice said: "Keep your eyes open." I'll never forget that. Then the ball began to pulsate in a reddish hue, which I had never seen before, then again in a greenish hue, which again I had never seen before—and suddenly I was in my "Self" or in my astral body, whatever you want to call it, which floated under the ceiling and I saw myself lying down there on the bed.

I panicked; I shot right back into my physical body in a frenzy! Immediately I opened a bottle of beer and simply had to get drunk. Yes—that's how I came to magic.

Yeah, and then something happened in the Barriere, the Bonn scene bar. I used to hang out there for drinks on the weekend. I was always the first patron to arrive in the evening and the last to leave. At some point I met a guy there, we talked about reading the cards—I don't remember exactly how it happened anymore. So I promised him that I'd read him the cards on Sunday. But I was so sloshed that I forgot all about it again.

Sunday evening was just around the corner—but I had an awful hang-over. So I thought I'd best send him straight back home. But I didn't really have the heart to do that and so I grabbed the cards and read them for him. Nothing svelte—simple down-to-earth stuff. I just wanted to get it over and done with. All I really did was give him some story.

Suddenly the room got quieter and quieter. I expected that he would break out laughing, pat me on the shoulder and say, "Come old man… you really have a lively imagination!"

Instead, he became very silent. I think I told him about his relationship and about his doing jail time, something I personally had known nothing about before. Also, I was far too buzzed to remember what he had told me about himself the previous day.

Then I look at him, he looks at me and asks how the hell I know all this. I say, "No idea—it was all in the cards…"

He left again—but he was totally shocked. I myself thought it was nothing but a coincidence.

And a few weeks later you were standing in front of my door. And you could speak English, that was the decisive point for me. Because I wanted to get at the great English books—okay, it wasn't just that, of course. I also needed someone to conjure with me—but your command of English was the most significant element.

Techniques of High Magic and stuff like that… Dion Fortune's *Psychic Self-Defence*… you read that to me in the evening chapter by chapter, translating it into German.

Yes—that's the way it was. That's how I came to magic.

And since then I have been—how can I say?—I'm still very skeptical about the whole thing.

[We both have to laugh heartily because Axel's inveterate skepticism and his constant doubts about magic have been one of our mainstays of conversation for years.]

Axel: Let me put it this way—some things actually do work, I'm firmly convinced of that, yes.

Harry: Well, that leads us to the next question: have you ever discarded magic and then stopped practicing it entirely—and, if so, why?

Axel: Yes, back when I had this kundalini syndrome. That's when I started with letter magic following the instructions in Zeisel's book—those exercises caused me to stop doing magic at some point.[10] I was already experiencing the first symptoms: my feet used to get hot, then the energy currents would stream upwards into my head.

Then at some point I was sitting in my new apartment in front of a candle one afternoon. At that time I was laid off. I had been imagining the fire tattva in the root chakra (*muladhara*) when I noticed how my feet were turning warm—that's when I stopped and thought it would end. But it didn't at all—I thought I was burning because my feet were getting so very hot.

My girlfriend got mad, she said: "You're crazy! You're only imagining it!"

I said: "I'm definitely not imagining it!"

That's how it went for a whole week. So I made contact with Frater U∴D∴, who was living across the Rhine at the time, and [I] drove to his place. He placed me in a tub with cold water, but that didn't make it any better. However, at some point it stopped on its own.

And after that I started drinking … that's how it went, yeah. Then came the incident with Hein—that was the tipping point! Hein was a buddy of mine who worked as a driver for the French embassy. He used to sniff a nose of coke in the evening and had a stiff shot in the morning until they caught him while driving the French ambassador: he had an accident and lost both his job and his girlfriend.

He sort of believed in me, that was because once when he and his chums were talking about me, suddenly his mirror fell off the wall—that made him a believer. He was actually a pretty rational person, but I for my part thought that he was totally kooky.

I visited him one day: he was sitting there, all depressive, in his digs. Then he told me: "My girlfriend Gabi has done a runner on me."

"Yes," I say, "that's the way it goes when you drink and sniff coke and lose your job—that's never a very good hand to play."

So he says: "Can't you do something to get her back?"

"What do you think I should do?" I ask.

He replies: "Man, you're always doing some things!"

---

10. See chapter 18, "German Letter Magic: History, Systems, Field Reports."

"Yeah, sure," I say. "I do some things—well, okay, so I used to do them, but I haven't done any in a good long time."

He says: "Just do something!"

I say, "You're nuts!"

But then I was at home and things were all boring anyway and I thought, all right, so I'll just do something. After all, the guy had said: "You're my friend—do something!"

And because he was my friend, I also felt obliged.

I did a bit of psychodrama there—he immediately forgot about all that afterwards. That was up on his beautiful flat's roof, it was like a balcony, you had a direct view of the Seven Mountains. So I waited there until it was full moon.

Then we did some ritual with parts taken from *Unicorn* magazine: Isis, some things I'd memorized a bit, the lyrics were by Gabi Kramer—I don't really remember it all that precisely... and I thought I'd put on a little show and then he'd have his peace and I'd be able to finish my beer—because at home I wasn't allowed to drink anymore.

And then I noticed, when I was wearing the robe—the one you sewed for me back then—that I was getting a different feeling somehow, kind of like a priest in church. Are you familiar with that?

Harry: Yes, I know that feeling quite well.

Axel: The feeling was there somehow, and I knew it would work. I just knew it! And the whole ritual came from my soul—really magical. And then I took off the robe again and put the staff aside—it was over and done with. So I polished off my bottle of beer and went home.

The next afternoon I came back to Hein—there he sat all depressed in his digs again. And so... what I'm telling you here, it's totally true! There he was and had opened a beer and I wanted to have a beer, too. Suddenly the phone rang.

And I said to Hein: "Watch out—that's Gabi!"

He answered it and yes, it was actually his girlfriend. Me, I thought: "Just a coincidence!"

Then I went home and a short time later the whole thing with his girl-friend was trickling down again.

So Hein says to me: "You have to do another one for me!"

Okay, so I did another one—another ritual. It wasn't quite as effective anymore, but at least, in the end they were back together again.

And at some point he came back to me and said: "You have to do me yet another one!"

I said: "I won't, no, this whole thing's just too devious for me!"

Exactly on that same evening I was invited by a former colleague of mine, but I wasn't at all up for it because actually I absolutely wanted to do another ritual—I was so addicted to doing that. Suddenly my colleague rang me up and canceled the meetup. These were all such strange coincidences...

So instead I went up to Hein again and performed another ritual—and from then on everything—how does that nice expression go again?—went down the drain.

His girlfriend separated from him, he lost the apartment, while I split up with my own girlfriend, too. Everything was a total mess and I wanted to have nothing more to do with all that stuff anymore—it was all just too fishy for me. Well, so then I stopped doing magic for a while.

Harry: And did you start again? Did you resume formal magic after that? If so, why exactly? And what was different afterwards?

Axel: Actually I did, yes. There I was in the Palatinate, working as a geriatric nurse. At that time I always performed the Lesser Banishing Ritual of the Pentagram in the kitchen because my girlfriend let me be alone there. I did so just to stay in practice.

And then—I remember it was in summer—my girlfriend was out, on a night shift or something, and at first I just wanted to go to bed and lie down in the living room with only a blanket covering me.

That night I woke up and everything was somehow different... sort of in a different mood... I tossed the blanket aside... Mind you, I had taken nothing, no drugs, nothing at all, neither was I drunk—but suddenly I could look right inside me! I looked into myself and saw some energy that was running there—it was streaming into my heart, which stopped beating for a moment. That was so scary... Suddenly the energy gushed into my head... then it flooded my belly... my consciousness was no longer in my head but in the belly. To be more precise, I was now actually thinking from my belly. Then the energy rushed on and suddenly it all stopped…

I still remember that it was definitely not a dream that I was having—and afterwards I suffered an awful bout of diarrhea.

Then I remembered that next day I would have to go to work again—and if that ado should happen to start again, they'd immediately lock me away. So at first I said to myself: "No, sir!"

I mean, I never really stopped entirely, I kept getting books again and again, then I sold off my whole library for a song at one point, but I now have it all back in my closet—if not even more books than before.

So if you like, I never actually stopped doing magic. Mentally I didn't, in my head I was always there…

I also had some contact with the Church of Satan and the Temple of Seth. I even performed some fire-breathing for those guys in the Black Metal scene—they recorded videos of me doing it. It was in the Heidelberg castle, at night—that was great! Unfortunately I never saw the video myself. I don't know if it's still circulating somewhere in the underground scene.

And after that performance—I remember this well—we were in a cemetery…I thought that was totally silly! They were really heavily into it, these guys. They were also very much right wing, part of the right-wing scene. They maintained contact with this Swedish fellow, the one who committed those murders at the time, in the Black Metal scene, where they set churches on fire…

They wanted to drive me home from Heidelberg in the evening because I didn't have a car. So we came past a cemetery.

I asked: "What do you want there?"

That's what they said—and I thought it was pretty cute, that's what they said: "We're doing a movie."

So I ask: "What kind of film are you shooting?"

When we entered the cemetery, there was a figure of St. Mary there, so they poured gas all over it, set it on fire and filmed it—I thought that was so bloody dopey!

What's more, they were all so dumb about it, they splashed the fuel on the hedge right beside it—the hedge suddenly caught fire and those Hard Metal jerks suddenly got all frightened and wanted to hoof it.

So I said: "You bunch of idiots!" and I doused the fire—it was too damp anyway to burn properly... But before the cops came, before it really started to blaze, it was I who actually killed that fire, because they were already stampeding away...

Finally, we returned to the car and then I broke off with them. I didn't want to have anything to do with that kind of thing: desecrating churches and stuff, that was just too creepy and daft for me, I couldn't reconcile that with my morality, it just wouldn't work! I don't think much of the church, but I don't spit on crucifixes or conduct some Satan hullabaloo or... that's just not my way. Well, those were my last contacts with that scene.

And then I started doing drugs, smoking cannabis. At that time I only had a part-time job.

It was on a Sunday, I got bored, which actually happens very rarely, when my nephew gave me some grass. So I opened a bottle of beer and thought by myself: drink a couple bottles of beer, smoke a pipe of grass, maybe it'll rock my day a bit. So I smoked the grass and there I was, sitting on my couch in a doozy, feeling like an idiot.

I thought: is that all? People go to jail for that shit! Me, I was just feeling smattered... But suddenly I noticed a blow hitting the bottom of the crapper. At first I thought I was sitting wrong... So I just sat down once more, but then it hit me in the coccyx and I thought: "What the hell is that?"

So then it crawled higher and I thought, "Shit, now you're gonna have a heart attack, a stroke!"

And it kept creeping up and then it popped out of me and I didn't even know what to do. I had absolutely no control over it anymore.

So I sat down cross-legged in front of my bed—that wasn't me, that wasn't what I wanted and did—and I pressed my tongue against my palate and straightened my head... and next the energy shoots right into my head—and before, exactly before that, I abruptly had to close my eyes—it felt like there was a hand shutting my eyes for me, and I just couldn't bear it anymore.

Next, I saw the energy that had jetted above my head and that had then collected somewhere in space or in the cosmos or whatever you want to call it, I just don't know—it then shot through my feet and again back up. This went on for about half an hour ...

Then I bent forward, made a hump, with my head on the floor, and it continued to buzz through me incessantly: *ssst*. That's what I heard, and after about half an hour, maybe three quarters of an hour, it stopped again.

First, I was really scared, then I thought: "Man, this is madness!"

Later, I tried to get hold of grass once more. But by then I was 55 years old. At that age, you can't just walk across some schoolyard saying: "Hey, guys, gimme some weed, will ya!"

Instead, I went to Holland on the Senior Citizens Express because I wanted to repeat the experience.

I thought to myself, my God—merely four puffs of grass ... That was just a mere harmless starter: what the hell may happen when you start doing some of the other stuff?

Then I started with salvia, with divining sage, with blue lotus, and with some other herbs to which I reacted far too violently, so eventually I stopped doing that stuff again.

I have high blood pressure, so who knows. It was a little scary: if I take my medication, adding some strange herbs for good measure—that can obviously scare you shitless.

So then I stopped—and yes, it works, but it also works without drugs.

This was all really just like I'm telling you. It's no lie, not some made-up tall story.

Harry: How do you deal with doubts about the effectiveness of magic in general or your magic in particular? What are its limits? What's missing?

Axel: So it definitely has limits—I'm not omnipotent. Frater U∴D∴ once wrote an article—what was its title again? "Coincidence, of course," exactly, it was in *Unicorn* ... "Magical success control" or something like that was the subtitle, I remember that one.[11]

Yes, some things, like this love spell that summoned back the girl-friend of this friend of mine—was that a coincidence? You can't determine that for sure. I do think doubt is quite appropriate.

With crystal magic, i.e., astral travel using a crystal ball, mirror magic (also used for astral travel) ... that one worked for me once. I've done it a hundred times, a thousand times—I don't really know how often ... but it never worked again. Still, I'm sure it does work in principle.

It's the same with this astral body thing: I'm a hundred percent sure that it works. I don't know whether it can be called up at will, though—I have my doubts about that.

Equally, whether love spells work, conjuring up a partners reunion—that's where I tend to nurture my doubts ...

I mean, there *are* limits somewhere—that's what I think.

Kundalini now, that one really exists, I'm quite sure of that. It's safer than my money in the bank. And you do need the right technology for that ... I don't know whether you can actually awaken it for everyone—I have my doubts about that, too. You need a certain disposition ... And you can also use it to wreak havoc—I did notice that as well.

And yes, here's something that I have to tell you! Without any drugs, I started again with the letter exercises and with the Middle Pillar of the Golden Dawn. That didn't do me any good, so I let it go again.

As for the drugs, okay: that was the drug that pushed up the energy—and the effect faded away again as soon as the stuff's impact had vanished.

But these visualization exercises—they do have a lasting effect. It's not suitable for everyone and I for one won't touch them.

I really have to say that I'm not tough enough to follow through with this ... because you really have to pursue it to the end—you can't simply stop midway, you have to follow through with it ... and I just can't keep that up—and it really can happen that your psyche will collapse.

---

11. "Zufall, natürlich! Das Problem der magischen Erfolgskontrolle" in *Unicorn: Spirituelle Wege und Erfahrungen* (No. 7, Winter 1983), 225–229.

It's like an initiation: either you can cope and go along with it or you can't, in which case it's over. As for me, I just can't hazard it. I simply have my limits.

I don't strive to be able to do that either—I want to stay the way I am, I don't want to become an initiate or whatever you want to call it, or a guru, or some wise person—I have my limits and it's good that I actually know what they are.

Harry: How do you feel about magic today, based on your many years of experience?

Axel: Well, in the beginning I wanted the kick—which I certainly got out of it ... possibly a kick or two too many, even.

I never wanted to develop my personality or become a guru or a great magician. What fascinated me were guys like Crowley. Think whatever you like of him—his way of life, that's what impressed me, and I wanted to imitate it a little bit ... but then again I'm not a Crowley and I didn't manage to do it, either.

My experience with magic is this: it does exist somewhere in some way. You can't grasp it, though, you just can't. But it's there—that's my experience. And I do know—I've tried it. Some things work and some things don't ... and now I'm content with that and it's all good for me.

Harry: You've always stayed yourself, like you said. And you were always looking for the kick. So what would you advise magicians today?

Axel: Try it out. Just try it out. You have to try what you think suits you. And if you think you need the kick, hell, just go for the kick. Sure there are approaches where you should be careful—but you'll have to decide that for yourself. That's what I would advise today's magicians to do.

And they should try things that work. By that I mean mirror magic, for example, for astral travel. Could be it works, could be it doesn't, but hey, what ever actually works a hundred percent? Everyone has to try it out for themselves.

Harry: Our summonings of demons were actually all very entertaining ...

Axel: Everything was entertaining, if you want to view it that way, sure—but did we actually *see* demons, did we really *materialize* them?

Harry: I was satisfied with what happened—more of it would have been way too much!

Axel: Well, I don't have that on my screen anymore—it's been a long time … I remember that the dog was barking. [*Axel's dog who was there during the summoning.*] I do remember that … when we stood there.

Harry: The red lights floating across the path, the light blue flashes up in the tree, the coughing next to us that didn't come from either of us, the lovely smell of sulphur all the time—that was enough for me. That's why I said at some point: "Hey, I want to stop now, it's just too much for me!"

Axel: I don't remember that anymore, really, I merely remember how we stood at the crossways in the woods, and then the chief forester came along.

Harry: That was during our second try …

Axel: That's when we broke it off. So why did we actually break it off? I mean, there's nothing illegal about it, is there: summoning demons?
    I wonder why we broke it off—we didn't do anything illegal, after all …

Harry: Well, there was just the little bother of the forest warden standing right by …

Axel: Yes, well, he could simply have fucked off too, but he wanted us to stop and so we did. Okay, we were a bit out of concept … I'll put it this way.

Harry: Yes, that's a better fit, sure … And he also thought we were poachers—he really wanted to have a look at the bag with our ritual utensils that you were carrying over your shoulder.

Axel: It wouldn't have worked anymore after that anyway.

Harry: True … So here's another question. Can people actually learn magic, or do you think one must have it from birth as a talent? If the former or even if both, what role do traditions play in magic? Magic books? Personal teachers? Magical orders, lodges, associations, etc.?

Axel: That's a tough question. A very difficult one … I feel it has to be anchored a bit in your personality. There must be some disposition for it. Yeah, I'm firmly convinced that it doesn't work for everyone, no.

Staudenmaier was a chemistry professor, it worked for him, too—and he was a really rational fellow. Do you know his book? *Magic as an Experimental Natural Science*?[12]

Harry: I believe I had a look at it at your place once.

Axel: He was a chemist, he tried it out on himself, and he had pretty bad experiences with it. He was actually a rationalist, but his experiences related in no way to his rationalism...

You have to be ready for it, I think...

Harry: Good point, yes.

Axel: If you're not ready... You also have to be a romantic—otherwise you just can't do it. Otherwise it won't work, no. Imagine a rationally thinking person standing at a crossways, conjuring up demons... No, that just won't work! Either you're slightly cracked or you're batshit crazy or you're a romantic who wants to experience something weird, yeah. Otherwise it just won't pan out.

I can't imagine my sister standing at a crossways performing a Wicca ritual—it just wouldn't fly. Or her significant other—my God! He's such a rational guy—nah, perish the thought! Me, I'm slightly gaga, I'm quite aware of that—I'm rather disturbed... and for people of that sort it actually works.

I mean, Crowley was also quite deranged, I'd say, because of his upbringing, and it worked for him, too... You have to have a problem of that kind, otherwise it won't work out for you.

Harry [laughing]: I wouldn't really agree with that—that's your very own personal interpretation.

Axel: Well, I won't claim that it's true for everyone else, it's really only my personal experience: I do know that I have a bee in my bonnet—well, I've taken good care of it all my life... I never wanted to get rid of it, it's just who I am! In some ways I'm actually proud of it.

---

12. Ludwig Staudenmaier, *Die Magie als experimentelle Naturwissenschaft*, 2nd exp. ed. (Leipzig: Akad. Verl.-Ges.), 1922.

I've not done much good, really. I mean, okay, so I was active in the nursing profession—within that context I've actually done some good things, but else… Let me put it this way: I've never made it in the bourgeois sense, but I don't regret that either. *[laughs]* It couldn't have gone any other way; it wouldn't have fitted me otherwise.

A social worker once said to me: "Mr. Büdenbender, I can't imagine you in a suit. You are just the way you are." He was right about that, really—that's just how it is.

Harry: Did certain traditions, books, teachers, magical orders, or the like play a role in your life?

Axel: That's rather arguable. Crowley always fascinated me, but then again he didn't teach me anything—not really. As for traditions, magic books, personal teachers… There's really only you—from you I have learned a lot. Let's put it this way: magical orders, lodges, associations—they have always interested me, from the intellectual point of view, I mean. I always found the Fraternitas Saturni exciting—what they did… The Golden Dawn… Arthur Machen's *The Great God Pan*—that story always fascinated me.

Who would ever consider opening a girl's third eye by surgery? And then she sees the great god Pan and goes mad? Who thinks up stuff like that?

Even Stephen King, the great Stephen King, who says that even to this day a shiver runs down his back when reading this story… It was precisely this narrative that awakened my obsession for the great god Pan—it comes from there.

And do you remember how I fell into a trance during a Pan ritual in my apartment? How you came and had to exorcise me? How bloody scared I was—do you remember that?

I called you late at night—I was fully into glossolalia, I just started ranting, suddenly there came sounds I had never heard before… and a remaining sane fraction of my mind said: "Before you go all crazy, call Harry!" And then you came to the rescue… Weird times…

Where was that Pan ritual from? Did it come from the Fraternitas Saturni? No, no, it was actually homemade, a homemade ritual.

Harry: Yes, we performed these Pan rituals over a long time: you summoning Pan while I played the flute.

Axel: Yes, and this tale of Arthur Machen's, this story, it inspired me. He was in the Golden Dawn himself. He never hit it big there, though, he didn't advance highly within their ranks.

This story was decisive, such stories … like the stories of Lovecraft.

Harry: What did the Bonn Workshop for Experimental Magic mean to you, then?

Axel: Look—it all gets lost in booze … no, man—I never went there sober …

Harry: Probably not …

Axel: No, I wasn't very sober at that time … So I must confess, I don't remember much about it anymore …

I do remember that we were in the Seven Mountains area once—I still have that on my screen if ever so vaguely.

And we were also once in the Kottenforst [an extensive forest area near Bonn on the left Rhine side] and did a Pentagram Ritual or something like that …

Harry: In the Kottenforst we summoned Pan—just the two of us.

Axel: Yes, so we did.

Harry: With the yew hammer. That's when Pan started playing the flute in the woods—I never heard anything like that again … My hair stood on end.

Axel: No—I meant with the experimental circle. I can still remember that: we did a Pentagram Ritual because it had started to rain—then it suddenly stopped. I remember someone there saying, "See, it worked."

And I said: "You must be off your rocker!"

I remember that—we were huddled in a shelter there—I remember that. Who else was there? Someone called M.? Was there an M.?

Harry: Yes, M. and her mate R.

Axel: Josef was there too, I think... and G. I was actually halfway sober at the time. But as for the rest—I was mostly smattered... It's what I needed back then to survive at all. No, I can only remember very little...

What's still important to me: I was born on October 12, like Aleister Crowley—I'm very proud of that. There must be a connection somewhere!

Harry: What would you say were your three most important experiences in magic?

Axel: That was the first one with the crystal ball—it made me really start off.

The most important thing, hm... that's really a tough one... There were so many important things...

The Pan ritual that I did upstairs in my room—where I got to see how I was drifting away...

Yes, and the kundalini experience—that I realized there really was such a thing.

Those were actually the three most important things I would say that worked—that I could really determine for myself that this stuff was for real.

Harry: So which books were important for you?

Axel: Well, Francis King's *Techniques of High Magic*—that's an important book, also because it helped me gain access.

Another nice book is *Psychic Self-Defence* by Dion Fortune—it's a rather funny adventure novel, not too bad. I don't know if everything it says is true, but it reads excitingly... let's put it this way: I think she has an active imagination, that lady—whether she really experienced all that, is another question. But that's what makes the thing just so exciting—you keep asking yourself: can this actually have happened or not? And I think she gets it across well.

That was a pretty important book to me. I always said she was crazy, the old bat—okay, so I never quite put it that way, but I always thought it couldn't really be true: "She's bonkers!" I have it at home now in German—I got myself a copy again. It's a great book.

Let's see, are there any others? Kenneth Grant...nobody understands him anyway, I certainly don't understand that man. I have his *The Magical Revival*—that one's actually quite good, I would still recommend it.

So there's these three books, right.

And not to forget: John Symonds, *The Great Beast*. [*laughs*] Why Crowley chose him as his biographer will remain an eternal mystery to me—but it does read well.

Finally, Daniel Pinchbeck, *Breaking Open the Head*. He went through a Balché ceremony and then everything changed. That book was also very important to me.

So these are five books. And *Techniques of High Magic* is a good book for practice, a good book for the practitioner.

Harry: I think so, too—this is also one of my two most important books. The other one's *The Golden Dawn*.

You always used to say "the main thing is that it sizzles and makes you dizzy"—are there any other experiences with magic that fit into this category? Anything worth mentioning?

Axel: Hold on a minute, let me think. There's so many things I can't remember, that's what boozing brings with it...Nah, I can't really think of anything else at the moment—I've already told you the most important events. Could be that some other stuff did happen, but if so I'm afraid I don't have it on my screen anymore.

Chapter 6
States of Consciousness

Harry Eilenstein

The tool of the craftsman is their body—the tool of the magician is their consciousness. A good understanding of one's own consciousness can accordingly be conducive to magic.

All of us are probably most familiar with the waking consciousness. This consciousness thinks, out of it we speak and observe the world, out of it we make decisions etc.

The second-best-known consciousness will be dreaming—images in sleep that are remembered in the morning.

Deep sleep is a rather abstract concept: in the dream state there are images to remember at least, whereas deep sleep is apparently "void" and hence one can only remember this "void" as such, which is a bit hard to do.

Then there is the state of ecstasy that occurs spontaneously during orgasm, in panic, in the course of addiction, in combat, and similar extreme situations.

This description of the four states of consciousness is initially based solely on the way we experience them, assuming we can speak of actively "experiencing" deep sleep at all.

However, the four types of consciousness can also be described more generally in terms of their structure and function:

The **waking consciousness** contains the information that is necessary for dealing with the current situation. All other information such as the date of birth of one's grandmother, the size of one's shoes, the sense of touch on one's butt while sitting in front of the PC, etc. are accessible, but they are usually not part of the waking consciousness. The waking consciousness coordinates the situation-relevant information.

In **dream** you become "immoral" and "honest": you don't hold back; you experience how you do things you wouldn't do otherwise; you experience past situations and emotions, etc. You can also concentrate in the waking state and access the dream area and then remember things that happened a long time ago. Dream consciousness contains all information, i.e., all perceptions and memories. They are there on an equal footing and are not sorted or selected according to the situation. However, this information can be charged with emotions to different degrees and can accordingly be of varied import.

In **deep sleep** nothing happens, at least no contents of consciousness are active in deep sleep. Deep sleep is thus the canvas on which dreams and the waking consciousness have painted their pictures.

Ecstasy boasts the simplest structure of them all: concentration on a single subject.

Ecstasy is thus suitable for directing all force and attention to a single theme and accordingly being as effective as possible in one's own actions.

Deep sleep is without contents of consciousness, the dream state contains all contents, waking consciousness contains the situation-relevant contents, and ecstasy contains only one single content.

Apparently there is a division of labor here: deep sleep is the framework of the whole, the dream state is the information archive, the waking consciousness is the coordination center, and ecstasy is the concentration on the current task.

This can be illustrated by an image: deep sleep is like a large house in which the archive of the dream state is located and from which the information currently needed is constantly brought to the office of the waking consciousness, where the most important thing is always right in the middle of the desk in the bright light of the desk lamp.

Most forms of magic and meditation can be described as the coordination of two of these states of consciousness, though the waking consciousness is invariably one of the components involved: else, one would not be able to consciously perceive this state of coordination of two forms of consciousness.

Waking and dream: dream journey, light trance, conscious telepathy, conscious telekinesis, remote hypnosis, etc. This state is experienced as extended attention and as an inner contact to something on the outside.

Waking and deep sleep: silence-meditation or void-meditation (Zen, no thoughts, merely a consciousness that is aware of itself), conscious experience of one's own soul, etc. This state is experienced as being fulfilled, warmth, being right, self-love, inner peace, and joy. One is simply there, thinking something for a moment from time to time, but acts out of one's own heart chakra (soul).

Waking and ecstasy: trance dances, tantra, sigil magic, sex magic, Tummo meditation (i.e., Tibetan kundalini fire meditation), mantra meditations, chanting, and others. This state is experienced as perfect concentration, as unity and fulfillment.

Evidently, the coordination of more than two states of consciousness is also conceivable, but in actual practice this occurs only rarely.

Two interesting points are the soul and the trauma. The soul seems to be connected to deep sleep; the inner encounter with the soul evokes the same feeling as silence-meditation.

A trauma is not another state of consciousness but a memory that has in some way become isolated and largely autonomous. This encapsulation is usually brought about by a violent emotion (mostly fear of death), in which one is then "stuck", i.e., that has failed to dissolve again after the termination of the threatening situation. A trauma is, as it were, a psychic spasm.

If you have a trauma in your psyche and learn magic or meditation, you will very likely encounter this very trauma—a chance for a comprehensive healing.

We can arrange the four states of consciousness mentioned on the Middle Pillar of the Tree of Life:

• Awake state	Malkuth	material world, everyday life
• Dream state	Yesod	psyche, vital force
• Deep sleep	Tiphareth	(soul)

Ecstasy is not found on the Tree of Life—it should be below Malkuth. It can also be seen as an aspect of Malkuth, if you prefer.

If deep sleep is soul consciousness, then it follows that the soul contains the information about all its previous incarnations—which one can experience by dream journeys (for example to Chesed). However, these memories are obviously not part of the "normal memories" of Yesod, but are located in another "space": after all, one experiences the Tiphareth state as stillness (deep sleep).

If there are these four states of consciousness that correspond to Malkuth, Yesod, and Tiphareth, the question arises of which consciousness is found in Da'ath. Some characteristics of this consciousness can be derived from our previous reflections:

The area of Yesod can be understood as the psyche of a person created by the soul in Tiphareth. Analogously, Da'ath can be seen as the psyche of the world created by God in Kether.

In Yesod, the human dream images can be found. In Da'ath, the archetypes of the gods can be found.

To Yesod belongs "ordinary magic," which emanates from the human psyche (body of vital-force). Therefore, we should find an "extraordinary magic" in Da'ath, which emanates from the gods.

Since the area of Da'ath is without boundaries, Da'ath consciousness should also be without confines.

If in ecstasy there is only a single content of consciousness, in waking consciousness there is the situation-relevant content, in the dream state there are all perceptions and memories, and in deep sleep there are the memories of all previous incarnations of one's own soul, accordingly, in Da'ath, consciousness there should be the memory of everything that has happened so far in the world. Da'ath is, to put it more poetically, the memory of the gods.

From these considerations a rough sketch of the state of consciousness in Da'ath can be derived:

Da'ath consciousness differs from the other four forms of consciousness as so far described in these reflections.

Consciousness in Da'ath is unlimited, i.e., all information is accessible.

Individuality is not defined by a boundary but by one's own quality.

We experience ourselves as part of a larger whole—as part of an area without boundaries.

There is a close connection between one's own consciousness and the gods. This connection can be experienced as our own "protective deity", i.e., as the "sea of the deity," of which our own soul is an integral droplet.

Instead of the "currents" in our own psyche that generate our own motivation, there are the "currents" in the world (or in God's psyche, if you prefer this term), which cause the "motivation" underlying the events in the world. These formulations may arguably not be entirely precise yet (and also a little elegiac), but with their help a first sketch of Da'ath consciousness can be made.

The effects of the magic that emanates from this Da'ath consciousness should be far greater than the "ordinary magic" that emanates from a person's psyche or vital-force body: hence, "extraordinary magic."

Pursuant to these considerations, the experience of the ego should step into the background in Da'ath consciousness, and should only be an "auxiliary function" in everyday life, but no longer the fulcrum of one's self-image. This does not mean that you have lost your egoism, but only that you are moving as part of something greater—you are no longer moving in the world or even *against* the world, but as part of the world.

Such a consciousness has the world behind it; we move with great support, or, to express it in a more figurative language, we act in friendship with the gods. The effects of our own actions will thus be correspondingly greater—an effortless and extraordinary magic.[13]

---

13. Read more about Da'ath consciousness and magic in chapter 2, "My Path from Wish Magic to Da'ath Magic," in chapter 11, "Da'ath Magic," and in chapter 15, "Some Questions on Magic."

Chapter 7
The Fetish of Legitimacy, or Magical Clubbiness

Frater U∴D∴

The Golden Dawn—Some Corrupted Myth

William Wynn Westcott, Deputy Official Mortician of the City of London, High Grade Mason, and leading member of the Societas Rosicruciana in Anglia (S.R.I.A.), presented in 1887 a bundle of occult documents allegedly of German origin, which he had personally deciphered. They were supposed to have come from the estate of the respected researcher of Freemasonry, Kenneth R. H. Mackenzie, and were forwarded by the Anglican clergyman A.F.A. Woodford (himself a member of the S.R.I.A.) to Westcott.

The texts, henceforth known as "Cipher Manuscripts," contained a series of magical ritual structures, detailed explanations of a grade system, and a magical training plan on which it was based, as well as the corresponding symbolism, and numerous other references, such as sigils, drafts for tarot cards, the cards' assignment to the kabbalistic Tree of Life, instructions for geomancy, alchemical and astrological material, and many other hermetic items. The grade system largely corresponded with that of the S.R.I.A. as well as that of the German Order of the Gold and Rosicrucians.

The manuscripts also contained the contact address of a certain Fräulein Anna Sprengel in Leipzig. To this aged adept of the Gold and Rosicrucians, so the fama will have it, Westcott established contact by letter and received prompt reply. Finally, so we learn further, the Leipzig Fräulein, together with Westcott's S.R.I.A. brother Samuel Liddell MacGregor Mathers, who had helped with the translation of the correspondence, issued him a charter for the foundation of a London lodge of the order. Thus, in 1888, the Isis-Urania

Temple No. 3 of the Hermetic Order of the Golden Dawn (Hermetic Order of the Golden Dawn, in the following abbreviated as GD) was established under the direction of Westcott, Woodford, and Mathers. It is well known that the Golden Dawn was to develop into the most influential magical order of the turn of the century and still makes its mark on the Western history of magical orders today.

Three years after its foundation, the contact to the mysterious Anna Sprengel ended and it didn't take long until Mathers finally took over the sole leadership of the GD: Woodford had died shortly after the foundation, and Westcott was put under pressure by his employer and had to give up his membership once it had become public.

The organization, which was open to both men and women, hit the nerve of the time with pinpoint accuracy and immediately met with great approval among the upper social classes both at home and abroad. Accordingly, it was soon able to register a number of prominent members whose number grew steadily over the years. Among them were the Irish poet, playwright, and later Nobel Prize winner William Butler Yeats; the Irish freedom fighter Maude Gonne; the actress Florence Farr; the writers Gustav Meyrink, Algernon Blackwood, Arthur Machen, Bram Stoker, Pamela Colman Smith, Constance Mary Wilde (a children's book author and also the wife of Oscar Wilde), and Evelyn Underhill; and finally the—already at this time quite wicked—young Aleister Crowley.

There is no doubt that the Rosicrucian founding myth contributed significantly to the reputation of the Order and its great popularity. At that time, the Rosicrucian saga exerted a great fascination throughout Europe, above all on the artists of Symbolism, but also on the educated middle classes as a whole: by way of an example, consider the celebrated art exhibitions of the *Salons de la Rose+Croix* in Paris (from 1892) instigated by Joséphin Péladan, Stanislas de Guaïta, and their *Ordre Kabbalistique de la Rose+Croix* (founded in 1887), which was also joined by the later advisor to the czar's court, Papus (Gérard Encausse)—or even the S.R.I.A. itself, from whose circle of members the Golden Dawn initially emerged.

Unfortunately, the whole story proved to be terribly tainted from the outset: the Cipher Manuscripts were a forgery, and the contact to Anna Sprengel and her resulting foundation of the order purely a legend. Later forensic, graphological, and linguistic investigations have proven this beyond doubt, and it is now considered indisputable in contemporary research. After all, none other than Mathers himself had to admit at some point that at least the correspondence with Sprengel was forged. There is a remote possibility, though it seems highly unlikely, that he himself knew nothing about the forgery of the actual Cipher Manuscripts.

There is less agreement on the question of who is to blame for these counterfeits and under what precise circumstances they arose. But these historical details and the related controversies that have been fought out to this day do not need to occupy us here any further.

"Old = Good" in Antiquity

The formula "old = good" is not an invention of the nineteenth century. It appears quite early in antiquity over and again. For example, the Jews in the Roman Empire were expressly excluded from the generally mandatory emperor's cult because they could assert that their religion, which prohibited such a cult, was significantly older than the Roman one. At the turn of the common era, Rome saw the emergence of a large number of new cults that differed markedly from the established state religion and drew their inspiration primarily from Asia Minor and Egyptian sources. But none of them were capable of converting a majority of Roman citizens—with one exception: Christianity. For only that which demonstrably went back to ancient roots in the distant past was really taken seriously by the majority of society, and only after Christianity had propagandistically succeeded in asserting its claim to represent the legitimate continuation, indeed "completion," of Judaism, the way was finally cleared for its elevation to the sole state religion under Emperor Constantine.

And it wasn't only religion; indeed, the entire ancient spiritual world operated according to the premise that every new thought, every propagated theory, every innovative explanation of nature could only claim correctness and veracity for itself with recourse to older, recognized authors. For the general consensus held that actual wisdom was to be located only with the "ancients", i.e., the ancestors. Accordingly, a predominant part of antiquity's discourse consisted of a multitude of quotations from recognized authorities of ancient times, with which one's own position was invariably underpinned in each and every case.

One may, with some justification, see in this a later form of archaic ancestor worship. It was to keep Western intellectual history firmly under its control in the fields of theology, philosophy, medicine, and observation of nature right up to medieval scholasticism. Indeed its offshoots can still be observed today in religious fundamentalism and creationism, for example.

Transmission Lines

We find similar things in all world cultures. Very often it is not just a question of referring to older role models and worldviews of a general nature. Just as significantly, great importance is attached to the personal mediation sequence of religious and spiritual teachings. Just as, for example, Catholicism refers to apostolic succession in its sacramental priestly ordination, the Vedic religions and spiritual schools abide by the principle of *guruparamparā*: the uninterrupted succession of spiritual teachers (gurus), who only in their entirety create a valid handed-down tradition. In Vajrayana Buddhism, the so-called transmission lines of the respective schools and sects, i.e., the transmission of traditional knowledge and magical-spiritual skills from one "lineage holder" lama to the next, play a central role. And in rabbinical Judaism and in Sufi Islam in its different forms we can observe such views again and again.

Freemasons, Rosicrucians, Templars

Freemasonry (FM), historically documented since the seventeenth century, was for a long time a structural model for Western magical orders of all kinds. In its own mythology and symbolism it refers on the one hand to the biblical Temple of Solomon. On the other hand, it claims to be the direct successor of the medieval cathedral works guilds since its foundation. It was primarily in its early days that attempts were repeatedly made to prove an uninterrupted historical line of succession to the cathedral builders. In view of the historical unsustainability of this assertion, current, regular FM has meanwhile largely moved away from it. Expectably, this did not happen overnight, and even to this day there are irregular Freemasonic orders and obediences who insist tenaciously on clinging to this mythical romanticization.

The same applies to a multitude of Rosicrucian and Templar orders. Thus, for example, in the promotional literature of the Old Mystical Order of the Rose Cross (AMORC), founded in New York in 1915, the claim can be found to this day that the organization goes back to ancient Egypt, that both the Pharaoh Ramses III and the Greek philosopher Socrates were members of the Order, etc. Harvey Spencer Lewis (1883–1939), the founder of the AMORC, also operated, similarly to the founders of the Golden Dawn, with forged documents, in this case from alleged French Rosicrucians, in the pursuit of legitimizing his order.

The Thriving Occult Patent Trade

It is a well-established fact that whenever a market is created, it will eventually be served. In the world of orders at the turn of the century, one can reasonably speak of a generally prevailing fetishism of legitimacy. As in ancient times, it was thought that a magical order was only worth its salt if it had a venerable charter (often termed a patent), ideally one that was as old as possible. This practice was also borrowed from Freemasonry. It also explains the widespread falsification of such documents and deeds, which, whether genuine or not, were also widely traded.

Theodor Reuss and John Yarker

The opera and variety singer, journalist, Prussian secret agent, and serial founder of occult orders and lodges Theodor Reuss (1855–1923) proved to be particularly active in this field. He developed the patent trade into a real profession. It is known, for example, that he sold a patent of the Mysteria Mystica Aeterna (MMA) to Rudolf Steiner, former secretary of the German section of the Theosophical Society and founder of anthroposophy, for the stately sum of 1,500 Reichsmarks, i.e., the German section of the Ordo Templi Orientis (OTO) which Reuss meanwhile headed. Steiner was then supposed to have held the highest degree to date within the OTO, namely the X° *Rex Summus*. (The XI° was to be installed only later by Aleister Crowley.)

In fact, Reuss had a huge assortment of different lodge and grade patents that he liberally offered for sale. (The sources speak of at least forty-four lodges, of which the majority were pure vaporware.) He represented a new edition of the Illuminati Order; muscled in on the S.R.I.A. until his expulsion in 1907;

was first a regular, then an irregular Freemason, notably of the Memphis-Misraim and Swedenborg Rite; published material in the OTO magazine *Oriflamme* regarding order-specific sexual magic; propagated the Martinist Order of Papus; and worked quite incidentally, albeit clandestinely, for the German imperial Abwehr, possibly as a double agent, but also for the British Intelligence Service.

As a vendor of orders and patents he worked closely with an even bigger, long-established professional in this field: the English High Grade Mason and writer John Yarker (1833–1923), probably the biggest pertinent hustler of all time, whose largely commercial interests he finally officially represented in Germany.

Yarker, who had been mentioned several times by H. P. Blavatsky in her first work *Isis Unveiled* (1877), immediately awarded her, accordingly flattered, honorary membership in his Old and Primitive Rite of Memphis-Misraïm. Following a personal meetup she returned the favor by granting him honorary membership in the Theosophical Society.

Careers such as those of Yarker and Reuss were only conceivable in an occult world that was formally obsessed with awards, diplomas, patents, affiliation certificates, and similar instruments of legitimation. But this was by no means a unique selling point of the nineteenth century.

Cagliostro—Great Cophta and Arch-Charlatan

Thus, for example, in the run-up to the French Revolution, the impostor, swindler, and quack Alessandro Count Cagliostro, whose real name was Giuseppe Balsamo (1743–1795), had already achieved some fame for himself by inventing a supposedly Egyptian tradition of Freemasonry—the forerunner of the Memphis-Misraïm rite still practiced today—as a framework to establish lucrative lodges and sell grade elevations throughout half of Europe.

Cagliostro didn't end well. Time and again exposed as a fraud, he had to constantly change his place of residence. He was finally arrested by the papal police in Rome in 1789 (then still part of the Papal State) and sentenced to death for heresy, freemasonry, and sorcery. In the meantime, however, he had effectively propagandistically sworn off Freemasonry and accused it of being the secret driving force behind the French Revolution in the best conspiracy theory style—thereby underpinning the ideological position of the Catholic

Church. You've got to hand it to him: the dreadfully confused and pathetic cock-and-bull story that he served up to the church authorities, and which was tied to this assertion, must eventually have saved his head after all. He claimed, for example, that he had been appointed—against his will and indeed without his knowledge!—one of the secret Grand Masters of the "Illuminati" (whom he equated with the Freemasons in his tale). It is not known whether his ecclesiastical inquisitors actually bought this brazen claim. But at least his fantasy story seemed to fit seamlessly into the Counter-Enlightenment propaganda of the papacy, and was hence evidently highly welcomed by the curia for political reasons.

In any case, his death sentence was commuted to life imprisonment, which he served in the Angel Castle until he died four years later in Fortress San Leo near San Marino. Thus he became the epitome of the arch-charlatan and swindler to whom Catherine II, the Tsarina of Russia no less, dedicated three personally penned comedies, Friedrich Schiller his novel fragment *Der Geisterseher*, and Goethe the comedy *Der Groß-Cophta*.

Some Notable Exceptions

In the world of magical orders there are also exceptions to this neurosis of legitimation, albeit not too many. One example: the Magic Pact of the Illuminati of Thanateros (IOT), known for its chaos magic and formally founded in 1987, defined itself as early as 1978 in its still conceptual form as the "magical heirs" of the Zos Kia Cultus allegedly developed by Austin Osman Spare, but never laid claim to being part of some actual uninterrupted historical tradition. Thus, no legitimation was claimed here with reference to any history that could only vainly appear objectifiable. Accordingly, there were neither dubious pompous patents nor sweepingly decorated foundation and grading documents of older, purportedly preceding instances being flourished.

Neither did the venerable Fraternitas Saturni, itself at ninety-three years (as of time of writing) a veritably venerable institution now (founded 1928): even though initially the brotherhood seriously pursued the possibility of digging up some assumed Scandinavian forerunners from the distant past, it was perfectly clear from the outset that these could at best be of an idealistic, not an organizational, nature. And thus this seminal magical order never played with loaded dice, either, by faking an ancientry that existed solely in the devious minds of its inventors.

The Experimental Path

Remembering the problems outlined above, which had only led to an immense number of magical and masonic associations embarrassing themselves and exhausting each other for centuries, awash with involuntary comedy of sheer clubbiness, our own experimental magic working group in Bonn dispensed from the outset with the myth of some ancient brotherhood: this was considered to be entirely superfluous and expendable by now.

A conversation I had with a friend in 1980 did go to prove that the legitimation fetish described here was still quite virulent outside our circle, though. My friend was an extremely experienced and well versed old esoteric, a proven connoisseur of the history of magic and its orders and himself a long-standing member of a renowned magical brotherhood to boot. When we talked shop for a bit and I told him that I had recently performed several extremely powerful Pan rituals together with friends, he asked in complete amazement: "But where did you get the ritual texts?" It took some considerable persuasion until he was convinced that we had actually developed these rituals ourselves, without recourse to any supposed "secret archives" of any "ancient" order—for him a hitherto unheard of, entirely unthinkable idea.

Tradition and Balderdash,
as well as: the Master Question

There's no denying that authentic, intelligent tradition has its value. It helps us collect and bundle knowledge, to pass on experience in condensed form, and to avoid needless additional efforts and aggravation. In short, it ensures that we don't have to reinvent the wheel all the time. Thus it can also be a considerable efficiency factor for practical magical work. But when it is merely confused with mundane formalities and their vapid self-celebration, we inevitably find ourselves confronted with fruitless counter-productiveness.

Therefore, in case of doubt, every magician should rather rely on their own experimentation instead of uncritically, gullibly, and lazily surrendering themself to any supposedly authoritative organizations.

A short meditation on the old question "Who initiated the first master?" may also be of assistance.

Chapter 8

Telepathy for Everyday Life

Harry Eilenstein

Telepathy is one of the basic elements of magic: receiving or sending information. Whether this analogy to sending a letter with the postal service precisely describes the processes can well be argued about—but the clarification of this specific question is not the concern of this chapter

The simplest proof of telepathy is the phenomenon that people who are intensively stared at from behind will turn around searchingly. This is a helpful old reflex that dates back to the time when people used to be occasionally ambushed by a hungry tiger or two.

The following is an experiment to prove the existence of telepathy to one-self and others when needed. But you will need at least five people, preferably an even larger group of people, to carry it out.

Get yourself two dozen postcards with striking imagery and put these into envelopes and close them so that the postcards cannot be seen.

Then four people each receive an envelope which they place on the table between them. Next, they mutually concentrate together for three minutes on the postcard in their respective envelope and write down their perceptions.

Now, the perceptions that occur to at least three people are combined: e.g. sand, warmth, predominantly blue, a light or yellow spot at the top right. This may result in a beach scene with the sun at the top right corner.

This picture is then supplemented by the motifs that have appeared for at least two participants: e.g. a palm tree and some white and angular white in the middle of the picture, right in the blue. So now it seems to be the image of a palm beach along with a yacht bearing a white sail.

Finally, each group opens its envelope and takes a look at the post-card they have described telepathically before.

This simple method makes it possible to distinguish the telepathic perceptions (which are identical for several people) from the associations (which only appear individually for one person).

With a little practice and, above all, some experimentation, we can find all sorts of practical applications of telepathy in everyday life.

One of the most useful methods is the "transfer of consciousness", i.e., the sending of one's own consciousness to another place, to another person, or to another object.

A few years ago my acquaintance Beate called to tell me that her boy-friend had left his laptop computer somewhere in town.

So I concentrated on her boyfriend first off and from there I switched my concentration to his laptop computer. Then I looked at the surroundings of this laptop: dark, slightly dusty, a lower shelf in a narrow aisle, possibly behind a shop counter in a small room.

With the help of this description, Beate's friend recognized the newspaper kiosk where he had been. When he drove back there, he got his laptop com-puter back from the kiosk owner.

On another occasion I got a call from Silke, who told me that she had lost her wallet. When I couldn't see it by the method described, I tried something else: I projected my consciousness into her wallet and then looked where I was. This proved to be easier. It was completely dark, so the wallet was within or under something. It was dusty to dirty and pretty musty; it smelled metal-lic; it wasn't in a house but maybe in a car?

So she looked in her car and found her wallet under the mat.

A few weeks later Silke called me again and said that her son Giacomo had lost his front door key.

I looked at employing the "old method" and felt that the key was inside something: it was dark, slightly dusty, and musty. Giacomo initially sus-pected the drawer of the cupboard in the hallway at his girlfriend's, but in fact the key wasn't there.

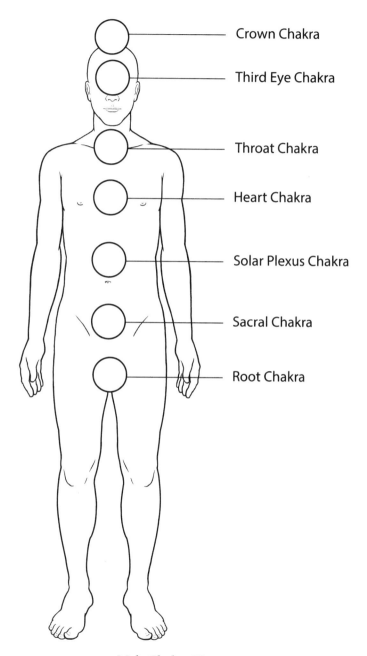

Crown Chakra

Third Eye Chakra

Throat Chakra

Heart Chakra

Solar Plexus Chakra

Sacral Chakra

Root Chakra

Male Chakra Figure

When he called me again, I tried the "new method" and projected my consciousness into his front door key. The environment was still dark, dusty and musty, but I could now see that it was soft and firm as well—neither wood nor metal. Next I expanded my consciousness to this solid soft shell and looked at the environment it was in: in Giacomo's room, on the right when you enter the door.

There was his guitar bag and the key proved to be in the bag's small outside pocket.

A short time later Silke called once more. This time her car wasn't driving properly, and she had no proper explanation for what was wrong with it.

So I checked and projected my consciousness into the engine of the car: unfortunately everything was dark and motionless there. All right, so the car was just standing still in front of her house. So I told Silke to imagine starting the engine. When we both realized what I had just said, we threw a fit of laughter.

Yet the idea was good: I could now see the flow of the electric current in the engine, the movement of the parts, and so on. For quite a while I looked for something that looked as if it wasn't quite right: I roughly know how a car engine works, but I'm not a car driver myself and certainly not a car mechanic.

Then I discovered something on the upper right hand of the engine which I thought was the alternator because it looked like a dynamo. The spinning part inside the dynamo seemed brittle and the spindle of this part was wobbling.

This diagnosis of the decrepit alternator was later confirmed by the garage.

The transfer of one's own consciousness to another person, however, occurs, at least in my personal everyday life, far more frequently than the transfer to an object. That's presumably because I counsel people.

This "consciousness-transfer" can be experienced in any family constellation, even when it isn't systematically trained and happens more or less intuitively.

There are very practical applications for these transfers of consciousness. The following episode, however, was more a case of a "consciousness escort."

A banker whom I had counseled for a while had an important meeting coming up with an Indian colleague, and he wasn't particularly confident that everything would go well. So he asked me if I could support him.

I told him that while I could well be there internally, I wouldn't try to get his colleague to do something he didn't want. Instead, I'd be there and would be able to call up some clarity, mitigate approaches to disputes, promote mutual understanding, and do the very same for the Indian banker.

After the negotiations had taken place, he rang me up and I told him how the meeting, which had lasted for about half an hour, had gone—all of which he was able to confirm in full. Unfortunately, in the end this negotiation didn't actually bear fruit, which was rather a pity because otherwise I would probably have been able to go on a trip to India with my banker.

There was a second experience with another banker. Eliot, an acquaintance of mine, had a negotiation meeting with a banker in America coming up and didn't really know whether these negotiations would pan out well. So I offered to describe for him the character of the banker in question and his values if he sent me a picture of him.

I looked at the picture and felt into the banker, just as I look at people when I meet them to see who it is I have in front of me. I then sent Eliot the description, which he found very helpful.

With such telepathic information retrievals, it is important to me to always look closely at what things feel right to me and what makes me feel like I am trespassing across some borderline. For example, I wouldn't have looked for the banker's weak points, where you could emotionally grab him and get him to do something he didn't really want.

What I wish to do is to remove obstacles and help people both to be themselves and to express themselves, but not to bring anyone to do something they don't want to.

From time to time it happens that one of the people I counsel rings me up and is about to panic. I'll generally try to calm them down with words and bring them back on track, but sometimes that's not enough and just won't work.

So at some point I came up with the idea of asking them for permission to transfer my consciousness into them. There I took a look at which chakra was going crazy and which one had collapsed: in a panic attack the third eye usually went crazy and the hara would collapse.

So I tried to calm the third eye of one lady suffering a panic attack and acted to revive her aura. When calming the third eye I discovered that it is a great help to imagine Buddha Amitabha there (i.e., in the pituitary gland, the "root" of the third eye) and to ask him for help.

The hara can be assisted by calling the spirit animal of the person concerned, connecting this spirit animal with the mother goddess of this animal species (e.g. the Great White Wolf in a wolf-spirit animal) and then asking the spirit animal to take a seat in the hara of the person concerned.

If a person seeking counsel displays rather diffuse symptoms and doesn't really know what's going on, I sometimes ask if I may look at their chakras. The condition of the chakras shows at least the general orientation of the condition of the person concerned:

- energy congestion in the root chakra / lack of energy in the crown chakra => addiction
- energy congestion in the crown chakra / energy deficiency in the root chakra => asceticism
- energy congestion in the hara / lack of energy in the third eye => offender
- energy congestion in the third eye / lack of energy in the hara => victim
- energy congestion in the solar plexus / lack of energy in the throat chakra => superstar
- energy congestion in the throat chakra / lack of energy in the solar plexus => fan boy/girl

In all these cases, the heart chakra is usually a little darker than usual. As a rule, the heart chakra can only shine and radiate properly again when the polarity in the three chakra pairs has at least been mellowed and partially healed.

A task that always gives me pleasure and usually makes the person seeking counsel laugh is the transfer of consciousness to an organ of the client.

If one of their organs hurts or is ill, I will project my consciousness into this organ and offer it to speak through me.

Usually it will start to do so right off the hook, and in a quite emotional and uninhibited manner so that the organ's problem becomes clear immediately. The language of the organs is usually so drastic and their narrative is so accurate that people have to laugh—both because they feel caught and because they feel acknowledged and hence liberated.

This form of counseling is real fun and I speak in a way I would never speak otherwise. Each organ has its own style, so there is a great variety.

The transfers of consciousness that I have described so far have all been conscious. But there are also unconscious transfers of consciousness … if that is the right term for it.

I experienced the most drastic case about a week ago before writing these lines: I was hiking up the hill into the forest, and in front of me a woman was pushing her bicycle uphill. I found that this woman had a strange kind of charisma about her—just as if something was wrong with her … something missing, a bit domineering, beholden to applause … I tend to perceive such things quite frequently but in this case I didn't take it any further.

Then I remembered a conversation I had recently had with a girlfriend. We had talked about a hike in the Seven Mountains region a few years ago, at the end of which she fell on her back in a very weird manner, as if in slow motion, which had caused a lot of things to break open in her psyche, making them visible.

So I walked up the hill mustering the woman who was walking in front of me, at the same time remembering the fall of my girlfriend. All of a sudden the woman before me fell to the ground as if in slow motion and her bicycle tumbled down on her. When she finally lay on the ground, she started to laugh because she obviously thought her mishap to be quite funny.

It seemed that I had transferred the image of my girlfriend falling onto the woman in front of me, merely by looking at her while I was musing about my girlfriend crashing to the ground.

On the one hand, it seems that one should be careful with regard to deliberate transfers of consciousness, while on the other hand there's an indication that such unintentional transfers of consciousness are probably taking place more frequently than we may believe

Chapter 9
Some Questions on Magic

Josef Knecht

Question: How did you originally come to magic?

Josef Knecht: It depends on how we want to define "magic." In a broader sense, I have been interested in the subject ever since—due to my interests in the natural sciences at school—I came across the fact that the scientific world also has its limits and that there are a number of phenomena that cannot be explained satisfactorily by science.

This may sound strangely trivial today, but it was a surprising and fascinating discovery for a young person with an ordinary school education in the 1970s. At first I was extensively occupied with parapsychology and read everything about it the city library could furnish me with. Then a friend came over with Rudolf Steiner, my next eye opener, with whom I stayed for quite some time. This was certainly not yet magic in the stricter sense, but at any rate my interest was guided in the direction in which magic, too, can actually be encountered. Although my own approach has always been more oriented toward insight and understanding rather than practical application, Anthroposophy eventually proved too cerebral for me. I met too few people there who could actually experience themselves all that Steiner was talking about, let alone comment on it from personal observation. I needed at least that much practice to be able to determine for myself whether the experiences claimed were basically replicable.

Further searches investigating Gnostic groups and various forms of meditation finally led me to Neopagan cults that inspired me with that devotion to the world and love of nature that I missed in Eastern and Gnostic approaches. In so-called Neopaganism and in the Wicca cult I also found the ecological commitment that was important to me. Here, I finally came across magic in the narrower sense: rituals and a practical implementation of spiritual ideas.

The experimental magic workshop group in Bonn constituted the apex of this "magical phase" in my life. The personal encounters and the close friendships that developed within the group were certainly just as decisive for the lasting effect the workshop had on my life as the practical experiences within that framework themselves.

Question: Have you ever completely abandoned magic and given it up altogether? If so, why?

Josef Knecht: Abandoned is not the appropriate term. At times I did lose interest and other things gained priority. And again, it depends on how you actually understand magic. For me, magic has always been a means to an end, mostly to better understand the world, to try out possibilities for changing the limitations of my consciousness. Sometimes, other approaches proved of greater help to me: meditation, dream work, inner journeys, and so on, though obviously these can also be regarded to pertain to magic in a broader understanding of the term.

If you mean by magic in general everything that could be termed spiritual, holistic, or depth-psychological, then I never stopped, and I even made a living of it by practicing homeopathy as a healing method. If you want to confine it to ritual or ceremonial magic in the strict sense, then I stopped not long after the termination of our workshop.

And if we speak of magic in the sense of Frater U∴D∴'s Ice Magic, as a radical breaking away of the will, severing our conventional connections to the world, then I have never actually practiced such an approach. Considering the great interest in Gnosticism that I have always retained, I can see the thrust of this effort and have great respect for it. It was never my own thing, though: I'll fall out of the world soon enough.

First and foremost, I am interested in exploring the world's possibilities further than is usually the case. And sometimes, I'll admit, I'm also interested in comfortably arranging myself in it, though such phases are usually quite limited.

Question: Did you resume formal magic after that? If so, why exactly? And what was different afterwards?

Josef Knecht: Within the basic understanding explained above, the magical plane is simply part of the everyday experience of the world and oneself, which I would not be able to give up at all even if I intended to do so. Yet the active way of dealing with it will shift according to the circumstances and possibilities of life.

What actually has changed over the years, as in all other life contexts, is that I have become more patient and the time perspective is losing its importance. Unless this tendency leads to becoming complacent and "falling asleep," it is really more helpful because it provides a fundamental sense of ease.

Question: How do you deal with doubts about the effectiveness of magic in general or your magic in particular? What are its limits? What's missing?

Josef Knecht: I have never had any doubts about the effectiveness of magic itself, though certainly [I have] regarding the efficacy of my own magic. This means that I would never even think of doubting whether magic works in general or whether there are inexplicable phenomena or talents to bring it about. I have simply experienced too much myself that defies any other reasonable interpretation. You'd also have to be quite naive, dumb, or inexperienced to deny magical phenomena per se.

But my own ability to make it work remains quite modest. By way of an example, if I'm not particularly gifted to play the violin, I might learn the basics and develop some simple skills, but I will never become a virtuoso even with the most exhaustive effort. But that doesn't imply that I'll categorically doubt people's ability to make music.

My limits lie in the fact that my perceptions in the extrasensory realm are not very precise and will rarely function on demand. And what's more, my interest in it remains within correspondingly narrow limits. As I said, for me magic is more of a tool to gain insight, just as scientific knowledge and skills or the ability to think logically are such tools. For me, it's quite enough to experience what works and what doesn't, and how it works. This is how I form my view of the world. But to magically influence my environment is not my primary concern.

Question: How do you feel about magic today, based on your many years of experience?

Josef Knecht: This really follows from my previous answers. I think I would still use magical techniques, let's say in emergency cases, when no other measure would achieve a certain goal [that] I have a deep intuition that it would be good to [attain]. This would mainly relate to supporting a healing process in some way.

On the other hand, when it comes to so called "high magic" rituals, I prefer quiet, more meditative approaches than before nowadays. In a way it's nevertheless magic, though, provided you expand your understanding and terminology enough to encompass different and untypical methods.

What I miss most about magic today is the magical atmosphere that permeated my life in those days. It was only much later that it became clear to me how deep this went—something I actually realized only due to the lack of it.

Question: Coming to magic and everyday life: has magic proved useful or helped you in your everyday life and if so, in what manner? Where did it fail?

Josef Knecht: We once had a time when we tried out all sorts of things, performed rituals for this and that, constantly laid cards or consulted other oracles. That was interesting and very romantic and certainly enriched my life more than many other activities. But I have learned that it is not a great idea to influence everyday things on the basis of my own limited insights. Of course you can achieve a lot with a powerful ritual, even in everyday life, but the question is whether you will actually fancy the final result with all its consequences.

In general, I did not get the impression that those amongst my acquaintances and friends who practiced a lot of magic were able to cope with everyday life any better than those who did not. I found it interesting to read that Frater U∴D∴ judges this similarly, albeit certainly on a much broader basis of experience than I do.

As a tool, I find magic rather unreliable and cumbersome. I have experienced other forms of endeavor as being more effective. And above all, I have come to the conclusion that those instances of my being which are largely unconscious to me but which control my destiny—and my body as well, which are thus maintaining the essentially automatic part of my system, to which that small section of consciousness which I call "I" can and must constantly fall back—that these instances have a better understanding how to regulate the course of my life than my attempts at gaining some advantages based solely on my modest conscious understanding of things.

Quite frankly, one failure of magic sometimes consists in the fact that "nothing happens," or at least nothing that feels or can reasonably be classified as a magical effect as far as I am concerned.

But the other failure can also repose in the fact that what has been formulated as a wish will indeed manifest exactly as targeted, with me only realizing after the manifestation of such "success" that I had actually imagined something entirely different and had forgotten essential components in the formulation of my objective. Those fairy tales of the fairy granting three wishes to someone which then, to the regret of the recipient, are fulfilled in a most literal manner, illustrate my point precisely.

I still remember an incident when as a student I "wished" for a very cheap apartment, close to the forest, with a lot of space, my own kitchen and separate entrance—an actually quite utopian request in view of the then as now difficult living situation in the city. The magic worked exactly as I had wished. I found the most unusual apartment, directly by the forest, with a landlord who did not make any unreasonable demands but instead asked me what I could actually afford to pay. Unfortunately, in my list of desirable qualities I had forgotten to add that the apartment should also be bright and dry, not murky and damp ...

Question: If you still practice magic today: what do you focus on? Has this changed in the course of your life (perhaps with increasing age)? If so, in what way? And why is that, do you think?

Josef Knecht: If for once I classify magic in the traditional manner into "low" and "high" magic, a very debatable distinction indeed but somewhat helpful in terms of answering this question, then I must state that I have lost interest in the "low" approach of influencing the environment according to my personal wishes. By contrast, "high" magic in the sense of continued growth of personality and finally transcending it (whatever that may actually imply) is still an essential part of my life's core. Today, however, I no longer deploy ritual methods but rather meditative ones in the sense of purely inner processes.

Why? In my current life, extensive rituals or ceremonies could only be accommodated with great effort and would create friction in my environment, provoking incomprehension, disapproval, wisecracks, and other unnecessary stumbling blocks, merely prompting a waste of energy. To be sure, the tendency to provoke or outrage my environment with radical decisions and actions has definitely subsided in the course of my life.

Question: What would you advise magicians today?

Josef Knecht: Advising other people, especially those you don't know personally, is always a delicate matter. From my long experience as a therapist I know that advice, if any, only makes sense on an individual basis. If one person experiences a cold curd wrap as helpful and healing for a sore throat, while the other needs a warm potato pack and the third requires essential oils and a woolen scarf, what should I actually advise someone? It is best to point out a few possibilities to stimulate creativity and encourage people to try them out. But even that, as nice as it sounds, can be a total overtaxing for some, if for them only clear, definitive instructions and a set framework of action can be of help.

I suspect that some of those who are reading this would be very happy and feel inspired in an experimental, open circle as I have experienced it, when in fact for others it would all be far too chaotic, and they would feel much better off within some more rigid religious structure.

For people who are on a similar wavelength as I am, a self-responsible and rationally well manageable form of search and research will prove very useful, whereas gurus, orders, and rulebooks may rather provoke their resistance.

What will probably prove to be very supportive for most people is a group of steady and reliable buddies, close friends even. Knowing that, in case of suddenly surfacing inner problems, which can always occur during intensive exercises—especially when there is a lack of previous experience to absorb them properly—there are people around who are unconditionally ready to support and help you, is an emotional buttress that simply cannot be overestimated.

Question: Can people actually learn magic, or do you think one must have it from birth as a talent? If the former or even if both, what role do traditions play in magic? Magic books? Personal teachers? Magical orders, lodges, associations etc.?

Josef Knecht: Of course you can learn magical skills like everything else. However, the real question is: how much actual effort is it worth? How far can I get with it? And that, in turn, depends very much on what talents I'm bringing along—as with all other skills in life. Everyone can learn to elicit certain sounds from a violin, no question about it. Whether it's worthwhile to make this activity the purpose of your life is another matter. So I know from experience that every person can learn to become aware of perceptions that are rated clairvoyant. But only a few may have sufficient talent to achieve a degree of precision that makes it interesting enough to invest a lot of energy into pursuing this course. The same applies to all other skills that can be useful in a magical way: meditating, concentrating, visualizing, dreaming, thinking, feeling, intuiting, directing energy, exercising willpower, etc.

If we take the field of perception, you'll observe during nuts-and-bolts seminars that some people seem to be blocked because they fixate themselves on the expectation of experiencing "extrasensory" perceptions in the form of luminous colorful images, as is often portrayed in literature. But since only a few people have a strong talent for pareidolia, all others tend to overlook or ignore the particular perceptions they do have. This affects all perceptions that make use of the analogy of hearing, touching, feeling, of premonitions and memories. Hence, an essential step in experimenting is to first find out which inner channel is the most successful and/or easiest to use. Then, you can decide if you want to prioritize or if you'd prefer working on those that seem to be more difficult initially, just as some right-handers may want to practice writing with their left hand.

Question: What is your conclusion today, forty years later, regarding the Bonn Workshop for Experimental Magic? Would you advise today's magicians to establish something similar? Regardless of your advice, what mistakes do you think they should try to avoid?

Josef Knecht: Under the limitations discussed above, I would tell those who have a similar temperament as we had then: I'd definitely advise anyone interested in magic or other similar experiences to get together with like-minded people and try things out, broaden their horizons. Central to this, in my opinion, is an undogmatic approach, a desire to experiment, well balanced with common sense and objectivity, plus smooth cooperation within the group. Only if you can firmly rely on each other will you want to venture further out to sea. Otherwise, the censor will kick off a lot earlier to suppress the experience, or else you may completely drop out and lose all control.

My conclusion is: the workshop group was the best thing that could have happened to me at that time in terms of my personal development, and these few years rank undoubtedly amongst the most influential phases of my life. The work within the group brought with it an opening into a multi-layered world experience. Without this time, these encounters and experiences, my life would have turned out completely different.

Question: How did you define magic at the beginning of your magical career? How do you define it today?

Josef Knecht: At that time I contributed to an article with the title "Magic as a Path to Soul Integrity." This was more or less my current definition then, which, however, was more of a should-be than a factual assertion, as I tended at that time to think about the world in wish categories rather than in observational ones. That has certainly changed.

Today I'm not living in a community anymore where the word "magic" rings familiar and is accepted without some explanation. So I don't think of what I am doing as "magical" any longer and would only use the word in tandem with a definition of what I'm actually talking about—except when meeting with old friends from the magical scene, of course. And that definition could be different, depending on the respective context, and would in most cases not point to magical techniques or rituals proper in the sense that we are referring to them in this book most of the time. Rather, it would be more of a kind of metaphorical meaning, pointing to a certain way of experiencing or understanding life.

Chapter 10
What Magical Orders Are Definitely Not (Anymore)

Frater U.·.D.·.

The history of magical orders is long and sometimes very chaotic. They are often referred to as secret societies or brotherhoods and for good reason, which will have to be discussed in more detail. In many cases, the Eurocentric view of the world, owed above all to imperial colonialism, has obscured the view that such organizations with structures that can hardly be distinguished from one another have actually been found across many cultures and among numerous indigenous peoples around the world since time immemorial.

Magic Secret Societies in History

It is well known that there have been many different secret societies in the history of the world, and they still exist today. Most of them are quite mundane in nature and do not pursue any explicitly magical or esoteric agenda. Instead, they go after purely political, economic or even, in some cases, criminal interests. Magical orders, on the other hand, are dedicated to the study and application of magical practices, but may also pursue other metaphysical, mystical, Gnostic, or spiritual goals. Sometimes, however, the boundaries between the two types are quite blurred, which we have to take into account in our following examination.

The Venerable Golden Dawn: A Nineteenth-Century Terrorist Organization?

The best-known magical order of the nineteenth century, the English Golden Dawn (GD), for example, was not quite unreasonably suspected by the British security authorities of its time of being a conspiratorial terrorist organization, as Richard B. Spence plausibly documents in his extensive study.[14] In fact, apart from its magical-esoteric orientation, the GD seconded as a reservoir for a large number of political underground activists who were classified by the British government as highly treasonous and alarming: Irish freedom fighters, Scottish legitimists, supporters of the Spanish Carlists, as well as (presumably) some employees of foreign intelligence services were streaming in and out in the GD's premises. The situation was even more opaque with regard to those members of the order who were foreigners or living abroad, located across numerous foreign countries. Although the Golden Dawn itself could not be validly assumed to be an operatively active organization in the political arena, it was regarded by the security authorities as a potential initiation and contact center, thus functioning as the facade of the various subversive groups represented within its membership.

Accordingly, Spence also considers it proven—and substantiates his claim manifoldly and convincingly—that the young Aleister Crowley, freshly recruited by the British secret service, acted under official orders to infiltrate the GD, to spy out its members, and finally to destroy or at the very least decisively weaken the order as agent provocateur in a sabotage operation by exposing it to ridicule in all publicity, which, as is well documented, he eventually managed to accomplish with a vengeance.

The Ancient Egyptian Priesthood

The ancient Egyptian priesthood, which was hermetically sealed off from the rest of society, was already a veritable ritual secret society of the greatest caliber, albeit demonstrating full public presence and enjoying the highest esteem both among ordinary people as well as among the ruling elites. This privileged group saw itself not only responsible for religious and magical matters, but also exerted a considerable political influence on the affairs of state. This finally prompted the Pharaoh Akhenaton, driving the preceding initial efforts of his father Amenophis III to extremes, to completely deprive them of power by implementing the first (albeit in the end rather short-lived) effectively monotheistic religion of world history, whereby he elevated

---

14. Richard B. Spence, *Secret Agent 666: Aleister Crowley, British Intelligence and the Occult.* Los Angeles, CA, London: Feral House; Turnaround [distr.], 2008.

himself to be the—now no longer only nominal—supreme secular as well as spiritual ruler over the giant Egyptian empire and thus ruthlessly sidelining his clerical political opponents.

The Freemasons

Freemasonry (FM) cannot legitimately be considered a magical order— at least, regular FM has always vehemently opposed such a categorization. However, since FM works ritually under formal secrecy, its opponents repeatedly accuse Freemasons of exactly this in the course of their three-and-a-half-century existence, a situation that has also for a long time driven FM's active persecution on a global level. More decisive for these reprisals, however, was FM's presumed political influence, which to this day has turned the organization into an easy whipping boy for numerous authoritarian and quite frequently antisemitic regimes, by blaming Masons for almost anything under the sun that happens to displease the rulers, or appears to jeopardize the political status quo from their point of view.

It is also true, however, that especially in the early days of historically documented FM, many of its members belonged to the political elites who actually wanted to leverage the brotherhood to push through a humanistic enlightenment agenda on a societal scale. In the seventeenth and eighteenth centuries, for many progressive feudal rulers and their aristocratic courts it was quite hip to be a member of one or even several Masonic lodges.

The conspiratorial machinations of the Italian Freemason lodge *Propaganda Due* (P2), which in the 1970s organized a broad network of members of the police, military, business, politics, and mafia organizations, actually planned a right-wing coup d'état and carried out a large number of false-flag terrorist attacks aimed at discrediting the political left. Expectably, this caused quite a sensation in the media. Although regular Freemasonry was in no way directly responsible for these conspiratorial and subversive activities, the personal and structural interconnections between these groups can hardly be denied.

The Germanenorden and the Thule Society

The German ariosophist Teutonic Order (*Germanenorden Walvater*, GO), which focused on practical rune magic and Aryan lore, founded the Thule

Society as a camouflage organization under its grandmaster Rudolf von Sebottendorf,[15] through which it exerted significant political influence on the electoral platform of the emerging Nazi party (the NSDAP) after World War I. Sebottendorf and the GO were also to exert a decisive influence on the ensuing civil war in Bavaria and other parts of the Reich, with both the Thule and his notorious Freikorps Oberland fighting league, which he personally set up and armed.

Templars, Assassins, Indian Warrior Monks

The fusion of occult practices with the craft of war within a fraternity framework can already be found in the European-Christian, Arab-Islamic, and Indian-Hindu Middle Ages.

Thus the Knights Templar, quite arguably with some justification, were said to have an internal magical cult of a possibly heretical nature, as were their Muslim adversaries, the Assassins, and their modern-day successors, the Ismaelites. On the Indian subcontinent, before the introduction of firearms, entire mercenary armies of meditation-hardened, ash-covered ascetics fought as frontline shock troops, often dressed only in loincloths or entirely naked. These too were organized in strictly closed fraternities. Following their eventual demilitarization, we owe them the present day Kaula, Nath and other Sadhu brotherhoods as well as the development of yoga, which originally emerged from their ranks as a soldierly fighting and defense technique of physical training and a conduit for the evolution of paranormal abilities (siddhis) that were to be deployed in armed conflict: yoga as a decidedly martial art.

The Ghost Dance Movement

If we let our gaze wander to North America, in the second half of the nineteenth century we notice the cross-tribal Indian revival movement of Ghost Dancing. At first, this was also organized as a closed shop brotherhood. From its inception it had made it its concern to restore access to the lost magical knowledge of the ancestors with the help of trance techniques including, above all, the eponymous "ghost dance," which would often last for several

---

15. For Sebottendorf and his extensive, uniquely seminal political activities, see chapter 18, "German Letter Magic: History, Systems, Field Reports."

days. Soon it turned into a veritable mass phenomenon covering large parts of the country and its Indian reservations, culminating in the last great battle of the Indian wars. The most influential prophet—i.e., visionary—and leader of this movement was the Sioux chief Tatanka Yotanka (actually *Ťhatȟáŋka Íyotake*), commonly known as Sitting Bull.

The Turkish Dervish Orders

At the beginning of the twentieth century, after the dissolution of the Ottoman Empire and the introduction of secularism by the Young Turks, the magically-mystically oriented dervish orders came under general suspicion under the Ataturk regime of being conspiratorial hotbeds of political revisionism, and of pursuing counter-revolutionary efforts. Their public performances were for the most part banned or, at best, still permitted in strictly regulated form for the sole purpose of promoting the tourism industry.

To this day these orders constitute an essential rationale for the fact that the Turkish republic maintains a national religious authority which supervises, among other things, the mosques of the country, the imams' approbation, supervising their public sermons, and censoring them if deemed necessary.

Voudon in Haiti

We can also find the magical brotherhood as a political issue in Haiti. The only successful slave uprising in the world that brought independence from France to this part of the island of Hispaniola in 1803 and established the first "black republic" would have been unthinkable without the subversive activity and support of the well-organized Voudon priesthood and its numerous cultic communities.

Even today, Haiti has the unwritten law that no ruler, including democratically elected politicians, can hold on to power if he messes with the Voudon *houngans*, *bocores*, and *ambos*. Even the longstanding dictator François Duvalier ("Papa Doc") cultivated relations with the various Voudon brotherhoods with great intensity, and repeatedly identified himself as a supporter of the Voudon cult, even though Haiti officially defines itself as a Roman Catholic country. Indeed, he even systematically spread the rumor that he himself was the dreaded cemetery *loa* and death spirit Baron Samedi and claimed to be under the special protection of supernatural forces.

Mau Mau and Simbas in Kenya

Similar to Haiti, the anti-colonial Mau Mau Uprising (also termed the Mau Mau War) in Kenya in the 1950s was supported by magically-oriented brotherhoods. In addition to the Mau Mau themselves, who originally started out as a secret society and made use of the local tradition of publicly performing and regularly renewing magical vows in order to ideologically fortify and numerically expand their followership, there were also the Simbas or "lion men"—initiated members of the lion clan who "transformed" themselves mentally into lions through magical practices such as donning lion skins, but primarily through trance techniques before combat. Their actual military impact remained rather low key, but in the course of this guerrilla war they provided valuable support in the fields of logistics, communication, and intelligence reconnaissance due to their extensive nationwide networking.

Although beaten militarily before the beginning of the 1960s, the uprising ultimately achieved its goal by forcing the British colonial power to release Kenya into independence at the end of 1963.

The Apprehensions of Orthodoxy

The examples given should suffice to support our observation above that the boundaries between political and magical secret societies are by no means always as clear-cut as the undiscerning observer might imagine. Perhaps they will also contribute to a broader understanding that magical orders are usually viewed with great suspicion by the ruling agents of politics, society, and clergy—in short: the establishment—and are hence frequently persecuted violently and brutally.

As a magician, you should get to know and understand these connections. After all, some precautionary measures can be derived from this, which are to be heeded if you want to avoid getting into great, possibly even life-threatening, difficulties simply because of your belonging to a magical order, no matter how apolitically oriented it may be.

The most important of these precautions is that you should keep as quiet as possible about your own membership in such an order. However, this will always depend on your own specific life situation. For example, personally I myself never had to make a secret of my membership in the Fraternitas Saturni (FS) after having decided early on to publicly take up the dispute over magic. However, my specific choice of career allowed me to do this without any inhibitions.

But this by no means holds true for everyone. Anyone who has to fear serious disadvantages at work, in their family, their circle of friends and acquaintances, or in general in society due to such openness, is well advised not to shout their magical alliance from the rooftops. In any case the names of other members of your brotherhood—as well as any other internal affairs—should never be put into the limelight!

In the following we will now devote ourselves to the "pure" magical orders, that is to those who do not pursue brazenly conspiratorial political, economic, or even criminal goals behind an occult façade, be it in reality or even only as a sideline e.g. as part of their overarching esoteric ideology.

So What's "Secret" Anyway?

There's an old dialog quip: "Do you know any secret orders?" "Yes, some." "Then they're not." This, of course, displays a fundamental misunderstanding, at least as far as magical orders are concerned. Indeed, for mundane secret societies that pursue revolutionary or criminal goals, secrecy actually begins with the fact that their very existence must not be revealed. The less their opponents know about it, the safer they are from persecution.

But this does not necessarily apply to magical orders unless they are outlawed and forbidden by the state, or when even mere membership is punishable by law. Where this is not the case, it is usually possible to speak quite openly about their existence. Then, as is often said of Freemasonry, they are not a "secret" fraternity but one "with a secret," which is not at all the same thing.

Now even Freemasons are never particularly edified when their "secret" rituals are publicly propagated ("profaned"). Nevertheless, this does not really jeopardize the effective exercise of their art. For what no number of ritual texts, however extensive, can reproduce in the public media is what is termed the "secret of the dimension of experience." Reading about a ritual is one thing. It's something entirely different, however, to experience this ritual with body and soul itself. Even the most linguistically skillful and artistic depiction can never really reproduce this experience because it is a highly personal, completely individual experience that unfolds its effect above all in the emotional and spiritual realm. Neither can the feeling of being in love, the horror of a panic attack, the surging emotions when listening to a Beethoven symphony or a rock concert, the ecstasies of sexuality or the rush of taste when sampling an excellently prepared meal ever be so adequately expressed linguistically that pure reading would constitute a full substitute for the experience itself. This is what is meant by the saying "True secrets protect themselves." It is therefore obvious that, at best, we will be able to exchange information about this in an approximate manner, and even this will be very imperfect. If the interlocutors share the same, albeit certainly never completely identical, experience, this can at least lead to a constructive, enriching dialogue and a strong empathic connection among themselves. This is often the case among members of the order.

However, such conversations are pointless with people who are completely unfamiliar with what is described and for whom it remains inaccessible due to their sheer lack of experience. Most of the time these discourses will end in an uncomprehending shrug of the shoulders at best, at worst in frustrated and frustrating aggravation. In this sense, too, secrets do protect themselves—if necessary, even from their bearers.

The Magic Order as an Academy of Life?

In the early 1950s, the aspiring adept found detailed information on daily body hygiene, laundry care, etc. in an early edition of the official, publicly distributed Fraternitas Saturni journal *Blätter für angewandte okkulte Lebenskunst (Papers for Applied Occult Art of Living)*. From today's point of view this may seem banal, bizarre, or even ridiculous, but in the devastated Germany of the post-war period and the reconstruction phase, the leadership of the lodge obviously saw it as a necessity for the war generation, many of whom were regarded—probably rightly—as being severely brutalized. Apparently in this particular historical situation such self-evident civilisatory behavior could no longer be taken for granted from every aspirant.

This episode, however, helps clarify something else as far as the perceived function of magical orders is concerned. It is not uncommon for them to have appeared in the past as "schools of life," and some of them actually still do so today. In this respect they hardly differ from the established religions that will equally assert to regulate the lives of their followers in every minute detail as far as possible. In the vast majority of cases, however, such brother-hoods are strictly hierarchically structured and thus betray a fundamentally antiquated, paternalistic view of humanity. Aspirants, novices and members of lower grades are thus often treated by their respective governing elite as immature children who are constantly to be patronized. You might perhaps like that sort of thing, but you don't actually have to …

Those who do not should, before joining the order, obtain as much trans-parency as possible about what awaits them in this respect. Of course, you won't be able to learn everything in advance, but clarifying conversations with various members, possibly also with alumni who have left the order, extensive research in internet forums, as well as consulting any literature that may be available on the subject, can certainly help avoid unwelcome surprises. Obviously you should proceed with understanding and tact. Bal-anced, fair assessments are unfortunately extremely rare. It isn't always the organization's fault if a former member starts to badmouth them. Likewise, uncritical, rapturous judgments of followers and admirers can be equally misleading. Here, a profound understanding of human nature, rationality and prudence are called for. And it certainly can't hurt if an aspirant knows how to read between the lines.

Frequently, especially beginners will try to get in touch with a magical order because they expect it to provide them access to secret knowledge. Often this is based on a romantic misjudgment of which the orders them-selves are not always innocent. If an organization systematically tries to cre-ate the impression that its archives conceal the most fabulous treasures of knowledge, which are supposedly only available to its own initiates while the poor rest of the world will have to do without them, there is only one reason-able piece of advice: run for it! Here, the earnest, legitimate thirst for knowl-edge of the unwary is being shamelessly abused. This approach is nothing but vile obscurantism. It was the young Aleister Crowley who, at the end of the nineteenth century, mocked the fact that the twenty-two letters of the Hebrew alphabet were revealed to him under the seal of secrecy in the course of his inauguration into the Golden Dawn—to him of all people, who already at that time probably possessed far more profound knowledge of the Kab-balah than all members of the order put together!

The Magic Order as a Lending Library?

There was a time when esoteric and certainly magical literature was incredibly difficult to get hold of. This was especially the case before the invention of book printing and the evolution of general literacy, but it was still quite true several centuries later. Not everyone could afford books, especially considering that magical works were often very expensive, as indeed some of them still are. Those who did not have an esoteric specialist bookshop in their vicinity regularly encountered major hurdles when attempting to procure relevant literature even as late as the 1990s. The situation was often aggravated by the fact that many interested parties, especially in small towns and villages, had to reckon with social challenges when they ordered magical titles through their local bookshop and word of this spread among the community. Under such circumstances, it was certainly reasonable to hope that joining a magical order would provide easier access to pertinent literature, provided that the organization maintained a well-stocked library.

Things are very different today, however. Mail order and online bookstores have become extremely efficient, as have antiquarian bookshops, and the Internet offers free, fully legal access to a veritable myriad of classic esoteric titles in many languages, no matter the specific subject. In addition, there are a large number of online forums where like-minded people from all over the world can exchange ideas to their heart's content in all openness as well as under the protection of anonymity. Anyone who wants to join a magical order today primarily in order to become better acquainted with the classics of astrology, alchemy, dowsing (radiesthesia,) or even ritual magic, to name just a few examples, may not be in the right place there.

On the other hand, of course, you can expect an order to furnish you with specialist knowledge about the order's own world view and magical practice, if necessary also offering a corresponding education. This may include research results, pointers, and advice that are actually available nowhere else in the public domain. After all, the most reliable way to access expert knowledge is to contact the experts themselves.

However, those who are chiefly interested in an ideologically neutral, nonbinding general education of an esoteric or even magical nature should first look elsewhere before committing to the frequently rather strict obligations that a membership in a magical order almost invariably entails. To summarize, today's orders are definitely no longer general academies of life or utile lending libraries, even if that used to be undoubtedly one of their functions for many people in the past, for sheer lack of viable alternatives.

The Force Field

Being in a group, ideally practicing solidarity with one another, constant exchange with like-minded people who may be more advanced on the mutual path and have more experience, regular worship, the common language and symbolism, but above all the collectively experienced dimension of experience—they create what many magical orders call their force field.

If you ask ten magicians how they define this force field, you will most likely get ten different answers, even if they all happen to be members of the same order. One magician may perhaps understand it quite literally as an energetic phenomenon, the other considers it to be a form of empathic cohesion, yet others may view it as the emanation of a protective spirit watching over the order, a form of karmic connectedness or transpersonal networking. Thus everyone perceives the force field in their own way, but as a rule everyone will probably agree that it exists in reality, no matter how subjectively and differently it may be perceived.

For many members of magical orders, the force field is a source of inspiration, of revelation, of encouragement, of commitment, of perseverance— and more often than not it constitutes the actual, existential reason for their loyalty to the order.

In view of the intensive, life-changing experience of the force field, education, curricular content, and ideology, as well as their specific technical form must take a back seat. Because ultimately magic, if it is to be a real enrichment, can only be lived and experienced. To make this possible is the actual function of the force field and thus ultimately constitutes the order's very right to exist itself.

Freestyle Magic versus Magic Orders?

The brotherhood format may not always be the appropriate way to progress on the path of magic. Our own experimental magic workshop in Bonn, for example, had nothing in common with a magical order. There was no common constitution, no fixed ideological or philosophical framework binding to all participants, no claim to a historical line of tradition, no grade system, no hierarchy of power, no pompous oaths of accession, loyalty, and secrecy.

And yet: about one third of us, myself included, were to later become members of the Fraternitas Saturni. But this only happened at the express invitation of this brotherhood, and when we finally undertook this step we did not take it as humiliated, intimidated "seekers" but as self-confident, experienced personalities who had freely decided to work on a good and great cause in order to learn and develop themselves in an entirely different way. One of us even advanced to become the Grandmaster of the FS a few years on.

Conclusion

Not everyone will like the loose, rather noncommittal format of such a free-style working group; not always will the happy serendipity of favorable circumstances make such a meetup possible. However, whenever the latter is the case, the mage should seize the opportunity. Certainly it is often preferable to do this before formally joining a magical order eventually. However, as I myself can confirm, and I am certainly not alone in this, the one does not have to exclude the other.

Chapter 11
Da'ath Magic

Harry Eilenstein

How can you tell Da'ath magic? If it's not conspicuous, it isn't Da'ath magic…

The magic emanating from Da'ath includes materializations, more heavy-duty forms of telekinesis (going beyond merely moving tiny objects), spontaneous healing, walking on water, non-physical ignition of fire, and similar effects. The typical trait of this magic is that it evidently overrides the laws of nature temporarily—in other words, it is a "miracle."

Seeing that our own experience is the only thing that can demonstrate that such things are possible at all, the inspection of Da'ath magic as presented here will probably seem to have a purely hypothetical character for some readers. I myself have not yet experienced all the occurrences described in the various "miracle stories." I've seen materializations, fairly hefty forms of telekinesis, I have lain naked in the glowing embers during firewalks, eaten pieces of embers, and I have experienced some other minor phenomena—enough for me to take those reports about "miracles" seriously.

Of course, the question arises how something like that "works" and how to "do" or perform it. The following are the known elements of this form of magic as far as I'm currently aware.

If you look at the various stories about saints, yogis, shamans, magicians, and similar people, you will notice that this form of magic appears to be quite effortless.

A tensed-up desire wouldn't fit very well with Da'ath's demarcationlessness either…

A second element is confidence in a deity, which can be observed in almost all incidents of miracles. A not quite as effective version of this is "wishing and forgetting," while "looking forward to the result" is in fact an escalation.

Since Da'ath is the domain of the deities, this connection comes as no surprise.

There is another element connected with trust in a deity: relaxed one-directionality. This aspect, too, is quite plausible, since there would have to be borders or delimiters between the respective contradictory components for a non-pinpointed directionality—which plainly would not fit in with Da'ath.

A fourth element is the fading of the I, the ego, or however you want to label that part of the psyche that has the tendency to draw boundaries around itself, to cling to things, and to reject everything else instead of getting involved in the flow of life.

These four elements can be observed, for example, in the miracles that Jesus performed. When he raised Lazarus from the dead, he completely trusted in God, thanking him preceding the miracle that God would make happen next, and in doing so he did not exert any particularly great effort, merely charging Lazarus that he should rise. Here, too, the eclipse of the "ego" is quite obvious: Jesus didn't even shrink back from his own death.

The same attitude can be observed with the two prophets Elias and Elisha; with the Mahasiddhas Tilopa, Naropa, Milarepa, and other yogis; and with many saints, magicians, and the like.

Lao Tzu described this Da'ath attitude most clearly. He named it "Wu wei," which can be translated as "non-doing" or "non-interfering." He trusted in the flow of life being wiser than himself.

How can one approach this possibility of doing miracles? Fortunately, we can almost always discover a simple method to go one step further. In this particular case, the simple method is to perform a dream journey to a person who has performed a miracle. This can be Christ's transformation of water into wine, the storm spell of the bard-druid Taliesin, the drinking of glowing copper by some Mahasiddhas, the healing of the Sufis, and many more.

Since the stories from the Bible are best known in our culture, I will take the walk of Christ over water as an example.

Sit or lie down comfortably and mentally watch Christ climb a mountain in the evening to pray to God after feeding the five thousand.

He has instructed his disciples to cross Lake Galilee to the other shore. Imagine standing nearby and watching.

The next morning, Christ descends from the mountain and walks in the direction of Lake Galilee. Next, imagine walking up to Christ and watching him. Continue walking by his side as he walks over the waves of the lake. Inwardly, connect with Christ and perceive in which inner state, in which consciousness he is currently.

If you wish, you can ask Christ if you may enter his consciousness. Feel his consciousness as he walks across the water—how does that feel? Take in this feeling, savoring it deliberately.

Undertake the same experiment with other people who have performed miracles and absorb the state they were in when they executed them.

This special form of dream journey is also highly recommended for therapeutic purposes for people who are uncertain about themselves or no longer have clear goals. This Da'ath state of consciousness, however, is also generally very helpful and extremely pleasant in everyday life: it makes life easier and, beyond that, it facilitates doing what you want to achieve in a focused and trusting fashion.

Of course you can also take a dream trip to Da'ath to get to know this area. If exploring these phenomena is important to you, it is best to undertake both kinds of dream journeys, as both experiences are quite different.

Now we have a first description of Da'ath magic as well as a first impression of the "flavor" of these wonders. Next, a guide to actually learning Da'ath magic would be useful. Since people are very different (starting off with their diverse horoscopes), there is no general recipe, but at least two general rules can be formulated.

One aspect that is certainly part and parcel of every Da'ath path is the supposition that you should have familiarized yourself with the demarcationlessness of Da'ath. Because if you are still in fear of it, you won't be able to act in or coming from Da'ath.

A second, also largely universal, aspect of Da'ath magic is the necessity of healing the psyche: in Da'ath there are no walls behind which you can hide or repress anything deriving from your own psyche. Accordingly, Da'atl presupposes that you accept yourself as you are.

This aspect, however, is not entirely universal, since it seems that even "ordinary" people can perform miracles if they are adjusted to a specific situation, such as, for example, lifting up the vehicle under which a person is trapped following an accident. Obviously, the one-directionality tied to such a situation is sufficient to perform something "impossible." For the general ability to effect something like this, a predominantly healed psyche that can be directed at a single point at any given time is certainly quite convenient.

From the relationship mandala described in my other chapters in this book results a further step that is beneficial for accessing Da'ath and acting from out of Da'ath: the union of the inner man with the inner woman, which presupposes the prior healing of the polarization of the psyche and the images of the inner man and the inner woman.

This aspect of the path to Da'ath is also found in kundalini yoga and tantra yoga. There, the seven main chakras are connected by a middle channel (sushumna) and two lateral channels (ida and pingala) respectively to the left and right of the main channel. In order to activate the flow of kundalini in the sushumna, the life force must be directed from ida and pingala into the sushumna. Ida and pingala contain the image of the inner man and the inner woman: when both unite, the image of one's own soul appears in the middle of the sushumna. The same process can also be found in the healing process of the relationship mandala.

If the psyche is replete with fears, addictions, and false (i.e., unrealistic) ideas, the life force cannot flow freely; the circulation of the vital force (kundalini) is hindered. This state obviously corresponds to the "normal" state of the psyche with its many boundaries, blockades, and even traumas. The free-flowing kundalini, on the other hand, is very similar to the unlimited consciousness in Da'ath.

Hence, it is a good idea to start out with kundalini yoga if you want to reach Da'ath.

In some Indian rituals ida and pingala, the inner man and the inner woman, appear as Shiva and Shakti. But the most effective way to unite ida and pingala is to get to know your own inner man and your own inner woman by dream journeys, meditations, rituals, and the like.

It follows from the fact of Da'ath being the realm of the deities that invocations of deities can be helpful. During an invocation you first imagine the deity in the outside and describe it: "It is ..." Then you proceed to address the deity directly and to imagine a flow of light from it to yourself: "You are ..." Finally, merge with the image of the deity and experience yourself as the god: "I am ..."

Such invocations can be an effective aid if you carry them out more frequently, becoming, in doing so, increasingly absorbed by the image of the deity.

With the aid of the kabbalistic Tree of Life, we can expound quite a bit further on the path to Da'ath.

We start out in Malkuth (earth), in the here and now, in everyday life, with our body.

Then we get to know the area of the vital force and the psyche in Yesod (moon).

Next follows the area of thinking in Hod (Mercury) which also appertains to the psyche.

The area of feelings in Netzach (Venus) is assigned to the psyche as well.

In Tiphareth (Sun) begins the realm of the soul; here we find the intentions of the soul for its present incarnation.

In Geburah (Mars) all contents of consciousness of the soul are bundled for one life. This area can also be understood as the karma sphere.

In Chesed (Jupiter) you will find the "memory" of the soul. Here, you can see its previous incarnations and likewise the balance of our current incarnation.

In Chesed there is an interesting preliminary stage to the demarcationlessness in Da'ath, namely, transparency: we can demarcate ourselves in Chesed, but we cannot hide anything and we can perceive everything on which we direct our attention.

Then finally Da'ath (Saturn) follows as the first of the three delimitationless areas of the deities.

Binah (Uranus) is the second aspect of the divinity realm. There we can experience ourselves as belonging to a community. This is not a formally "founded project community" like in Chesed, but a "natural community" to which we belong because of the nature of our inner being. Here we find trust and inner connectedness: this is the source of the trust that characterizes Da'ath.

Chokmah (Neptune) is the third aspect of the divine realm. It can be experienced as a light storm: an entirely unhindered self-expression. This is the source of one-directedness and the urge for self-expression that characterizes Da'ath.

Kether (Pluto) is the unity behind the multiplicity of the world, commonly hailed "God." Since this oneness is also the One and the All, there is nothing that could limit it in any way. This perfect freedom is the source of the possibility to perform things in Da'ath that contradict the laws of nature.

This kabbalistic "Tree of Life"-way is not the only conceivable description, but its basic structure is essentially the same as that of most other path descriptions, such as the Rosy Path of the Sufis or the Lamrim ("stages of the path") of the Tibetans.

A further description of the path to Da'ath can be formulated with the help of the kind of perceptions on the Middle Pillar, i.e., on the central part of this path:

In Malkuth one sees things from the outside.

In Yesod one sees things inwardly (dream, dream journey, etc.). There is a "fog of light" everywhere that makes everything visible. Most images are rather blurred and grey, only now and then strong colors will occur (more or less, anyway).

At the transition from the psyche (Yesod) to the soul (Tiphareth) there are three striking effects: 1. the important things begin to shine from within and are colored; 2. contouring becomes extremely keen; 3. all forms are steadily and fluidly transformed into other forms.

In Tiphareth (soul) things shine from within and are colored and there are often "standing images" that are immovable ("visions").

In Da'ath (deities) one experiences contours within the light.

In Kether (God) there is finally only bright glaring white light.

This manner of optical perception refers to the experience you will have once you have really arrived in a specific area. A dream journey to Da'ath, for example, leads to visions that are common on dream journeys, i.e., to Yesod images.

A striking peculiarity of Da'ath magic is that once you have learned it, you will no longer have a particularly pronounced need to actually make use of it: at this point you will have stopped striving for power etc., instead flowing with life.

In general, especially in Indian culture, it is emphasized that one should not strive for siddhis, i.e., the ability to perform miracles, and that when siddhis do occur, it is best to ignore them. This gives the impression that one has to completely give up one's own will, one's own ego, in order to reach Da'ath.

With the Buddhist yogis called "Mahasiddhas" about one thousand years ago, however, the ego—i.e., one's own fears, addictions, fixations, needs, etc.—is actually made use of to attain Da'ath. To this end, the meditation is captured in images that correspond to the psyche of the meditator: the glutton dissolves their demarcation to the world by imagining in the course of their meditation to devour, piece by piece, the entire world; the musician persistently concentrates on the silence behind all sounds when performing music; the toilet cleaner regards their work as an expression of their love for all beings etc.

There are a number of magical phenomena that do not allow us to determine clearly whether they are a part of Da'ath magic or not. The boundary between the "ordinary magic" emanating from the psyche in Yesod and the "extraordinary magic" emanating from Da'ath isn't always entirely apparent. This is probably best described by a few examples.

My great-grandmother once said, when she was at the fair with my siblings and me, and I only drew blanks in the raffles, that this couldn't be and that she would now draw a prize for me. My parents and grandparents tried to explain to her how the drawing of the lots actually worked, but she wasn't interested and instead drew the main prize right away with a single lot. She repeated that stunt twice again later—which may be "only" telepathy, but a very reliable brand of telepathy to be sure.[16]

My grandfather decided to play the lottery when he and his wife had a very violent quarrel with my great-grandmother. He had a six numbers main hit in the lottery off the cuff, purchased a house, and moved out with my grandmother, thus actually saving his wife's life. Can that reasonably still be considered "normal telepathy"?

At a later point, my grandfather experienced knee pain and went to see a healer. However, when he entered her kitchen, all the feathers of the chicken she was just plucking flushed in a burst toward my grandfather. Upon which, the healer declared that she couldn't heal him because he obviously possessed

---

16. See my view on telepathy in chapter 8, "Telepathy for Everyday Life."

greater powers than she did. The flushing of chicken feathers clearly goes beyond "normal telekinesis."

When I was seventeen, there was an (invisible) poltergeist in my parents' house for a year: it ran up and down the stairs and sometimes it sounded as if it was chopping up all the furniture in my room. Every now and then, it would talk to one of my sisters at night, which disturbed her sleep a bit, though she did eventually get used to it. Here, too, you can't say for sure if this is still "ordinary magic."

It also doesn't seem to be mandatory to maintain contact with deities, as I have on two occasions experienced lights floating through the forest, flashes of light in the trees, the smell of sulphur, the coughing of an invisible person between the two of us, and the flinging of a candle across the room while evocating demons in tandem with Axel.[17]

Why would you need Da'ath magic when you have largely dissolved your ego on the way to the ability to use it? Da'ath magic is rarely planned, but it sometimes just so happens that you will use it—or that it flows through you. It arises out of a given situation, it is part of the flow of life, it isn't "volitional magic."

And why do you need the Da'ath magic in the new epoch that corresponds to Da'ath? Probably the apposite opportunities will also show up in this respect. All sorts of scenarios can be devised that may sound like science fiction, from conflict de-escalation or collective meditations to effect a fortification of the ozone layer in our atmosphere to clinics mainly featuring capable spiritual healers. But which of these is actually realistic and which isn't, cannot readily be assessed ...

At least we can say for sure that magic will be integrated into the new world view that is currently emerging.

Note: The description of Da'ath magic in this chapter is an attempt to sketch its essence and describe its properties as best as possible, but a truly ascertained, reliable, and detailed representation is not yet conceivable—at least not as far as I am concerned

---

17. This was Axel Büdenbender: see his contributions in this book.

Chapter 12
Magical Healing
in the Hermetic Tradition

Josef Knecht

Nowadays, when you hear the word "magic" you don't usually think of healing, but rather of spells, conjurations, witchcraft, and so on. We tend to associate healing in a somehow magical sense with shamanism, whose representatives, even before they became "shamans" in the last twenty years, were usually called "medicine men" or "witch doctors." (This at a time when generally male ethnologists had not yet noticed that these medicine "men" were to a very large extent actually women). These terms reflect the primary activity of those tribal magicians of all peoples.

Of course, healing was one of the main concerns of people everywhere in the world plagued by sickness and adversities. And healing has always been connected with the supernormal, right up to the common locution "demi-gods in white"—as doctors are often called e.g. in German—even for the modern doctor, working on the basis of technology and pharmaceuticals.

Obviously the search for healing was also part of the European traditions of spirituality outside conventional Christianity, within which we have to classify our traditional hermetic magic. In alchemy, spagyrics developed with its plant and mineral essences which are still used for healing purposes today. As the most important and best-known healing method of the hermetic sciences, we have had homeopathy for more than two hundred years. In addition, a broad spectrum of energetic methods has developed, from mesmerizing or magnetizing to modern bio-energetic therapies. Further, there is a tradition of mediumistic and spiritual healing that can equally be attributed to magical healing methods. The occidental tradition of hermeticism or esotericism thus has a lot to offer in terms of healing methods that can look back on centuries of experience and are well proven. Only those methods that contribute to healing with alchemistically-prepared drugs will be discussed in more detail here.

The classic among the hermetic healing methods is spagyrics (commonly also known as "spagyric medicine") as a direct offshoot of the alchemical tradition. The concept of spagyrics goes back to the *ars spagyrica* of the renowned physician Paracelsus, who is also regarded as one of the forefathers of homeopathy. This special production method of herbal remedies has been carried on until today, and there were several important alchemists in the twentieth century, such as Alexander von Bernus, Carl Friedrich Zimpel, Frater Albertus, or Manfred Junius, who occupied themselves in detail with this doctrine and published treatises on it.

Spagyrics is about transferring the essence or spirit of a plant into the medicine. For this purpose, an often-complex alchemical procedure of ashing, dissolving, distillation, and so on is employed, which requires special education and cannot unfortunately be described in more detail here.

Alongside individual remedies for specific ailments, alchemy has also always dealt with the universal remedy, the so-called elixir that was deemed to cure all diseases and confer immortality. This is the Great Work of the alchemical path and not a remedy in the proper sense but the embodiment of the spiritual goal itself.

Within the spectrum of alternative healing methods, alchemical spagyrics has been able to hold its own quite well, thus preserving the legacy of an originally hermetic method, but it has not achieved a greater degree of popularity, and is rather overshadowed by the great alternative medical systems such as Traditional Chinese Medicine (TCM), Indian Ayurveda, and especially homeopathy, which developed from similar roots but eventually pursued entirely different paths.

Even if today it is considered good form and necessary for social recognition to identify oneself as "scientific," we cannot help but recognize that homeopathy is also firmly anchored in those structures and laws of nature, as described by hermetics, that transcend our current understanding of science or, if you will, have embarked on a different, parallel path of knowledge.

While homeopathy—contrary to constantly repeated false claims—has succeeded excellently in providing scientifically sound proofs of efficacy according to all current rules of this art (double-blind, replicated, published with peer review), its actual roots are located neither historically nor factually within this framework.

The stumbling block for scientific recognition is usually seen in the high potentization levels that chemically imply such a high dilution that irrefutably no molecules of the original substance can be found in its remedies. From this it appears that the mechanism of action of homeopathic medicinal products cannot be a chemical one. But no more than that.

However, homeopathy proves to be hermetic not by this potentization but rather by the law of similarity for which there is no counterpart in today's natural sciences.

The rule of similars in homeopathic diction is: *similia similibus curentur*—let similar things be healed by similar things. Of course, here we easily recognize the "as above, so below" of hermeticism or the principle of so-called sympathetic magic as ethnologists would label it.

The universally valid principle of micro and macrocosms implies that things, living beings, or processes connected on an analog level can have an influence on each other if this connection is activated in an appropriate and effective way. Such an analogy connection is neither causally nor locally tangible, but subject to the natural law of analogy, which cannot be classified scientifically so far and for which, in the scientific view of the world, there are only cautious attempts at understanding on the basis of non-local entanglements (as they are known from quantum mechanics), or of synchronicities within the framework of depth psychology.

For the hermetic, magician, or shaman, however, working on the basis of such analogies is not a questionable connection but an easily comprehensible and applicable law of nature. Like all laws of nature, it cannot be questioned or explained, but only determined in its effect. Even gravity can only be observed but not justified or explained. In contrast to scientific laws, however, the principle of analogy does not seem to be subject to mathematically detectable regularities.

In homeopathy, the activation of the analogous effect takes place on the one hand in the anamnesis, i.e., the explorative conversation between the practitioner and the patient, by means of which the pattern of their ailment, their complaints, or their life problems can be determined. Aforesaid anamnesis is a complex and often tedious process, since such a basic pattern is not easily recognizable. If that were different, or if the pattern were more conscious, it would not cause such problems in the first place. The word an-amnesis says it all: to retrieve from oblivion. The aim of such an in-depth conversation is to reach a level that reaches beyond daily consciousness and only expresses itself through physical complaints or emotional disorders.

This pattern is then confronted with as similar a pattern as possible of a substance or living being of nature by imbibing the same in potentized form. Then, if successful, the healing takes place, which also extends to the physical complaints. Homeopathy is particularly effective when treating severe chronic and systemic diseases.

The other side of finding the adequate analogies relates to the substances used. Homeopaths have to discern the patterns that unfold in contact between certain specific substances and a human system or organism. For this purpose, the homeopath undertakes a kind of shamanic journey, which is referred to as remedy proving: individuals or groups will take the appropriate remedy or expose themselves to it in other ways (meditation, contact, trituration) and meticulously record what they experience during the contact and afterwards: every emotion, every body reaction, every fantasy, every dream. The work and art of conducting the proving then consists of finally reviewing the accumulated pile of individual records, filtering out what is relevant, and structuring it into a recognizable and applicable pattern.

The homoeopaths therefore get to know the "spirits" with which they treat by personal experience, well in accord with good shamanic tradition. They expose themselves to the experience and try to find out the energy patterns for themselves, which they then strive to recognize in their patients. Of course, this can only be carried out by select examples out of the infinite abundance of possible remedies. Still, those remedies whose effect one has experienced oneself will always remain special, and you will maintain a very special relationship with them in the treatment.

Above all, the practitioners themselves will undergo changes during their "journeys" into the medicines, just as someone can only become a shaman by changing deeply within their self. Magical healing is not a mechanical process and cannot simply be executed rationally. Rather, it requires the whole human being, both on the part of the patients and on the part of the practitioners.

In addition to the principle of analogy, the de-materialization of the remedies is a clearly recognizable alchemical principle. Here as there it is a matter of freeing the essence from the carrier substance and thereby making its effect all the stronger. Potentization does not directly follow known alchemical processes, but it pursues the same goal in its own way.

It is known that the founder of homeopathy, the physician Samuel Hahnemann,[18] was well acquainted with classical alchemy and was also a Freemason. Although he devised his own method of de-materializing his remedies, he consciously stood on the ground of the spiritual tradition of hermeticism.

An interesting feature of homeopathy is its combining two of the interpretation models of magical events presented in the chapter "Models of Magic"[19] in a very pragmatic fashion: the energy model and the information model.

In an attempt to somehow link homeopathy to scientific thinking and to make its effect plausible in established terms, it is often stated that the globules transmit or contain "energies." The exact nature of these "energies" is not clear, though. From a physical point of view, globules only have kinetic energy, which is released when they fall, and chemical energy, which is released when they are burned. If someone is given to associate other forms of energy with the small white globules, these are certainly not forms of energy that occur in physics, not even in quantum physics, which is frequently drawn on for pseudo-explanations, because hardly anyone commands sufficient knowledge to be able to clearly say where the fallacy of this line of argument is located.

Not to knock the metaphorical use of scientific terms: we are frequently given to using the expression "energy" in everyday language in a figurative sense. But when I say that I feel so "energetic" today, I am aware that this is not a physicist's statement and does nothing to explain anything on this level

---

18. Christian Friedrich Samuel Hahnemann was born in Meissen, Germany in
    in Paris, France in 1843 at an advanced age as an acclaimed physician.

19. See chapter 20, "Models of Magic in Practice."

The "energy" that can be spoken of in homeopathy is the life energy, which is called by different names in differing cultures as prana, chi, manas, etc., and is called *dynamis* by Hahnemann in the homeopathic doctrine. But this is not stored in the globules—how should this even be possible, seeing that it is supposed to be "dynamic"?—but it is the *dynamis* that keeps the organism healthy and which, in case of illness, should be brought back into balance by a homeopathic remedy. The life energy is informed (literally: formed inwardly) by the drug, and its structure is influenced by it; the disease-causing pattern is mirrored by as similar a pattern of a natural substance as possible, and this—so posits the homeopathic idea—brings it back to itself, to its own balance.

At the same time, the early homeopaths were very aware that the life force, whose "morbid derangement" they sought to heal, first had to be present in sufficient quantity. Accordingly, Samuel Hahnemann followed the teachings of Franz Anton Mesmer (1734–1815) and started off by magnetizing those patients who basically lacked vitality, in order to subsequently administer homeopathic remedies to them.

The doctrine of homeopathy ingeniously combines two concepts here, namely that of an energy underlying all life processes, as postulated by vitalism, and a level of patterns that keeps this form of energy in a meaningful flow and determines its properties.

Both can be influenced, and both have to function properly for the organism to be healthy.

Admittedly, today´s homeopathy as currently practiced almost exclusively takes into account the informative aspect of the prescribed remedy and, at best, provides for the required vitality itself merely by recommending a healthy lifestyle. But in the original construct of this healing art, a direct influence on the life force was equally intended, as is the case in numerous other energetic healing systems.

In view of the widespread ambivalence of magical or shamanic actions, the question arises whether, in spagyrics or homeopathy, there is also a conceivable deployment of their procedures in the "opposite direction", i.e., in the sense of consciously damaging other people, as we know it from spells—i.e., in analogy to black magic a sort of "black" spagyrics or homeopathy. However, the specific type of influence within the homeopathic application of remedies is not particularly suited to such practices because the effect is by definition energetically not invasive; rather, it should only trigger the self-healing powers of the organism, which will consequently direct the system toward a better balance according to its own inherent rules.

This aside, homeopathic treatment can indeed have adverse effects, namely the so-called "proving symptoms," so defined because they occur during remedy provings and are used to identify the intrinsic pattern of a given substance. This only works by causing symptoms in a healthy, balanced person, i.e., by temporarily unbalancing the system. Such symptoms may be quite protracted and very troublesome if you happen to respond strongly to a certain remedy. But this occurs only rarely and cannot be predicted reliably. As a rule, such effects will quickly recede again because they are not produced in accord with the patterns of one's own organism.

Chapter 13
Some Questions on Magic

Frater U∴D∴

Question: How did you originally come to magic?

Frater U∴D∴: My magical path began as a child, at the age of nine, to be precise, when an uncle encouraged me to practice yoga, which he had just discovered. Hypnosis and self-hypnosis followed soon, and so it went on and on. I also dug into other disciplines of parascience, such as dowsing, telepathy, telekinesis, astral travel, and the like. For a significant time, however, my main focus was on the Eastern teachings, especially meditation and mysticism. Some years later, during a particularly intensive phase of meditation, I also set out on a program of letter magic according to Sebottendorf. However, that didn't go too well. After I had advanced to the level of the raven's head, I began to feel worse and worse: depressive bouts, dizziness, nausea, and more. So I had to break off the series of exercises and consequently took a break from practical magic for quite a while.

After having found an occult topic for my dissertation in English literature in the course of my university studies (though all that actually became of it finally was a master's thesis in comparative literature), I had enough time and leisure to familiarize myself with Western magic in a systematic manner. At first this was focused on the Golden Dawn and Aleister Crowley, and as I didn't want to restrain myself to the theoretical realm alone, I began to actually implement and practice what I had read as well. Soon enough I hit upon the sigil magic of Austin Osman Spare, which immediately fascinated me because of its high effectiveness. It was this that finally convinced me of the validity of magic in general.

In October 1979, together with two fellow students, I opened the Horus esoteric bookshop in Bonn. Shortly afterward, the Bonn Workshop for Experimental Magic was formed, where, for the first time, I came into regular contact with a large number of other practitioners of magic. Our focus was on the practical exploration of different approaches to magic, which of course gave my own practice a tremendous boost. Since then, the subject has never let me go.

Question: Have you ever completely abandoned magic and given it up altogether? If so, why?

Frater U∴D∴: No, I've never really stopped practicing magic since. Of course, there were individual disciplines that I couldn't finish. I've already mentioned one example: Sebottendorf's letter magic. Years later I took it up again, incidentally, but had to terminate it for exactly the same reasons I did so the first time. Of course, it's really not so much practical magic as a form of "philosophic seething," as they say in alchemy. After all, it is not primarily concerned with effecting changes in the world and manifesting magical goals. Rather, it focuses on bringing about other states of consciousness—inner transmutation. In this respect, letter magic is actually more precisely categorized as a branch of mysticism or metaphysics, as many of its major authors such as Kolb and Waltharius tend to emphasize.

But be that as it may, this misadventure did not detract from my fundamental preoccupation with magic for good. To be true, there were phases in my life in which the practice was rather pushed onto the backburner in favor of theoretical studies. On the other hand, from a certain point on magic was always embedded in my everyday life as a standard routine.

For example, I mentally performed the Lesser Banishing Ritual of the Pentagram for about twelve years every evening before falling asleep. Many years ago I ran up an approximate tally indicating that I could look back at about 4,500 rituals at that time. Of course, this number is quite meaningless by itself; I only make mention of it here because it helps to illustrate to what degree magic can be embedded in everyday life if it is actually taken seriously. And even though my understanding of magic has developed and changed considerably over the years, I never bade it farewell.

Question: Did you resume formal magic after that? If so, why exactly? And what was different afterwards?

Frater U∴D∴: Even though it never really affected me myself, I can empathize with anyone who chooses to wave goodbye to magic for a while. Some practices are simply very intense and can't always be processed easily, let alone immediately. Often enough, it is certainly anything but a mistake to allow yourself a period of processing and convalescence, perhaps also of quiet gestation and maturation. Not everything's suitable for everyone. My experiences with letter magic described above are but one case in point. After conducting some fairly intensive demon magic, I experienced so many personal issues in everyday life that I simply had to let it go for a while. The exceedingly strong emphasis on magical protection so common in Western magic is there for a reason, after all.

I don't really place too much value in the common platitude that magic can drive us crazy, whatever that may actually mean. On the other hand, it cannot reasonably be denied that people with hefty mental issues will rarely find magic to be particularly helpful. Unfortunately, many of them do feel very strongly attracted to magic, which might go to explain some of its excesses and maybe even the odd magical mishap. After a break—be it voluntary or involuntary—your experience with certain magical practices will usually change. As your understanding of the actually essential aspects and nuances of the magical process expands, so will your resilience as well as your mastery of the practice itself. Most of the time, however, this does require some patience—not necessarily most magicians' strongest point!

Question: How do you deal with doubts about the effectiveness of magic in general or your magic in particular? What are its limits? What's missing?

Frater U∴D∴: I only nurtured fundamental doubts about magic at the very outset when I ventured into this, to me, entirely new and unknown field. However, these were quickly dispersed by the unbelievable effectiveness of A.O. Spare's sigil magic, as well as by a myriad of the craziest magic experiences (admittedly not all of them successes…). What has really steadily evolved within me over the decades, however: a fundamental skepticism toward many of the basic assumptions Western magicians have become inordinately fond of. Not every changed state of consciousness, not every trance, not every ecstasy, and not every accidental event can be termed magical, in my opinion.

What are the limits of "magic"? Who can really say for sure? From the point of view of the natural sciences, magic is utterly impossible anyway. Ironically, I actually agree with that in principle—though for entirely different reasons. Because if magic, as I'm firmly convinced, is about doing the impossible, it cannot, by definition, be possible itself. But that is no reason to forego it! And it is precisely this that has become the essence of the matter to me over the years.

Am I myself omnipotent as a magician? Of course not! In fact, I'm not at all interested in what I may be capable of accomplishing in magic. Rather, I find it of far greater interest to attend to what I cannot as yet achieve.

Question: How do you feel about magic today, based on your many years of experience?

Frater U∴D∴: For me today, magic is first and foremost an expression of the struggle with human powerlessness, human impotence. Right from the outset, as far as we are able to determine, magic was a tool that served human survival: it was about killing, protecting, and provisioning. If you like, that is the basic formula of Stone Age hunting magic. Essentially, nothing has really changed in this respect to this day. Whether magic has always actually achieved what humans expected of it is, of course, a different matter.

In contrast to common wisdom, I don't believe that we can really learn from our mistakes. For all they go to show is that we have done something wrong, and we already know how to do that or else we wouldn't have done it. However: those who shy away from making mistakes are fundamentally misplaced in magic, because our almost total human powerlessness is an undeniable fact, and as magicians we have to deal with it constantly. In this respect, mistakes can, of course, be a great incentive to expand our abilities, to wrest them from reality, i.e., from what exerts its effect on us.

Ultimately, magic is always about power in the sense of "being able to do"—which shouldn't, however, be mistaken for petty domination and exploitation of weaker and otherwise inferior beings. The bottom line is that for the magician, as I understand him or her, the world and reality as we know them and as they are constantly agonizing and harrying us, are simply not enough. Indeed they are and will remain fundamentally alien to the magician. Neither do magicians wish to repair them, nor do they want to appease some other, supposedly higher agency of alien heteronomy. Rather, the magician (at least in my view) wants to overcome them. This is entirely unrelated to morality and ethics. It is nothing less than the pursuit of sovereign self-determination, i.e., real freedom. It is in the nature of things that the world and reality will not allow this to happen undisputedly, for after all the gods have never been man's friends.

Question: Coming to magic and everyday life: has magic proved useful or helped you in your everyday life and if so, in what manner? Where did it fail?

Frater U∴D∴: People who operate with what is called success or results magic will usually employ it for everyday concerns. Of course, there are other magical approaches that are primarily concerned with access to knowledge, cognition, spiritual development, and the understanding of cosmic correlations, as well as, quite frequently, with achieving mystical or spiritual goals. But from an historical point of view these are a comparatively late development in magic. In its most probable original form, i.e., hunting magic, magic or sorcery was always about tackling the problems of everyday life.

For me, everyday or success magic has always played an important role. Because only here can you objectify what magic—or the magician themself—is actually capable of. Higher states of consciousness, cosmogonic insights, the unio mystica, or the experience of the "divine will" can always be endlessly argued about till the cows come home. It's also a prime way to deceive yourself. By contrast, a money, love, or healing spell either works or it doesn't. Admittedly, this is a highly simplified representation, the more so as the effects of magic will often look like strange coincidences. But essentially, success magic, correctly applied, will effectively resist self-deception.

So my answer is quite simple: yes. Whether it was the acquisition of an apartment that was difficult to get, the receipt of very unlikely sums of money despite the most adverse circumstances in times of financial distress, the search for a parking lot in a crowded city during the rush hour, the virtually blind automatic navigation without any external tools such as maps or satnavs to an unknown address in a foreign place that was completely unfamiliar to me, the sudden healing of decades of short-sightedness impairing friends or acquaintances, the successful averting of legal as well as massive, existentially threatening economic hazards both for myself and for others, the spontaneous release of a restaurant table for my companions and me in establishments that normally require months of prior reservation—the examples are legion. And the same applies to all practicing magicians, shamans, sorcerers, witches, or whatever we want to call them, whom I have met in my life so far.

As far as failure or errors are concerned, all reasonably self-critical magicians will, of course, make this experience again and again. However, I am loath to attribute this to "magic itself." Let's never forget that there should be no magic at all if we abide by the unanimous vote of rationalism, which is currently the predominant ideology in the West (though not only there). From this point of view, every, even the slightest, magical effect represents an unheard-of scandal that must therefore be vehemently denied and disavowed. For it calls into question the fundamental premises of our collective worldview and reality-production.

Other cultures may perhaps seem to be slightly more relaxed in this regard, at least at a superficial glance. But even there, magic is very often loaded with panicky fear and prohibitions, witches and magicians—real and supposed—are being persecuted even in the twenty-first century, and quite frequently they are actually being put to death as we speak.

Finally, the question of which limits are inherent to magic or which failures are primarily due to my own inability cannot really be answered conclusively. I have frequently observed that my magical operations on behalf or in the interest of others were more likely to fail than those I performed for myself. But there is no reliable rule that can be derived from this. Because for every such observation there are slews of counter-examples. Thus, at the end of the day, there is only one thing left for us: to push on with our research!

Question: If you still practice magic today: what do you focus on? Has this changed in the course of your life (perhaps with increasing age)? If so, in what way? And why is that, do you think?

Frater U∴D∴: Like so many other experienced magicians, today I am more inclined toward what is somewhat misleadingly referred to in magic literature as the "techniques of the empty hand." By saying "misleading," what I mean is that these are not clearly defined, definable techniques. Even a common term like "mental magic" describes this process at best approximately, without really doing it justice. To fall back on Ice magical diction, I would therefore prefer to speak of "goal-released engagement," though I'm well aware of the fact that not everyone will be able to relate to this rather abstract-sounding formulation, at least not right away.

I used to have a dedicated temple for magical workings wherever I lived. Like every serious hermetic magician, I would operate with magical weapons and tools, robes, pentacles, incense, and so on. This is no longer the case today, even though I would recommend every beginner intent on following the Western tradition of magic to engage vigorously with these tools and methods. The Ice Magic approach, of course, is an entirely different one, but that's not our concern here.

Question: What would you advise magicians today?

Frater U∴D∴: I would advise the beginner to read as much magical literature as thoroughly as possible. You will encounter numerous contradictions, sometimes even bitter backbiting between different magical factions. Of course, you should never be concerned with clearly determining which of these views is "true" and which is "untrue," because experience has shown that this won't really lead you anywhere. Yet, critical skepticism is definitely called for. Paper doesn't blush, as they say, and all that counts in the end is your own practical experience. That is why unbiased, open-ended experimentation should always be your priority. This will often require some courage, but without it there's no success in the offing.

I would recommend the advanced practitioner to dig even further into magic literature, but to set their own priorities, or, to put it another way, to specialize increasingly.

Whether we regard planetary magic, talismantics, element magic, evocations, sex magic, money magic, oracle techniques, chaos magic, astromagic, theurgy, necromancy, thelemic magic, Saturn gnosis, shamanism, Wicca, letter magic, Kahuna magic, atavistic magic, rune magic, Voudon, Juju, Hoodoo, Macumba, Candomblé, Santería, Ice Magic, and all the other countless sub-disciplines, systems, schools, edifices of teachings—any magician's life is far too short to cope with all these areas in equal measure. So we are compelled to economize on our finite life resources and focus on what we individually regard as the most promising.

Assuming that "old hands" are game with taking any advice from me at all, perhaps it might be this: don't stop at what has been achieved, the path will never end, continuative questions are always more conducive than conclusive answers.

Question: Can people actually learn magic or do you think one must have it from birth as a talent? If the former or even if both, what role do traditions play in magic? Magic books? Personal teachers? Magical orders, lodges, associations etc.?

Frater U∴D∴: Can you learn magic? Certainly! I myself am an example of this, hailing from a family in which there was maybe an occasional touch of rudimentary superstition but no serious and certainly no hereditary magical talent or activity. Neither did I know about talking off warts or card reading from family experience, nor did we discuss any supernatural experiences.

From both my parents' sides, my family comes from the petty bourgeois artisan milieu, which by itself, of course, says nothing about any magical propensity. However, a rather hands-on, materialist, anything-but-metaphysical-or-hypersensitive view of reality prevailed throughout. Even as a child I was not encouraged in my occult inclinations, though my family never proactively restrained me either. So it's no exaggeration to say that I'm primarily an autodidact when it comes to magic, and that I've trained myself in the main by studying books.

On the other hand, I know a fair number of magicians who have inherited a lot from their respective families in this respect, including some quite remarkable magical talents. So there definitely is such a thing. Via my contacts with both British and Russian special forces, I'm also aware that these military units will often recruit people with such talents. So there are both: the natural magical talent and the magical scholar or self-taught sorceress.

As far as the role of tradition is concerned, this is a rather complex phenomenon that I'm discussing in greater detail at various points in this book. Let us just note here that traditions provide a frame of reference within which individuals can feel both rooted and protected. At the same time, however, they will also exclude alien elements. Vide for example folk magic and magically oriented families where knowledge and skills may only be transferred to blood relatives.

Magic books rarely play a prominent role in folk magic, which used to be practiced mostly by illiterate people throughout history. But obviously they are of utmost importance within what I like to term library magic, which has historically been the privilege and object of interest of clerical and intellectual elites. Of course, magic books are also indispensable for today's magical autodidacts like me.

Personal teachers are rather rare in magic despite all common myths. Evidently some sort of apprenticeship will frequently develop between experienced and inexperienced practitioners over a limited period of time. But this is almost never of a permanent nature. I myself have also benefited from a few teachers, especially in the field of shamanism and in what later manifested as Ice Magic. Ultimately, however, every magician must and will develop their own approach. In this respect, the teacher should be appreciated primarily as a source of impetus and occasionally as an eye-opener, but their role should definitely not be overrated. After all, teachers will usually pursue their own interests first and foremost, which do not always coincide with those of the acolyte—or if so, at the most over a fairly limited period of time.

I'm also dealing in more detail with magical orders, brotherhoods, and associations elsewhere in this book, so let me simply state here that, at least today, they have the primary task of offering their members a like-minded community, support, care, and sometimes what is generally characterized as their "force field."

Question: What is your conclusion today regarding the Bonn Workshop for Experimental Magic? Would you advise today's magicians to establish something similar? Regardless of your advice, what mistakes do you think they should try to avoid?

Frater U∴D∴: I owe a great deal to the Bonn workshop group. It wasn't so much the direct transfer of tangible knowledge, perhaps, but the experience of working together with magicians of widely different origins and worldviews. Our overall resolutely undogmatic approach, which respected virtually no taboos, as well as the unreserved preference of practice over theoretical speculation, plus the occasionally quite iconoclastic approach to established authorities of the magical tradition, was eminently formative for me at that time and still remains to be so. Furthermore, it was simply a hell of a lot of fun to work together in this manner!

So, unsurprisingly, I would advise every beginner today to start something similar from scratch, should the opportunity present itself. To be sure, any such a group will always make its mistakes. But so what, don't we all? Can you say adventure? All that's important is how they deal with it. In my opinion, the only thing that really matters is that individual ego trips don't get the upper hand. There's really not much more to be said about it, except: just go for it!

Question: How did you define magic at the beginning of your magical career? How do you define it today?

Frater U∴D∴: Okay, in a nutshell, then.

Initially: "Magic is the art and the science of bringing about changes through altered states of consciousness."

Today: "Magic means doing the impossible."

Chapter 14
Mistakes in Magic

Harry Eilenstein

I s it possible to make mistakes in magic? Well, you can do all sorts of things that don't lead to the desired result—so the answer is yes, you can obviously make mistakes. On the other hand, the result of each mistake reflects your own character—hence all mistakes are perfect...and they are possibilities and suggestions to change, i.e., to become more what you are, yourself.

Possible errors can occur in many areas and therefore have different effects. In the following, the types of errors are ordered according to their origin in a magical action: first the errors in motivation, then those in execution, and finally the long-term consequences.

Motivation

Motivation shapes the entire magical action and should therefore be as close as possible to your own being, your own soul, your own truth, otherwise you may do something that you do not actually want to do—and get something in return that you do not want either. A waste of time, power, and concentration...

The most important question is whether you really want what you think you do. A little listening to oneself, looking at the origins of the desire, can help to avoid the grossest mistakes.

The most common mistake is that what you think you want is actually merely a substitute for something else that you can't achieve...Hence, it can be useful to ask yourself a few questions before starting out on a magical operation:

- Do I act like an addict who desperately needs a lot of one specific thing to fill an old deficiency?
- Do I behave like an ascetic who wants to give up something and instead create some rigid forms?
- Do I act like a perpetrator who needs power and dominance to feel safe?
- Do I act like a victim seeking protection and help?
- Do I act like a superstar hungry for recognition?
- Do I act like a fan boy/girl hiding in shame?

You can also check out the role of magic in your life. For example, if you don't feel quite "suitable for everyday use" and magic is a means to get a piece of the cake for yourself largely unnoticed and without any squabble, then magic is a substitute for coping with everyday life. Probably you don't dare to show yourself as you are and you live in anxiety. Of course, it's still not wrong to practice magic, but you should also take care of healing your own anxieties.

It is a very common aberration to employ magic so as to escape from the world. Typically, everything dissolves into esoteric credulity, wishful dreams, diffuse fears, unfounded superstition, and the like. To the outsider at least it then becomes perfectly obvious that something is amiss…

In my early twenties I forged twelve magic snake rings plus a thirteenth, central ring. I passed them on to various magicians and witch circles in order to help stop the forest dieback together. I had talked to the trees before, who kept telling me that my plan wouldn't help them—but that's not something I wanted to hear. There was an unconscious feeling of powerlessness in me and an equally unconscious striving for magical power, of which I was not aware at all at the time…

I also didn't notice how much of Lord of the Rings symbolism was mixed into my rings either—nor that their root was my own repressed sexuality.

In the end, however, all these mistakes were noticed by others and the rings were dug up at the places of power and melted down again, in the course of which several accidents occurred: there was a lot of power in those rings and they fought fiercely against their destruction.

That was a huge waste of commitment, time, rituals, money, and more, for I hadn't truly and sincerely fathomed my motivation before starting out to forge the magic rings in the first place.

On the other hand, what I did learn from this action was how to forge such rings, how important motivation is, and what can happen if you attempt to destroy such rings again. Mentally, I was imprisoned for two years in the Lord of the Rings cosmos. And I learned a lot about my own personality, which I would not have done otherwise in such a graphic manner.

In that sense we may indeed say that you can also learn a lot of important things from major mistakes…

On another occasion Axel, my magic teacher,[20] and I conducted a midnight demon evocation at a crossroads. At that time I was still too daunted to declare that I didn't want to do that at all. When I separated afterwards from Axel in the city and returned home alone after this rather successful evocation, my hair stood on end.

I had never been so scared before. I only saw two possibilities: either the dread gets me or I'll get the dread. So I returned to this crossroads every day until I was actually able to lie down there and sleep in peace. In that half year I learned to deal with fear—but that wasn't actually my conscious plan.

On another occasion Axel and I each produced two *spiritus familiaris*, i.e., two artificial spirits, one for either of us. To achieve this, you form a figurine out of clay and beeswax as well as chamomile, aurum chloratum, and some other ingredients that symbolize the character of the spirit you want to create. Then you charge it with your own blood, with the vital force, with the four elements and so on.

This spirit could be sent off to perform one task or the other, to help someone, to bring about a coincidence etc. That worked quite well, but in the course of time the spirits became stronger and stronger so that it became clear at some point that we had to dissolve them again in order not to get into trouble ourselves. It wasn't at all easy, because the dissolving of my spirit and its material form felt like killing a beloved pet. That, too, had not been clear to me at the outset…

---

20. This was Axel Büdenbender: see his contributions in this book.

Research

It is advisable to truly explore magic and not simply take anything at face value merely because it happens to be printed in some book. After all, every book was written by humans. The most down-to-earth approach is always the experiment and thus your own experience.

So the book says that astral journeys are only possible if your head lies northward? Well, that's easy to check...

The extension of the "book faith" is the guru faith: only what the teacher says is true and reliable. Most of the time, however, your own thinking and, above all, your own experience are preferable to imitation.

Of course, this doesn't mean that you can't learn from others. If someone else is able to do something and you follow their instructions and achieve the desired effect, everything is fine. Obviously you can still check which parts of the manual you can omit, change, and supplement, and what effect this has. This way you develop expertise.

Foreseeable Consequences

Actually, this is a point that should be taken for granted, but as I have indeed overlooked it myself several times, I will insert it here anyway. The fulfillment of some wishes will have predictable consequences that you nevertheless didn't consider beforehand.

Many years ago, I wished I could finally have a heart-connection with a woman. I had only to wait for half an hour until I met her, but I didn't think that in the long run this could lead to a breakup of the relationship that I had at the time.

On another occasion I realized that I hadn't wept for some twenty years. Since I had the impression that this could not possibly be wholesome, I wished to learn to cry again. However, I had not considered how much suffering might be necessary to dissolve my weeping-blockade... nor that I would have so many weeping-attacks for a quarter of a year that on some days I was incapable of working. I still feel it's good to be able to cry again, but I had imagined an entirely different way of getting there.

Symbolism

In magic, we will often operate with symbols—and symbols have their own dynamics that are sure to prevail against your own intentions when working with them.

With the snake rings already mentioned, I forged the rings as a closed circle, i.e., as snakes that bit their own tails. However, this symbolizes captured vital force, and not free vital force. Thus they were a very fitting image for my own repressed sexuality and not for the freely flowing kundalini or for the freely streaming vital force in nature.

The meaning of a symbol cannot be transformed by a consecration that strives for another meaning of the symbol—the symbol prevails over everything else.

After the snake ring disaster I started to explore all mythologies to gain a decent overview of the meaning of symbols. I didn't want to make such a gross mistake again.

On another occasion, I went on a dream journey into the fire aspect of the earth element together with four other magicians. In a cave we met an earth spirit who had lit a fire in front of him. Curious as I am, I placed myself in his fire—without realizing that by this act I would symbolically put myself under his command. It wasn't easy to get rid of this bond again—and it was one of the roots of the thirteen snake-rings …

Structure and Development

Many magicians and witches have a tendency to look at either structures such as astrology, the tarot, the I Ching, etc., or to concentrate on developmental pathways such as chakras, the Kabbalah, etc. Both tendencies can lead to one-sidedness.

The intensive occupation e.g. with astrology leads to the fact that we perceive the existing structures, the imprints, the fixed, the predetermined rhythm … so where does that leave freedom of choice?

The intensive occupation e.g. with the chakras leads to the fact that we perceive above all the possibilities of transformation, the development potential, the endless metamorphoses … where then does that leave the knowledge of the individual?

I've never met anyone whose character didn't correspond to their horo-scope, but I don't know of anyone who wouldn't have been able to learn, either. The combination of e.g. astrology and chakras results in a structure that develops to a higher level.

Or to say it with Goethe: "shaped form that develops alive."

Sensible Procedure

The consideration of the possible errors can be supplemented by the consid-eration of some useful strategies.

Experience Instead of Regulation

A very essential element is your own experience. Experience works, whereas regulations have to be followed. Therefore, experience is always preferable. If, for example, I have pressed nails into walls with my thumb for years and then someone comes along to show me what you can do with a hammer, the next time I want to hang up a picture I won't have to struggle hard to use a ham-mer again. Rather, I will pick it up immediately because I have experienced that it is easier that way. From experience comes insight, and insight shapes behavior.

It is thus advisable to experiment with telepathy, telekinesis, wishes, etc., to calculate horoscopes, take part in a fire walk and try out similar things and gain experience. In this way you will amplify the toolbox of your own possibilities for action with valuable tools that you will then use as a matter of course because you have experienced that they work. You will become a magician, quite unspectacularly, merely by the way.

From Wish to Wish Fulfilment

A completely different aspect of this useful procedure arises from the under-standing of your own actions.

In the beginning, there is a feeling: something pleasant that we want to achieve or something unpleasant that we wish to avoid—without such a feel-ing nothing will get to move.

If we believe that this sensation has nothing to do with ourselves, still nothing will move—we will either suppress this sensation or blame it on oth-ers. But when you realize that it belongs to you and actually concerns you, it becomes a will: I want to change it, I want to have it, or similar. The sensation and the ego have combined to form a will impulse.

If you think that what you want is impossible, still nothing will happen. However, if you consider the goal to be attainable, an intention to act arises. In this third step, the will connects with the trust in yourself and with the trust in the world. This trust (however it may manifest) is an important foundation of magic: only if you think it is possible to reach your own goal can you perform magic effectively. One approach is to wish and then forget the wish; a better way is to wish and then look relaxed and calmly at what is happening. The best way is to trust in magic, in your soul, in a deity, etc. that they will fulfill your wish.

Finally, there is a fourth point: the first step on the way to the goal. This step has an inner side and an outer side to it.

The inner side can, for example, be a daily meditation on your own soul, by which you keep contact with yourself. Only if you are true to yourself can life become a mirror image of what you really are … and if the world is a mirror image of what you really are, you can actually enjoy the world.

The outer side is a first step in the right direction. You don't have to know the whole way, but you do have to make a movement in the right direction. As the Kabbalists say: if you take one step toward God, he will approach you ten steps.

Even these four steps should not become the rule, but you can try them out and see whether your own actions become more effective if you follow them.

Your Own Style

With magic, as with all other matters, it is beneficial to do things in your own style. If you are spontaneous, choleric, and egocentric, you should act in a spontaneous, choleric, and egocentric manner—nothing can be more effective than this behavior.

Of course it makes sense to distinguish between what you do out of fear, addiction, and wrong ideas, and what you do out of joy of life, creative urge, curiosity, joy of discovery, love, and so on. Only what comes from the heart, what is "true," can be effective.

In order to recognize your own style, it is helpful to seek contact with your own soul, to know your own spirit animal, spirit plant, and spirit stone, to study your own horoscope... Here again there is no recipe, but the basic direction is simple: be true to yourself.

The Pleasurable Way

Finally, there are all sorts of details, but they will look different with everyone.

An example of this is the widespread reluctance to sit there for hours and concentrate on one symbol. Of course, the ability to imagine a symbol and concentrate on it is very useful in magic, but many people find it exhausting, boring, and will wander around with their concentration.

Most people, on the other hand, find dream journeys extremely exciting and informative. If you go on dream journeys often to get to know yourself, to find a lost key, to find out the cause of a friend's illness, or simply to meet dragons, you will learn to see in the area of the vital force, to concentrate on this area, and finally to consciously steer the vital force itself.

Dream journeys have the advantage that you don't have to follow an abstract meditation instruction, instead moving with the flow of your own motivation: you can travel inwardly to your right knee because it hurts and ask what is going on there. Once you can restore peace to your knee in this fashion and continue walking, you will always discover new opportunities where dream journeys are helpful—and, by the bye, become more and more practiced in dealing with the vital force.

Chapter 15
Some Questions on Magic

Harry Eilenstein

Question: How did you originally come to magic?

Harry: This happened quite unintentionally during my first major life crisis. After a suicide attempt out of love-sickness I thought that it's actually stupid to kill yourself if you don't really know for sure if you're actually going to cease to exist thereafter—the existence of ghosts and the stories about reincarnation make that at least doubtful.

So I decided to live for a hundred years and fathom this life right here and this world: what's going on here and why?

A short time later, when I was sitting in the city park of Bad Godesberg, now a township of Bonn, Germany, musing on all these matters, suddenly a voice behind me said: "Learn magic!" But there was nobody actually standing behind me who could have said that. Later, I came to the conclusion that my soul must have spoken to me.

On the evening of that day I met a lady in whose flat I in turn met Axel[21] who eventually accepted me as a sorcerer's apprentice. With him I quickly experienced quite a lot of things of which I had not suspected anything until then.

Question: Have you ever completely discarded magic and stopped doing it altogether? And if so, why?

Harry: I never rejected it because its existence was quite obvious to me. However, I did stop doing magic once for a few months because my girlfriend at

---

21. This was Axel Büdenbender: see his contributions in this book.

the time handed me a choice: "It's either magic or me!" Not the most glorious episode in my biography...

In my life it was Axel who assumed the role of a doubter, who questioned the very existence of magic at least once a week. When our endless debates became too much for me, I wrote him the *Encouragement for the Doubting Occultist*, my first book. Axel's doubts, however, were very valuable to me because they made me think through my experiences more thoroughly, and they were also the impetus for me to start writing books and to discover that I tend to deliberate things more thoroughly when I write a book about them.

Question: How do you deal with doubts about the effectiveness of your magic? What are its limits? What is it that you lack?

Harry: My telepathic perception almost always works when I need it.[22] My structural observations, i.e., astrology, the kabbalistic Tree of Life, and various mandalas, are also very dependable. In the course of magically summoning things and events, I have more and more gone over to healing my psyche, to be faithful to myself, and to trust in "the ones above"— then I don't need to explicitly wish for anything anymore as things then come to me by themselves.

If something is not the way I would like it to be, I will check whether I am really sincere and faithful to myself and then ask "the ones above" to send me what will do me good right now—this may be what I wish for right now, or what shows me where I stand at the moment and, above all, what is really required at the moment.

I don't really see any boundaries of magic that would hinder me, and in that respect I'm not missing anything.

If I can repose in my self-love, nothing is missing from the outside, because the outside always reflects my inside.

Question: Based on your many years of experience, what's your stand on magic today?

Harry: To me, it's normal everyday life... and extremely practical.

---

22. See Harry's views on telepathy in chapter 8, "Telepathy for Everyday Life."

Question: Magic and everyday life: Has magic proved useful or helped you in your everyday life and if so, in what way? And what has it failed in?

Harry: On the one hand, magic gives me the opportunity to recognize things and to understand situations by the use of telepathy, or with the help of analogies such as the Tree of Life, astrology, mandalas, and the like; on the other hand, the "magical desire" inside me has expanded and transformed to become a general trust in "those above", i.e., in my soul and the gods.

Moreover, the gods have become an important help in my consultations—they give me the opportunity to show a person seeking advice the whole, sound state of that about which they have a question: I determine which deity is "responsible" for it and then conduct a dream journey or something similar to this deity together with the person seeking counsel. This is usually quite effective.

Question: What would you advise today's magicians—beginners, advanced, and very experienced practitioners with many years of experience?

Harry: I don't find that easy to answer because I would tell everyone something different—everyone has a unique biography, is in a different situation, thinks and speaks differently, has their own distinct horoscope... "Every carnival reveler is different," as they say around here in the Rhineland.

But of course there is also the universally valid, of which each individual is a singular manifestation. So what would I say in general?

Know yourself. Search for your soul. Dance your power animal. Grow as your spirit plant. Shape your life as your spirit stone. Be true to yourself. Be courageous. Enjoy life. You are your own source and your own meaning and your own fulfillment.

Check your motivations. Look further around than you have done so far.

Be egoistic, but with as much foresight as possible so that you will also have an overview of the consequences of your actions, especially the long-term ramifications.

Be in the here and now, but with an overview of the whole—otherwise you will miss out on your life.

Visit the gods, talk to them. Don't be small with them, but look how big they are and *what* they are.

To beginners:

Stay independent. Learn from others but test what you have learned. Is there another way? What do others say? What does my own experience tell me?

Many experiments are the best way to gain expertise. It has its advantages to simply try something out, but it also has its advantages to look closely at what you are planning to do. You need both courage and caution—the two can be combined into proactive prudence.

Your psyche muscles in on everything. Hence it makes sense to take a close look at our own psyche over and again—otherwise we tend to do things out of distorted motivations, things that will lead to results we didn't wish for at all.

And above all: Who am I? What do I want? Stay true to yourself, don't make yourself dependent. Keep your heart, your eyes, and your hands open for the fullness of life.

To the advanced practitioner:

Well, what can I tell you? If you have already experienced some things, you will usually have clearer ideas about what you want and also about what goes and what you can do—as well as what isn't your forte.

The best advice would be not to stop, but to look again and again whether you have already seen everything that can be realized in and about magic, what you can realize concerning yourself.

To recognize oneself and one's own style is actually the essential thing. Matter with its causality is there—and so is the soul, so are the spirit animals, the gods etc. with all their magic—the only real question is how well you have recognized yourself and the world, and how effectively you can consequently move in the world being yourself.

And for experienced magicians and sorceresses?

I find it even harder to say anything to them. After all, everyone travels their own way and the further someone has pursued this path, the more individual any suggestions to someone like that will turn out to be.

I would most likely suggest that they look at the formless, the delimited that lies behind all limited forms—i.e., what the Kabbalists call

"Da'ath," what Buddha talks about again and again, and from where "extraordinary magic" is practiced.

I am not concerned with the superior power that can be found there, rather with the greater peace that awaits us, the connection with everything, the experience of unhindered self-expression.

As far as I can see and make a judgment call on this, there are a few quite meaningful "arrangements" in this area. For example, we can only really be at home in the delimited when we have largely dissolved our own apprehensions and addictions, our deficits, our striving for power, our megalomania, etc. This at least largely helps prevent someone abusing the great magical potential in the delimited area for psychosis-driven objectives, and so on.

I'm not sure if this is a really safe arrangement, since people with anxieties can be rather cozily embedded in them, but as such people can't open their borders to the entire world, this arrangement will in any case prevent the gross abuse of power.

Finally, I can forward a suggestion: it is beneficial not to see yourself as an isolated being, but as a part of the whole. Though perhaps this is merely my personal formulation for an insight that would sound fairly different to others.

Then there is probably another generally valid dynamic: the more magic you practice and the more you approach Da'ath or feel at home there, the more your own psyche will fade into the background. The psyche won't dissolve, but it will no longer be the center and source of your own actions.

This development starts way before: if you look at your psyche and get to know it better, the origin of your own actions shifts from the here and now in everyday life to the psyche—you now better discern your own motivations and their origins, and you will thus be capable of making more meaningful and effective long-term decisions.

The second step is triggered by the encounter with one's own soul. The soul has created the psyche: the soul is the entrepreneur, and the psyche is the manager. We will begin to align the psyche with the soul because the soul is the source of the psyche. Thus all the violent feelings in the psyche will relativize themselves a little. Instead, the resplendence of the soul will move into the focus of attention more and more.

The third step is the recognition of the deity, of which one's own soul is a modest part. Thus we reach the delimitationless realm: a deity is a precise quality, but it is boundless and omnipresent at the same time. With this step, our own magic also changes—our actions begin to flow out of the deity through the soul and then through the psyche into the here and now. This attitude is what Lao Tzu calls *Wu wei*, "non-doing" or "non-interference."

Finally, there is a fourth step that leads from the deities to the oneness, to the origin, to God. What can we say about this? We can only experience it. There it is, as it is … glistening white light or shining blackness … simply being. It is worth searching for.

Now I have, without planning to do so, described the Middle Pillar of the Kabbalah. It is a good guide to whatever you may do and to the possibilities of magic. The "practice of the Middle Pillar" is quite simple: the light flows from above, from the oneness of the white sphere Kether down through the rainbow-colored sphere of the deities of Da'ath, and through the golden sphere of the souls in Tiphareth, and the violet sphere of the psyche of Yesod, to the brown sphere of the material world in Malkuth.

For me, this is a map of the world that I have recognized as true, and an attitude that I experience as meaningful.

As a beginner, you can start with the simple meditation of this "practice of the Middle Pillar": it can gradually expand and deepen over time and become ever more meaningful.

Question: Can you actually learn magic, or do you think it must have been there from birth, as an innate talent?

Harry: All I can say definitely and decisively to that is: I just don't know! For this I would have to know the biographies of considerably more people and equally the biographies of their forebears.

I suppose that, as with everything else, one, there is a basic ability in every human being; two, there actually are different talents, e.g. horoscope-related talents; three, there are probably certain abilities that can be inherited; and four, curiosity, experimentation, experience, and practice are extremely beneficial.

I can only speak for my own family. I was born in Holstein, an area in northern Germany, and there they say that the son inherits these things from the mother whereas the daughter inherits them from the father. It seems as if our clan had stuck to this rule—at least as long as they still lived in Holstein…

My great-grandmother drew the main prize three times at the fair with a single lottery ticket for one of her great-grandchildren who had gone away empty-handed when she drew her own lottery ticket. Her son, my grandfather, hit six numbers in the lottery when he really urgently needed money—indeed it was a matter of life and death at the time. My mother, the said grandfather's daughter, always knew when my grandparents came to Bonn unannounced from Holstein and cooked a more sumptuous lunch and baked a cake for them in advance. Well, and I myself have obviously become a magician. Here the "Holstein cunning folk sequence" actually applies: great-grandmother—grandfather—mother—son. These were just a few examples of the magic I have observed in terms of my ancestors within this framework of "sequential magic" that switches regularly between male and female relatives.

Two of my sisters also have at least rather pronounced telepathic talents but have never trained them systematically or used them in a targeted way. My other three siblings never had a particular inclination towards magic or the like. One of my sisters did ask me about these things once, but I am not aware that she actually conducted anything practical along these lines.

The Holstein "father-daughter / mother-son" rule no longer applies to my sisters as they are my mother's daughters—however, as I insinuated, they weren't born in Holstein either but in Bonn. And my brother, to whom this rule should apply, has no esoteric tendencies whatsoever—but then again he was also born in Bonn after all.

My own children do not follow the "Holstein rule" either, because my son in particular has a great talent for magic and uses it completely naturally in his everyday life—incidentally, he was born in Bonn, too.

This gives the impression of there being regional differences in the rules as to whether and how such a talent can be inherited. But it seems extremely unlikely to me that there actually might be different rules from place to place.

As I said, in order to really be able to say something meaningful about the question of inherited magical talent, a large-scale investigation of many people and their ancestors would be required.

One would also have to determine whether all the children in a family have inherited this talent. That doesn't seem to be the case in my own clan. For example, my mother's sister has a son, but I haven't been able to detect any esoteric-magical tendencies there.

Then there could also be the latent talent that has never been used and developed. My ancestors only ever noticed spontaneous magical actions which are not based on any exercises let alone some specific training.

I feel that all this speaks more for an imprint by the horoscope, by role models, and by practice than by a genetic inheritance of magical abilities.

Apart from all these considerations, I don't find this question particularly interesting myself, because in my experience so far on a practical level it's more that some people feel the urge in themselves to learn magic and will then either realize after a while that magic is a substitute for something else in their life, or that they actually have the talent to learn magic.

Question: What role do traditions play in magic? Magic books? Personal teachers? Magical orders, lodges, brotherhoods etc.?

Harry: Again, I can't answer that in a general manner—people are just too different for that. Without preserving and passing on knowledge, everyone would have to start all over again. But without experiencing and testing things themselves, one would also take on a lot of mistaken or narrowly biased ideas. Hence, books are useful but they're not a truly reliable source of information.

Traditions arise when a culture exists for a longer period of time. I personally enjoy the many different cultures and traditions we can observe. I would find it a pity if, for example, there weren't this variety of gods, myths, and styles that are a part of these traditions.

Personally, I feel very much at home in the culture of ancient Egypt as well as in early Germanic mythology, equally in some other cultures such as the Dakota tradition—and I wouldn't want to miss the two books *The Golden Dawn* and *Techniques of High Magic*, which also belongs to the Golden Dawn perimeter, as they inspired me very much.

Personal teachers are not really my cup of tea. I prefer experimenting together with others and exchanging ideas at eye level. This has also been the case with Axel, even though I do like to refer to him as "my magical teacher."

I got to know some "teachers" and also learned the odd thing or two from them, but you can hardly call that a valid "teacher-student relationship" because these encounters have always been very selective and quite brief—more like a kind of visit.

That's different for other people. I can derive that from the fact that some people have learned from me, though I always experience myself as being at eye level with those seeking advice. Sure, I may know a bit more and have more experience, but does that make me "more"? Certainly not.

As far as magical orders and the like are concerned, in my opinion almost all of them have one big disadvantage: you are expected to commit yourself for life, to marry an association, as it were. I myself cannot do that because I don't know where my life will lead and what other insights I will gain along the road. I experimented together with Axel, explored all kinds of things together with Josef,[23] took part in the Bonn Workshop for Experimental Magic, took part in rituals in a witch coven a few times, but actually I have always looked for the conversation and the experiences in twos—that has always proven to be the most effective approach for me.

From my point of view, the question of authority and tradition is a question of epochs: in the Paleolithic period, which corresponds to the oral phase of the baby, you will simply do what you have experienced as actually being able to do—folk magic, if you will.

In the Neolithic age, which corresponds to the anal phase of the infant, everything is arranged according to the rhythm of the seasons and

---

23. This was Josef Knecht: see his contributions in this book.

of life. This is tradition with its seasonal festivals, its rules, its security in the endless cycle, and in the role model of the deities.

In kingship/monotheism, which corresponds to the phallic phase of the child, everything is centrally controlled and shaped, including the transmission of knowledge and power. This is the system of authorities, transmission lines, and initiations.

In materialism, which corresponds to the genital phase of the youth, everything is examined, tested, expressed in formulas and used in a practical, tangible manner—that's experimental magic.

In the era of globalization that is now beginning, corresponding to the adult phase of the grown-up, in which everyone is carried in trust by the whole and in which everyone bears responsibility for the whole, a sustainable system must be developed on earth and in every family that unites individuality and community—this form of magic is still in its infancy: namely Da'ath magic.[24]

In my opinion, tradition is therefore merely one of the five layers of human history. As such, it should be used, but always considered together with the other four layers: the spontaneous magic of the Paleolithic, the traditional magic of the Neolithic, the authority magic of the kingship-epoch, the experimental magic of materialism, and the Da'ath magic of the epoch now commencing.

Question: What is your conclusion regarding the Bonn Workshop for Experimental Magic today, some forty years on? And don't hesitate to be quite ruthless in your evaluation!

Harry: Again I find that difficult to say. There I met Josef and Frater U∴D∴ which I wouldn't want to miss either; there I experienced that there are even more magicians and sorceresses in the world and that they all come from different directions; there I led group rituals for the first time; there I saw that others also researched magic scientifically—though that was something I was still taking for granted at the time; there I learned via Peter's conjuring-up of my "clan being" that my encounter with my soul is

---

24. See Harry's take on Da'ath magic and consciousness in chapter 2, "My Path from Wish Magic to Da'ath Magic," more explicitly in chapter 6, "States of Consciousness," as well as chapter 11, "Da'ath Magic."

an experience that can also be found in other cultures; through the magazine *Unicorn* I experienced new aspects of writing…

There were many small encounters and experiences that enriched me,
and in retrospect these three years were something very special for me—
similar to the initial years with Axel, when we both didn't know anybody
else who also practiced magic, or the long years of regular meetings with
Josef later on.

Question: Would you advise today's magicians to set up something similar?

Harry: Well, again I can't answer that in general—people tend to learn in all
too different ways. I think it would be great if everyone had the opportunity to compare their own experiences with those of others in such a
manner in a group and to experiment together and support each other in
their own development.

Then everyone can see for themselves whether they would like to join
such a group of like-minded people or whether they rather wouldn't.

Question: Irrespective of your advice, what mistakes do you think they should
avoid?

Harry: If you have the possibility and the inclination within you to make a
mistake, you will make it in some way or another—otherwise you cannot experience and live out this part of yourself. Among other things, by
committing mistakes we become aware of ourselves and can thus express
ourselves more confidently and freely.

Of course, there are mistakes that are nothing but mistakes, blind
belief in authority, for example. But as long as there are people who are
stuck in the victim's attitude and who also have an inferiority complex,
and as long as there are also people who are dwelling at the opposite
pole, i.e., in the role of the megalomaniac, egocentric perpetrator, there is
bound to be the issue of dependency.

Of course I would like to see this and similar problems gone, but
what use is it really, warning of this problem? People will only ever learn
through experience.

I find it more helpful to look at how to "heal" yourself in the old sense
of "becoming whole" again. If you no longer have the "wound" of believing

blindly in authority, you will also be able to distinguish between the assumption of authority and its abuse, and the natural authority that comes from expertise and love of man.

Question: How did you define magic at the beginning of your magical career?

Harry: I didn't. I simply experienced it and I was curious about how it worked and what there was to discover.

Question: So how do you define magic today?

Harry: Actually, I still don't define it. Rather, I show people who care to ask what you can do by magic. Maybe you could describe it as "acting with the help of consciousness" instead of the commonplace "acting with the help of the body."

I'm more interested in what you can do and how to go about it, not so much in definitions. However, I do find highly precise and most comprehensive descriptions and well-assorted field reports to be quite enriching and stimulating.

Chapter 16

The Problem with Magic Is Not
Whether It Works, but That It *Does*

Josef Knecht

Numerous fairy tales and old stories seem to want to give us the hint: watch out what you wish for; it could actually come about! Or, to put it in the words of my favorite quote by Frater U∴D∴: The problem with magic is not *whether* it works, but that it *does*.

In the following, I will share with you a number of my personal experiences and reflections on the workings of magic. Based on their respective point of view and experience, my coauthors will show you entirely different perspectives in other chapters of this book. This diversity, too, is a fascination of magic.

Perhaps you are familiar with the fairy tale of the three wishes: a man observes that a neighbor is granted three wishes by a fairy as a reward for a little bit of friendliness. Out of greed, he surreptiously also secures three wishes for himself from her. But he can't make them work in his favor because his motives are not clear. Although every one of his wishes comes true as promised—the fairy religiously keeps her word—every one of them turns against him because he expresses it on the wrong occasion, and with the wrong intention, and because he cannot control his impulses. "Wrong" here is not meant as an external judgment call, but wrong in the sense of his own enterprise, which fails completely.

One can easily misunderstand this fairy tale moralistically and suspect the message to be that we should behave selflessly and "well" in order for our life to succeed. But I would rather see in it the knowledge and experience that magic just doesn't work the way this man wants it to. If I spit against the wind, then it's not a punishment but the disregard of a natural law when the spittle flies back into my face again.

Magic follows its own laws; and you'd do well to gain some insight about them before trying to spit against the wind.[25] When I'm handling electrical devices without knowing what to touch and what better not, I can easily take a hit. That's not a "punishment" either. Meaning: magic works the way it works and not the way I would like it to.

What does this mean in practice? In some respects, the functioning of our unconscious, or the working of magic, seems to me like a computer that, although technically speaking incapable of making any mistakes, nevertheless produces amazing or very undesirable results again and again, errors that come about because we didn't have a sufficiently farsighted overview when programming it. A computer "punishes" every tiny error relentlessly. The same can be the case with a magical task for the unconscious when it comes to effect specific changes in life.

As already mentioned elsewhere, I well remember a small ritual I conducted to "help" find a suitable, affordable, and pleasant apartment for myself. In the wish or order addressed to the "search function" of my subconscious, I had listed all the qualities that seemed important to me: the apartment should be inexpensive—at that time as much of a rarity as it is today, it should be quite large, and have its own kitchen. And please keep it close to nature without being too distant from the university. A highly unlikely set of qualities, which I conveyed to my subconscious by means of a small ritual and sent off as an order. Apparently, my inner search function did its job well, because after a reasonable time I found a nice basement apartment with its own entrance and a spacious kitchen, right next to the forest and merely a quarter of an hour away from the university. The landlord did not demand an exorbitant rental fee, as I had expected, but merely asked me quite benevolently how much I was able to pay. Everything was amazingly good so far; it was only after moving in that I was able to discern all those qualities in the apartment that I had not foreseen in my ritual. One room was exceed-

---

25. I would like to stress that the considerations presented here apply only to a world-immanent, i.e., non-gnostic, magic. Frater U∴D∴'s concept of Ice Magic (see my chapter 4, "Different Perspectives in Magical Thinking And Experiencing Magic") is based precisely on evading all laws and thus in principle evades the relevance of these thoughts.

ingly dark, and the kitchen had no daylight at all. It was also rather damp and smelled like a laundry room given the proper weather conditions. Here and there, the wallpaper hung from the walls, and the furniture was old and had apparently not been selected according to any obvious aesthetic criteria. I also had forgotten to mention that I had no need for small, crawling flatmates of the insectoid persuasion. I did finally get used to them and learned that such a magical "purchase order" apparently has to be implemented very precisely.

In this particular case the result came close enough to my wishes and nothing really bad happened, so I couldn't reasonably complain. But I had indeed figured out the lesson that my overview was far from sufficient to optimally assess my own life situation and to find the best solution for myself. And that was the case even with a mere trifle such as looking for an apartment! After I had made some further similar experiences, I decided not to interfere in my life anymore with my everyday mind and my superficial needs. It just didn't pan out.

There was a significantly more horrible ending to the story of a budding adept who thought he urgently needed money and sent this wish into the world with a little ritual. He had not thought about how the money could realistically come to him. Since he did not play the lottery or anything similar and didn't run any business that could have flourished vigorously all of a sudden, his "order" chose the only available channel: a relative of his died in an accident, and he inherited the desired money. Straight out of Goethe's sorcerer's apprentice. I don't think this story requires any further comment.

Apart from clarity in defining one's desires, there is another factor that should always be kept in mind when practicing success-oriented magic. In accord with C.G. Jung's concept, I will here label this the "shadow", i.e., that part of our psyche that always remains unconscious to us and embodies the bits that we do not like about ourselves and others, that we repress and deny.

In practice, it must be taken into account that an unsettled shadow tends to transfer itself into reality, even if our waking consciousness wants something different to happen. This is already the case under everyday conditions where it can show up as a Freudian slip, as illness, mishap, or accident. This law applies even more so when the subconscious mind is activated and "charged" by the energy boost of a ritual. A repressed desire is usually much more intensely charged with psychic energy and—precisely because it is not otherwise perceived—pushes more strongly into external reality than a conscious intention. Non-observance of this connection then leads to "magical ricochets", i.e., to intense but undesired consequences for the everyday personality. Since the impulse that was suppressed and thus removed from consciousness is the one that has prevailed, the event is not perceived and interpreted as a result of the ritual.

This regularity has a particularly fatal effect if the daily consciousness programs itself for success and cultivates a fanciful idea of its own grandeur. Its matching shadow is the feeling of inferiority and failure. When such a complex is magically activated and energized, the shadow likes to appear as a boycotter who lets all plans flounder. Since it usually seems as if this failure is a consequence of "external" circumstances, the everyday personality often intensifies its efforts and lends ever more energy to the complex, whereby the failure and the feelings of defeat will surface even more clearly and will correspondingly demand more effort in order to be repressed further. Such a loop can have a very paralyzing effect and—as seen from the point of view of the conscious personality who would like to expand and become successful—can eventually prove to be fatal.

Many magical and other spiritual systems consequently recommend working with the shadow at the very onset of spiritual work. The "shadow," so named by Carl Jung, is also called the "guardian of the threshold," a threatening authority that controls the transition between the waking consciousness and the unconscious and can intimidate the unprepared psyche so terribly that it directly withdraws from the threshold.

When we enter a Tibetan temple, which in many respects symbolically plays out the psyche's passage through its own underworld and makes it possible to experience this incident as an external process, we first encounter large demon figures appearing suddenly in threatening poses in the semi-darkness. Only when we have passed these do Buddha statues and images become visible. The laws of the inner path can be experienced in this environment in a very impressive and direct way.

In today's culture, however, there is no longer a general consensus about symbolic figures depicting the shadow. Our "demons" can be very diverse. The devil has long since served his time in this respect; and—as folklore so beautifully has it—one man's meat is another man's poison. So our challenge is often to recognize our own demons as such. Especially in the context of groups interested in magic, there are many who feel attracted by the dark side of the psyche, dress in black, and are fascinated by images and symbols, music and films that would commonly be perceived as "demonic"—vide Goths, Black Metal nerds, Satanists, etc. The people concerned are apparently fascinated by the collective shadow and tend to work their way through it. This has a very important function for society because the recognition of the shadow is always psycho-hygienically helpful. The more a force or power is repressed, the more devastating its implementation in everyday life can be. Recently, this could be observed very well in the Catholic Church regarding the subject of sexuality. The denial of an elementary psychic power does not make it disappear, but perverts it and makes it "demonic" in the true sense of the word. And the repression of the sexual and of the feminine as such was even more dramatic in the Renaissance and Enlightenment periods with their mass burning of witches. The brighter the light, the darker the shadow. Or as a friend of mine once put it: No war has ever been waged in the name of evil. The worst crimes of humanity were committed without exception in the name of good, true faith, and progress—all this constituting evidence for the rule that a suppressed shadow has a devastating effect. In this respect, any society can be grateful to those who bring to the surface all that no one else wants to see, and lend these forces and needs a voice and a visual expression.

However, it is critical to be aware that working on the collective shadow is by no means the same as working on one's own. Anyone who feels drawn to morbidity, illness, death, and decay, and loves to watch zombie movies, or attempts to conjure up dark demon figures, obviously exposes themself to a sphere—namely illness and death—that is currently taboo and strongly repressed in our society. But the shadow of the person concerned is an entirely different one, because they are aware of their tendency to morbidity and able to express it. Their own shadow lies in what they themselves find unbearable and repulsive and tend to avoid in their consciousness. Perhaps they have a "white shadow" that lies in their longing for bourgeois recognition and a nice, decent family, in all that they strongly abhor and avoid in their daily consciousness.

Even in the Middle Ages, illness and death did not reside in the shadow. The demons were not disfigured, decaying zombies, because illness and decay were an everyday experience of the people and they were eminently conscious of it. Rather, medieval demons were sexually attractive succubi and incubi (i.e., coitus demons) that seduced people and enticed them to all sorts of sins that were considered unspeakable at the time, and which nobody would be upset about today.

The price for avoiding the personal shadow is stagnation in emotional and magical development. Those who cannot get past the guardian of the threshold won't enter the realm of magic and the unconscious, but will remain attached to their own imaginary world and the specters of their own dreams of desire or fear.

If this is the case, the functioning of magic is only directed at a private fantasy world that is fortified and inflated by rituals, paraphernalia, and activated imaginations. In the occult tradition, there used to be talk of the dangers of the astral sphere, C.G. Jung spoke of an inflation of the unconscious, and today we would more prosaically term this phenomenon escapism. Here, too, there is the problem that magic does work, but that it does not bring us closer to reality, instead leading us deeper into a dead end of private imagination and flight from the world.

If I believe that I can travel spiritually to any spheres that are real beyond my personal imagination, then it is useful to conduct some sober fact checking now and then, and to travel on the material plane to a place where I can afterwards verify the factuality of my spiritual perceptions. Adepts of the magical tradition always agreed that the material level was the easiest to handle. Anyone who does not get along here and has difficulty orienting themselves under the comparatively comprehensible laws of the physical and social world will encounter even greater difficulty with all other levels of being. If the "higher" levels are not experienced as more arduous and complex, then it is worth asking yourself where you have actually landed.

One of the first tasks for prospective adepts is to learn to master their life circumstances and to take their life into their own hands. Everyday life is the field in which karma is resolved and worked through, and in which an essential part of inner development must take place. In everyday life, import-

basic characteristics and abilities (such as intelligence, energy, determination, an eye for the essentials, empathy, patience, etc.) can be acquired, which are then indispensable for further "magical" training. These are qualities that are conducive to both material and spiritual development (if you actually want to distinguish between them). It is therefore no wonder when we hear from experienced magic teachers that top executives from business or academic researchers are among the most talented magic students once they have decided to pursue this path.

On the other hand, those who live a bleak everyday life and believe that they can achieve their spiritual goals in their "free time" only cheat themselves. Mental maturity has nothing to do with the mastery of magical (or for that matter other) practices. You cannot "acquire" maturity, you can only open yourself to experiences leading to spiritual maturity in the wide and colorful field of life.

These remarks can be read as an advice to rather concentrate on so-called "high magic", i.e., on the use of ritual, spiritual journeys, and further techniques for spiritual development and maturation in the same sense as other spiritual methods and schools do. In my opinion, magic directed at everyday success is suitable for trying out how far one's own powers will actually reach, or, in the case of notorious doubters, to convince themselves that "there are more things in heaven and earth than are dreamt of in your philosophy." No question: magic works. Everybody who has tried it and seriously dealt with it knows that. But it doesn't always look the way we imagine naively. And for coping with everyday life, it is a less suitable, arduous, and cumbersome tool—a rather inefficient use of energy.

So I would like to conclude with another story, which this time does not hail from the canon of fairy tales but is told of the Buddha: the Buddha is sitting under a tree, resting, when two of his disciples come running excitedly up to him. They enthusiastically tell him that they have heard of a yogi who, after twenty years of consistent meditation, has acquired the ability to walk on water. They even observed him crossing the nearby river on foot themselves. The Buddha clearly sees in their eyes the question why he refrains from teaching them such skills, too. Smiling, he responds, "Too bad about the wasted years. If he'd given the ferryman a coin, he'd have gotten over to the other side more easily."

Chapter 17
Magic and Science

Harry Eilenstein

When you have had so many experiences with magic that you consider it a given that it really exists, you will often feel the need to suss out the connection between magic and the natural sciences.

What does a worldview look like that includes both 3D printers and materializations? How can you describe the world without airplanes and levitation being contradictions? Is there a view of the world for which both the internet and telepathic information retrieval are valid aspects?

Da'ath, as mentioned several times in various chapters in this book, is a view of the world in which there are no boundaries.[26] In a Da'ath world description, therefore, no two contradictory world descriptions should be necessary or even possible.

If two people look at the same object from two different points of view, this object can seem very different to either of them. However, one should be able to assume that both will perceive something that is actually there, but that they see a different section of it.

The natural scientist's point of view is to look at the development over time: which cause has which effect?

The perspective of a magician is the contemplation of simultaneity: in astrology between the planetary state and the horoscope of a human being, in telepathy between the lost object and the image in one's own consciousness, in magic between one's own desire and the corresponding desired event: what happens in a meaningful context?

---

26. For my discussions of Da'ath magic, see chapter 2, "My Path From Wish Magic to Da'ath Magic," and chapter 6, "States of Consciousness," as well as chapter 11, "Da'ath Magic." There's also mention of it in chapter 15, "Some Questions on Magic."

Since the natural sciences look at the temporal course of events, and magic looks at the context of meaning between simultaneous events, quite different worldviews result from these two ways of looking at things. It follows from this that magic cannot be explained by the natural sciences, nor can the natural sciences be explained by magic.

It does not follow, however, that magic and the natural sciences must contradict each other; instead, we should be able to use the two different perspectives in order to design a more comprehensive view of the world. After all, the natural sciences and magic are both describing the same world.

If both describe the world from different points of view and have accordingly developed different descriptions and vocabularies, the question arises what could actually be compared with these two worldviews. In the magical worldview, the scientific causal connections do not occur, and in the scientific worldview, the analogies of magic do not occur either.

What both worldviews have in common, though, are the structures they observe and the angles between different things as the smallest structural element. Finally, there are also the laws of conservation, which should constitute a formative element in both systems.

The beginning of all things is the same in both systems: "In the beginning was singularity" and "In the beginning was God."

Note: The image used in this section of a primeval unity ("God") that unfolds gradually does not apply equally to all magical worldviews but to a good many of them. This primordial unity is found, for example, in the Kabbalah in the form of Kether as an essential element. By the same token the Quintessence, the "source of the four elements," can be understood as just such a primordial unity. After all, for a long time no distinction was made between religion and magic—instead, magic was an integral component of most religions and was therefore regarded as a kind of "effect emanating from the gods." (Vide e.g. theurgy.) Hence, the non-theist reader is advised not to be put off by my usage of the term "God," and is encouraged to view it as a fundamentally technical designation.

The next step is equally the same: "The world began with the Big Bang" and "The world was created by God's decision to create."

This next step happened very quickly in both systems: "The universe was created by the phase of the 'inflationary universe' in which the universe expanded at 1050 times the speed of light" and "The world was created in seven days."

These similarities do not explain anything yet per se, but they are nevertheless pleasing, since they do not contradict each other and form a first common basis.

So how does the story continue? In the scientific view of the world, events occur everywhere by chance, i.e., causally conditioned, though not following any definite pattern through which the world differentiates itself. In the magical worldview, the world appears as a complex pattern in which everything is connected with everything and in which everything is related to everything else.

If we combine both points of view, the result is the image of a world that unfolds causally as a complex, symmetrical image: an almost infinitely complex kaleidoscopic mandala, so to speak.

Unfortunately, there is a fundamental problem with further observation: we can only perceive the tiny part of the world on Earth that we can actually see, i.e., the contents of a sphere with a radius of eight billion light years: the universe is eight billion years old and from the things that are, for example, fifty billion light years away from us, no ray of light has yet reached us on Earth. And even in the tiny section we can observe, there are 1081 atoms, so it might be difficult to observe any overall patterns in space. But if the perception of this presumed pattern isn't possible, we can still look at the details and see whether something can be found there.

The angle as the smallest structural element is found in astrology as the aspects between the planets whose qualities are precisely defined. One can therefore see whether these angles, with their respective qualities as found in astrology, also occur in the natural sciences.

There are three basic forces: gravity, electromagnetic force, and color force.

Gravity pulls all things together—we can thus call it "unipolar." The "unipolar" angle in astrology is the conjunction (0° angle) that unites two things into one unit, which corresponds to the effect of gravity.

The electromagnetic force is "bipolar" (+ and -) and becomes neutral by the combination of both poles. In astrology, the "bipolar" angle would be the opposition (180°), which, just like the electromagnetic wave (light), is an oscillation, i.e., the constant alternation between two poles.

The color force is "triple polar" ("yellow" and "red" and "blue"). For example, it holds the three quarks together in a proton. If you want to remove one of these quarks from the proton, you have to invest so much energy in the process that a new proton is created from it. So you cannot separate these three quarks. The "triple polar" aspect in astrology is the trigon (120° angle) that holds together two planets that have zodiac signs with the same element (being fire, water, air, and earth).

The astrological square (90°) separates two planets in the same way that a tent pole separates the floor tarpaulin from the ceiling tarpaulin: the separation creates a space. This phenomenon can be observed, for example, in an electromagnetic wave whose magnetic wave is always at right angles (90°) to the electric wave.

The astrological sextile (60°) assembles similar elements into a group. This can be found in nature in various places: the water molecules in the snowflake form structures with 60° angles; the protons and neutrons ("spheres of equal size") are arranged within the atomic nuclei at 60° angles to each other; around any given planet six moons can circle in the same orbit at a distance of 60° from each other, etc.

The qualities of the angles in astrology and in the natural sciences thus coincide—which was to be expected but is nonetheless another pleasing discovery.

The central element of astrology is the zodiac. It actually has a very conspicuous structure: twelve equal parts that form a circle, sharply separated from each other and endowed with properties that can be described by aspects (angles): each sign is identical with itself (conjunction), opposite signs are complementary opposites (opposition), signs arranged in a triangle to one another have the same element (trigon), signs arranged in a square have the same dynamics (square), signs arranged in a hexagon form a common group (sextile), etc.

The central element of superstring theory, which today describes all physics, is "Heisenberg's spin chain." It has a very conspicuous structure: twelve equally sized parts that form a circle, which are sharply separated from each other and which also have properties that can be described by means of angles (aspects). This Heisenberg spin chain is like a string stretched in a circle, vibrating—six of the twelve sections vibrate downwards, the other six upwards (two group, which are alternating up and down), the twelve boundary points between them are always at rest. The two groups of six correspond to the two hexagons on the zodiac: the fire/air signs and the water/earth signs.

Hence, the basic "building block" in both astrology and physics features exactly the same structure.

The zodiac as the blueprint of the physical world reappears once again very clearly: the world is made up of four types of particles: the up quark, the down quark, the electron, and the neutrino. These four particles appear in three different sizes.

This structure obviously corresponds to the zodiac in which there are four elements that appear in three dynamics.

Natural scientists and magicians/astrologers are obviously living in the same world and conjointly describe this world in an accurate manner because they both find the same structures in this world, even if they happen to describe these structures from different perspectives.

The superstring theory used by physicists today is a very complex model. To describe it, a mathematical model is needed that not only uses the three space dimensions common in everyday life plus one time dimension, but also seven additional space dimensions that become visible only in areas far smaller than an electron. One of these seven additional space dimensions has the property of "enveloping" the other ten dimensions.

There is also an eleven-dimensional model of the world in magic: the kabbalistic Tree of Life, which consists of eleven Sephiroth (spheres, balls, areas). The highest of these eleven spheres (Kether) corresponds to the time dimension. The three spheres below it (Chokmah, Binah, Da'ath) correspond to the three "normal" space dimensions. The six following spheres (Chesed, Geburah, Tiphareth, Netzach, Hod, Yesod) correspond to the six "hidden" space dimensions. The lowest sphere (Malkuth) corresponds to the "summarizing" dimension.

It thus becomes apparent that the essential elements in both worldviews have the same structures.

There is a "coincidence" in the scientific model of the origin of the world, which has dazzled physicists time and again.

After the Big Bang, the universe, which was constantly expanding at the speed of light, was still so small that its inherent energy was so dense that everything was in a thermal equilibrium, i.e., it was equally bright and equally hot everywhere. Only seven hundred years after the Big Bang, the first atomic nuclei were formed from protons and neutrons, but it was still far too hot for electrons to bind to these atomic nuclei.

Ten thousand years after the Big Bang, two things happened at the same time, between which there was no physical connection: on the one hand, the previous thermal equilibrium ended, meaning that different places could be disparately hot and bright, and on the other hand, electrons began to bind themselves as a shell around the atomic nuclei.

This simultaneity of the end of the thermal equilibrium and the formation of electron sheaths, which is only a strange coincidence from a physical point of view, is, however, extremely conclusive on the Tree of Life.

The thermal equilibrium is to be found from Kether to Tiphareth, i.e., in the region corresponding to the deities and the souls. This perfect interconnectedness of all parts (i.e., the thermal equilibrium) corresponds to the interconnectedness of the souls. If you are in this area with your consciousness, telepathy, for example, works quite effortlessly.

The formation of the electron shell around an atomic nucleus corresponds to the formation of a psyche around an incarnating soul. This psyche isolates the soul from other souls, so to speak. On the Tree of Life the psyche is represented by Netzach, Hod and Yesod. The different temperatures in space after the formation of electron shells correspond to the different states of the psyches of the individual humans.

So this is up to now merely a contemplation of a meaningful correspondence between the physical evolution of the universe and the spiritual development of a soul (as far as one can grasp the latter at all with any certainty), but at least this examination goes to show that a physical curiosity within the magical world view can certainly make sense: for magic, in contrast to physics, considers simultaneities.

The laws of conservation are a core piece of physics: "Nothing comes from nothing." Or to put it more nobly: "Every cause has an effect, but with no process the whole becomes more or less." You could also say that nothing is ever lost.

This means, among other things, that every change in the world has one of two possible dynamics: either two parts join together to form a larger part, or a composite part separates into two subparts.

In terms of processes, this means that wherever something happens, its opposite also happens: *actio = reactio*. The impulse of the recoil of a rifle corresponds exactly to the impulse of the bullet fired. This principle goes so far as to allow for the possibility of an electron and an anti-electron emerging from nothing and then to extinguish one another again ("virtual particles").

The laws of conservation of physics thus give rise to many different opposing particles and processes in nature. We can also describe this mathematically: $0 = +1 + -1$. Or to speak with Frater U∴D∴: *ubique daemon∴ ubique deus∴*.

This principle is also found in the psyche: The three natural, wholesome qualities a child develops are trust, strength, and self-love. When these qualities are disturbed by stress, it isn't a simple deformation of these qualities that takes place but always a polarization, i.e., the opposition of two opposites of equal size: trust becomes addiction and asceticism, strength becomes power and impotence, and self-love becomes delusions of grandeur and feelings of inferiority. One of these two poles is lived and acted out consciously, the other pole is suppressed, and the psyche looks out for someone outside to take it over: no addict without an ascetic, no victim without a perpetrator, no star without fan boy or girl.

Of course we can now pose the question of what practical use such reflections are supposed to be.

First of all, an apparent contradiction within one's own world view can be quite disturbing: is the scientific world view or the magical world view the correct one? The dissolution of this contradiction enables us a more relaxed exercise of magic: because of the reality of physics, we no longer need to tackle fundamental doubts about magic. We now maintain a unitary world view. For this reason alone, the search for a "unitary magical-scientific world view" is worth the effort.

Furthermore, it is very likely that such a world view, assuming it is developed further than it has merely been sketched here, is sure to render some useful pointers for conducting practical magic.

One could then also describe the physical and magical processes by a uniform language, for example: "The accentuation of one element of the whole causes a clearly visible change in the pattern within this whole."

In physics, this would mean that pouring oil into the fire would increase that fire and its heat. In magic, this would mean that invoking Pan would lead to erotic adventures. Such a language that describes both sides of the world even-handedly could have some pleasant effects.

In the previous reflections, everything has referred to the magical control of chance, that is to meaningful cohesions. But what about the more extreme forms of magic such as materializations, i.e., objects that appear out of nowhere?

The common (physical) point of view is that effects always have a physical cause. In the previous description in this chapter, magic is merely an order of things that physics has not yet taken notice of, but that does not call into question the principle that "every effect has a physical cause."

If, however, the physical description of the world and the magic description of the world are the same, it should also be possible to achieve an effect by a change in the "pattern of the world" merely by magic. Basically, this is already the case with ordinary telepathy: if, by looking inside, we can find out where the house key is someone else has lost, then this is more than the congruence of two elements within a large pattern. Even if you make a paper wheel turn by concentration alone, this is a telekinetic effect without physical cause.

Thus, we can take the sentence "The accentuation of an element of the whole causes a clearly visible change of the pattern in the whole" quite literally: the (magic) concentration on a desired result, too, causes a real effect in the physical world which has no physical cause.

Now we can also distinguish between ordinary magic and extraordinary magic. The former is telepathy, astrology, the use of oracles, small forms of telekinesis, etc., while the latter is what one would commonly call a miracle, i.e., levitation, materialization, spontaneous healing, unscathed lying on glowing coals, etc.

If the sentence "The emphasis on one element of the whole causes a clearly visible change in the pattern in the whole" is actually formulated correctly, then a great magical effect should also be caused by high concentration. The difference between ordinary magic and extraordinary magic would then be the same as that between a rifle shot and an atomic bomb.

The rifle belongs to the lower part of the Tree of Life. It functions on the level of molecules (gunpowder), i.e., in the area of Netzach, Hod, and Yesod. An atomic bomb, however, functions on another level because it is based on the fission of atomic nuclei, which on the Tree of Life corresponds to the area of Chesed, Geburah and Tiphareth (atomic nuclei), and also to the area of Chokmah, Binah, and Da'ath (transformation of matter into energy).

The first of these realms (Netzach, Hod, and Yesod) also corresponds to the psyche, the second to the soul (Chesed, Geburah, and Tiphareth) and to the deities (Chokmah, Binah, and Da'ath). This would imply that the effect of magic would be greater if it originates not only from one's own psyche but is in harmony with one's own soul, or if the magical action even has a deity as a supporter.

At least my own experiences match up with the model sketched here. In the materialization that I once experienced, I completely trusted in "those above" and put my further life into their hands. And when in lying naked on glowing coals I had a complete "trust in everything."

Most people who performed miracles also had this trust. Jesus Christ, for example, always thanked God for his help *before* his miracles and not after the miracle had been performed. There's no more radical way to express trust ... And trust is ultimately nothing else but harmony, i.e., the connection with one's own soul or with a deity.

If a unitary description of the world can help us find this kind of trust, then it has already redeemed itself with an immense benefit.

This trust is also one of the two elements of the currently developing Da'ath world view: the individual bears responsibility for the whole and is in turn carried and supported in trust by the whole.

Chapter 18

German Letter Magic:
History, Systems, Field Reports

Frater U∴D∴

Orientalizing a Western Magical Tradition
Rudolf von Sebottendorf:
The Historical Classification of Author and Work

When we talk about letter magic or, more precisely, letter exercises in the following, this refers to a series of exercises presented to a broader public by the German theosophist, esotericist, astrologer, publishing director, writer, impostor, political activist, putschist, gun runner, and spy Rudolf von Sebottendorf (1875–1945). Here are a few facts that should serve to place the author and the work in their historical context.

Sebottendorf (often incorrectly written "Sebottendorff") was born on 9 November 1875 in Hoyerswerda as Adam Alfred Rudolf Glauer, son of the train driver Rudolf Glauer. After claiming to have graduated from the technical school in Ilmenau as an engineer—in fact, as is now assumed, he was merely trained as a mechanic in a nearby factory—he signed up on a merchant vessel as a heater and on-board electrician, and he spent the years 1897 to 1900 in Egypt in the service of the Khedive (viceroy) as a technician. He then studied, so he states, at the Polytechnic Institute in Zurich. From 1908 to about 1914 he lived in Turkish Constantinople (today Istanbul) where he acted as estate administrator of a pasha and was also commercially active running his own business. There he was adopted by a certain Baron Heinrich von Sebottendorf, assumed the name Rudolf Glandek Freiherr von Sebottendorf, and became a naturalized Turkish citizen in 1911.

The adoption—probably contrived according to contemporary research—was legally challenged by the Sebottendorf aristocrat family, upon which followed a legal dispute spanning years until the parties involved finally reached an agreement. Consequently he continued bearing his title of nobility until the end of his life, even though this was not officially recognized in his homeland, being rejected, for instance, by various German registration authorities.

He took part in the first Balkan war, was wounded, and returned to Germany. In 1913, in joint authorship with the Turkish lecturer at the University of Leipzig, he published the language guide *Turkish* with the renowned publishers Langenscheidt Verlag. The work was reprinted multiple times in a revised version.

He maintained his public image as a millionaire and self-made man. In fact, we find him in Vienna in 1915 where he married the affluent merchant's daughter Bertha Iffland, who hailed from Berlin—probably the real source of his fortune. The couple moved to Dresden to the elegant Kleinzschachwitz quarter, where Sebottendorf had a magnificent villa built for 50,000 gold marks—an astronomical sum even by the standards of the time. Soon thereafter he is put under tutelage for his financial extravagance, the assets of his wife being now administered by the renowned Berlin solicitor Max Alsberg, and thus protected from his access. Throughout his life, authorities and political opponents prosecuted him on suspicion of unethical financial machinations, fraud, and imposture, but he was never actually convicted.

Around 1916, he joined the nationalist antisemitic, ariosophist Teutonic Order Walvater (*Germanenorden Walvater*, GO, formerly *Reichshammerbund*), founded four years previously, and in 1918 became editor of the order's magazine *Die Runen (The Runes)*. In 1918 he founded the Thule Society (*Thule Gesellschaft*) in his function as Master of the GO. Purportedly an association for the study of Germanic folklore and history, it operated in actuality as a political camouflage organization of the GO, whose leadership he held until 1933. Prominent National Socialist members were Rudolf Hess (later to become the official deputy of the "Führer") and the NSdAP chief ideologist Alfred Rosenberg, who assisted Adolf Hitler during their joint imprisonment following the party's Munich coup d'état attempt in writing his work *Mein Kampf* as an unnamed coauthor. Rosenberg was later to succeed Sebottendorf as editor-in-chief of the National Socialist Party's highly influential daily newspaper *Völkischer Beobachter*.

In the political turmoil at the end of the First World War and in the years immediately following, Sebottendorf distinguished himself by his massive, hardly-to-be-overestimated support of the *Freikorpsverbände* (being right-wing paramilitary Free Corps units) in the suppression of the left-wing Munich Republic of Councils. After the founding and arming of the Thule Combat Alliance (*Thule Kampfbund*) in 1919, he set up the infamous *Freikorps Oberland*, which was integrated into the Black Reichswehr (*Schwarze Reichswehr*, the extra-legal paramilitary formations promoted by the German Reichswehr army during the time of the Weimar Republic) shortly thereafter and from which the core of the Bavarian *SA* (*Sturmabteilung*—the notorious Nazi Stormtroopers) would emerge in 1921 through subsequent organizations such as the *Bund Oberland* and others. The young Heinrich Himmler was one of its more prominent members. After its successful Munich operation in 1920, the *Freikorps Oberland* was first deployed in the Ruhr rebellion and, following this operation, in the suppression of the uprisings in Upper Silesia, where it set up its own death squad and was responsible for abductions and Vehmic murders.

Sebottendorf even plotted a coup d'état against Bavarian Prime Minister Kurt Eisner, which, however, was aborted, and he was eventually officially wanted for a time in the Free State of Bavaria due to his illegal activities, among other charges as a conspiratorial gun-runner of right-wing radical, antisemitic and anti-democratic militias. In 1918, he became editor-in-chief of the former sports newspaper *Münchener Beobachter*, which he acquired in the name of his lover Käthe Bierbaumer. In 1921, he renamed it *Völkischer Beobachter (Volkish Observer)* and finally ceded the highly indebted organ to the young NSdAP to use as its main propaganda vehicle until the end of World War II. Bierbaumer was also the formal owner of the Franz Eher publishing house in Munich, which specialized in National Socialist literature, and would later publish Hitler's *Mein Kampf (My Struggle)* as well as the *Völkischer Beobachter* itself.

Moreover, Sebottendorf exerted a decisive influence on Rosenberg's program for the new party that emerged under Hitler, originating from the DSP and DAP. Namely the NSdAP's legal political demand for Roman law to be

abolished in favor of "aristocratic" Germanic law is an ideological component of early National Socialism that Sebottendorf directly adopted from the
GO and contributed to the Nazi movement.

Expelled from the federal state of Baden as a foreigner due to his political
activities (for example he set up and armed a secret battalion storm troop
within the Freiburg residents' militia and supported the Berlin Kapp Putsch),
he lived from 1920 in Bad Sachsa with both his wife and lover in a ménage-à-
trois, above all as an astrological writer. He became editor of the *Astrologische
Rundschau (Astrological Review)* and head of the Theosophical Publishing
House (*Theosophisches Verlagshaus*) in Leipzig. He now kept out of politics
until 1933. After his divorce in 1928, he adopted a brisk travel activity: Mex-
ico, USA, Austria, Switzerland, Turkey (where he temporarily functioned as
a Mexican consul). It is highly probable that he was already working as an
intelligence officer, though these activities possibly commenced much earlier. Among other works, he published the novel *Der Talisman des Rosenk-
reuzers (The Rosicrucian's Talisman*, 1923), the main protagonist of which,
Erwin Torre, was unmistakably autobiographical. In it he reports on initiations into various dervish orders and extensive contacts with Jewish Freemasons and Kabbalists in Busra, Turkey. After the National Socialists seized
power in January 1933, he suddenly reappeared in Munich and published
his work *Before Hitler Came. Documents from the Early Days of the National
Socialist Movement (Bevor Hitler kam. Urkundliches aus der Frühzeit der
nationalsozialistischen Bewegung).*[27] In it he describes, from his point of view,
the predominantly conspiratorial events ascribed to the nationalist-esoteric
organizations that finally brought Hitler to power. Obviously he expected a
corresponding recognition by his political companions and idols, but in this
he saw himself sorely disappointed: instead of being hailed and credited for
his achievements, he immediately fell out of favor with the regime, his book
was banned, the second edition was confiscated, and he himself was expelled
from the country as a Turkish citizen following a short period of detention,

---

27. The German title *Before Hitler Came (Before Hitler Came)* was to be used again in 1964
for the tabloid style, crypto-historical book by Nazi and conspiracy theorist Dietrich
Bronder: Dietrich Bronder, *Bevor Hitler kam: Eine historische Studie*, Hannover: Pfeiffer
1964. Hence, the two publications with their identical titles should not be confused with
one another.

after which he found refuge together with Käthe Bierbaumer, first in Liechtenstein, then in Austria, and eventually in Switzerland. There are indications that from Switzerland Sebottendorf attempted to blackmail the Nazi government with a follow-up volume of *Before Hitler Came*, which he claimed to have already completed and which offered further incriminating material from the early days of the "movement." In any case, the Reich Treasurer of the NSdAP, SS-Oberst-Gruppenführer Franz Xaver Schwarz, one of the most important functionaries of the party, is said to have visited him there. It can be assumed that they agreed on the payment of some hush-money. Soon afterwards, Sebottendorf was considered an undesirable in Switzerland as well; he had to leave the country and removed to Luxembourg for a short while.

Finally, leaving his companion Käthe Bierbaumer behind in Austria, he returned to Turkey. Obviously, however, not all bridges to the Nazi state apparatus had been broken (unless the entire affair had been a large-scale legend of the German foreign intelligence service in the first place), because he remained in Istanbul until the end of the war as a subaltern agent of the German Abwehr under Canaris. He was managed under the tradecraft names "Greif" and "Hakawati" (fairy tale narrator) but lived in rather destitute circumstances. His senior officers persistently suspected him of working as a double or possibly even triple agent for the English and Turkish intelligence services. This, however, was never to be verified.

On May 9, 1945, one day after the unconditional surrender of the German Reich, he was found floating dead in the Bosporus. The official report maintained that he had committed suicide, but rumors continue to this day that he fell victim to a physical altercation with political opponents or agents of the Allies. According to other sources, after his fictitious death he was in fact immersed either in Turkey or, more likely, in Egypt, possibly with intelligence support, be it Turkish or British. His (speculative) date of death in Cairo is quoted as 1956 or 1957.

In view of this adventurer's vita it is certainly no exaggeration to state that the expression "dazzling personality" seems to have been specifically crafted for Rudolf von Sebottendorf's sake …

In 1924 he presented his letter magic exercises for the first time in his booklet *The Practice of Ancient Turkish Freemasonry (Die Praxis der alten türkischen Freimaurerei).* He claims to have taken it from the manuscript of a certain Walter Ulrich Paul Schwidtal (1875–1920), former secretary to the Turkish embassy in Berne, Switzerland, to whom he also dedicates the book. In 1913 Schwidtal is said to have brought the practice in the form of a typewritten text with accompanying photographs from Turkey to Switzerland, where he instructed some personal students in the system. This typescript is supposed to have been a revised copy of the older Arabic work *Ilm el Miftach (The Science of the Key)*, a manual consisting of about ten to twelve instruction letters. (Here we are possibly dealing with a generic title, though demonstrably unknown in Turkey at that time, which in the Arab language region signifies—more frequently referenced as *Miftah ul-Ilm*—until today different "keys to the understanding" of the Islamic Hadiths.) In addition, Schwidtal is said to have written another treatise based on said key, entitled *Oriental Magic (Orientalische Magie).* Both the mentioned manuscript and the Arabic original are considered lost so that Sebottendorf is actually the only witness vouching for their existence.

So much for the legend of its creation.

The Freiburg publisher Hermann Bauer published a new edition of the Sebottendorf book in 1954. Its rather baroque full title is *The Secret Exercises of Turkish Freemasons. The Key to Understanding Alchemy. A Representation of the Ritual, Teachings and Symbols of Oriental Freemasons. Arranged by Rudolf Freiherr von Sebottendorf (Die geheimen Übungen der türkischen Freimaurer. Der Schlüssel zum Verständnis der Alchimie. Eine Darstellung des Rituals, der Lehren und der Erkennungszeichen orientalischer Freimaurer. Bearbeitet von Rudolf Freiherr von Sebottendorf),* featuring the additional note: "Newly edited and with a foreword by Waltharius."

Waltharius (1905–1997), who, according to a personal statement he made during a phone conversation I had with him in the early '90s, was officially permitted to bear this single name following a formal change of name, was originally born as Walter Studinski. As a New Spirit devotee, Theosophist, Rosicrucian, and heir to the Pansophical archive of Rudolf Tränker, as well as an author of highly regarded works on mysticism and alchemy, he achieved a significant degree of fame in the German-speaking realm of the 1950s to 1970s.

In his introduction he writes: "I have completed [...] this booklet in some places by minor additions, mainly where the exercises in the first part are concerned, and have also given some important hints as regards the creation of the 'Shadow'."

Waltharius incorrectly states that the work *Oriental Magic*, allegedly written by Schwidtal, was never published and that the manuscript was in fact lost. In actuality, however, Sebottendorf did publish, under his own name, a multi-part article with the same title *Oriental Magic (Orientalische Magie)* in issues 4 to 6 of the German journal *Theosophie*, published from 1924 to 1925. In it, he deals primarily with Islamic magic, its various sub-disciplines, and forms of organization: Sufism and diverse dervish orders, ecstasy techniques, fakir phenomena, astrology, the summoning of jinnies, qur'anic surah magic and number mysticism, geomancy etc. In the final section, which he again heads *"Ilm el Miftach,"* Sebottendorf briefly paraphrases the letter exercises described in his first work as "The Way to Higher Magic," discusses their references to the kabbalistic *Sefer Jetzirah* ("Book of Creation"), and concludes: "The science of the key thus does not unveil the mystery of alchemy alone as I did in *Freemasonry* [this refers to his initial treatise on the subject; ed.]." In 2008, this article text was reprinted by the Graz, Austria publishers Edition Geheimes Wissen (copyright claim: Irene Huber) without detailing the original source and without a table of contents. This is apparently a scan performed with OCR software, only moderately proofread, featuring a significant number of abstruse scanning errors. Hence, this edition cannot, unfortunately, be considered as quotable, at least not by academic standards.

We are therefore dealing with a revised version of the "secret exercises," as Waltharius once again conveys, in which the editor, however, unquestioningly adopts the story of origin as narrated by Sebottendorf. This proves problematic in that a more in-depth historical investigation arrives at entirely different conclusions.

In fact, no reliable evidence is currently known to contemporary research that the letter magic exercises in their presented form are indeed of Arabic, Turkish, Oriental, or even Islamic origin at all, as claimed by Sebottendorf. Rather, they seem to come from another, perfectly Western tradition as will be shown below.

As far as the term "Turkish Freemasonry" itself is concerned, it should be noted that around the time of origin of the Sebottendorf book, numerous different authors of both Western and Middle Eastern provenance recognized a certain similarity between the practices of Turkish Bektashi Dervishes (Turkish: *Bektaşilik*) and Masonic customs, and hence spoke of "Oriental ," occasionally of "Muslim Freemasonry." In the 1920s, there was even an Ottoman organization created under the name *Tarikat-i Salāhiye* that was specifically dedicated to a synthesis of the Masonic and Bektashi traditions. And as early as 1868 a regular British Freemason in Turkey reported that the Bektashis understood themselves as Freemasons of sorts and tried to ally themselves with the Fraternity.

Nevertheless, Sebottendorf's assertion of a veritably existing "Turkish Freemasonry" is considered completely fictitious, i.e., mythical in today's dervish research for a variety of reasons that cannot be discussed at length here for lack of space. Rather, all evidence seems to suggest that this was a pure construct on Sebottendorf's part in which, however, a series of genuinely Sufi, Jewish-Kabbalistic, hurufistic, and generally mystical elements were interwoven within a Western-Masonic frame of reference.

In addition, there was a very distinct European source of letter magic exercises, quite accessible to Sebottendorf, which did not originate from the hardly penetrable shadowy circle of Oriental secret societies. This source shall now be examined in more detail.

Sebottendorf's Predecessors in the Nineteenth Century

In the first half of the nineteenth century, the Catholic theologian and later-to-be opera director Johann Baptist Kerning (1774–1851), actually Johann Baptist Krebs, worked pseudonymously in the German principality of Württemberg. He was considered a mystic and a reviver of Freemasonry in Württemberg, which at that time was almost entirely dormant due to official prohibitions. He was the founder and long-time Master of the Chair of the Stuttgart Masonic lodge "Wilhelm zur aufgehenden Sonne" ("William at the Rising Sun") and in 1840 endowed the still existing lodge "Zu den drei Zedern" ("At the Three Cedars"). Kerning distinguished himself as an author of Masonic writings with a strong theosophical bias and, which is of particular interest in our context, as the creator of a "Sabbath grade."

The International Masonic Encyclopedia (Internationales Freimaurerlexikon) notes:

> Doctrine clothed in Masonic ritual form ("Sabbath doctrine") based on the philosophy of Aristotle. God himself is will-less according to this doctrine, creative man can form new ideas and thus approach the Godhead. The positing of sound = force is peculiar. The central point here is the Logos of the Gospel of John. God = word, for Krebs further, the word = sound. The S. aims to render an introduction to philosophy. Sentences and words (terms) are transformed into sounds and perceived as such. The tones are parts of the primordial force, this is the sought-for unity (God). Spelling is the educational tool.[28]

According to the encyclopedia, the ritual was finally published in 1922 from the manuscript in an (unnamed) FM organ.

The general public learned of Kerning's system only posthumously via his student Karl Kolb and his so-called *Letter Book* (actual title *The Rebirth, The Inner True Life or How Does Man Become Blessed? In Accordance With the Sayings of Scripture and the Laws of Thought Answered by a Freemason (Die Wiedergeburt, das innere wahrhaftige Leben oder wie wird der Mensch selig? In Übereinstimmung mit den Aussprüchen der heiligen Schrift und den Gesetzen des Denkens beantwortet von einem Freimaurer, 1857).* A reprint of this book under the title *The Letter Book. Rebirth, The Inner True Life Or How Does Man Become Blessed?* was published in 1994 by my own Edition Magus, referencing "Karl Kolb & J. B. Kerning" as authors.[29]

Kolb's publication proved a great success. The treatise saw numerous new editions, most of them under the main title *The Letter Book (Das Buchstabenbuch).*

None other than the undisputed number one of German fantasy and occult fiction, the Austro-Hungarian author Gustav Meyrink (i.e., Gustav Meyer,

28. Eugen Lennhoff, Oskar Posner, Dieter A. Binder [edd.], *Internationales Freimaurerlexikon*, rev. & exp. Edition, Munich 2011, p. 733a s.v. "Sabbithengrad."

29. Karl Kolb, J. B. Kerning, Das Buchstabenbuch. *Die Wiedergeburt, das innere wahrhaftige Leben, oder Wie wird der Mensch selig?*, repr. of the 2nd ed. Lorch 1908. (Bad Münstereifel: Edition Magus, 1994).

1868–1932) dedicated the writing of an entire practical work to Kerning in 1907. Published under the pseudonym Kama and entitled *Kernings Testament*, this was an absolute rarity being an entirely practical work, given that Meyrink's overall literary oeuvre is internationally renowned for fantastical works that included *The Golem* (*Der Golem*), *The Angel of the West Window* (*Der Engel vom westlichen Fenster*) and *The Green Face* (*Das grüne Gesicht*). *Kernings Testament*, too, was later reprinted under its original title in 1993 in a limited edition by Edition Magus.[30] In his novel *The White Dominican* (*Der weiße Dominikaner*, 1921), Meyrink refers once again to Kerning's letter magic exercises.

Numerous exegists, imitators, and freeloaders followed. For example, the prominent Prague occultist, Theosophist, and personal friend of Meyrink's, Karl Weinfurter (1867–1942) incorporated Kerning's exercises into his long-standing bestseller *The Burning Bush. The Revealed Mystic Path* (*Der brennende Busch. Der entschleierte Weg der Mystik*, 1930). The aforementioned Waltharius also refers to it in his *Mysticism, Zen and the Colored Shadow* (*Mystik, Zen und der farbige Schatten*), published in 1954, and again supplements the observation of the system with his own elements, such as the use of Zen meditation. He also summarizes the exercises briefly in what is perhaps his most renowned work, *Mysticism. The World's Ultimate Secret. The Path to Immortal Self and to Union With God* (*Mystik. Das letzte Geheimnis der Welt. Der Weg zum unsterblichen Selbst und zur Gottvereinigung*, 1957). However, he makes mention expressly only of Kerning and Kolb, Sebottendorf now being demoted without further ado to the bibliographical appendix. A more detailed list of secondary authors who took up Kerning's suggestions and implemented them or simply gave them an unoriginal reference may be dispensed with here.

Nevertheless, there were critical voices to be heard as well. Franz Hartmann (1838–1912), arguably the most eminent German Theosophist of the turn of the century, took several opportunities to express himself in an increasingly pejorative manner to disparage the Kerning exercises which were enjoying a steadily increasing popularity: among American Christian Scientists, European Rosicrucians, in the "Inner Circle" of Adyar Theosophy, and, at least

---

30. Gustav Meyrink [Kama], *Kernings Testament* (Bad Münstereifel: Edition Magus, 1993).

temporarily, in OTO, whose co-founder Hartmann himself had been, after all. After initially having felt quite enthusiastic about the exercises, he finally arrived at a very snarky judgment: "This path leads to illness and madness."

As we can see, nothing much remains left of Sebottendorf's assertion of a Turkish-Oriental origin of his letter magic exercises. This is not to say that his variant constitutes blatant plagiarism and entirely lacks originality. While the Letter Book by Kolb/Kerning explicitly refers to the Kabbalah, if only marginally, Sebottendorf focuses more on alchemical classics such as Paracelsus and Khunrath, as well as some lesser-known authors from the alchemical tradition, in the same vein drawing on the mythical Hermes Trismegistos. Only in his later series of articles, Oriental Magic, as we have already seen, does he devote increased attention to the Kabbalah. Above all, however, the connection with Islamic-Sufist elements, first and foremost the inclusion of the fourteen mysterious undeciphered "preliminary letters" or phonetic formulas (*alam, alar, alamar, tsam, cham asak*, etc.), which are each trailed by altogether twenty-nine selected surahs in the Quran, undoubtedly originates with him. To this day, these formulas are a popular subject of study in speculative Islamic mysticism, and they constitute the doctrinal framework of various dervish orders and revival movements.

In addition, Sebottendorf links the series of exercises to the twenty-eight mansions of the Moon of Arab-Islamic astrology, which are assumed to mark the practitioner's spiritual path of development.

This "Islamization" of the exercises was of central concern to him insofar as he attached partook, like so many of his conservative, politically right-wing contemporaries—and significantly beyond the prevalent fascination with the Orient and Islam of Western occultists and conventional fancies of the "Wild East"—to the thought patterns of Western Orientalism as they emerged in the fading nineteenth century within the framework of European imperialism and colonialism, though they did indeed fall back blithely on romantic precursors.

In this spirit he confesses his unmitigated admiration for the unprecedented stamina of the Turkish population in the First World War (though being the inveterate racist he is, he doesn't fail to mention that they aren't even a "racially homogeneous people"), attributing it solely to the culture of Islam. The latter appears to him to be far more "vital" and "viable" than the culture of the Christian West, which he views as being decadent. By way of contextualization: Oswald Spengler's barnstormer *The Decline of the West (Der Untergang des Abendlandes)* had only been published as recently as 1918. Its fulminant success can arguably be explained less by its actual contents but by its very title, which happened to hit precisely the right nerve of the time for such a culture-apocalyptic work. In this respect, Sebottendorf's idiosyncratic portrayal was markedly critical of culture and anti-modernist, and thus pursued quite specific political goals—albeit in a rather veiled manner—even if these may remain fairly obscure to his readers today.[31]

An equally essential difference between Sebottendorf's presentation and Kolb/Kerning's *Letter Book* lies moreover in the fact that Sebottendorf largely refrains from the religiously edifying and long-winded theological discussions that characterize the work of its predecessors. Unlike them, he definitely doesn't strive for an extensive exegesis of selected passages from the Bible, but neither does he, as one might perhaps expect, resort to any petty interpretations of the Quran.

Indisputably, the commonalities between both approaches to letter magic are nevertheless great, including their sharing the central objective of the practices submitted: Kerning himself is concerned with the "revival of a prophetic force in man" as the mainstay of his system; Kolb's title hints at the aim of human beatification, while Sebottendorf explicitly states that his exercises are "nothing more than a working on oneself, for refinement, for the acquisition of higher knowledge."

It becomes clear, of course, that almost a hundred years have passed between the two treatises when we read in Sebottendorf: "I will not demand from the reader any faith in my words, but I will prove my explanations; I will prove that Oriental Freemasonry to this day faithfully preserves the ancient wisdom doctrines which modern Freemasonry has forgotten about [...]" Obviously the nineteenth century, with its materialism, positivism, and the general scientification of the zeitgeist, has left its mark on the latter author. Here, comprehensible proof claims the place of the mandatory act of faith and speculative metaphysical insight that inform the earlier work.

---

31. As an aside, it may be worth noting how this idealization of Islamic culture by early twentieth-century right-wingers contrasts with their present-day political successors' deeply entrenched Islamophobia.

Even Sebottendorf's fundamental critique of established Freemasonry, which is perceived as "toothless," rigidified, and conformist, utterly alienated from its spiritual foundations, is wholly in tune an occultist at the turn of the century. Both the British Hermetic Order of the Golden Dawn and its immediate predecessor, the Societas Rosicruciana in Anglia, the Ancient and Primitive Rite of Memphis-Misraïm founded by John Yarker, and the later Ordo Templi Orientis (OTO) defined themselves from the outset as rediscoverers and innovators of the "original" knowledge of Freemasonry that was considered to have been lost. The same applies to numerous other orders founded since the second half of the nineteenth century, the first precursors of which attitude can be found as early as the eighteenth century.

On the other hand, Sebottendorf, again ever the antimodernist, expressly speaks out against the monism of Häckel and Büchner, which were also given to set the tone in the nineteenth century, and reestablishes the link back to the religious by asserting toward the end of his preface: "The only demand I make is that the reader be aware of his unity with God, without this consciousness the exercises are worthless."

Finally, for the sake of completeness, it should be mentioned that Sebottendorf's original work *The Practice of Ancient Turkish Freemasonry. A Key to Understanding Alchemy. A Representation of the Rituals, Teachings and Symbols of Oriental Freemasons* (i.e., without the editorial changes and the preface by Waltharius) was also published in 1993 by my own Edition Magus in a limited edition as a reprint.[32]

A detailed comparison between Kerning's exercises and their Sebottendorf variant is still pending. However, this is not the right place for it. In any case, the political and historical connections discussed here cannot detract from the effectiveness of his series of exercises, as the following field reports will show.

> *Note: In the following section, two systems of German letter magic are explained in detail. There are a few more around that will not be discussed here as this would go beyond the scope of this book. This task*

---

32. *Die Praxis der alten türkischen Freimaurerei. Ein Schlüssel zum Verständnis der Alchemie. Eine Darstellung des Rituals, der Lehre und der Erkennungszeichen orientalischer Freimaurer* (Bad Münstereifel: Edition Magus, 1993).

shall be reserved for another work that will be devoted exclusively to this fascinating topic. In addition, it is the procedures presented here that we and other members of the Bonn Workshop for Experimental Magic were able to experience on a practical level personally.

Following on, three of us will present their relevant experience reports.

Harry Eilenstein

The Sebottendorf System

1. Duration:

These letter exercises, which primarily Frater U∴D∴ has dealt with on a practical level, are carried out over a period of three to twenty-five months. They should thus take a goodly two years at the most.

2. The Formulas:

The three vowels "I," "A," "O" are used, which in most cases are turned into "Si," "Sa," "So" by a prefixed "S."

They are used together with the postures described below.

3. The Postures:

Three hand postures ("Postures") are used in this procedure:

"I": stretch the index finger of the right hand, clenching the remaining fingers to a fist.

"A": hold the hand in a straight plane, fingers against each other, spread the thumb at right angles.

"O": hold the hand as a stretched plane, index finger and thumb are curved and form a circle

When executing these Postures, the arm is held straight from the elbow to the fingertips.

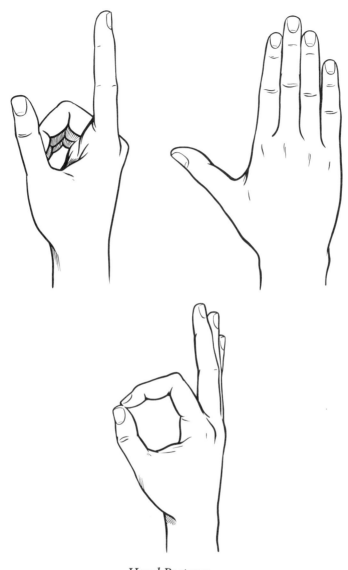

Hand Postures

4. **The Grips and Their Movements:**

Note: The description of the Grips and their movements are quoted here directly from Sebottendorf's original treatise.

In the exercises, four sections of the body are worked upon.

a. **The Neck Grip:** Place the angled hand on your neck so that the thumb touches the right artery, the index finger touches the throat and the other fingers are on the plane of the index finger. Pull off the angled hand by moving the index finger sharply over the throat until the hand is on the same height as the right shoulder, then lower the hand.

b. **The Chest Grip:** This Grip is performed with the right hand angled over the chest. You will get the height right if you place the angled hand as in the Neck Grip and place the angled left hand so that the thumb barely touches the pinky of the right hand. This is the correct height. The grip itself is positioned so that the tips of the four fingers will barely touch the left arm, the palm of the hand resting on the left side of the chest. Pull off with spread thumb until the fingertips touch the right side of the body.

c. **The Middle Grip:** This Grip is no longer known in Masonry today, it is carried out somewhat lower than the Chest Grip; the correct position can be determined by placing the angled right hand in the manner of the Chest Grip and again positioning the angled left hand in such a manner that the spread thumb barely touches the right hand's pinky.

d. **The Master Grip or Belly Grip:** This Grip is located lower than the Middle Grip by the width of the angled hand, it is positioned below the navel and is executed over the solar plexus just as the previous grips.

e. **The Final Grip (used only during Follow-Up Work):** The Grip is called the Final Grip by the masters because it concludes the entire work. It is in truth a shortened Master Grip. It is positioned to the left of the navel and pulled over it.

It is not required that the Chest, Middle and Belly Grips be performed on the unclad body, it can safely be clothed. However, silk clothing is not recommended.

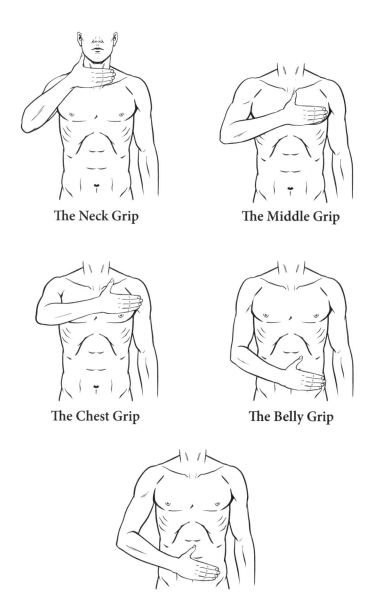

The Neck Grip

The Middle Grip

The Chest Grip

The Belly Grip

The Final Grip

The Grips

Author's comment: Sebottendorf's original text specifies both "below the navel" and "across the solar plexus," but the distance between these areas as measured by hand width indicate that the solar plexus must be implied.

5. The Preparatory Work

The exercise is performed in the morning and evening for about five to ten minutes.

Standing upright, raise your arm straight up or respectively stretch it horizontally forward and hold your hand in the "I" gesture until your finger turns warm. Then lower your hand.

Now perform the same procedure with the "A" gesture and the "O" Posture.

When performing these Postures you are to think/imagine the corresponding letter intensely inside of you.

Once the warming up of the fingers has been achieved, the syllables "Si," "Sa," and "So" are to be used in lieu of "I," "A" and "O."

However, you will now employ Postures different to the warm-up exercise of the Preparatory Work:

You warm up your finger in the "I" Posture with the syllable "Si" and let your hand sink once it has turned warm.

Then, you hold your hand in the "A" Posture and think internally of the "Sa" formula. After a while, you position your hand in front of your neck and charge it with the force in your hand. Subsequently, you perform the swift "left => right" motion before the throat with the syllable "Si" ("Neck Grip").

Next, you hold your hand in the "O" Posture and concentrate on the "So" formula. Finally, you charge the solar plexus with this energy and finish off again with the swift "left => right" motion ("Belly Grip").

6. The Main Work

a. Stage 1

First, the Preparatory Work is carried out for seven days. On the sixth day, check whether the index finger smells slightly of sulphur after its animation by the "Sa" formula.

If so, the next stage follows. If not, continue the practice for a further seven days. The smell of sulphur may not manifest for all practitioners. In that case, after fourteen days you will simply proceed to the next stage anyway.

b. Stage 2

This exercise is performed daily for fourteen days for about ten minutes a day.

Employ the "I" Posture together with the "Si" formula until the finger turns warm.

Then proceed to the "A" Posture, now using the formula "alam" instead of "Sa." After a while, perform the "Neck Grip."

Now hold your hand in the "O" Posture and concentrate on the "So" formula. Finally, you charge the belly section with this energy and finish off again performing the swift "left => right" motion, i.e., the "Belly Grip."

After fourteen days, the index finger of the right hand should taste of mercury sublimate. This taste may not manifest for all practitioners.

c. Stage 3

This exercise is performed for about ten minutes daily over a total of fourteen days.

The difference to the previous Stage 2 is merely the formulas used:

For two days: "alam"
For two days: "alamas"
For seven days: "alar"
For three days: "alamar"

The power is transferred with the swift motion to the right body side: the "Chest Grip."

The index finger should now taste salty after the exercise. This taste may not manifest for all practitioners.

After the three tastings, a black shadow will appear next in this phase. (*Note*: This shadow is commonly called the *caput corvi* or "raven head.")

d. Stage 4

After a short application of the "I" formula in tandem with the "I" Posture, proceed to the "A" Posture. The formulas this time are: "alar," "Kaha ja as," "taha," "tasam," "tas" and again "tasam"—no precise number of days is specified for this stage.

The force is transferred with the "Chest Grip."

The manifest effect is the coloring of the shadow from black to blue, next to a faint red and finally to a pale green that will gradually turn fresher.

e. Stage 5

The exercise is the same as before, but the formulas "cha," "cham asak" and "ka" are used and the power is transferred with the "Belly Grip"

The colors of the shadow change several times and will finally graduate from yellow to a bright white.

7. The Follow-up Work

The procedure is the same as before. The formula is "na" and the Final Grip is used.

The white shadow changes from a dirty grey to a full red.

8. Hints by Sebottendorf

You should keep silent about the exercise as long as you are performing it and talk about it only after achieving your goal.

Early in the morning, right after getting up, is the best time for conducting the exercises.

It is not recommended to practice for more than ten minutes a day.

The Grip should be used no more than three times a day.

With the Neck Grip, a glowing heat may develop in the neck.

The connection of the exercises to the chakras is briefly mentioned but not expounded on in detail.

9. Schematic Overview of the Work

Stage	Grip	Formula	Phenomenon
Preliminary work	Neck Grip	Si	warm index finger
		Sat	
	Belly Grip	So	
Main work 1	Neck Grip	Si	heat and sulphurous smell on index finger
		Sat	
	Belly Grip	So	
Main work 2	Neck Grip	Si	index finger tastes of mercury sublimate
		alam	
	Belly Grip	So	
Main work 3	Neck Grip	Si	salty taste on the index finger; shadow
		alam, alamas, alar, alamar	
	Belly Grip	So	
Main work 4	Chest Grip	Si	the black shadow turns blue, then red, then green
		Alar, Kaha ja as, taha, tasam tas, tasam	
Main work 5	Middle Grip	Si	
		alam, jas, sa, cham	
	Belly Grip	Si	the green shadow changes via various colors to yellow and finally to white
		cham, cham asak, ka	
Follow-up Work	Final Grip	na	white shadow changes quickly from grimy grey to full red

The Zeisel System

The letter magic method described by Johannes Zeisel, which Axel and I used, is very simple compared to the Sebottendorf method. It is actually a variant of the Weinfurter method.

Johannes Zeisel served as a soldier in the World War II and lived for several decades afterwards. Regrettably, neither his year of birth nor of death are known.[33]

He simplified the Weinfurter method and used the "alphabetical" letter sequence "a, e, i, o, u." Zeisel imagined the vowels one after the other optically, acoustically, and sensually in the soles of his feet. After some time he proceeded to the ankles, then to the knees, and gradually further upwards.

It is striking that he simply used the five vowels without assigning them (as did Weinfurter) a reference to the divine name Jehovah.

Harry Eilenstein
Field Report (Zeisel Method)
It was Axel who explained the letter magic exercises according to Zeisel to me and so I tried them out.

I lay down, imagining the vowels one after the other for a few minutes in the soles of my feet and humming them inwardly in my imagination as "endless sound."

Several phenomena occurred one after the other:

- I was relaxing.
- My body became heavy.
- My body became warm.
- The heat became more intense.
- A general vibration (appr. 6Hz) developed in my body.
- My arms or legs twitched: as I was lying under a blanket, I could perceive that these could not be my physical limbs; sometimes my right arm also twitched left through my body; by inference I actually perceived spontaneous movements of my astral body.
- Sometimes my body would start to sway as easily—probably a loosening of my astral body.

All these phenomena were extremely pleasant and beneficial and had an invigorating effect.

---

33. Johannes Zeisel, *Entschleierte Mystik. Ein moderner Weg von der Magie zur mystischen Erleuchtung*, Freiburg (Freiburg i. Br.: Hermann Bauer, 1984).

However, I also know of some experiences that resemble the letter exercise experiences of Frater U∴D∴ and Axel.

After listening to a radio program about meditation at the age of about twenty (that was before I knew Axel), I sat down in the evening in the lotus posture and tried out all the methods I heard of in the broadcast, one after the other: repeating a word constantly, becoming quiet inwardly, breathing quickly and deeply, holding one's breath for as long as possible etc.

In that night I dreamt that I was sitting on a bench in a castle, in front of a table, to my left the wall, so that I could only go to the right. A milky-white, foggy figure approached me from the right and came ever closer. That's when I panicked and woke up.

Apparently I perceived my astral body return to my body at the end of my sleep.

After hearing about astral travel from Axel, I performed relaxation exercises every day and tried to become calm, heavy, warm, vibrant, etc.

At a certain level of deep relaxation, however, I heard a "grey noise" coming in waves and consisting of pure fear—without any images being involved.

I returned to this place over and again, but I just could not bear this fear.

During my community service I rode my bike for a good hour every morning and evening and in the winter I conducted a fire meditation to keep warm. This first led to a one-directionality which was like an awakening from the waking state, and a few weeks later to the perception of an abyss into which I was supposed to jump—but it panicked me and blocked my path to this awakening and this abyss for many years to come.

With the help of rune exercises, during which I sang the name and the sayings to these runes (taken from the Spiesberger book) for at least one hour every day in the posture of a rune, the kundalini awoke in my solar plexus and rose up to my neck. As I was about to faint, I stopped the exercises at this point and lay down on my bed so as not to keel over.

Apparently the astral journey, the ascent of the kundalini, the abyss experience (on the Tree of Life this is Da'ath), the letter magic exercises, the fire meditation, and hypnosis as well belong together. (In hypnosis, the terms "relaxed—heavy—warm—tired" are commonly used as a suggestion to hypnotize the other person).

The common thread in these meditations could be the shift of conscious-ness from the physical area to the life force area—whereby one then also per-ceives the contents of one's own life force body.

In my opinion the awakening of the kundalini is connected with learning of astral travel because the first three quarters of the way is identical in both cases: the relaxation of the body and the alignment of the consciousness with the life force.

Since the shamans are essentially people who master astral travel and shamanism is the oldest form of religion, one would assume that the sha-mans generally also know the kundalini. This is actually confirmed by the kundalini depictions in the two early Neolithic temples of Göbekli Tepe and Nevali Cori (10,000 BCE).

For a few months now I have been exploring whether there is a gentle way to awaken the kundalini and to cross the abyss to Da'ath—this has also influenced the chapters I have written for this book.

What's just coming up in the context of the letter magic exercises of the four of us seems like the beginning of what I saw in the dream journey I undertook to determine why the four of us met again in the first place after all these years.

Frater U∴D∴

Field Report (Sebottendorf Method)

In 1975 I followed an intensive yoga and meditation program. This included up to four meditations a day, three to four, occasionally even six hours of asanas, a strictly vegetarian diet with four days of full fasting a month, no alcohol and nicotine, accompanied by regular study of spiritual, mostly East-ern scriptures, etc. At the same time, however, I had the feeling that I should also devote a little more attention to Western traditions as a counterbalance.

After I had discovered two classics of Rosicrucianism for myself, the *Chymical Wedding of Christian Rosencreutz* and the *Fama Fraternitatis*, I came across a small volume with the fascinating title *The Secret Exercises of the Turkish Freemasons* (to wit: *Die geheimen Übungen der türkischen Fre-imaurer*), published by Bauer Verlag in Freiburg. The author was a certain Rudolf von Sebottendorf, completely unknown to me at the time. Accord-ingly, I didn't know anything about his political involvement with the right-wing extremist volkish movement and the early NSdAP or Nazi party, the ariosophical Teutonic Order, his racist Thule Society, his frenzied antisemitism, nor any other of all the sordid details that characterized his life.

In his book, of course, nothing pointed to that. It soon became quite obvious that his purported "Turkish Freemasonry" was really neither here nor there: he referred to various dervish orders, which he obviously equated with Freemasonry, albeit without offering any further plausible justification, but which were in truth, of course, both historically as well as viewed from a religious studies perspective, solely attributable to Sufism. Overall, he used the terms "Freemasonry" and "Freemason" as placeholders to designate both regular and irregular Freemasonry, Rosicrucianism, late medieval alchemy, theosophical teachings, dervish orders, as well as Sufism in general and their respective followers and practitioners. Even in those early days of what was yet to become a magical career of sorts only many years later, this seemed far too vague, inaccurate, and ultimately misleading to me. Sure, he obviously wanted to boil things down to their purported lowest common denominator, the "inner truth" of all these doctrines and schools of thought, but that's exactly where you could—and still can today—differ vigorously.

And frankly, the alleged Islamic-Sufist element in these letter exercises didn't really interest me one bit. First of all, I personally never had any special affinity for all this anyway (born in Egypt myself, I grew up in Islamic countries and cultures both in Africa and in Asia and had garnered my own experiences with that particular brand of religiosity) and secondly, Sebottendorf himself didn't make a mandatory condition of subscribing to that particular mindset in order to be able to deal in more detail with the exercises.

This, by the way, also applies to all magicians I met later who tried out this system: not one of them paid much attention to the Islamic aspect of the exercise regime.

At any rate, I was fascinated by his simply described, altogether easy to understand, almost minimalist system of exercises in which it was merely a matter of intoning some vowels and syllables internally for barely a few minutes every day and imagining them in prescribed body regions, in the course of which a few finger and hand postures had to be carried out, the latter supplemented by a set of minor movements. Much of it reminded me of the yoga techniques concerned with of mantras and mudras with which I was already fairly familiar on a practical level. (I was a real badass yogi at the time, remember!)

According to Sebottendorf, certain perceptions were to manifest in the course of practice that doubled as confirmation signals to process the further stages. However, these weren't always that clearly defined. All right, so a shadow in the corner of your eye might still seem relatable, likewise a warm sensation in the index finger or a sulfurous smell on one's thumb, but who the heck could seriously claim to be able to determine beyond reasonable doubt the taste of "mercury sublimate," whatever that might be, on their forefinger?

Nevertheless, I plodded on, practicing the exercises diligently and unbiasedly until, after a few weeks and quite within the given time frame, I finally noticed the "raven head" or "shadow" as described by the author. I continued the exercises and eventually reached the level of the Middle Grip and the associated color perceptions.

But that proved also to be the end of me. At the beginning, the series of exercises actually seemed to me like a kind of process of mental alchemy set in motion internally, which at first quite captivated me and filled me with mild joy, but in the further course of the practice it was getting worse and worse for me: one depressive attack followed the next, my sleep was suddenly interspersed with nightmares as never seen before, and in general I was overcome by a persistent feeling of dull anxiety and aversion that permeated my entire everyday life and could no longer be shaken off no matter what I tried. (Well, to be honest I didn't opt for any psychotropic medication or therapeutic counsel at the time, but that was about the limit. In any case, what was I supposed to tell the doctor? "Oh well, you know, I've been doing these top-secret Turkish Freemasons' exercises and now I feel all crappy?" All things considered, I really wasn't that keen on getting to know some funny farm from the inside ...)

On the upside I didn't experience any distinct anxiety or panic attacks, nor did I have any problems with internal energy surges, hot flushes, kundalini phenomena, or the like, of which, as I learned years later, quite a few other practitioners were wont to report. Nonetheless, in the course of time things became more and more unpleasant, even scary, for me.

It would be a ludicrous exaggeration and a preposterous dramatization to speak of a sensation of "evil," but there was certainly a feeling of indefinite darkness at play here, at the very least of something that obviously did me no good, even if I couldn't precisely define or explain it.

The decisive external impulse to cancel the series of exercises was my execution of the Neck Grip. Although I had pulled back my hand quite gently according to the instructions, I suddenly felt a sharp, caustic burning sensation on my neck as if I had cut it with a blade. At the same time the inside of my mouth suddenly dried out like parchment paper. All this didn't last particularly long, but it did worry me deeply. Of course, Sebottendorf had described a similar reaction quite precisely and in this context had explained the meaning and wherewithal of alchemical "putrefaction" extensively. But bundled in a package with all those other icky side effects one certainty germinated in me from now on: this could not possibly be a healthy reaction! Not one to shy away easily from challenges, I did continue the series, as described above, for a bit, but there seemed to be no improvement of the symptoms in the offing.

In addition, my meditation practice was in the meanwhile strongly disrupted: I had ever greater difficulties with my concentration, my imagination was running amok, I could no longer properly maintain my mantras, all my inner centering was completely out of control—in short, regular meditation became a real torture. This had nothing to do with the usual initial difficulties of any new meditation regime: I had accrued enough pretty intensive experience to be able to judge this reliably.

Since meditation practice clearly constituted the center of my life at the time and had absolute priority, I didn't appreciate these particular "side effects" of the letter magic exercises at all and, as I generally felt more and more miserable, I finally decided to cut it out. So I eventually terminated the exercises, whereupon my psychological condition, including my meditation practice, improved again almost overnight.

It should also be mentioned, however, that apart from autohypnosis and autosuggestion, plus some attempts at telepathy and other psychic skills including telemetry and astral travel, I had no experience at all with distinctly magical practices (and as such, the letter exercises indeed seemed to me to be quite magical) up until then.

For a few years I kept my hands off it. After all, not every spiritual practice is suitable for everyone. While one given person may be more aligned with one specific meditation technique, another will prove to be only suited to an entirely different kind of practice in the long run. At that time I wasn't able to judge whether I was simply not ready yet for the letter magic exercises, or whether it might be a matter of a fundamental incompatibility.

Finally, five or six years later, I tried my luck again. In the meantime I no longer meditated regularly, didn't practice hatha yoga anymore due to an injury, was no longer a vegetarian, smoked like a chimney, and while I never drank excessive amounts of alcohol, cordially disliking that specific kind of buzz, I wasn't exactly a teetotaler either. By then I had also had some experience with sigil magic, ritual magic, invocations, trance and ecstasy techniques, and a whole range of other magical practices.

Again I started from the beginning and followed Sebottendorf's instructions meticulously. This time it could hardly be said that my—once fairly extreme—yoga practice had perhaps made me oversensitive, which is actually not all that uncommon. And yet the effect of the letter magic exercises was exactly the same: frequent depressive attacks, increased nausea, and to top it all, sleep disturbances that were actually totally foreign to me. And once again there was this constant feeling of dull anxiety that overshadowed everything else in the all-too-literal obnoxiously punny sense.

So I broke off the series of exercises again, though this time it happened early on after about two weeks of practice. Fortunately I recovered relatively quickly again, but ever since I have chosen to leave so-called letter magic to others who seem to be more suited to it than I.

Not to be too mawkish about it, I do have to confess that this series of exercises has instilled the utmost respect in me to this day. Nor have I yet found a plausible explanation for how such simple, at first sight seemingly harmless, practices can have such a dramatic, downright menacing effect.

In the meantime I have come to know quite a few magicians who have worked on the exercises with varying success. A few have actually executed them to the end described, some have even experienced them as being extremely pleasant. Others are quite enthusiastic, hailing them as the best thing since sliced mandrake. But many of them, be it at first try, be it at a repeated attempt, have broken them off just as I have, and more often than not for very similar reasons. It is still an unsolved mystery to us "failures" what was really going on at the time.

Hence it seems rather pointless to me to speculate about the specific reasons for this phenomenon as long as we still know too little about the actual processes that are triggered by the Sebottendorf letter exercises in mental as well as in physical inner life. So, for the record, this series of exercises is a form of practice which leaves virtually no one untouched who seriously engages with it.

And by the way: the term "letter magic," which I have used myself quite regularly in the past, does seem somewhat misleading at closer look. For it's not about a targeted influence on the world or the realization of concrete, tangible goals, the manifestation of a statement of will or similar, nor of doing the impossible: but, rather, of achieving states of consciousness or the soul that are basically more appropriately assigned to mysticism. There's nothing at all wrong with that in the principle, but the terminology used should perhaps reflect this more adequately.

Axel Büdenbender

Field Report (Zeisel Method)
(*Phone log*)

Axel imagined the letters in his soles until the feet first became warm and then hot. Next, the heat moved up his legs to his knees, whereupon he imagined the letters there. Subsequently, the heat became independent and climbed up to the hara without him imagining anything further. Then the heat suddenly "banged" into his head.

These exercises caused wild dreams that were so unpleasant that Axel has stopped performing the exercises.

He started again with these exercises every now and then, but invariably broke them off once more after a while.

Later he let the kundalini heat rise up to his knees and then called the energy down to Malkuth with the help of the Middle Pillar. This significantly increased the energy bursts, i.e., the ascending kundalini.

Through this form of meditation (letter exercises and Middle Pillar) a huge power potential was built up in the spine, which he could no longer control. He had the feeling that this energy was tearing him into an abyss.

On the following day, however, there was often a fear of death: fear of heart attack etc., a fear that felt as if it would tear him apart... This anxiety only subsided after three to four days.

According to Axel's estimation, you have to drive this force potential to its peak and then beyond—and then it will either tear you down into the Abyss or tear you apart.

The energy is like fire. As the energy rises, he sees flashes of light.

Without drugs, he sees the energy flow as if from the outside, and he gets scared.

With cannabis and divination sage, the kundalini is awake but the ego dissolves. Then there is also no more fear of either the kundalini or of death.

Today, when Axel even but reads about the kundalini, something changes, and it begins to stir.

The kundalini and the Abyss are closely connected—the same applies to the Abyss on the Tree of Life, being Da'ath on the Middle Pillar.

Chapter 19
Magical Mappings

Harry Eilenstein

There are various maps available in magic, such as the four elements mandala of the pentagram ritual, the slightly more differentiated mandala of the zodiac, the chakra system, the kabbalistic Tree of Life, etc.

There are also some other maps that can help us understand the development of magic, to grasp the meaning of Da'ath magic, to comprehend the effect (or non-impact) of one's own magic, and thus to become more effective in one's own actions.

Since Da'ath is an area in which all boundaries dissolve, it might be helpful to use a system that describes not only one's own development, but the development of human beings as a whole. These two developments, biography and history, can be compared with each other: just as every human embryo repeats the evolutionary ontogenesis from unicellular organisms to human beings, every human being mirrors the history of mankind in their biography.

In the beginning was the Paleolithic Age in which man lived as a part of nature within nature.

This corresponds to the baby that is breastfed and cared for by its mother: it lives, as it were, as a part of the mother.

Freud calls this stage of life the "oral phase": the child absorbs everything and puts everything into its mouth.

This phase can be characterized by a "Yes" to all things.

This was followed by the Neolithic Age during which people began to shape the world. On one side there was the village, the gardens, the farmland, and the pastures, and on the other side the wilderness. Humans lived in a rhythm determined by the seasons and in an order that enabled the preservation and nourishment of the village community.

This corresponds to the toddler who learns to walk and speak, can say "no," and clearly sees what is pleasurable and what is not. During this phase, children are also in need of order and set daily rhythms.

Freud calls this stage of life the "anal phase": the child begins to reject unpleasant things and to defend itself.

This phase can be characterized by a "No!" to all unpleasant things.

Next came the social form of kingship: the centralized administration of a larger country. For this purpose, a hierarchy was created, as were the script and an efficient numerical system. Royalty also shaped religion: the multiplicity of the gods received a king of the gods at its head who finally became the one, single (monotheistic) god. In the field of worldviews, philosophy emerged in this period, which derives everything from a first cause.

This corresponds to the child who has learned to say "I," who experiences themself as an independent being and has clear ideas of what they want and do not want.

Freud calls this stage of life the "phallic phase": the child places itself in the center of its world and ideally begins to radiate in self-love.

This phase can be characterized by an "I!!!"

Then follows materialism with its research, technology, and industrialization, which is entirely oriented toward the outside and its use for mankind's own purposes.

This corresponds to the young person who sets themself apart from their parents, who begins to discover the opposite sex and has become curious about the wider world.

Freud calls this stage of life the "genital phase": the young person begins to discover and live out their sexuality.

This phase can be characterized by a "You?"

The next step is the epoch that began approximately after the Second World War: people have acquired the possibility of destroying themselves with their nuclear bombs; environmental pollution exerts an equally destructive effect on all people; global warming also threatens the vast majority of countries, albeit in different ways; all distances have become shorter as a result of air traffic … the earth has become a village in which everyone is affected by the actions of everyone else.

This corresponds to the adult who, together with a partner, founds a family whose prosperity depends on the well-being of all family members.

This stage of life can be called the "adult phase" in the manner of Freud: the adult begins to build a stable life plan that supports itself without harming its environment.

This phase can be described as a "We."

Probably two more phases will follow in the future:

The first stage in future will be the phase of mature people who begin to explore the diversity of the world and who become the teachers of the younger ones ("tutorial phase").

This phase can be described by "Other …."

The last phase will correspond to the old man or woman who withdraws and looks at the whole, experiences it, and becomes wise ("gerontic phase").

This phase can be described as the "All."

Thus, the development of both mankind and the individual human being can be described by seven words: "Yes."—"No!"—"I!!!"—"You?"—"We."—"Other …"—"All."

Note that there are four static states that are connected by three dynamic processes, and which alternate with one another. The "Yes," the "I!!!!," the "We," and the "All" are stable states, while the rejection of the "No!," the search of the "You?" and the expansion of the "Other …" are developing the previous state further.

We can find the sequence of the four static states on the Middle Pillar of the Tree of Life again:

- Malkuth is the body, i.e., the development toward man.
- Yesod is the security of the "Yes" of the Paleolithic Age.
- Tiphareth is the self-centered "I!!!" of the soul.
- Da'ath is the "We" of today's epoch.
- Kether is the wise "All" of the distant future.

The three dynamic developmental phases correspond to the three pairs of Sephiroth (realms) on the Tree of Life:

- Hod is the development of speech and Netzach is the evaluating of the Neolithic: the "No!" of the toddler.
- The struggle of Geburah and the creation of Chesed are the characteristics of materialism: the "You?" of puberty.
- The security of Binah and the unhindered expansion of Chokmah correspond to the mature human with his "Other...."

The important point in these deliberations (i.e., in the present time and in this chapter) is Da'ath: humanity has just begun to develop a "We" feeling and to understand itself as a greater family. As with all transitions, there is a prolonged back and forth movement, which currently takes place between dull, short-sighted egoism and far-sighted global action.

What is needed is the perception of oneself as part of the whole—to be connected to the whole and to carry the whole: responsibility; to be connected to the whole and to be carried by the whole: trust.

Trust and responsibility are the two elements through which a family can thrive and through which humanity on earth can have a chance to survive for a while longer.

For this, a coordination between individuality and globalization must be achieved. This corresponds to the individuality in Da'ath that is no longer defined by its borders but by its quality. Thus trust in the continued existence of one's own individuality is needed, even if one opens the borders—the personal borders and the borders of the states.

Da'ath consciousness is obviously also a political affair and, hence, probably so will Da'ath magic be.[34]

If we strive for a goal like Da'ath consciousness, Da'ath magic and a Da'ath politics, it is helpful to know the possible mistakes and errors on our way to that goal. This question leads to yet another map or, rather, to an extension of the map of the seven steps: "Yes."—"No!"—"I!!!" —"You?"—"We."—"Other..."—"All."

In the Paleolithic Age and in the oral phase, the wholesome state is snug security. If this security is lost, the person in question either becomes louder

---

34. For more detailed discussions of Da'ath magic, see my chapter 2, "My Path from Wish Magic to Da'ath Magic," and chapter 6, "States of Consciousness," as well as chapter 11, "Da'ath Magic." There's also mention of it in chapter 15, "Some Questions on Magic."

and louder and develops into an addict; or they turn quieter and quieter and become an ascetic.

In the Neolithic or anal phase, the wholesome state is clarity and power. If this clear power is lost, the person will either wax louder and louder and become the perpetrator; or they turn quieter and quieter and become the victim.

In the kingship or phallic phase, the wholesome state is the self-expression carried by self-love. If this self-love is lost, the person concerned either becomes louder and louder and develops into a megalomaniac star, or he becomes quieter and quieter and becomes a fan with an inferiority complex.

The six extremes of these three polar deviations from the three wholesome states can increase ever further until they finally become a completely one-directed fixation. Then they are trapped in a painful and anguishing ecstasy:

- the *addicts* who can only think of their heroin
- the fanatical *ascetics* who wants to impose their world view on the entire world
- the violent *perpetrators* who will grab everything they want
- the panicked *victims* who just want to escape it all
- the megalomaniac *superstars* who cannot bear anyone else beside them
- the *fan boys/girls* who consider themselves absolutely worthless and want to turn themselves invisible

All "good feelings" are on the path of the seven phases of life, whereas the six "wrong paths," which, polarity-based, branch off from the first three phases of this path to the left and right, are full of distressing feelings.

These six deviations, i.e., the addict, the ascetic, the perpetrator, the victim, the superstar, and the fan boy/girl, are at the same time the six obstacles on the path to reaching Da'ath awareness, to practicing Da'ath magic, and to realizing Da'ath politics:

- The *addict* is fixated on lack and therefore cannot break open their limits to Da'ath consciousness; he/she cannot practice effective magic, because of the deficiency image in themselves they will always just add more deficiency into their own life; and they cannot think for the welfare of all because they believe they must take something away from others to have enough for themselves.

- The *ascetic* is fixed on renunciation and a hard, rigid order, and therefore cannot open his/her boundaries to the diversity of Da'ath because then they will fear their own death; they cannot exercise effective magic because they see nothing but their own fear and their rigid ideas; and they cannot look at the welfare of the whole because they believe that only their own opinion is right.
- The *perpetrator* is completely fixated on their struggle for survival and therefore cannot open themselves to the boundlessness of Da'ath because they consider everyone on the outside to be their enemies; they cannot exercise effective magic because they think only in terms of coercion and fear and thus will isolate themselves more and more; and they cannot strive for an equal existence for all human beings because all they seek is their own advantage.
- The *victim* is also completely fixated on their own survival, but they try to achieve this by adaptation, hiding, silence, and evasion: the victim goes into hiding, i.e., they isolate themselves and hence cannot reach Da'ath; they cannot exercise effective magic because they don't dare to stand by and show themselves; and the victim cannot pursue a policy of autonomy and equality because they dread the perpetrators.
- The *superstar* is egocentric and narcissistic and must always place themself in the center of events, hence there is no space left for others and certainly none for experiencing Da'ath's lack of demarcation from all other beings; they cannot exercise an effective Da'ath magic because they remain trapped in themselves and have no access to Da'ath; and they cannot exercise politics for everyone because they only see and look after themselves.
- The *fan boy/girl* is fixated on their shame and wants to hide and bathe in the light of someone else, so they do not perceive their own quality clearly enough to be able to rest in this own quality in the unlimited Da'ath; they cannot exercise effective magic as they would

have to be connected to their own soul first; and they cannot execute politics for everyone as they are not independent at all and instead seek someone who can function as a substitute ego for them.

Self-healing is a prerequisite for being able to reach Da'ath—and also to feel comfortable and to be able to spend a greater part of one's own time there.

The six polar, extreme states are deviations from the three basic wholesome states of security, power, and self-love.

From the previous considerations another structure results that we will encounter on our way to Da'ath: the relationship mandala. This mandala has a quite simple structure, which, however, can shape your entire whole life:

- In the beginning is the soul that decides on an incarnation. It is the center of the human being created by it.
- Then the soul settles down in the fertilized ovum and now shapes the vital force with its own quality and intentions. It is reflected in the vital force that creates two images because the vital force is polar: the inner male image and the inner female image. This inner man and this inner woman are the innermost circle of the psyche that encompasses the soul.
- When the person concerned experiences something violent, their psyche will polarize into an addict and an ascetic, into a perpetrator and a victim, or into a superstar and a fan boy/girl. In this way, two inner male images, polarized in the same way, and two female images, equally polarized in the same way, are created. These four images form the second circle of the psyche, which encompasses the soul and the inner circle of the psyche, which in turn consists of the whole inner man and the whole inner woman.
- If the person concerned is a man and has experienced something violent in terms of security and has embarked on the path of retreat, he will identify himself with the image of the ascetic self.

However, since he also carries within him the image of the addict, but does not live it out, an addict will appear in his life who connects themself with this part of his psyche, and who lives this part in lieu of the addict—and thereby makes life hell for the person concerned, as the addict is the opposite of the ascetic ...

There will also appear in his life an ascetic woman who lives the corresponding inner image of the person concerned and will become his friend—he gets along with her, but there is no erotic tension.

There will also be an addicted woman who lives this inner image of the person in question. She is the opposite pole to the ascetic, both in terms of gender and orientation (addicted instead of ascetic)—consequently he chooses her as his partner ... A wise move?

Finally, he can also meet people who, like himself, are ascetics and make friends with them.

These people now perform together the life-drama of the person concerned, who in turn returns the favor by taking on a role in the life-drama of the others. Of course, all this goes on unconsciously.

It is obviously necessary to end this life-drama because it is full of deficits, limits, and self-doubt. How can we expect to push on without this healing process into the demarcationlessness of Da'ath, to feel comfortable there, and then to exercise magic there and be able to conduct Da'ath politics?

The first step in ending this painful drama is to recognize the people who have embodied roles from your drama. Fortunately, this is quite simple to discern: they are the people who trigger emotions in you.

The second step is to retract the projections, the roles that the others have taken on, and to assert: "This is a part of me." This is the most difficult and unpleasant task of all ...

The third step is to bring the two polarized male images together. Once they meet, they will fight, and finally dissolve one another so that finally the "phoenix of the whole male image" can arise from the "ashes of the two extremes." The same happens with the two polarized images of women that the person concerned carries within himself.

The fourth step happens almost by itself: the inner man and the inner woman unite with each other, whereupon one's own soul becomes visible.

Obviously, this is merely a brief basic sketch outlining the sequence of the seven development phases with the six polar aberrations, as well as the relationship mandala as a contribution to magical mapping. Hopefully it will inspire some readers to investigate this subject in greater depth and arrive at further, possibly path-breaking, conclusions.

Chapter 20
Models of Magic in Practice

Frater U∴D∴

Initially, I presented my models of magic in an English article entitled "Models of Magic" in the British magazine *Chaos International* (issue 4, 9/1990). Since then, it has become my most plagiarized brainchild. Again and again, other authors have appropriated the concept and acted as if it were entirely their own. Of course we all know that imitation is the most forthright form of flattery. But in order to spare the reader time-consuming searching and looking up stuff, I will take the liberty of plagiarizing myself for a change and to refer to the content here once more, albeit rewritten and supplemented by some additional remarks pertaining to actual magical practice within this framework.

If we look at conventional—i.e., historically handed down—magic in its entirety, we will notice some basic, fundamentally different approaches that can be represented in structured form as models of the Dark Art.

However, before we go into detail, there are two caveats to consider. On the one hand, the models discussed here are by no means procedures that originally evolved in a strict chronological order, even if we can legitimately simplify matters by assigning them to approximately certain epochs.

On the other hand, these models will by no means always manifest in their pure form. It is not at all uncommon for overlaps and hybrid forms to occur. We will take this into account in more detail when reviewing their practical application.

The Spirit Model

Probably the oldest form of magic is the spirit model. We find it in prehistoric as well as in today's shamanism and animism. In addition to the material world perceptible with our sensory organs, there is also a generally invisible level of existence, usually called "subtle" in the traditions of Western esotericism. It is populated by various beings that can be summarized as "spirits."

Since these spirits are not subject to the laws and restrictions of the physical world, they are able to impact events and bring about effects on the material level that are not possible for man himself to achieve. For example, they can penetrate and influence matter, they are neither bound to the time axis nor can spatial distance impede them, and so on. In short, in most areas they are more powerful than humans.

The magician, shaman, or sorceress is in turn a human being who has the ability to gain access to the world of spirits and to communicate with them. This is usually effected by inducing a trance via techniques of ecstasy: drumming, rattling, dancing, fasting, self-mortification, entheogenic drugs, etc. During their extensive travels in the spirit world, the shaman makes friends and forges alliances with various of its inhabitants. (However, it is also conceivable that the shaman may make enemies in the course of these forays.)

For example, they establish contact with their personal power animals, with protective spirits, helpers, etc. whereas they may also impart knowledge and insights to the shaman, for example, regarding the usage of medicinal plants, stones, magic objects, visions of the future, or ways of attracting prey.

Essential for the spirit model is the fact that it is not man himself who causes the desired magical effects. Rather, it is always the spirits that will effect this for the shaman or the medicine man. Thus, the principal function of the tribal wizard or the witch doctor is primarily to move the spirits to bring about the desired event, or to avert imminent danger.

As is common knowledge, the word "witch" derives from the Old High German *hagazussa*. This technical term is usually translated as "fence rider" ("Zaunreiterin"). This refers to the "fence between the worlds": namely between the world of humans and that of spirits. The witch or the sorcerer are thus, unlike the normal human being, border crossers who are at home in both worlds. This is what enables them to perform magic.

The Energy Model

In Western culture, the energy model began to take hold on a grand scale with the public appearance of Franz Anton Mesmer (1734–1815). This medical doctor, who hailed from the Lake Constance region and received his doctorate in Vienna, initially enjoyed great success there with his magnetic cure, the effect of which he attributed to the concept of "animal magnetism," which he had developed. Unquestionably, he was a brilliant, charismatic self-marketer with a distinctive business acumen. On the other hand, he also offered free treatments for the poor throughout his life, and actually did so on a large scale. Eventually, however, he fell out of favor with the medical faculty of Vienna University and was forced to relocate to Paris.

There, he worked highly successfully over many years. Among his followers and patrons belonged, among many others, the French king and his consort, and the renowned general Lafayette. However, he was less well received by the medical establishment, which, like its Viennese colleagues, considered his methods to be mere charlatanry. Consequently, they persistently agitated and intrigued to get rid of this irritating outsider.

Finally, the pressure exerted by his adversaries showed effect. Fearing the looming French Revolution, Mesmer, now an established millionaire, returned to his German homeland. Travels to England and Italy followed, sojourns in Switzerland, as well as over and again in France.

Through his numerous public performances and "magnetic salons" in which he magnetized viewers and influenced them with powerful suggestions, he conveyed to the Western intellectual world a concept largely unknown to his epoch: namely, that the processes in the human body were by no means completely self-sufficient and autonomous in the manner of a soulless machine completely independent of the spirit, as the prevailing mechanistic image of nature and man claimed, but that the human spirit was able to exert a decisive influence on them. Thus diseases could be successfully treated without the use of drugs or external therapy aids.

In Mesmer's time, therapeutic treatments with magnets had already been around for some time, so he did not actually invent magnet therapy. Rather, his original achievement was to attribute the healing effect not to the metal magnets themselves, but to an innate human fluidum, the said animal magnetism. It is therefore a postulated internal energy that can be concentrated, controlled, and thus used in a targeted manner.

This concept, too, had many precursors spread across the world's cultures. Consider the *prana* of Indian yoga lore; the *chi* (*qi*) in Chinese acupuncture and martial arts; the *manas* of the Polynesians; the *n/um* of the San or !Kung bushmen of the Kalahari desert, etc. We can find similar concepts already rudimentarily in ancient Egypt and in many forms of shamanism. Mesmerism itself was to be followed by various other variants of the principle: *Vril* (Edward Bulwer-Lytton—after which the English meat extract was named "Bovril"), *Od* (Karl von Reichenbach), *astral light* (Eliphas Levi), electro-magnetism (Bardon), *Orgone* (Wilhelm Reich), and the *Magis* I myself so named. More generally, occult literature is replete with references to "vitality," "essence of life," etc. The spectrum of effects of the Mesmeric teachings and their later parallels ranges from radiesthesia, hermetic talismantics, and spiritual healing to positive thinking and the sexual magic of the OTO.

The reference to the historically antecedent, sometimes millennia-old precursors of the magical energy concept suggests that its chronological classification cannot be determined exactly. So it is quite conceivable that it came into being at about the same time as the spirit model of magic, possibly in parallel to it.

The magic energy model requires no spirits. Instead, the inner "subtle" energy, which is tagged with various names (see above), is regarded as the magically effective agent. It is assumed that it can also bring about magical effects in the field of coarse (i.e., non-subtle) matter if it is bundled, polarized, and directed accordingly. Just as it can be absorbed from the outside, for example by the elements, the planets, plants, and animals, it can also be projected outside: into objects, onto living entities, and onto life situations.

Here the magician is a choreographer of energy movements, who can do entirely without the help of subtle entities such as spirits.

The Psychological Model

The psychological model of magic also owes much to Anton Mesmer, albeit rather indirectly. Its influence comes to bear via the detour of (primarily medical) hypnotism and the depth psychology emerging toward the end of the nineteenth century. As we have seen, Mesmer had opened the eyes of his contemporaries to the fact that the strict separation between body and mind that Descartes had postulated until then was not really tenable on closer inspection. In this sense, he can also be regarded as a precursor of psychosomatic medicine that formally emerged only at the beginning of the twentieth century.

The first known representative of the psychological model of magic was the English artist and occultist Austin Osman Spare (1886–1956). Born in London, he was already obsessed with graphics, sketching, and painting at a young age, and he was able to celebrate great success early on. In later years, he would claim to have been the actual inventor of surrealism.

Celebrated exhibitions, academy scholarships, awards, an appointment as an official war painter in the First World War (from which he returned strongly traumatized by shell shock), editor of highly respected art magazines of his time—for a long time he was regarded as the great hope of English painting, until his star sank again, the sales of his works declined perceptibly, and he finally, financially bled white and shaken by personal crises, withdrew to the southern parts of the city at the end of the 1920s, where he spent the rest of his life, quite the ingenious eccentric, as a kind of urban semi-hermit under impoverished conditions in the run-down working-class districts of London.

He was extensively involved with automatic drawing, relished in using occult and magical symbols as well as ancient Egyptian iconography, and impressed Aleister Crowley himself, at least for a while, to whose order Argenteum Astrum he belonged as a probationer for two years, until he and the Master Therion split up in a quarrel. Crowley accordingly labeled him a "black brother," while Spare dismissed Crowley in turn as a pompous charlatan.

In his work *The Book of Pleasure (Self-Love): The Psychology of Ecstasy* (1913), which was strongly influenced by Taoism, Spare described, among many other things, the basic elements of his own magic system, which he would later develop further after World War II under the influence of his friend and sponsor, the English magician Kenneth Grant, who designated it the "Zos Kia Cultus."

His highly idiosyncratic, often very cryptic suggestions, mystified by his eccentric private language, were partly taken up again many years later by the chaos-magic order of the IOT in a kind of freestyle mode. In this *Book of Pleasure*, he also presented what was to remain his most lasting contribution to Western magic history to this day: sigil magic.

Despite all his fame as an artist, his influence on his occult contemporaries was actually minimal; he was stuck with being a kind of insider tip. In his late phase of social marginalization, he made ends meet by assembling and repairing radios, but occasionally he also carried out magical commissions, for example, for Gerald Brosseau Gardner (1884–1964), the founder of the Wicca cult. He exhibited his art with varying sales success almost only on his own initiative in pubs, not in regular galleries. It was not until the mid-1970s that the English magician, writer, and Crowley student Kenneth Grant (1924–2011), the founder and head of the New Isis Lodge and the Typhonian OTO, an offshoot of Crowley's OTO, discovered him and his work, and presented him to a wider occult public when he published his lavishly illustrated book *The Images and Oracles of Austin Osman Spare* (1975). Grant and his wife Steffi, who was also an artist, had met Spare shortly after World War II, sponsored him extensively, and encouraged a kind of renaissance of himself, thereby making a decisive contribution to reawakening both his artistic and magical ambitions. Inspired by this turn of events, he penned a number of other books, which, however, only appeared posthumously.

Spare's psychological approach has numerous facets. It is essentially based on Sigmund Freud's depth psychology, which he learned about relatively early by English standards. (It is commonly accepted that Freud is considered to be the real discoverer and pioneering theorist of the subconscious. However, he actually did not discover or invent it at all. In fact, the concept of the subconscious and the hidden forces and creative resources within it was really the dernier cri among psychological researchers, physicians, occultists, and spiritualists in Europe from about 1886—Spare's year of birth—till around 1910; instead, Freud systematized it, integrated it into a therapeutic superstructure, and finally made it academically acceptable.)

Spare takes up his observations and theories to create his own magical system without naming his source of inspiration.

In his sigil magic, the magician encodes sentences expressing his will graphically or acoustically beyond conscious recognition. This is how the individual, operation-specific sigils are created.

Next, they are "inoculated" into the subconscious mind in different ways with the help of trance techniques. Next, the practitioner has to forget them as fast as possible. It is the subconscious that is now responsible for the realization and manifestation of the magician's will. As Spare puts it: "Sigils will flesh", i.e., they strive to "incarnate."

Thus Spare turns Freud's theory of repression upside down. Once the Viennese psychiatrist had discovered that numerous neurotic behaviors in everyday life (e.g. ablutomania or washing compulsion) were a consequence of the suppression of traumatic and other unconscious psychological issues into the subconscious, Spare drew the following conclusion: if the subconscious can be made to cause unwanted coercive behavior and the resulting life situations by repression, it should also be possible to induce the subconscious to produce desired effects by employing targeted repression. Thus, after their "charge," the sigils represent a kind of programming of the subconscious caused by targeted suppression of their intended content.

According to Freud's teaching, the psyche essentially consists of the superego, the consciousness, the intermediate censor, and the subconscious. The censor's main task is to prevent unfiltered communication between consciousness and subconscious. It is therefore not enough simply to think up a will or wish: if this is found to be inadmissible by the moral censor, who is akin to a moralistic governess, he won't allow the will or wish to be anchored in the subconscious.

Spare avoids this very problem by first enciphering the formulated will or wish as described so that the censor cannot understand it and therefore cannot censor it. Thus the message is smuggled into the subconscious in the shape of an abstract sigil of no discernible content, effectively bypassing the censor. Since the subconscious was involved in the encoding process at least in an observing form—as in all human activity—and thus represents the "omniscient memory" of the individual, it is not difficult for this psychic agency to decipher or understand the instructions for action anchored in this manner. The oblivion to be effected after charging (actually: after uploading the encrypted message to the subconscious) is intended to ensure that the sentence of will won't rise again into consciousness in decoded form and provoke censor-related resistances.

The immediate goal of any sigil magic operation is furthermore "atavistic nostalgia" or "atavistic resurgence." By this, Spare indicates a reactivation of psychic atavisms that are latently present in humans. These atavisms are primal spiritual forces, remnants of earlier, mostly animal, stages of development.

"The soul," he later writes in his strange syntax, "is the ancestral animals. The body is their knowledge." Here, in addition to Freud, Darwin's doctrine of evolution is echoed, albeit very idiosyncratically and theosophically reinterpreted. These atavisms are also the executive agencies that implement the magical operation in the outside. The desire encapsulated in the sigil activates the corresponding atavism, thereby it becomes embodied, thus organic, and the body (Zos) in turn reifies it: thus it is manifested.

For the sake of completeness, it should be mentioned that, according to the statements of several of his friends, Spare reported several years later about a letter from Sigmund Freud in which he purportedly congratulated him on his Book of Pleasure and paid tribute to his deep, unique insight into the functioning of the subconscious. Spare also claimed that Freud had adopted some of his core ideas. Fiction or truth? After all, it is an undeniable fact that Spare sometimes tended to exaggerate and mythologize himself and his own achievements, and he was anything but averse to swaggering. In addition, he almost never drew a distinction between his inner and his outer life; dreams and visions were as real and objective to him as anything that occurred in the material world. In any case, so far such a correspondence between Freud and Spare could not be established by contemporary research.

After the collapse of the Golden Dawn, much of Anglo-Saxon magic, especially British magic, took a new direction in the twentieth century. Until well into the 1980s, apart from a few exceptions, most authors preferred a decidedly psychological approach: Israel Regardie (a former private secretary of Crowley's and himself a trained Jungian depth psychologist and psychoanalyst), Dion Fortune, Walter Ernest Butler, William Gray, Francis King, David Conway, and several more. Although they generally do not specifically fall back on the magic of Austin Osman Spare, they do have one thing in common with him: the core target of their magical approach is always to trim the subconscious (in today's more common Jungian diction: the unconscious) toward magic by suitable exercises to be repeated as often as possible, and by the simultaneous use of associated symbols as well as external stimuli and objects such as colors, scents, metals, precious stones, numeric structures, temple construction and design, ritual clothing, and of course invocations and conjuring formulas.

In the psychological model, therefore, neither the spirits nor the subtle energies are required to manifest magical effects because it is the subconscious or the unconscious alone that is deemed to be responsible for magical effects to be manifested. Accordingly, magic consists in successfully manipulating this mental agency.

Personally, I tend to refer to the psychological model as a pragmatic intermediate one, because it doesn't even begin to bother to really explain the way magic works, no matter how plausible or not such an explanation might prove to be. It solely defines the performing instance of magic, namely the subconscious/unconscious, without saying anything about the mechanics underlying this magical manifestation.

The Information Model

The information model of magic takes into account the core statement of information theory, which states that matter itself is "stupid": in order to structure itself in any orderly manner, it requires information. Only this informational input can put an end to the indeterminacy of the chaos state.

An example of this is a television tube which has not been set to a specific channel: the white noise to be perceived is generated by electrons that are distributed in a completely random and disorderly manner, i.e., chaotically. Only when they receive the corresponding information from the preset TV station will they sort themselves into recognizable images and patterns.

Accordingly, information magic is about bundling the necessary information in a structured way (so-called "clusters") and transferring it to a target object or receiver. The Cybermagic developed by me deals primarily with this. For example, knowledge of foreign languages or healing knowledge can be transferred from one magician to another, making it much easier for the recipient to expand their knowledge in the field in question in the future if the operation is successful: the acquisition of knowledge is much faster and often seems more like remembering than acquiring new data. Conversely, the magician can "suck" information from other living beings by activating it and transferring it to himself.

While this computer science-oriented concept may seem very modern and innovative, there is nothing really new under the sun and this view of matters is no exception.

For example, one of the standard practices of Indian spiritual schools is for the guru to come together with his designated successor for a joint meditation shortly before his demise. In the course of this immersive spiritual exercise, he will then transfer all his knowledge to the chela in a non-discursive form. From the outside, nothing at all seems to happen between the two, there isn't even so much as a conversation taking place, and as a rule this process will be conducted without any physical contact. Once the transmission is complete, the guru usually enters *mahāsamādhi* either immediately or soon after, leaving behind his mortal shell.

Tibetan "lineage holder" lamas follow a similar procedure when appointing their successors within the particular transmission line they happen to administer.

In ancient Greece, a related process was known. There it was a matter of the philosophical teacher, within the framework of education, transferring to the pupil his own *daimonium* or the sum total of his knowledge, life experience, and ethos, which would frequently be conducted in a sex-magical manner.

The fact that the respective traditions of these processes do not explicitly mention an information model shouldn't divert us from the fact that these processes are actually very similar in nature.

In this model, too, the magician renounces the elements and active instances used in the other approaches: neither the spirits nor the energies are needed, nor is there any manipulation or programming of the unconscious taking place.

The Metamodel

The metamodel, as its name implies, does not describe a specific approach to magic but rather the handling of the other models described above.

Its only requirement is quickly described: "Always work with the model that seems to be most suitable for the task at hand." There are no objectifiable or normative criteria for this; instead, the magician's individual suitability, inclination, and experience are decisive. For example, in the course of their practice they may find that they can heal best if working within the energy model. On the other hand, the sorceress may operate most successfully within the spirit model to influence a court hearing. If the wizard wants to ensure a successful final audit of his daughter, he decides, based on previous experience, on making use of the information model, and so on.

His magical colleague, on the other hand, could be quite different. She may prefer the energetic charge of a talisman for the successful academic exam of her child, heal most successfully with the help of the spirit model, and decide to work with the psychological model to achieve a desired court decision.

So it depends solely on the magician themself which model proves to be the most suitable and most promising.

Finally, as already mentioned, there are also hybrid forms and overlaps. For example, a magician may use one of his power animals (spirit model) to both lend a patient strength and balance his subtle energies (energy model). Likewise, he can first charge himself energetically (energy model) and protect himself in a separate action with the help of sigil magic (psychological model), before he attempts a demon evocation (spirit model).

It is obvious, however, that the practical handling of the metamodel will only succeed if the magician can resort to appropriate extensive experience. Any magician will hardly be able to successfully apply a model that they do not really know from their own experience.

By Way of Illustration: A Dialog

"Are there actually spirits?"

"In the spirit model, sure."

"And in the energy model?"

"That's only about actuating energies."

"So what about the psychological model, then?"

"There, it's solely about projecting actively manufactured contents of the unconscious into the outside world."

"So what do things look like in the information model?"

"In the information model, information clusters are crafted for controlling matter."

"Okay, but are there actually spirits now or not?"

"In the spirit model, sure."

As chaos magic posits: "Nothing is true—everything is permitted!"

Some Notes on Practical Application

The practical implementation of the various models as depicted through the burning glass of the metamodel requires only one basic condition: a precise knowledge of their respective procedures. The less theoretical and abstract, the more practical and tangible, the more promising the project will be. Those who work toward this goal have considerably more useful options for action at their disposal than those magicians who operate with one or, at best, two models alone—which, unfortunately, the vast majority of magical practitioners are currently still given to.

After all, the old truism that the map should never be confused with the landscape still applies. The concept of the 4+1 models, as presented above, serves mainly as an illustration and guidance. It cannot and will not replace the experience of practical inspection.

Pushing On

It can also be used to create a plausible, coherent training system, even one in which the magician, the mage herself, holds the reins and progresses at exactly the pace that best suits her needs and abilities. All doors are open for trials and experiments.

Here are two examples.

A Training Curriculum

(12 months)

Month #1

- Week #1: Working in the spirit model
- Week #2: Working in the energy model
- Week #3: Working in the psychological model
- Week #4: Working in the information model

Month #2

- Week #1: Working in the spirit model
- Week #2: Working in the energy model
- Week #3: Working in the psychological model
- Week #4: Working in the information model

... etc. up to and including *Month # 12*

In this way, a rich experience routine develops, revealing the respective strengths and weaknesses of each model. At the same time the changeover between the models is trained extensively.

An Experimental Curriculum
(6 months)
   Month #1
   - Week #1: Healing (spirit model)
   - Week #2: Healing (energy model)
   - Week #3: Healing (psychological model)
   - Week #4: Healing (information model)

   Month #2
   - Week #1: Clairvoyance (spirit model)
   - Week #2: Clairvoyance (energy model)
   - Week #3: Clairvoyance (psychological model)
   - Week #4: Clairvoyance (information model)

… etc.: proceed abiding by the same structure, e.g. *Month #3*: Remote interference; *Month #4*: Money spell; *Month #5*: Procurement of specific objects; *Month #6*: Acquisition of knowledge or hard-to-come-by intelligence.

In this manner, it will become clear how the various models are proving themselves in different areas. At the same time, the process will show you which models seem to be most suitable for certain tasks subjectively.

The above implementation plans are merely suggestions: they can be modified as required, be it in terms of frequency, duration, sequence, or content—but once decided upon, they should be implemented consistently.

Chapter 21
Political Dimensions of Magic

Josef Knecht

If there is a tendency to rail against all spiritual movements because they are alleged to be "apolitical," then magic will certainly be perceived as a particularly unworldly activity. But that's simply not true.

For these musings, I generally assume an understanding of "politics" that is not limited to the current party politics and their media echo chambers. Instead, any action that takes place within a social context and refers to it is regarded as political here.

To this effect, we will first of all have to take a look at what magic does to the person who works with it and how they are changed in the process.

In her work *Dreaming the Dark* (see bibliography at the end of this chapter) the Californian witch Starhawk makes the distinction between "power from within" and "power over," a critical distinction within the English language.

According to Starhawk's understanding, magic is generally not suitable for exercising power over others, since it has its source solely in the unconscious, in the deeper self, and is subject to its own laws. This may at first seem surprising, seeing that all pertinent fantasy narratives combine the exercise of magic and sorcery with the execution of power. And in Harry Potter's world there is even an entire dedicated government department for sorcery.

In our reality, however, there are more effective methods of exercising power and manipulating the will of others than the relatively elaborate exercise of magic, which is also more often than not quite unreliable and whose effects can hardly be scaled to very large masses of people, or replicated as often as desired.

One could, of course, define the concept of magic so broadly that it encompasses influencing of people by means of propaganda, medial brainwashing, etc. as well. But that would only misguide the discussion at hand and shall hence be avoided here.

As a technique of shaping, strengthening, and expanding consciousness that predominantly emanates from the individual or the small group, magic is, however, highly suitable as an aid to resistance against politically repressive claims and systems.

"I define magic as the art of changing consciousness at will. According to that definition, magic encompasses political action, which is aimed at changing consciousness and thereby causing change" (*Dreaming the Dark*, p. 13).

Why is this important, and why should it be considered at all in the context of this collection of essays? What relevance does it have for spiritual practice?

On the one hand it is, of course, decisive for immediate political reasons, because even magically or otherwise, spiritually active people usually do not live alone in some wilderness but within social communities, hence they are influenced by their developments and are subjected to certain framework conditions. When spiritual freedom is restricted and life is more and more supervised down into the private sphere, the application of any spiritual practice becomes more laborious and, in the worst case, also hazardous at some point. We therefore have a fundamental interest in participating in the preservation of the most open and livable political conditions possible. This can—depending on specific interests and individual character makeup—demand eminently variable forms, but every activity aiming at the social realm will profit immensely from a well-trained consciousness, clarity of goals, and an adequately coordinated inner power structure, all of which constitute essential components of personal magical development.

On the other hand, the ideological environment should not be underestimated as a decisive factor in terms of one's own practice. The beliefs with which I grow up and which are considered universally binding have a considerable influence on what the censor of the unconscious allows to happen and what is filtered out, regardless of whether we consciously adhere to it or not. I remember a book title from the '90s: *Shaman in the Guts, Christian in the Head* (in German: *Schamanin im Bauch, Christin im Kopf. Frauen*

Asiens im Aufbruch—see bibliography at the end of this chapter). In it, an East Asian woman talks about her spiritual development, in the course of which she had to discover that her Christian education had never reached her deeper strata and that she was still filled in-depth with the shamanic religiosity of her homeland. That sounded good in the '90s. For us Central Europeans, however, the opposite is usually true: the magical or shamanic view of the world, which we encounter at the earliest during puberty if not much later, often takes place only in our heads, while the deeper layers of the unconscious continue to be determined either by the established forms of Christianity or by a fundamental disbelief and doubts about everything that is "between heaven and earth" as we have inherited it from the Age of Enlightenment.

Both prove to be very obstructive in magical practice and consume a lot of energy by way of resistance and doubt. Therefore, it is very useful to deal with this early on and to strive for an inner distance to the given ideological framework, which always has political consequences as we liberate ourselves from our intellectual-cultural straitjacket. Collective patterns of thought, feeling, and behavior exert a strong binding force that should not be under-estimated, because the more these influences are repressed, the more dependent we become on them. This is shown in a very naive way, for example, by Satanists who believe that their cult has escaped the established religion to a particularly far extent. In actual fact, however, it usually constitutes merely an internal counter-movement, an essentially Christian reaction of defiance that still remains shackled to the same view of the world and solely adopts its opposite polarity. At the end of the day, Anti-Christianity is still Christianity.

In this sense, magic can justifiably be seen as a stronghold of the subversive and a bulwark against the disenchantment of the world. Interestingly, in the rejection of the esoteric, the occult, the unbound spiritual and—worst of all—the magical, the Christian churches and the secular powers shake hands. For different reasons, admittedly, but just as vehemently, everything is antagonized and defamed by both sides that can neither be integrated within scientism nor within the Christian church.

Magic is only tolerated on the fictional level and can solely be lived out in the fantasy of novels, games, and cinema, thereby, however, becoming more and more excessive. Never before has the market for books and movies been so inundated with magical and mythical figures, powers, and stories as it is today. One might well be given to suspect that this is a welcome distraction of the subversive forces of ideological unease in a barren, disenchanted, and ultimately disappointing world with little worth living for. This, by the way, has always been the case in the European and many other traditions. There was plenty of magic in myths and fairy tales, all legends were replete with it. But if it dared to tangibly manifest itself in live social reality, it was at least viewed with suspicion or straightforwardly persecuted.

Magic is always about self-empowerment. It does not turn against anyone in particular and only wants to be able to pursue its own goals in peace. But it seems that magical individualism is always being perceived as turning against a centrally controlled world. Recourse to one's own forces and one's own thinking gives freedom; and from a certain political perspective freedom is always regarded with apprehension and rejection and, in case of doubt, suppressed.

Among the accusations against magic, the ethical or moral dimension always played a major role. Magic has invariably been considered morally reprehensible, even evil. The magical and witchcraft-based tradition owes most of its mortal casualties to it. The last stakes may have cooled down by now, but the campaigns against alternative medicine in recent years indicate that the fundamental attitude of some of our contemporaries has hardly changed at all.

Indeed the ethics of an independent spirituality or magic rests on a fundamentally different groundwork than the predominant conventional one: their guiding principle of ethical action is not defined by obeying authorities or principles, but by integrity, the inner conformity of action with one's own convictions. This may sound abstract at first, but it has essential practical consequences, since all actions are based on an entirely different motivation than the conventional one.

The concept of "not getting caught," for example, completely loses its meaning here because there is no acceptable authority other than one's own conviction that could evaluate, i.e., judge, one's behavior. It also means that I would always act in the same manner, regardless of whether someone was watching me or not. (Unless I intend something to occur within the observer that is in accordance with my own will.) And my actions are also independent of their effect. "What's the point? It doesn't change anything" is no longer a meaningful counterargument if I stand up for something. It is only of import that my commitment is coherent for me and reflects my attitude.

Integrity as an inner compass means to always remain in harmony with the inner core, be it when talking or when taking action. This core, of course, needs to be recognized and realized as such in the first place. To do this independently of possible advantages or disadvantages lends us great inner strength and commitment toward others. It also implies an end to all whining and self-pity, since life and fate are not passively endured but experienced as an expression of one's own deeper will—ideally, at any rate.

A well-known example of such ethics is Crowley's "Do what thou wilt shall be the whole of the Law." Often misinterpreted as an invitation to hedonistic arbitrariness, this formula points precisely to such inner integrity. If acting according to arbitrary and hedonistic impulses actually corresponds to my inner conviction, then of course this will by inference also be the only yardstick, but even in this case it will be free from hypocrisy, trickery, and inner conflict—and also bereft of self-pity when consequences occur as one would expect. Usually, however, the deepest convictions of healthy and sane people will be of a different nature and will equally be socially quite well anchored ("Love is the law …").

But whatever the beliefs may be in detail, integrity is integrity and always accords much greater strength, concentration, and clarity than obedient compliance and moral codes will. And this is exactly what every form of magic and spiritual development is all about: releasing as much strength and concentration as possible for one's own actions and avoiding fruitless ambivalence and inner resistance, to drain energy from the superego.

When reading a title that combines politics and magic, many conventionally biased readers will probably first associate the machinations of Freemasons and secret societies pulling the strings in the background and manipulating the world to their advantage by means of dark rituals. As much as historians have always tried to deal with this fascinating topic over and again, they have never brought to light anything concrete or verifiable supporting this view. Either the secret societies are really secret, or they don't exist in this form outside the Illuminati novels. In either case, there's nothing much to talk about. We will refrain from individual influences of political adventurers such as Sebottendorf—as discussed here in the chapter on letter magic[35]—because they do not constitute a systematic phenomenon, being, from a historical point of view, merely anecdotal figures.

As sobering as this may be, there are nevertheless considerable other influences impacting the development of society that emanate from magical thinking. "In the seventeenth century, the mechanist view of the world as composed of dead, inert, isolated particles was still being challenged by views expressed in systems of magic, such as alchemy, astrology, hermeticism, cabbalism, and ritual magic," Starhawk writes in *Dreaming the Dark* (p. 216). This counter-position then continuously lost strength for two hundred years until, in the middle of the twentieth century, a secular, scientifically oriented, and rationalistic culture prevailed in all industrialized countries. The great successes of modern technology and medicine simply spoke for themselves, and the hopes of young people were directed more toward conquering distant worlds with material spaceships than toward exploring the inner world, or even imaginatively immersing oneself in archaic myths.

This movement lost its dominance in the 1950s when the hippie movement set completely new accents, first in the USA and then in Europe, challenging the prevailing materialist paradigm. Certainly there were forerunners in Romanticism and Art Nouveau, but they were not threatening the established worldview because they continued to fit rather well into the bourgeois world. The hippies, and with them the wave of expansion of consciousness through drugs and other psychological means, no longer did so.

At the moment, it seems as if the setback of the materialistic forces is gaining the upper hand worldwide, but I tend to opine that this is the last twitch of a sinking paradigm, which can admittedly cause a lot of damage and make a lot of noise. But the "re-enchantment of the world" in the sense of Berman's book from the '80s cannot be stopped. Even though the mechanistic image of the world still presents itself arrogantly and power-consciously to the outside world, it has long since run out of business and lost its plausibility philosophically, scientifically, medically, and socially, and way before the dramatic ecological consequences of this predominant mindset became indisputably obvious.

---

35. See chapter 18, "German Letter Magic: History, Systems, Field Reports."

Since the end of the twentieth century, we have seen the return of magical and mythical ideas in countless novels and films. The fantasy genre is booming almost unceasingly, and even technically highly equipped science fiction sagas can no longer do without magic. Nothing reflects more clearly what occupies people's imagination and dreams than mainstream movies and novels.

Materialism has tried to distort the essence and perception of people completely, disappointing and ignoring their very hopes and needs. The time is clearly ripe again for a worldview that suits us and the world, and for this reason it will undoubtedly prevail again.

Bibliography

Berman, Morris. *The Reenchantment of the World.* Ithaca, NY: Cornell University, 1981.

Chung, Hyun Kyung, with the assistance of Dorothea Dilschneider. *Schamanin im Bauch, Christin im Kopf.* Frauen Asiens im Aufbruch. Stuttgart: Kreuz Verlag, 1992.

Crowley, Aleister. *The Book of the Law.* 1904.

Evans, Arthur. *Witchcraft and the Gay Counterculture.* Boston: Fag Rag Books, 1978.

LaVey, Anton Szandor. *The Satanic Bible.* New York: Avon Books, 1969.

Marks, Stephan. *Hüter des Schlafes. Politische Mythologie.* Berlin: Hofgarten Verlag, 1983.

Simos, Miriam/Starhawk. *Dreaming the Dark: Magic, Sex and Politics.* Boston: Beacon Press, 1982.

Chapter 22

The Magician in Revolt:
Powerlessness as Scandal

Frater U∴D∴

There is an essential difference between religion and magic that is rarely reflected upon. Religion is always affirmative in one form or another: be it that it positively approves of the world as a whole, be it that, while it may define the here and now perhaps as a vale of tears and an uncomely transitory station through which life passes, it awards the following hereafter on the other hand all the more encomium and promissory utopian value. In any case, it pays homage to its deities and defines man as a secondary, subservient being who is utterly at their mercy.

Even if via earthly good conduct man is finally promised eternal life in the glory of God, becoming one with Godhead or the never-ending pleasures of paradises beyond, this does nothing to change the fundamental equation "Godhead first—man second." Thus, on the one side there is power, on the other powerlessness, clamped down for all time. Man must submit unconditionally to this hierarchy; everything else is but blasphemous sacrilege.

Wherever magic was domesticated by religion, which is invariably the case in all so-called high religions, it seconds this affirmation as a matter of course. Indeed, magic is only regarded admissible if it agrees with the divine will, however defined, and thus subordinates itself to it and participates in the divine plan postulated by priesthood and theologians. It is then happily ennobled as "high magic" that should at best unfold its effect in cosmic terms and as related to the salvation of the believers' souls, but as good as never in profane everyday dimensions.

Her shabby little sister is "low" magic, which suffered very badly under the predominant representatives of the religious and secular hierarchies, often even being extremely brutally persecuted: a discipline that dedicates itself primarily to coping with everyday life. (In today's magic literature it is usually betokened, less derogatory, "success magic.") In view of its central importance, we have dedicated a separate chapter to this fundamental problem in this book.[36]

It is, at the very latest, since serious shamanism research took its hold that we may assume that magic and magical thinking actually preceded ritually organized religion in history, to all likelihood indeed even by thousands of years. Hunting, protection, and healing spells are fundamental survival techniques of nomadic tribal cultures. In this sense they are, like the rest of "low" magic, craft instruments for mastering mundane life unencumbered by metaphysical-spiritual or moral-ethical, i.e., religious, salvific demands.

In spite of its almost total appropriation by conventional religions, "low" magic has survived, at least in significant remnants within the framework of folk magic as well as in covert subversive spiritual currents: despised by the elites, fought against, menaced with torture and the death penalty or, unless otherwise possible, tolerated grudgingly at most, it was yet never entirely exterminated. And so we can still find it in scientistically- and materialistically-dominated cultures such as ours today: repressed, marginalized, and condemned to a subcultural underground existence, but quite virulent nevertheless, and anything but extinct. Staying alive and kicking is the low magician's fundamental remit, after all.

The terms "survival technology" and "coping with everyday life" refer to one of man's core problems, namely humankind's fundamental impotence. Man enters the developmental stage as a rational being, increasingly capable of reflection, who sees himself at the mercy of his environment. Gravity, metabolism, physical- and health-related fragility, the never-ending necessity to procure daily sustenance, and the abundant perils of nature: scarcity of hunting spoils, threats from predators, storms and lightning strikes, earthquakes and volcanic eruptions, meteorite impacts, deluges, conflagrations, periods of drought, frost and searing heat, famines, poisonous plants and

36. See my analysis in chapter 1, "Folk Magic vs. Library Magic: Genetics or Enlightenment? Of Low, High, Black, and White Magic."

fungi, as well as contaminated food, climate and environmental changes, diseases and epidemics, accidents, and, last but not least, brutal conflicts with rival groups of people, finally his own mortality—his chances of survival are infinitesimally small indeed, considering his unavoidable death, they are ultimately zero. Thus humanity's existence has always teetered—and teeters still—on a knife's edge.

From the very beginning, magic may have been the result of human efforts to face this powerlessness. In principle, it doesn't differ from other cultural techniques and crafts. Whether it is the development of hunting techniques and weapons; the manufacture of weatherproof clothing; the use of fire to generate heat, prepare food, and deter predators; the construction of safe housing; the manufacture of tools, vessels, and receptacles; the development of trade, barter, and means of transport as well as the associated skills of navigation and social organization—the discovery and maintenance of magical processes is a seamless part of *Homo faber*'s effort to wrest from his environment what it is unable or unwilling to offer him voluntarily within the overall context of the struggle for survival.

In contrast to mundane craftsmanship, however, magic deals with the invisible, materially and sensitively incomprehensible world of spirits, with subtle or immaterial energies, with the processes of chance and its hidden laws. In a later stage of civilization, the "Secret Doctrines" are hence not labeled such primarily because they must be kept secret from the uninitiated but because they deal with what happens in the secret realm, what is not immediately perceptible.

In this sense alone, magical action can be viewed as an act of revolt against the world as-is: the magician or sorceress does not accept their own powerlessness unchallenged, and does not allow themself to succumb to fate, to be knuckled down by the prevailing conditions, or by any other power, for that matter. They both confront the actual state of the world with its desirable state: purely secular and world-based. The success magician coldly refers the question as to whether this may possibly violate some "divine plan" as claimed by whomever to the priest or the mystic. At best, the magic gang are interested in this issue only in terms of how it may technically confront them with obstacles or possible counterforces, and how to deal with these effectively.

The opponents of magic in the religious and mystical camp will ever and again reproach it for seducing man into megalomania. Apart from individual exceptions typically based on specific pathological personality structures, however, the exact opposite is actually the case. In his essay on the dangers of mysticism, Aleister Crowley pointed out a century ago that it is by no means the allegedly humble and modest mystic, but rather the magician, who is constantly confronted with his own limits. Whereas the mystic expeditiously unites himself with the "Absolute," thereby adopting all its fain attributes and simply shaking off his human limitations as in an act of metaphysical legerdemain, the magician, on the other hand, has to deal with his failure over and again. And no matter how many operations he may succeed in accomplishing, the limits of his prowess are always all too obvious. He, the Great One, writes Crowley, the Ruler of the Universe, is incapable of running a mile in three minutes. While it may be that many magicians are initially driven by a childish or romantic mania of omnipotence, realistically this remains pure wishful thinking. In addition, it also primarily characterizes the beginner and almost never the experienced magus.

However, in pre-religious, non-cultic magic, this reflected self-criticism has nothing to do with cringing submission to the divine, purportedly superior powers. When all is said and done, man stands here quite simply set against the gods, assuming that the existence of the latter is accepted at all.

This tendency can also be found in the ancient philosophical and theological speculations regarding theurgy. For a long time, researchers were agreed that ancient theurgy was a sort of magical "compelling the gods": the magician should be able to make the gods subservient to his will through his art. This interpretation, however, can no longer be seriously defended in view of the current state of research. Instead, the present prevailing consensus describes theurgy (literally "work of God"), far less belligerently, as an essentially tame system of religious rites and practices to connect with and receive help from divine beings.

However, the earlier interpretation of theurgy as an aggressive compulsion of the gods was by no means contrived out of thin air. The view of the theurge as the subjugator of the gods did actually exist, even if it remained a minority doctrine. Here the late antique Neoplatonist Maximos of Ephesus (ca. 310–372 CE) comes to mind, who was already in his early years a close friend, advisor, and teacher of the later-to-be Roman emperor Julian. As an oracle reader and miracle worker, Maximos caused quite a stir. Legend has it that he was also a commissioned magician, a trade that was generally frowned upon by the Neoplatonists of his day. It is well known that he followed Julian's imperial call to the court at Constantinople despite highly unfavorable omens, remarking that he would nonetheless fulfill his duty and that, by the way, it was quite possible to force the favor of the gods. It was probably mainly thanks to his influence that the originally Christian-baptized emperor finally turned away from Christianity and restored traditional Roman paganism as the state religion (hence his sobriquet "Julian the Apostate"). This undertaking proved to be a short-lived attempt, however, as Julian died in 363, after a regrettably short reign, of a battle wound on his Persian campaign, on which he was, by the way, accompanied by loyal Maximos. In our context, however, it is interesting to note that the ancient view of theurgy as a constraint on the gods was by no means without massive, eminently tangible political influence.

More importantly, in Maximos we have a historically documented, prominent magician who on the one hand was fully integrated into the society of a major civilization, even acting as imperial advisor to the court in the highest honors, and yet maintained an unabashedly contrarian attitude toward the gods of his time based on—magic.

With the emergence of sedentary civilizations, organized religions, and their priesthood castes, the unbiased, self-evident deployment of success magic as an indispensable survival technology had lost its societal traction. For it could not be reconciled with the affirmatory reflex already discussed of state-supporting, conformist cults stabilizing the societal power hierarchies and their fundamental affirmation of the world. In Greek antiquity, magic or sorcery (*goēteía*) therefore had a very bad reputation, in general being considered highly immoral. In Rome it was indeed proscribed under the death penalty. Maximos himself was initially tried in 363 for sorcery against both Emperor Valentian I and Emperor Valens, but the charges were eventually dropped due to lack of evidence. Almost a decade later he unwisely interpreted an oracle for a group of conspirators to the disadvantage of Emperor

Valens, whereupon he was first banished to his hometown of Ephesus for supporting the conspiracy, and eventually executed there.

Although equating magic with evil devil's work threatening society as a whole is quite typical for Abrahamic religions, it is also found in other cultures in a correspondingly modified form, ancient Greece and Rome being but two examples. What culminated in the bloody persecution of witches over hundreds of years in the European-Christian context is still reflected today, for example, in the vehement aversion of Hindu orthodoxy in India to magical sadhus, a bias that even shapes the Indian entertainment industry: in contemporary Bollywood cinema, for example, the figure of the yogi, flat out equated with the sadhu, is usually an insidious villain who deserves to be bludgeoned. In Western sensational media, the old fairy tale of the "satanic magician," which has been a common trope since the late medieval Witch Hammer, is boiled up at regular intervals. As a rule, the only accurate base for this is the fundamental spirit of rebellion against the status quo, embodied in Christian mythology by the "fallen angel" Lucifer, whose battle cry *Non serviam!* ("I will not serve!") is also prevalent in forms of magic not appropriated by established religiosity whenever its practitioners refuse to resign themselves to the perennial scandal of human impotence and mortality.

Finally, the magician manifests himself in revolt wherever he breaks taboos from a conventional point of view: for example, in the tantric sexual magic of *vamachara* and the *aghora* practices of India, in Jewish necromancy, in medieval demon evocation within the Christian context, or the conjuration of jinnies in heretical Islamic sorcery. The Greco-Egyptian magical papyri and the magical side of ancient Gnosticism are also worth mentioning here. In addition, the amoral-technocratic postmodern chaos magic and, finally, the dialectical fundamental critique of both conventional magic and the commonly prevailing narrative of human reality as proposed by Ice Magic are cases in point.

The bottom line remains this: although the aspect of magic as a subversive "ontology guerrilla" should perhaps not be overemphasized, there are numerous examples indicating that magicians do not allow themselves to be uncomplainingly classified into the herd of system-compliant, conformist subjects and "average citizens."

They counter the silence of these intimidated lambs with the trumpeting roar of their barbaric names of evocation, with the frosty, oyster-eyed calculus of their sigils, the exalted guffaw of their techniques of ecstasy, their thundering runes, their unreserved negation of ekpyrosis, and their never ever bridgeable, contourless foreignness.

Chapter 23
Magic and Astrology

Harry Eilenstein

Magic and astrology are important elements of "non-physics based world-views" that have been combined in various ways in the course of history.

Astrology is used, for example, to find "auspicious times" for a magical enterprise. This practice has a long tradition in different cultures, but it doesn't always work the way one would like it as "chance" or "contingency" will often prevent the planned action from actually taking place at the time and in the way it should. It's usually no big problem to perform a sweat lodge ceremony exactly on a full Moon to use the tension of the Sun-Moon opposition for the ritual, but more specific astrological wishes can sometimes not be realized.

To take an example, there once was an astrologically minded couple who wanted a child—but no Scorpio! The two employed contraception in a manner making a Scorpio birth extremely unlikely, but then it happened that a Scorpio birth became indeed conceivable nevertheless. So the woman did everything she could to ensure that the birth would still take place in the sign Libra, but despite all labor-inducing gymnastics, it simply didn't work out. And so the child was actually born a double Scorpio (sun sign and rising sign).

As with magic in general, the external events don't only correspond to the magical desire but to the overall picture of the magician's psyche—and a great apprehension of Scorpios leads to summoning a Scorpio into one's life.

In addition to this application of astrology as a tool to promote the effectiveness of magic, there is also the possibility of looking at a person's style of magic through the lens of their chart.

To facilitate the understanding of the following astrological representations, here is a brief description of the most important astrological elements.

A horoscope is like a stage play: the ascendant is the set, the planets are the actors, the signs of the zodiac are the roles of the actors, the houses are the areas of life in which the actors are active, and the aspects between them are the script. The conscious self should take over the role of the director, and if they don't know what to do, they can turn to the playwright: to their own soul.

The ascendant is one of the twelve signs of the zodiac that also represent the roles of the actors (planets).

The planets: Moon the little child, Mercury the pupil, Venus the youth, Sun the king, Mars the warrior, Jupiter the manager, Saturn the keeper, Uranus the inventor, Neptune the artist and Pluto the magician.

The signs of the zodiac: the spontaneous Aries, the bon vivant Taurus, the curious Gemini, the sensitive Cancer, the egocentric Leo, the artisan Virgo, the aesthetic Libra, the intense Scorpio, the idealistic Sagittarius, the realistic Capricorn, the intellectual Aquarius and the trusting Pisces.

The astrological houses: the here and now of the first house, the possession of the second house, the encounters of the third house, the home of the fourth house, the self-expression of the fifth house, the workshop of the sixth house, the living room of the seventh house, the battle arena of the eighth house, the viewpoint of the ninth house, the administration office of the tenth house, the clubhouse of the eleventh house, and the village square of the twelfth house.

The aspects: the marriage of the conjunction, the friendship of the trine, the acquaintance of the sextile, the separation of the square, the complementary opposition of the opposition, the constant rearrangement of the quincunx, and the endless development of the semi sextile.

So what do the planets do in magic?

The Moon stands, among other things, for the life force and for the inner images.

Mercury stands for the understanding and use of language in magic.

Venus stands for emotion and therefore also for a good part of motivation—at a certain point you can't progress any further in magic or meditation without emotions.

The Sun stands for the ego, which is why it describes the role of the person concerned within magic.

Mars stands for energy, which is why you can tell from its position how active someone is in magic.

Jupiter stands for organization and therefore for the tendency to join an order or to set up a new magic system.

Saturn stands for life experience, worldview, and firm rules, which can also be found, among other things, in a magical order.

Uranus stands for the sudden, the new, and the spontaneous, an essential part of magic that, from Uranus' point of view, could also be described as "doing the impossible."

Neptune stands for the connection to the whole, for the dissolution, the expansion—the four "boundless states" as e.g. Buddha describes them.

Pluto stands for one-directionality and transformation and is therefore one of the most essential planets in magic.

It is, of course, not possible to describe all possible nuances of magic in the horoscope within the framework of a limited chapter in this book. The forty-five possible formations of pairs within the group of ten planets alone would be too much—apart from the fact that there are 315 different encounters between two planets in seven different astrological aspects (conjunction, semi-sextile, sextile, square, trine, quincunx, opposition). And this doesn't even take into account the signs of the zodiac and the houses!

Hence, the following considerations can only give a first impression of how to proceed.

- The ascendant describes the general view of magic.
- in the here and now, Aries does what they want.
- Taurus seeks the beneficial.
- Gemini simply tries out everything.
- Cancer protects the life force in their own family circle.
- Leo uses magic for self-expression.
- Virgo uses it above all for healing.
- Libra wants to create encounters and harmony with magic.

- Scorpio strives for maximum intensity through magic.
- For Sagittarius, magic is a tool for improving the world.
- Capricorn uses magic to consolidate the desirable state.
- Aquarius uses magic to bring their utopia to reality.
- Pisces tunes themself into the magic of life.

These descriptions all refer to the ascendant and not to the sun sign, i.e., the position of the Sun in the chart.

The planets in the first house of the birth chart work in a similar way since they participate in everything the person concerned does:

The Moon sees the actual essence of magic in the handling of the life force—it should quite simply produce the living state.

Mercury sees the use of magic names and mantras and magic formulas as the alpha and omega of magic—for him, words are the carriers of magic power.

Venus concentrates on the emotions—magic leads to the desired result, if the emotions are contradiction-free and intensive.

The Sun sees its own will as the measure of all things—even in magic, which is therefore above all self-expression and self-representation.

Mars focuses on concrete action and is thus oriented toward motivation, strength, struggle, and generally toward action and tangible experience—including in magic.

Jupiter emphasizes the side of productive construction in magic, i.e., the pursuit of an intention, a goal, a master plan.

Saturn emphasizes the rules, the cooperation, the order structure, the tradition, the instructions by experienced teachers, the following of instructions in grimoires and yoga books and the like.

Uranus wants to reach the goal by a leap, i.e., he practices magic as the triggering of sudden changes—magic, for Uranus, is the working of miracles.

Neptune feels into the world and acts in harmony with the whole, he lets the whole act through himself and even sees his own personality as a pattern in the whole, which is not separated from the whole by its substance.

Pluto transforms; he is the sorcerer among the planets, he has one-directionality, he knows and experiences and lives the essence of life.

The character of the eight different aspects is quite striking as well:

- The **conjunction** (0°) is like a marriage—a firm connection of similar things.
- The **semi-sextile** (30°) is like a next step—the endless development of all things.
- The **sextile** (60°) is like an acquaintance—a loose connection of like-minded people.
- The **square** (90°) is like a tent pole—the separation of things that belong together but which are aligned differently.
- The **trine** (120°) is like a friendship—a firm connection of different things.
- The **quincunx** (150°) is a tidying up and tension—the constant new grasp of the omnipresent.
- The **opposition** (180°) is a swing—a set of supplementary opposites vibrating in rhythm.
- The **isolation** (-°) is the lack of aspect to other planets—an independent solo.

From the ascendant and from the planets in the first house, of course, there is also a connection to certain deities, which one then prefers to call upon in magic. In the following overview some deities repeatedly are listed with various zodiac signs/planets. This is because deities usually have a more complex character than mere zodiac signs or planets. This synopsis is, of course, only a suggestion and by no means a comprehensive list.

Aries/Mars: Pan, creator deities, war gods, Ares, Indra, Mars, Rudra, Cernunnos as fertility god, Freyr, Khnum

Taurus/Venus: Aphrodite, Venus, Mother Earth, Freyr, Freya, Demeter, Persephone

Gemini/Mercury: Hermes, Mercury, Alcis, Ashvins, trickster deities like Loki, Iktomi and Ananse

Cancer/Moon: Mother Earth, Luna, Moon, Isis, Hathor, Maria, Tezcatlipoca, Demeter, Pte-san-win, Thoeris, Hapi

Leo/Sun: Zeus, Tyr, Papaios, Belenus, Lugh, Sun, Christ, Osiris, Dhyaus

Virgo/Mercury: Lugh lamfadha, Mercury, Weyland, Hephaestos, Vulcan, Persephone

Libra/Venus: Apollo, Baldur, Bragi, Venus, Orpheus, Dagda as harpist, Ma'at

Scorpio/Mars/Pluto: Odin, Pan, Dionysus, Shiva, Mars, Pluto, Ananse, Iktomi, Loki, Lucifer, Devil, Persephone, Orpheus, Christ, Xipe tlaloc, Quetzal-coatl, Sebek, Osiris

Sagittarius/Jupiter: Zeus, Dagda, Shiun, Vishnu, Dhyaus, Tyr, Odin, Tuncashila

Capricorn/Saturn: Cronos, Reaper, Saturn, Creator Gods, Geb, Ptah

Aquarius/Saturn/Uranus: Wambli, Iktomi, Loki as cunning inventor, Saturn, Uranus

Pisces/Jupiter/Neptune: Brahma, Wakan tanka, Jupiter, Neptune, Poseidon

A phenomenon that is quite easy to observe is the handling of the life force represented by the Moon. Of course, everyone has their life force (if you want to apply this model), but everyone has a different style of dealing with it, too.

People with the Moon at the ascendant usually have a strong tendency to get the moods of other people. The Moon is also the psyche, the subconscious, the closeness, the dreams, the sensitivity…

With a conjunction, a trine, or a sextile between Moon and Neptune, the psyche (Moon) is opened to the outside (Neptune), which means that these people are very receptive to telepathic perceptions. If a conjunction, a trine, a sextile, or an opposition from one of these two planets to Mars is added, this telepathy also becomes active, i.e., these people can not only perceive telepathically, but also send out thoughts and images themselves.

If these two or three planets are connected by squares, quincunxes, or semi-sextiles, the same abilities abound, but they are less easy to steer, more volatile, or will only occur in emergency situations. This general quality of these three aspects applies to all planetary combinations.

Mars in this Moon/Neptune/Mars constellation probably also describes a tendency to telekinesis—but I'm afraid I haven't studied that subject thoroughly enough yet to expound any further on it.

Since every human has the Moon in their birth chart, obviously everybody can learn telepathy. Even if the Moon stands isolated, i.e., has no aspects to other planets, this is possible. In this case, one simply has to deal with one's own life force again and again through dream journeys, meditations, life force guidance, kundalini yoga, rune incantation, letter magic exercises, pranayama, etc. in order to become familiar with it and to learn how to deal with it consciously.

When the Moon is connected to Uranus, the life force phenomena such as telepathy, telekinesis, consecrations, healings (e.g. with the help of Reiki) etc. become more spontaneous and are less easy to plan. Instead of the "touch" of Neptune, a sudden change occurs in Uranus.

In combination with Pluto, the Moon becomes more intense and ready for fundamental transformation—everything is staked on one card.

To understand the attitude of a person to magic, the relationship between the four outer planets—Saturn, Uranus, Neptune and Pluto—is essential:

- Pluto is the one-directionality that makes magic effective.
- Neptune is the dissolution of the boundaries through which consciousness can connect with its goal.
- Uranus is the leap beyond the limits of what is physically possible.
- Saturn constitutes precisely these limits of the familiar, beyond which the three trans-saturnians transcend.

The basis for the magic attitude of all people today is the sextile between Pluto and Neptune, which has existed since 1942 and will continue doing so until 2039. This means that all people born after 1942 have this aspect in their chart. In the beginning, this aspect was still imprecise, i.e., with a deviation of 5°, but then it quickly became more exact.

When the first people with this Pluto/Neptune-sextile turned about 20 years old, they started to create a new magical, spiritual, artistic, ecological, and social worldview: the hippie movement and a little later (when these people had grown older), then the foundation of the ecological parties, and a little later yet the revival of the old magical orders.

Pluto gives Neptune an existential meaning in this collective astrological aspect: the connection of the individual with all things leads to a sharpening of the view of threatening ecological catastrophes, to an increase in social commitment, to the foundation of the peace movement, to the growing importance of alternative healing methods such as homeopathy or Reiki, to the renaissance of meditation and esotericism and magic in the West, the widespread experimentation with drugs to expand consciousness, the reintroduction of the "ancestor cult" in the form of family constellations, Josef Beuys' principle "everyone is an artist," the propagation of "free love"—the list could go on almost endlessly.

This Pluto/Neptune sextile is the basic tone of all magic in today's world. This keynote is differentiated and individualized by the relationship of Uranus and Saturn to these two planets in the chart of the individual human being.

Since Pluto and Neptune have a sextile to each other, the other planets can only have two harmonic aspects (conjunction, trine, sextile, opposition) or two disharmonic aspects (quincunx, square, semi-sextile) to these two planets—this follows from the geometry of these aspects.

This means (in simplified terms) that each of the other eight planets in the horoscope either seeks the proximity of Pluto and Neptune or evades these two planets.

Saturn, as the planet of life experience, natural laws and social rules, religious laws etc., tells us a lot about the relationship of the human being concerned to the rules of the world through its respective position in relation to Pluto and Neptune.

If, for example, Saturn stands next to Neptune (conjunction), one's own worldview (Saturn) is shaped by magical, spiritual, artistic, social, drug-related views. If Saturn stands next to Pluto, however, the worldview (Saturn) receives an existential power of persuasion (Pluto) which can go as far as becoming revolutionary or demagogic.

In both cases (Saturn/Neptune conjunction or Saturn/Pluto conjunction) the person concerned will also actively represent their weltanschauung in the world—simply because it happens to be their conviction. If Pluto or Neptune are also located at the ascendant or in the tenth house (or both), the person concerned will also become active in public with their magic views.

To a large extent, what has been described here for the conjunction applies as well to the trine and to the sextile.

With the opposition, things are also quite similar but more dynamic—whereby the opposition of Saturn to Pluto or Neptune automatically implies a trine to the other of the two planets. The two planets in the opposition (Saturn–Pluto or Saturn–Neptune) alternate rhythmically: a constant alternation between Saturn's rule-controlled everyday life on one side of the swing and Pluto's basic beliefs or Neptune's expansion of personality on the other. These "opposition people" have two sides, but they are in harmony with each other with the person concerned switching back and forth.

When connecting through a square, quincunx, or semi-sextile from Saturn to the Pluto/Neptune sextile, the tension is greater: one may be in an inner conflict because one experiences Saturn's everyday life and Pluto/Neptune's magic as two fundamentally different things—possibly as two entirely independent worlds.

Another form of living this kind of disharmonic aspect is simply the independence (square) of the practice of one's own magic (Pluto) from any traditions and rules (Saturn).

A person with harmonious aspects between Saturn and Pluto/Neptune, on the other hand, will tend to develop solid forms that will then hold (possibly common) magic.

Uranus describes the form in which the element of the sudden and spontaneous contributes to magic.

If Uranus has two harmonious aspects (conjunction, trine, sextile, opposition) to the Pluto/Neptune sextile, the magic, i.e., the expansion (Neptune) of one's personality in both perception and action, suddenly manifests itself—a spontaneous magician.

While in the harmonic aspects this spontaneous expansion can be directed and sometimes even planned and deliberately brought about, in the disharmonic aspects between Uranus and the Pluto/Neptune sextile, this is less likely. In the disharmonic constellations, the sudden (Uranus) stands against the magical (Pluto/Neptune)—thereby making the practice of magic more unpredictable, harder to plan and, above all, deliberately more spontaneous. Which by no means rules out the possibility that magic always works exactly when you really need it …

If both Saturn and Uranus have a connection to the Pluto/Neptune sextile, the situation becomes even more complex—and even more interesting and creative. For example, if Saturn is close to Neptune, this means that magic (Neptune) is given a fixed form (Saturn) and is perceived as the essence of life (Pluto). If Uranus then has a square to the Neptune/Saturn conjunction, magic is experienced as a leap (Uranus) out of reality (Saturn)—i.e., as the creation of one's own, self-determined reality.

If, on the other hand, for example, Uranus is located near Pluto, one is convinced that all essentials (Pluto) can only occur spontaneously (Uranus). If Saturn then has e.g. a square to this Pluto/Uranus conjunction, the person concerned will hold the opinion that magic must break up the common reality or at least fundamentally transform it—the essence of the world is the chaos (Uranus) behind the apparent order (Saturn).

The relationship between Saturn and Uranus can generally be expressed as "tradition and experiment." The study of this relationship was an essential aspect of the Bonn Workshop for Experimental Magic—a large number of the people in this circle had, besides the Pluto/Neptune sextile, which all humans born after 1942 have simply due to their similar birth date, a square between a Saturn/Neptune conjunction and the Uranus in their charts.

Of course, the other planets also play a role in their relationship to magic. For example, I know a woman who has a Pluto/Mars square in her birth chart. Because of the collective Pluto/Neptune-sextile, she has a rather remarkable magical talent, especially with regard to her telepathic perception, but also, unfortunately, for absorbing emotions and illnesses from others. However, due to her Pluto/Mars square and the corresponding Neptune/Mars quincunx, she is anxious about becoming magically active herself. The square and the quincunx separate her power (Mars) from her spirituality (Pluto/Neptune sextile). Nevertheless, she has found a solution: on the one hand she will often implore Christ or the Virgin Mary for a miracle (she has Uranus in her first house), or she will ask me for magical assistance—which, of course, due to her Leo-Uranus in the first house, should not be a step-by-step manual healing, but a solid magical miracle.

It is particularly the planets in the first house that will strongly influence one's own attitude to magic, no matter if they are connected with Uranus, Neptune, and Pluto by aspects or not.

Moon in first house can lead to a preference for the Wicca cult and for life force healings.

Mercury in first house can make you inclined to mantra magic and lead to a weakness for very long invocations.

Venus in first house will feel most comfortable in an emotional form of magic.

Sun in first house can lead to a "magic of unhindered self-expression."

Mars in first house can e.g. lead to a preference for tantric rituals and combat magic.

Jupiter in first house can cause you to require a circle of like-minded people to lead.

Saturn in first house can make you feel most comfortable in a magical order.

Uranus in first house can have the consequence that one can be magically effective only in spontaneity.

Neptune in first house can indicate that one always searches in magic for the tuning-in with the whole.

Pluto in first house can lead to a preference for Chod rituals, evocations and a "revolutionary magic" in general.

The position of Pluto and Neptune in the signs of the zodiac and in the houses is also important. One can downright observe a change in the attitude toward magic depending on this position of Pluto and Neptune, which changes only very slowly.

At the transitions between these basic collective magic phases, which are described in the following, Neptune sometimes changed to the next sign earlier or later than indicated in the overview. To see the precise position of the two planets in the transition phases, you can look it up in an ephemeris.

From 1942 to 1958 Pluto stood in Leo and Neptune in Libra. For the people born in this period, magic is a form of existential self-expression (Pluto in Leo) that can restore collective harmony (Neptune in Libra): the hippies.

From 1958 to 1972 Pluto stood in Virgo and Neptune in Scorpio. For the people born in this period, magic is a form of existential order (Pluto in

Virgo) that must be restored through a collective transformation (Neptune in Scorpio): the healers.

From 1972 to 1984 Pluto was located in Libra and Neptune in Sagittarius. For the people born in this period, magic is a form of existential harmony and beauty in all things (Pluto in Libra), which must be achieved by striving for the best for all (Neptune in Sagittarius): the do-gooders of the world.

From 1984 to 1996 Pluto stood in Scorpio and Neptune in Capricorn. For the people born in this period, magic is a form of existential ecstasy and general transformation (Pluto in Scorpio) that will bring the material world into a permanently stable and sustainable state (Neptune in Capricorn): the peaceful revolutionaries.

From 1996 to 2008 Pluto stood in Sagittarius and Neptune in Aquarius. For the people born in this period, magic is a form of existential idealism (Pluto in Sagittarius), which is the basis for the design and realization of the utopia of a new humanity (Neptune in Aquarius): the "Fridays for Future" movement and other initiatives that declare: "Something must happen—now!"

From 2008 to 2024 Pluto stands in Capricorn and Neptune in Pisces. For the people who were born or are yet to be born in this period, magic is a form of existential reflection on the reality in which we live (Pluto in Capricorn), through which we can achieve a prosperous coexistence of all living beings on this planet (Neptune in Pisces): man as a responsible and trust-carried member of the "earth family."

From 2024 to 2039 Pluto stands in Aquarius and Neptune in Aries—afterward this ninety-seven-year-long phase in which the Pluto/Neptune sextile prevails comes to an end. For the people born in this period, magic will be a form of existential cosmopolitanism (Pluto in Aquarius) which is the spontaneous recreation of a variety of spiritually, magically, ecologically, artistically, and socially sustainable ways of life (Neptune in Aries): the life-creatives.

The then-members of the Bonn Workshop for Experimental Magic, and hence also the four authors of this book, belong to the collective-astrological phase in which Pluto is located in Leo and Neptune in Libra: the Bonn Workshop for Experimental Magic thus also embodied a striving for the attainment of as comprehensive as possible an individual self-expression (Pluto in Leo), for which the variety of approaches and conversions of this self-expression was an enrichment and not an obstacle (Neptune in Libra). Only the "nestling" in our circle had Pluto advanced into Virgo as well as Neptune in Sagittarius and therefore already belongs to the "healer generation."

Naturally, we usually assume that the world is the way we experience, structure, and understand it, how we act in it, and how we perceive it functioning.

Astrology offers us the possibility to understand the variety of ways in which one can experience the world, and the phases in which the collective aspects of this worldview evolve (such as the Pluto/Neptune aspect).

This isn't always easy, because the forms of magic sketched in this chapter are not mere abstract worldviews: magic actually works for humans in the way they experience and describe it. That's why people are possibly convinced that "magic works for everyone in exactly the same way."

The distinction between the general rules of magic and one's own "astrological lens," through which one sees magic as well, can sometimes be quite relaxing.

Of course, the question poses itself once more whether we can actually distinguish "magic per se" from the individual way in which we experience it. But even to this question each birth chart renders a different answer …

Fortunately, for a fulfilled life we do not need a definitive answer to the question of "objective truth": it is sufficient to express what we are—no matter whether that may be the soul, life, God, or whatever, wherever one is, whatever one is.

But of course everyone views this matter differently, as based on their respective birth chart.

Chapter 24
Why Magic Isn't for Humans

Frater U∴D∴

As the contributions in this book go to show, there are very different, sometimes quite contradictory views on magic. Here follows mine—without any claim to consensus.

Any experienced magician will confirm that, with increasing practice, magic proves itself to be a radically life-changing discipline. The term "practice" here doesn't refer to the timid, superficial, and ultimately only short-lived finger exercises of those who are a mite curious at best. Rather, it is about a serious effort spread over many years, even decades, to come to grips with magical art and its possibilities. But what exactly does that actually mean—"life-changing"?

Nobody is born an accomplished magician, not even so-called native talents. Even they require instruction, experience, and experimentation. Magic is often described as an art. Case in point: I myself have just done so. But we must not forget that, like all arts, it also has its tradecraft component. Even if a given young person may have what it takes to become a true piano or violin virtuoso at world level, to take an example, they will not be spared the task of initially mastering the basics of their art like any other beginner: music notation, music theory, aural training, finger training, etudes, etc. The same applies respectively to the painter, the sculptor, the opera singer, or the gifted ballet dancer.

However, such analogies also have their limits. For, unlike conventional mundane craftsmanship, magic isn't really about technical skills and the precise knowledge of any objectifiable laws of nature and rules of procedure. Both dogmatic library magicians and very many folk magicians are repeatedly struck with this fallacy. This is not particularly surprising, seeing that humans will always describe the world solely within the framework of what they are familiar with. Thus, their access to magic will almost invariably merely represent an extension of what they already know.

This becomes abundantly clear, for example, in the classic grimoires, whose authors tend to fabulate with an impish joy of attention to detail about princes, dukes, counts, and baronets of hell: a direct reflection of the feudal society of that time, projected into the spirit world in all unreflected naiveté. Today, hundreds of years later, we may well be amused by this. But if, instead, we try to understand magic as psychotechnology or as a flavor of applied quantum mechanics, this, too, is but an expression of our epoch and a linear continuation of its domineering culture and way of thinking. Indeed, such explanatory models tend to say a lot about ourselves, but almost nothing about magic proper.

Rather, the real craftsmanship of magic, as it is conventionally passed down, lies in the intuition that alone is shaped, trained, and refined by experience and involvement, enabling us as magicians to divine generally concealed cause-and-effect relationships, qualities of time, courses of events, and control mechanisms and, on occasion, to make use of them successfully.

One can label this, and it has indeed been done quite frequently, a form of "mental development," which in turn bridges the gap between "low" and "high" magic so-called—at least inasmuch as the latter makes the spiritual evolution of the magician's personality or soul its core concern. After all, no one is barred from becoming a bit wiser in the course of practicing their magic...

However, you cannot and will not salvage the same old person you used to be in the process. Shamans, witch doctors, medicine women, magicians, witches, Mgangas, Siddhas, Houngans, Mambos, Brujos, Curanderas, Vitkis, Cunning Folk, Marabous and so on—the names are legion—have always been, despite all the attention they were rendered in myths, fairy tales, and legends, an eminently exceptional phenomenon and have remained so until this very day. To put it in biologistic modern terminology: the human gene pool just doesn't (perhaps yet?) seem up to rendering more.

It is quite obviously not given to "normal" humans to devote themselves seriously and consistently to magic and to make it an integral part of their own life, let alone allowing it to completely penetrate and determine said life.

To propose this statement, this has nothing to do with fatuously arrogant elitism, because it is patently no judgment call but rather focuses solely on the otherness of the magician. Thus it can happen that experienced magicians regard themselves and their colleagues to be a genus if not a species in its own right: at most superficially similar to their fellow human beings, they are actually just as remote from their kindred as are, e.g., reptiles or deep-sea fauna.

Even if you should not agree unreservedly with this view, there's no denying that no one who, whether out of anxiety or even for plain lack of imagination, chooses to cling to the delineations of their familiar bourgeois existence and their associated self-definition as well as the purported "normality" of their specific narrative of reality, will progress particularly far in magic.

Magic is always the monstrous, the "unheard-of event" of which Goethe spoke in connection with the novella. Seen in this light, it is not for humans and has never been—at least not for those who hanker to be and remain what the overwhelming majority of their species understands by being human.

Those who actually do get involved will start to perceive, emote, feel, and think differently sooner rather than later, will set different standards and develop different values. The further this process progresses, is strengthened, and stabilized, the less it can still be communicated and meaningfully understood by those who remain excluded from it. Thus, in the end, only one truly characteristic term remains to describe this process and those who expose themselves to it: alien.

And thus the Golden Dawn adept Gustav Meyrink manages like no other to express the sentiment of the entire magical guild when he lets his novel's protagonist Bartlett Green say to John Dee in The Angel of the West Window—albeit in this particular case with an unabashedly elitist bluster: "To the pack that only sees the outside and stays lukewarm from eternity to eternity, we […] have been exalted from the very beginning."

Select Recommended Reading

Conway, David. *Magic: An Occult Primer.* London: Cape, 1972.

Dukes, Ramsey. *SSOTBME Revised: An Essay on Magic.* London: The Mouse That Spins, 2019.

———. *Uncle Ramsey's Little Book of Demons.* London: Aeon Books, 2005.

———. *What I Did in My Holidays: Essays on Black Magic, Satanism, Devil Worship and Other Niceties.* Cape Town: The Mouse That Spins, 2011.

Fortune, Dion. *Psychic Self-Defence: A Study in Occult Pathology and Criminality.* Newburyport, MA: Weiser, 2011.

———. *The Sea-Priestess.* Newburyport, MA: Weiser, 2003.

Grant, Kenneth. *The Magical Revival.* London: Starfire, 2010.

Hine, Phil. *Condensed Chaos: An Introduction to Chaos Magic.* Tempe, AZ: Original Falcon Press, 2010.

King, Francis, and Stephen Skinner. *Techniques of High Magic: A Manual of Self-initiation.* Singapore: Golden Hoard, 2016.

Knight, Gareth. *A Practical Guide to Qabalistic Symbolism.* Newburyport, MA: Weiser, 2001.

Lachman, Gary. *Politics and the Occult: The Left, the Right, and the Radically Unseen.* Wheaton, IL: Quest Books, 2012.

———. *Dark Star Rising: Magick and Power in the Age of Trump.* New York: TarcherPerigee, 2018.

Millar, Angel. *The Three Stages of Initiatic Spirituality: Craftsman, Warrior, Magician.* Rochester, VT: Inner Traditions, 2020.

Pinchbeck, Daniel. *Breaking Open the Head: A Visionary Journey from Cynicism to Shamanism.* London: Flamingo, 2004.

Regardie, Israel. *The Golden Dawn: The Original Account of the Teachings, Rites, and Ceremonies of the Hermetic Order of the Golden Dawn (Stella Matutina)*. St. Paul, MN: Llewellyn, 1978.

Sherwin, Ray. *A Theatre of Magick*. London: CreateSpace, 2012.

Symonds, John. *The Great Beast: The Life of Aleister Crowley*. Revised and updated and incorporating [chapters from] "The Magick of Aleister Crowley." St Albans: Mayflower, 1973.

U∴D∴, Frater. *High Magic: Theory & Practice*. St. Paul, Minn.: Llewellyn, 2005–2008.

———. *The Magical Shield: Protection Magic to Ward Off Negative Forces*. Woodbury, MN: Llewellyn, 2016.

———. *Money Magic: Mastering Prosperity in Its True Element*. Woodbury, MN: Llewellyn, 2011.

———. *Practical Sigil Magic: Creating Personal Symbols For Success*. Rev. and enl. special ed. for the Americas. Woodbury, MN: Llewellyn, 2012.

———. *Sex Magic: Release & Control the Power of Your Erotic Potential*. Woodbury, MN: Llewellyn, 2018.

———. *Where Do Demons Live? Everything You Want to Know About Magic*. Woodbury, MN: Llewellyn, 2010.

Webb, Don. *Overthrowing the Old Gods: Aleister Crowley and the Book of the Law*. Rochester, VT: Inner Traditions, 2013.

———. *The Seven Faces of Darkness: Practical Typhonian Magic*. Smithville, TX: Rûna-Raven Press, 1996.

———. *Uncle Setnakt's Essential Guide to the Left Hand Path*. Smithville, TX: Rûna-Raven Press, 1999.

To Write to the Author

If you wish to contact the author or would like more information about this book, please write to the author in care of Llewellyn Worldwide Ltd. and we will forward your request. Both the author and the publisher appreciate hearing from you and learning of your enjoyment of this book and how it has helped you. Llewellyn Worldwide Ltd. cannot guarantee that every letter written to the author can be answered, but all will be forwarded. Please write to:

Frater U∴D∴
℅ Llewellyn Worldwide
2143 Wooddale Drive
Woodbury, MN 55125-2989

Please enclose a self-addressed stamped envelope for reply,
or $1.00 to cover costs. If outside the U.S.A., enclose
an international postal reply coupon.

Many of Llewellyn's authors have websites with additional
information and resources. For more information,
please visit our website at http://www.llewellyn.com.

Notes

Notes

Notes